ABOUT THE BOOK

The Scribes is set in Rome in the years 179-180 A.D. Its protagonist is Justin, a young scribe of the Roman church, named after Justin Martyr. He is helped in the copyist's tasks by two friends, Marcus and Rufus. His teacher in Rome had been Irenaeus, Bishop of Lyons, who was beginning to write his *Against Heresies* when the novel takes place.

The story begins when the Roman church receives a visit from a wealthy ship merchant from Alexandria in Egypt and his daughter, Juliana. This appealing young woman is a student in the catechetical school in Alexandria, and is also a scribe for her church. Justin is attracted to her, but troubled by her manuscript. Her St. Mark begins differently. He has the longer ending (Mark 16:9-20) and she does not. etc. For Justin this is very unsettling. His primary aim in life is to copy with scrupulous fidelity the text of the gospels, as the church in Rome has receeived it. But the church in Alexandria has preserved a different type of text. He is determined to get to the bottom of this puzzle, and as he does, he develops a romantic interest in Juliana. But she has returned to Alexandria. How will he pursue the relationship?

The opportunity comes when Bishop Eleutherus of Rome sends Justin and Marcus to deliver letters to various churches throughout the empire. Their final destination is Alexandria.

TRAVEL... with Justin and Marcus as they visit churches in Cornith, Athens, Ephesus, Antioch, and Alexandria.

MEET... the remarkable leaders they encounter: Dionysius of Cornith, Athenagoras of Athens, Pinytus of Cnossus, Theophilus of Antioch, the aged Hegesippus and the young Clement of Alexandria.

JOURNEY... with them to exotic places like Cnossus in Crete, Oxyrhyhchus in the Nile Valley and Crocodilopolis in the Fayum in Egypt.

EXPERIENCE... with them the many hazards that could befall a traveler or a manuscript: storms, pirates, arrests, theft, greedy customs agents, eager booksellers, heretical groups, unscrupulous innkeepers, scribes who improve the style of their texts.

JOIN... them as they face the challenge of different readings in the texts, different methods of copying, different interpretations among the churches, and strange gospels among the Gnostics.

To the Congregation of St. John's Church, New Haven.

CHAPTER 1

It was too dark to travel, but Justin was determined to get home. He could see the lights of his city, the city of Rome, the capital of the world. Dangers from beasts and from brigands could not deter him. He pressed on for the last few miles, with the cool summer breeze blowing in his face.

It had been a long journey of several months, and Justin was eager to return to his home and his work. He had never been on so long a journey in the thirty-two years of his life, and as he walked in the twilight he felt tired but pleased. He had been on a long trek to Lyons, in Gaul, in the North of the empire on an honored errand for his bishop, Eleutherus, to deliver a copy of the four gospels as a gift from the Roman Church to their new Bishop of Lyons, Irenaeus.

Justin had been the copyist of the codex. The task had taken the better part of a year and had occupied every moment of his spare time. Whenever he was not at the carpenter's bench and his daily chores, he had devoted himself to the codex. The book from which he copied had been in the possession of the Roman Church for over sixty years. It had been made, at least in St. Mark, from the original gospel, the very autograph. Justin felt himself part of something much larger, much grander than he had ever imagined. He was receiving the tradition and handing it on.

His father had done the same and had paid a price for it. For almost fifty years he had been chief scribe in the Roman Church and had been loved and respected far and wide. He had founded the small scriptorium, or scribes' chamber, in a room at the back of their house in the village. There several would meet to join one another in the work of making copies of the scriptures for the church and for private use. Among those who knew and

1

respected the father was Justin Martyr, the great apologist, after whom the son was named. None in that previous generation had done more to tell and re-tell the Christian story in a way that made it available to the world. But he, like Justin's father, had lost his life, a martyr to the story.

Now returning on this late summer evening in the year A.D. 179 Justin pondered the voices he had heard on his journey. There was the haunting voice of the simple Christian from Lyons, who had witnessed the martyrdom of his friends and had lived to tell the tale:

"You should have seen Blandina. She was submitted to every form of torture one could imagine, and still she made a simple and bold profession of faith: 'I am a Christian, we do nothing to be ashamed of.' And Oh the wonder of our aged Bishop Pothinus, over ninety years old! The Governor asked him, 'Who is the God of the Christians?' He replied with breathless confidence, 'If you are worthy, you will know.' And then there were others...Marturus and Sanctus and Attalus, led with Blandina into the Amphitheater to be exposed to the beasts, It was horrifying, I tell you, and yet it was wonderful to see their witness."

The stories reminded Justin of that day he would never forget, when as a boy of 17 he had seen his own father put to death for the simple and bold profession: "I am a Christian." The father's voice still rang in Justin's ears on this summer evening as if the words had been said on that very day. And it was joined by the voice of that other Justin, the great man after whom his father had named him:

"We believe in the God of the Christians, whom alone we believe to be the maker of the whole world from the beginning, and also regarding Jesus Christ the Child of God, who was also foretold by the prophets as one who was to come down to mankind as a herald of salvation and a teacher of good doctrines." How Justin Martyr's voice rang out! How his face shone!

And there were other voices. There was the voice of Irenaeus, the new Bishop of Lyons, who had been young Justin's teacher in Rome. Justin recalled his joy at hearing Irenaeus

2

declare, "Well done!" when he received and poured over the four gospels codex which Justin had prepared and brought to Gaul. And he recalled his teacher's unforgettable words, said often in lectures at Rome, and repeated during this recent visit to the north: "Justin, always copy faithfully the gospels as you have received them. Do not be tempted to 'improve' or 'strengthen' them by adding to them, or subtracting from them or altering them in any way, for this is to destroy them. Resist all pressure to add to the scriptures, even where it would seem to strengthen our case in the defense of the truth. The Gospels as they stand bear faithful witness to Christ, and our task is to preserve them for the church, until the Lord comes again in glory."

Justin came to the brow of the hill, and in the dusk his house could now be seen. His thoughts turned from many voices to many questions. What lay in store for him upon his return? One always has this feeling after a long journey. What business would need immediate attention? Would someone have fallen sick or died? Was there a new threat of persecution, a storm that was always just over the horizon? He had just heard first-hand accounts of the horrors of the persecution in Lyons. Might it happen in Rome as in the days of Nero, and of his father? Would he stand firm as had Peter and Paul and his father and his namesake, the Philosopher-martyr? He could only trust that he would, and pray that it might not happen. He sang to himself the words of Psalm forty-four, cited by St. Paul,

"For thy sake we are being killed all the day long
We are accounted as sheep to be slaughtered."

The mention of sheep reminded him of Marcus, his dear friend the shepherd, who in his spare time helped with the copying. He would be eager to see Marcus, slightly younger, and newer at the task of copying, but deeply committed the Lord and his church, and gifted with extraordinary accuracy in transmission. He would be glad to see Rufus, full of zeal, and somewhat impetuous, but never willfully inaccurate in the scribe's work, since the day of his severe scolding for "improving" a text. Rufus' eagerness to defend the true faith, with a word, or with a sword was at once dangerous and endearing. These three comrades in the work would take up

3

some new task together, and although Justin would do the bulk of the work, he rejoiced in the fellowship and help given by the others, and sought yet more colleagues whom he could trust and train. Would they be able to continue this work unhindered? So far no move had been made to seize the books of the Roman Church. The leadership had been left unharmed. The scriptorium was not in the city but in a village, and tucked out of the way. But how devastating it would be for each of them to have spent months in painstaking copying of the scriptures, only to have them snatched away and destroyed. As the darkness fell, Justin reached his house.

On opening his door, Justin got that sense one often feels after a long trip, of a place that seemed both familiar and foreign. There was all his furniture and belongings, undisturbed, and yet the door seemed to creak more and the floor-boards reacted more loudly to steps, like a man long asleep, and suddenly awakened to duty. The smells too had a strange newness to them. For months he had been in the open air, with the strong scents of earth and flowers and trees. This had been his environment, and now he stepped into the close quarters where he had lived his whole life, quarters whose familiarity would soon make woods and flowers smell strange and foreign. He sat on his chair, which gave its own audible response, and he gave thanks to his God for a safe return.

A letter from Marcus had been slipped under the door. Justin dropped his satchel and opened it. He lit his lamp and read, "Marcus to Justin, Greetings in the name of the Lord. Come at once, if you can. Not much is new, except that Rufus has been detained, and a new task awaits us. The Bishop is eager to see us about it. Grace and Peace."

Rufus detained? No doubt his zeal had got the better of him, and an incautious remark to a person of influence had led to his arrest. Pray God this was not the beginning of a fresh wave of persecution. Justin's feet were so tired he felt he could not move another step. Yet without hesitation he rose and almost ran over the hill to Marcus' door.

"Welcome, my brother, come in, and God bless you!" Marcus cried. "It is wonderful to have you here, safe and sound.

4

I want to hear all you have to tell, but first let me explain my note."

"Yes do," said Justin breathlessly.

They sat together at Marcus' simple table, and shared some wine, while Justin listened.

"Last week in the market-place Rufus found himself in heated discussion with some aggressive Valentinian Gnostics. They were going on about Aeons and Pleroma, and I don't know what all else. I heard the commotion and went to see what was happening. You know how Rufus is. He simply will not let such teaching go unchallenged. Voices were raised all round, and it ended in a fight. Rufus did not hit anyone, nor say anything insulting (so far as I could tell) but it was rumored that he was the cause of the trouble, and off he was taken. Disturbing the peace or something like that. He is detained under house arrest, and will probably be there for a while. I was able to visit him the other day, and he was cheerful, and being treated with civility. Someone in that household is a Christian, and therefore we can hope for the best. He will probably be released within a month."

"And do they know he is a scribe?" asked Justin, recovering his breath.

"O, I don't think anyone knows or cares among those who are holding him, and he hasn't been interrogated, at least not as of my visit. But it is troublesome, and we all do have to take care, and keep guard. We can go to see him tomorrow, perhaps, but first we must go to the bishop."

"Yes, tell me Marcus," said Justin in eager anticipation.

Marcus yawned, for he too was tired. Then he said, "He is very eager to see you and have news of your journey to Gaul and your time with Irenaeus. And you must tell me all this too. But he also has a new copying task for us, one of great interest. It seems that there is a visitor from the East, from Alexandria, who is here in Rome on important business. He has brought with him his daughter, who is in possession of a fine manuscript of the Gospel of Mark. She desires a copy, and asks if we might make it. I think I have the story correct. The Bishop will tell you the details. I actually heard it from the deacon, who was asking after

5

you on the Bishop's behalf. I told him I would inform you as soon as you returned."

"So, a manuscript from Alexandria, and they want a copy made." said Justin, "A bit unusual, since Alexandria is the copying center of the world. Why come to Rome for this? It's a little puzzling, but at the Bishop's word we will set to work. Yes, some more wine would be all right, but then we must pray and call it a night. I can hardly move."

"We will go to the Bishop at mid-morning tomorrow," said Marcus, "So we had better do what sleeping we can. Oh. Justin, it is the joy of the Lord to see you again, and to know you are safe! Was it a hard journey?"

Justin looked up, lost in thought and prayer. He was silent for a moment, and then he spoke.

"I often thought of the apostle's words, 'dangers from rivers, dangers from robbers,' and once or twice my life, and our precious Gospels codex was in danger. But God preserved me...and it."

Justin made his way back down the familiar village street, and crawled into his own bed, almost asleep before his head hit the pillow.

CHAPTER 2

The dry, crisp clean breezes of Oxyrynchus had always refreshed Juliana's soul. But never had they been so refreshing as now. As she sat in the garden of her country house she thought about the events of the past year. She and her father Demetrius had come to the country for a few weeks' rest after an especially trying time in Alexandria. For him the trial was the endless details of the large landholdings, in the Fayum and in the delta, and a shipping business of which he was the owner. A poor crop season and a dissatisfied workforce were the constant headaches of the year, and imperial taxation policy had also taken its toll. He had prospered, it is true, but it seemed to him that he had had to work harder than ever.

For Juliana the trouble had been with Hermas. He had proved a fine gentleman and friend in the first year of their acquaintance. But then he began to be possessive, and to want to press their relationship beyond the bounds of Christian morality. Her refusal meant tension. Then one day in early spring he announced that he had found Chloe, a woman, so he said, who really knew what love meant, a woman with whom he could really share. So Juliana found herself spurned. She had tried to talk to Apion, her cousin and close friend. They had grown up in the same house and had talked about all sorts of matters over the years. But now Apion was in the midst of a spiritual crisis, and was unavailable. Juliana felt very alone.

There in the garden, in Oxyrynchus, in the early summer, she sat and thought about her life of twenty-four years. On one level it had been a life of tremendous privilege. The only child of a prosperous Alexandrian shipping merchant, she could have had anything she wanted. And her father's considerable fortune and broad outlook meant that she had freedom in choosing a marriage partner, an uncommon privilege for an Egyptian girl. Surely she was the envy of many of her neighbors, suffering from arranged marriages in their early teens. Those girls lucky enough not to be exposed at birth, faced an equally great danger in abortion. But a Christian home shielded Juliana from these horrors. Her mother, a Jewish woman from a prominent family of Roman citizenry was loving and cultured, and from Juliana's childhood they had known the Christian hope and had been active in the Alexandrine church. The bishop was Juliana's uncle. Her father had lavished attention on her, providing tutors and a governess, and as she grew older, two trusted servants, Rhoda and James. She grew up knowing the great writers of Greece and Rome. She also had traveled much. When her father's business took him the length and breadth of the great sea, she would often go with him. Thus she visited many of the schools and churches of the empire. Wherever she went, men sought her company, attracted by her beauty, or her intelligence or her money. But none of them seemed to be right for Juliana.

But all this wealth and privilege could not shield Juliana from tragedy. When she was ten, her mother died of the fierce plague that swept across the empire, killing a third of the populace and eventually claiming the Emperor. The loss left a permanent mark on Juliana. Then there was the revolt that had broken out when Juliana was seventeen. While traveling to her country estate in Oxyrhynchus, Juliana witnessed first-hand the bloodshed and cruelty. The relentless Roman forces crushed the revolt. Several times she feared her life was in danger. Then it was over, and she was left to sort out the cruelty and senselessness of it all, and to ask, "Why, God, why do you allow these things?"

A year later Juliana suffered another great fright. An intruder broke into their house in Alexandria, intent on stealing the goods and violating the women. Had not Juliana's strong servant James intervened, what had been a moment of fright might have turned into a life of shame.

Despite all this, Juliana's life was one of hope and joy and encouragement.For her twentieth birthday her father had given her the most remarkable gift: a beautifully copied codex of the Gospel of Mark, for her own private use. A Christian scribe in Alexandria, who had been schooled for many years in the best classical methods, had copied it. He was part of a group of scribes in the Egyptian Church who had a keen interest in presenting Christian manuscripts which on the level of style and elegance could stand alongside the great classics, Homer, Sophocles, Plato, Demosthenes, etc."The best book must have the best treatment," they would say. Juliana had learned the copyist's trade from some of these scribes and shared their vision of commending the Christian faith with her cultured friends. And the copy of Mark which Juliana held as she sat in the garden and thought was of a quality second to none. In moments of perplexity and disappointment she turned to this manuscript for comfort. She had practically memorized the text. On that morning in the dry, crisp, clean air she had thought on the words, "The kingdom of God is like a grain of mustard seed...."

"Juliana!"

Her father's voice called her back from deep thought. "Juliana, we have had some news today from Alexandria. My clients in Rome want me to come and spend some time with them this summer. We shall leave in two weeks time, and will spend a month or so there. I do want you to come."

"Father, I do love travel with you, but I am just not up to it now," she complained.

"It will help you to...." He stopped, knowing that any paternal lecture about getting over Hermas would only make matters worse.

"...to see the Roman Church," he said hopefully, "and to look at their manuscripts, and to show them yours."

Demetrius knew he had struck a positive note, and so he waited, not wanting to ruin the idea by over-playing it.

"Well, I'll think about it, Father, I'll think about it."

Not much thought was necessary. By dinner she was full of questions about Rome and chatter about the church and its copy methods. She had learned so much in recent years from the scribes of Alexandria, and had aspired herself to be a copyist of the Gospels and the letters of Paul. To learn the Roman

9

methods, and above all, to boast of the splendid Alexandrian scribal work filled her with eager anticipation.

"Do you really think they will be willing to teach and take the time with me? " she asked.

"We can try, " said her father. "I'll obtain a letter of introduction from our bishop to theirs, and that should surely smooth the way."

CHAPTER 3

The hot Italian summer sun had almost dried the early morning rain as Justin and Marcus began their three-mile walk from the village to the city. After their visit to the Bishop, they would try to see Rufus, whose house of detention was not much out of the way. They reached the modest villa where Eleutherus lived, and were greeted with great warmth. The Bishop was eager to hear news of Gaul, and of his friend Irenaeus, and of the progress of the mission since the devastating persecution. Justin handed him a pack of letters, and began to speak of the church.

"What remarkable courage and faithfulness, and unwavering..."

Just then the deacon at the door announced in a loud, and slightly officious voice, "Our visitors from Alexandria. Demetrius and his daughter Juliana."

The door opened wide, revealing a distinguished man in his fifties, well groomed and dressed, and a woman in her mid-twenties. She was very striking indeed, with flowing black hair, and large, brown eyes. Demetrius stepped forward, offered the kiss of Peace to the three Romans, and spoke;

"How kind of you to welcome an eastern brother and his daughter. I am a merchant from Alexandria. I am here in Rome to settle some business. My daughter and I are members of the Christian church in Alexandria, and we bring you greetings, and letters from our Bishop, Agrippinus."

"A joy to have you in our fellowship." said the Bishop.

Then with a glance to the scribes, Demetrius said, "I hear you have a fine scriptorium, and some able scribes."

"Able indeed," said the bishop, pleased at their growing reputation. "Justin, in fact is the second generation. His father was our chief scribe for many years before he suffered a martyr's death. And this is Marcus, his colleague in the work."

"And allow me to introduce Juliana." She stepped forward and bowed to the men, with a broad smile. "She has a request to make. She has been learning the copyist's trade herself, and would like to observe and learn your scribal methods here in Rome."

Justin and Marcus caught each other's glance, and wondered at each other's thoughts. As each started to speak, the Bishop, in a voice full of sympathy and authority, said,

"I am sure, Demetrius, that our scribes will be entirely at your service."

Juliana reached into her satchel and brought forth a codex. It was about six inches by nine inches, covered by an attractive leather and tied with thongs. "This is my prize possession, my greatest treasure, " she said in a voice full of sincerity and charm. "My father gave it to me, a special present on my twentieth birthday, and it has been my constant companion. It is the Gospel of Saint Mark, copied by one of the ablest scribes in Alexandria, and made from a manuscript, which they believe to have been copied from the original gospel. I wonder whether I might learn more of your trade by observing how you copy this treasure."

"It would be an honor, madam, lady... how do you prefer to be addressed...."

"Oh, Juliana! Christians can use Christian names, and may I..."

"Justin, and this is Marcus, and there is a third named Rufus, who is away just now."

The Bishop cleared his throat and shifted his position, annoyed at the mention of Rufus. "May we have a look?" he asked.

Juliana carefully placed the codex on the table, untied the string and opened it in the center, Their eyes fell on the page that began, "For the Son of Man came not to be served, but to serve, and to give his life as a ransom for many."

It was the most beautiful Christian manuscript they had ever seen. Justin and Marcus stood speechless before it. The beauty lay in the finely wrought Greek letters, and the carefully formed columns. On each of the pages, which were about the size of Justin's hand, there were two columns. The letters were in a "book hand" rather than the utility, or document hand, normally used by Christian scribes. Justin had only seen a few books of this quality, and they had been copies of classical texts, on which time and expense had been lavished. To any scribe of their day this was a work of art. It had clearly been a labor of love, and a Father's lavish gift to his only and beloved daughter.

"It is splendid," said Justin, and turning fully toward her, he added, "I doubt that we could produce anything so fine as this. But if it is your desire to see how it is we copy, you are welcome and we will start at once. You will bring the codex when you come, then?"

"No, you may take it now. It will be safe with you. I will find my way to your scriptorium tomorrow morning, as I believe we are staying in the village just next to yours. This way you may have some opportunity to familiarize yourself with the book, indeed get to know and enjoy it, before you show me how you copy it."

"Well, I am honored," said Justin, "But I feel a great weight of responsibility, and I shall guard it with my life. And we may expect you mid-morning tomorrow?"

"If all this is agreeable," said the Bishop, "I must beg a few minutes alone with Justin, to learn of his journey to Gaul, and of the church there. He has only just returned, you see."

"We understand," said Demetrius, "And we are deeply grateful for your generosity to your sister from the East."

"I will give it my very best," said Justin, as the visitors were shown to the door.

Justin's visit with the bishop lasted for an hour, and ended with fervent prayer and the singing of some psalms. Then he and Marcus were on their way. For a while neither spoke.

Finally Marcus said, "Well, what do you make of it all?"

"Beautiful!" said Justin, almost shouting to be heard above the street noise.

"Do you mean the script or the scribe?"

"Both" said Justin.   And it was a statement above contradiction.

"I have one nagging concern, Marcus," he went on, "You will recall the last time we in the Roman Church welcomed a wealthy shipping merchant from the East. It was in my Father's generation that Marcion came from Sinope, a port on the Black Sea. Well, remember how he threw his money around, and made himself out to be a teacher. In the end he proved to be a great distorter, rejecting the whole of the Old scriptures and much of the new. And what little scripture he kept he mangled. He attracted a great following, and while in the end the church gave back the money and sent Marcion packing back to the East, we are still sorting out the difficulties. It may just be coincidental that this Demetrius is an Eastern shipping merchant, but I couldn't help drawing the parallel. He seems quite humble, and his daughter more eager to learn than to teach. I'm sure there's nothing in the thought, so I'm sorry I even said it. I said, I will take heed to my ways, that I offend not with my tongue...." Justin mused in the opening words of the thirty-ninth Psalm.

"I had actually had the same thought, but I doubt we have anything to worry about. But what is the good of friends if you can not share your thoughts, your fears, and your hopes? In any case, the danger here is not so much doctrinal as personal."

"Yes," said Justin after hesitating.

So they walked on in silence.

14

CHAPTER 4

The bustling Roman streets led Justin and Marcus to the edge of the city, where they found the villa they sought, a basilica structure, set in fine grounds. They made their way down the long corridor bounded by high walls richly embowered with flowers and vines of every kind. The strong scents seemed to compete with one another for the bees that were plentiful and active. The path led to the main entrance, where a servant seemed to expect the visitors.

"This way, sir" he said to Marcus, and the two followed down a columned hall. Halfway down they passed a stately room, where it appeared that three senators were conferring on some weighty matter over lunch. The whispers revealed the importance, but not the content of the discussion. At the end of the hall a door opened onto a small chamber, and it in turn led to another. The servant unlocked the door, and showed the visitors in. Rufus sprang to his feet, greeting Justin with a holy kiss, and exclaiming loudly his joy at seeing his brother.

"You have a half an hour," said the servant as he shut the door behind him.

The three scribes sat together and talked. Rufus told his tale of arrest in vivid detail, and with frequent denunciation of Gnostics, and their challenge to the faith of the church. Justin told of his travels and adventures, and the things he had learned from the survivors of the persecution in Lyons. The faith must be defended, and their friend, the new bishop there, was engaged in a major work to defend it against the Gnostics, of all types. But persecution was dreadful, and should never be invited. Not only did it threaten the church of this generation. It threatened the scriptures, and the handing on of the faith for all subsequent generations. Christians should not shrink under trial. But they

15

must do all in their power not to provoke the powers that be, which, as the apostle had written, were "ordained by God."

Rufus seemed humbled but unconvinced. Marcus broke in to say that a visitor had come from Alexandria to learn the methods of the Roman scribes. But he and Justin had decided on the way not to mention that the visitor was a woman. Should Rufus be released, and join them, they would deal with that issue as it came up. For now, they just spoke of " the visitor" from the church in Alexandria.

"Alexandria," said Rufus, "I have heard that they are famous for their zeal."

"And their wisdom." Justin shot back. "They have the finest scriptorium anywhere in the world, I am told. Their copyists have trained, some of them for years, in the finest schools, and they produce the most finely scripted texts. In fact, we saw one today that was crafted in the most splendid hand. The visitor has brought it, and we may learn more than they will learn in the next month."

"With God's speed I may join you again before the month is out," said Rufus, "and I am pledged to control myself, and avoid future arrests. It was so good of you to come..."

All too quickly the servant returned, and Justin and Marcus found themselves returning the way they had come. But now the chamber was empty, and the only sign of life was the sound of two children playing a game in the garden. Back down the long scented corridor, still busy with bees, they reached the open way and took it uphill for the two-mile journey home. The mid-afternoon heat invited a long nap, but both scribes had much preparation to do before nightfall, and needed to be ready for the morning. A vitally important month lay ahead of them, and they would have to be as free as possible. They parted company in the village, but agreed to meet at nine in the morning at the scriptorium. It was hard for either of them to imagine what the dynamic of the scriptorium would be like. Especially Justin, who would spend most of the days with Juliana, wondered what he might have to teach her. The codex that he held in his satchel, when copied, would provide a stronger link between the churches of Rome and Alexandria, and it was this worldwide profession of the truth, from the earliest times till now, that was so important. At least this is what he had learned and received from his friend and mentor, Irenaeus. To strengthen that link was vital in the face of the many challenges to the church, whether Gnostic or docetic or separationist or adoptionist or Marcionite. On all sides, it seemed, and increasingly from within the church, new movements seemed to be gaining momentum. In the face of that challenge his faithful copying of the scriptures, in coordination with other faithful copying, all round the world, was of critical importance. He felt called by God to be a faithful scribe at just such a time as this.

There was no time, when he reached his house, for Justin to rest. He would not even take the time to enjoy the new codex with its beautiful script. Carpentry had to be cleared, the scriptorium needed rearrangement for the new work, and several letters that had come in his absence could not wait. Still tired from his long journey, he would need sleep. He busied himself with these chores until late into the night, took Juliana's codex from his satchel and laid it on the copy desk beside a fresh and ready quire, and went to bed.

CHAPTER 5

Justin could not sleep. It was a little after midnight and a long time until dawn. His mind was filled with thoughts of the manuscript and its owner. He had been caught off guard by his reaction. His glance at Marcus made it clear that he too was taken aback. The prospect of spending the next few weeks in the scriptorium, day- by- day with such an attractive, intelligent and interesting woman was undeniably pleasant. She sought to learn from him not only the skill of the scribe, but also the craft of the reed-pen. But what more was in store: many conversations on theology, the endless contrasts between East and West, the playful banter over disputed points? They would think the same thoughts, breathe the same air, drink of the same spirit for the better part of a month.

The whole idea of a woman scribe was new. Rufus, of course, with his rigorist views, would not have approved. The thought of women in the church, let alone in the scriptorium, would be suspect, and from his point of view, put the whole Christian enterprise in jeopardy. "Flee from meat and wine and women!" he would often cry in heated debate. And although he was, alas, not present to protest, and was in any case the newest member of the scribal band, he was nonetheless a valued brother, and Justin was aware of what he would think and what he might say. He chided himself for thinking it a relief that Rufus was detained.

Was Justin investing too much in the eastern visitor? Was this striking woman with her beautiful manuscript to be honored any more than another visitor to Rome? It was her faith and love of learning that had led her to seek out the local scribes and learn all she could from them. Why should he entertain for a moment the notion that any special friendship might develop, any affection or---something more--- he dared even to think it? He must be entirely sensible and get on with his work. The rigorism of Rufus was not for him, but it did have its point. Single-minded zeal for the task at hand was what was called for, and he must keep guard over his heart.

But it did surprise him that she was willing to leave her precious copy of St. Mark there with him at the scriptorium. It was her special private possession, used for devotion. She felt it would be safe with him. It certainly bespoke a high degree of trust in a man she had only just met. Had she thought it a great generosity that he invited her to come each morning to the scriptorium, to join and aid him in his work? Had she been impressed with his eagerness to read and copy this beautiful manuscript from Alexandria? Whatever her reason, there it lay, in the room adjacent to his own. No wonder he couldn't sleep! He lit his lamp, dressed himself and went into the scriptorium. Several hours without disturbance lay before him, when he could read and enjoy the splendid codex. He carefully untied the string and opened to the title page.

"The beginning of the Gospel of Jesus Christ..."

Something was missing. In every copy of St. Mark that he had ever read were the words "Jesus Christ, the Son of God." Why was this splendid Alexandrian manuscript different? Surely they believed in Alexandria that Jesus was the Son of God? Perhaps it was a scribal slip, caused because in Greek "Christ" and "God", written in abbreviation, ended in the same letter. So some Alexandrian scribe had inadvertently left out the precious words. Justin had caught himself in just such a mistake some time ago. He had left out a line in St. John, and found his text reading in the great prayer of Jesus "I do not pray that thou shouldst take them from the evil one." But what had Mark originally written? Mark had had links with the earliest churches in both Rome and Alexandria, but was reputed to be the founder of the latter. Had some early copyist, eager to honor the Lord, or to underline the Gospel's emphasis added it? What, perhaps, could Juliana tell him? He needed to know, but he hardly dared ask her, knowing how much this particular manuscript meant to

20

her. Yet the faithful handing on of the faith depended on the faithful transmission of the text.

True, St. Mark spoke elsewhere of Jesus as "Son of God." But it seemed vitally important to get it right at the outset. Did the Evangelist affirm that Jesus was the "Son of God" from all times, or were some heretics right, that Jesus only really *became* the Son of God at his baptism? The designation in the opening line had often provided him with the support he need in debate on this point. But was it original?

And then another thought crossed his mind. How did this manuscript end? There were two endings of Mark known to him. The one that he knew and received from the Roman Church, told of Jesus' of resurrection appearance and his commissioning of the disciples. But in one or two manuscripts he had seen these reports were missing. He had always been a bit puzzled by this but had received the Roman text with confidence. But what of this splendid Markan text from Alexandria, bearing all the authority of that church, even if it seemed to have been produced for private use? He turned carefully to the end of the codex. The last words it contained were

"...for they were afraid." (Mark 16:8)

Justin sat puzzled at the codex. The most beautiful book, copied by the most able hand, could nonetheless be wrong. If the exemplar, from which it had been copied was faulty, the codex itself would be faulty too. And this codex seemed to be at fault. Was not its ending of the Markan gospel very abrupt, quite unfinished? And had not his friend and mentor especially noted how Mark ends his gospel with the Lord Jesus, ascended into heaven and seated at the right hand of God?

Perhaps there were more irreconcilable differences between the texts and the traditions. He returned to the first page. Then he reached for his own valued copy of Mark, which he had carefully copied from the great codex of the Roman Church, and from which he had made the presentation copy, in the second gospel for Irenaeus, and the church of Lyons. This copy he had come to consider authoritative, representing as best he could discern, what Mark originally wrote. He set the two along side each other, and in the early hours of the morning he poured over them noting any difference, however great or small.

Mark begins his gospel with the ministry of John the Baptist, and shows how that ministry is according to the word of the prophet Isaiah. Juliana's Mark ended the quotation "Make his paths straight." But the manuscript of the Roman Church read, "Make straight the path of our God." Now Justin knew that this was the reading of the Old Testament, and as a passage dearly loved and often read in the church the Isaiah text could very easily have caused a change in one of the early copies. Alexandria might be right here, but how was he to be sure? Perhaps this was the place to point out a difference to Juliana. It might make for a pleasant and friendly way to explore differences of a minor sort. But the task before him, at his Bishop's bidding, was to copy a manuscript which clearly had been corrupted somewhere along the line. Perhaps the thing to do was to copy the text as is, but then to note in the margin all the places where it differed from the text known to the Roman Church, giving the variant reading. It would, of course be a less elegant work, in the end, and he could even make those notations after Juliana had gone. He sat thinking it over for a long time.

The early morning light told Justin how much he had lost track of the time. Desiring some sleep before he received his visitor, he closed the beautiful and perplexing book, extinguished his light and tumbled into bed. He did not wake until he heard Marcus knocking at his door.

A very drowsy Justin opened to his equally drowsy friend.

"Have you just awakened, my friend, that is not like you," said Marcus, "But I got very little sleep myself. Early in the morning I was awakened from the most fantastic dream, the most vivid dream I have ever had. There I was in an open field of dry, brown grass, and suddenly, as from nowhere, an immense lion sprang forward to devour me. I was defenseless. I was as good as dead. Then at once there appeared a great eagle, who swooped down upon me, dug his giant talons ever so gently into my back and lifted me from danger, carrying me to a pleasant meadow by streams of living water."

"And its interpretation?" asked Justin with a yawn.

22

"Well, it must be telling us that Mark is Dangerous and John is safe, but then, neither gospel is dangerous and neither safe."

"Yes," said Justin, "Unless we believe the tradition current among us that Mark is the Eagle and John is the lion! But what is a dream? A dream is a mist, a phantom, a figment. It is present but a moment and no more. It distorts, it distracts, it disorients. It knows all we question and questions all we know. A dream makes the unreal real and the real unreal. Dreams may be our master while we sleep, but when we awake, we despise their phantoms."

"But Justin," replied the impatient Marcus, "Did not God speak to our fathers in dreams. Did he not through a dream speak to Joseph in the old covenant, and Joseph in the new? Did he not instruct Jacob in his travel, and the wise men in theirs through a dream? Did he not thus save his people and spare their savior? If he spoke thus to men of old, would he not also speak to us in the same way?"

"Perhaps your dream is to be heeded, Marcus, but let me tell you, I have just this night been subject to something more fantastic and challenging than any dream."

"And what could that be?" asked the incredulous Marcus.

"I have spent most of this night pouring over the beautiful manuscript entrusted to us by Juliana, the one we begin copying this morning."

"And what could be challenging and fantastic about that," asked Marcus.

"Marcus, look..." Justin opened the codex with the same reverence and care as before, but with a heavy heart, "Look here at the first line of the Gospel. Do you see it is defective? It lacks the crucial phrase, prized by us, "The Son of God." And look here, at the end. Look how it ends so abruptly, with nothing about our Lord's appearance, and commission, such as we have known. Only the abrupt, 'for they were afraid...' Fear? That's not the way the Gospel ends, surely. Awe, maybe, perhaps worship, but not fear! And there is more, but now is not the time, Juliana will be here any moment, and we must begin the task we have promised. But Marcus, it is to be the copying of a defective

23

manuscript. Under her watchful eye there will be no chance to correct it in the copy. Marcus, what shall we do?"

Marcus had seldom seen Justin so perplexed. This leader among their scribal band had always been the one they looked to for confidence and assurance. Had the journey to Gaul really shaken him more deeply than was evident at first? It is true, the Alexandrian omissions were troubling, but as far as Marcus could tell, they were patently errors, and need not be published in the Churches of Rome. Let the Alexandrians have an extra copy of their own manuscript, and a private manuscript at that. Marcus did not see the situation to be as difficult as Justin apparently did. So he said, rather lightly.

"So then, copy the Alexandrian text and return text and copy to Alexandria, and don't give it too much thought. We'll stick by what we've received."

"But what if...what if some of their readings are right? Oh, I'm sure we've got it right at beginning and end, Marcus, but what about this? Look at the story about John the Baptist. This codex reads "Make his paths straight." Marcus, don't you see how easy it would be for us to begin writing the wording in our manuscripts that is so familiar to us from that great song we sing from the prophecy of Isaiah? Here *they* may be right and we may be wrong.

"Justin, " pleaded Marcus, "It really is a minor difference, a trifling, and I don't..."

"A trifling!" shot back Justin, and then he was interrupted by a knock on the door. It was Juliana, accompanied by two servants, one a man and the other a woman. All were well dressed and finely groomed, and were eager to see the scribes and their scriptorium.

"Welcome to our scriptorium." said Justin. "We hope that what we have to offer will be adequate. We had not expected three, Marcus, will you be kind enough to run round and fetch some extra bread and drink..."

"Really, " said Juliana, "we do not wish to be a burden. My Father has sent provisions for us and gifts for you and we will all be well looked after. May I introduce Rhoda and James? They will serve and assist us as needed."

24

Justin led the way through to the scriptorium, now filled with morning sunlight. There on the copying table lay Juliana's precious codex. The pens and papyrus quires were carefully arranged. All was ready for the work, except Justin's heart. But he put on his best front, determined to keep his secret to himself, and cheerfully opened the book, perhaps exaggerating care and reverence.

"This is indeed a beautiful hand, Juliana, and mine will be plain by contrast, a utility script, but here we are. I first take this quire of papyrus; I dip the pen in this ink. Now as I sit over the document, I attempt to keep the pen as upright as I can..."

"I am used to more of a slant," said Juliana, "And find it enables me to round the letters off more carefully, and to control their shape more easily."

Just then Justin thought to himself, "What does it matter how beautiful a text is, if it is wrong? You may have the most perfect margins, the most elegant script, the most learned scribe in the world, but if the text he produces is faulty, what use is it?" But he controlled his tongue and stuck to his task. He dutifully, slowly, copied out, "The beginning of the Gospel of Jesus Christ..."

The following day he would go and lay his dilemma before the Bishop.

CHAPTER 6

Shortly after midday Marcus had to leave to attend to the family business. His father was a sheep farmer on a modest holding on the edge of the great city, and with every passing year more and more fell to Marcus and his brothers to do. Their father and mother, now in their seventies, and still active, were pleased that their sons were eager to carry on the trade in sheep. It was not an especially lucrative business, but it kept them comfortably, and they had managed even in times of hardship. The family had been long time members of the Christian congregation at Rome, and all were active with the exception of the youngest brother, Junius, who was eager to express his freedom from Christian faith and morals. Pleasant but heated debates between Marcus and Junius often punctuated the tasks on the sheep farm.

Walking from the scriptorium to the farm, Marcus pondered the events of the morning. The visit from the strikingly beautiful Juliana and her two servants was pleasing but disorienting. Yet more jarring was the dream of the night before, still vivid in his mind, but not entirely clear in meaning. What was he to make of the lion and the eagle? Which was Mark and which was John? Or were they both meant to symbolize Mark? Was the gospel manuscript they were now copying both a danger and a blessing? And then he remembered that he was behind in his regular recitation of the psalms. He knew most of them by heart, some in Greek, some in Latin (from the old Roman Psalter). He had ended at the sixth psalm, so he took up with the seventh,

> "O Lord my God, in thee have I put my trust: save me from all them that persecute me, and deliver me; lest he devour my soul like a lion..."

27

"Nequando rapiat ut leo animam meam..." There the lion lurked again, ready to pounce. Perhaps Justin was right, and he should not put so much stock in the dream, but everywhere he turned, it seemed, the lion stared him in the face.

And then there was the unsettling discovery that Justin had made. The beginning and the ending of Mark in this beautiful copy were defective (or so it seemed to them). Had he made too light of it? He had never seen Justin so rattled, nor had they ever disagreed so sharply. The impending arrival of the scribe from Alexandria, and that a woman scribe, had, no doubt added to the tension of the moment. It gave him lots to think about as he tended sheep.

Marcus and Justin were the best of friends, but they had known disagreements in their years of work together in the scriptorium. Marcus remembered the time when they were copying St. Paul's letter to the Romans for use of a new congregation on the other side of the city. It was meant to be a major project, producing a large codex of all the known epistles of St. Paul, made from the Roman Church's exemplar. They had reached the section where Paul speaks of "life in the Spirit," and had taken turns copying and checking each other's work. They came to the place where St. Paul wrote, "Who is to condemn? It is Christ, who died, yes, who was raised, who is at the right hand of God, who indeed intercedes for us."

Justin and Marcus noticed that the manuscript from which they were copying was unusual. There were no less than three marginal notations in this one sentence. In an obviously different hand someone had written in the margin "Christ Jesus" in the customary abbreviations (XS IS). Below it were written the words *ek nekron*, "from the dead," to clarify the word "raised." Yet another notation added the word "*kai*" (the Greek for "also"). Should any or all of these marginal notes be included in the text they were copying? Should they be copied in the margin, in imitation of the exemplar? Or should any or all be rejected? Simply to include them in the new copy of Paul would leave no trace of the doubt they felt on finding them in the margin. Furthermore another complication had arisen, which both the scribes, and their new companion, Rufus, had spotted

28

straightway. All three, extra readings, if original, greatly enhanced the usefulness of the verse in controversy against the Gnostics who taught a "separationist" view of Christ. This was the view that Christ came upon Jesus at his baptism, and left him at the crucifixion. This to them was the import of the cry from the cross: "My God, My God, Why hast thou forsaken me?" So forcefully did some Gnostic "separationists" push this interpretation of the cry that a few championed the strange alternate reading "Why hast thou persecuted me?" But the teachers of the Roman Church, and Irenaeus in particular, would not be drawn. "The original text must be copied," he insisted, "whether it helps or hinders our cause!"

Marcus knew how deeply this teaching of Irenaeus had impressed Justin, for he was fond of quoting it, and they both considered the word of the great teacher unimpeachable. No one cared more about the refutation and overthrow of heresy than Irenaeus. Yet none was more committed to the preservation of the text of scripture, as it came from the hands of the prophets and the apostles. To distort scripture, even in a good cause, was to distort the faith of the church, and ultimately to destroy it. Was not this the fundamental error behind Marcion's system, as he rejected the Old Testament and selected only an expurgated Lukan gospel and some of the letters of Paul from among the apostolic writings? This was a gross distortion, but even the slightest deviation was a danger. Granted, there were places where the text was uncertain, and there probabilities had to be weighed, but where the text was clear, no addition or omission could be tolerated, however slight or tempting the alteration might be.

"I think we should keep them in the text." Rufus had exclaimed in youthful enthusiasm and admirable zeal. "They offer just what we need against those Gnostics, and all in one verse! Jesus Christ was and is one and inseparable, his resurrection was a real rising from the dead, and these were events, his death, his resurrection, his exaltation, that happened in sequence. They were not, spiritually speaking, blended into one another."

"That makes them all the more suspect!" snapped Justin. "It would be only too tempting for someone to improve the text of Paul in this way." Justin had reacted sharply, and Marcus, true to form, had tried to mediate.

"They are small and harmless alterations, and the first sounds like St. Paul's way of writing. It is a bit of a puzzle to find them in the margin, but it's not worth too much worry. If we keep them, they are consistent with what St. Paul wrote elsewhere. If we reject them, their teaching is guaranteed elsewhere in St. Paul. At least we should note them in the margins, I think."

"But Marcus," Justin retorted sharply, "We do not know them in any other copy of St. Paul, and we are usually rigorous about not including marginal notes. You forget the danger once we start being lax. Where do we stop? I will admit none of them."

Tempers cooled and the storm passed from the scriptorium. Marcus decided that given a growing tendency to falsify texts in their time, the scribes had best be as unbending as Justin. Too much was at stake. The sound of trouble in the sheepfold warned him of some more immediate danger to be attended to.

CHAPTER 7

The twin libraries of Trajan were without peer, without rival, at least in the West. These Bibliothecae Ulpiae rose high above the Basilica in the Forum of Trajan, and faced each other across the Forum. The one housed Greek manuscripts, the other Latin, together with the imperial archives. Each building opened on to the rectangular court through a rank of columns. Once inside the buildings the reader found a large central niche for a monumental statue. The manuscripts themselves were housed in cupboards, each of which was decorated with a bust of one writer or another whose writings had given them fame in one of the two great languages of the empire. At the center of the quadrilateral between the two libraries arose the Column of Trajan. The architect of the group, Apollodorus, whose work had been dedicated in January 112, had conceived of a work of grandeur, calculated to inspire any reader or scholar. Entering under the arch from the southeast, the scholar at once felt a sense of human achievement. And as the whole was built into and against the slopes of the Capitoline and Quirinal hills, a sense of natural stability and power added to the feeling of awe. From every corner, and to all the senses, the message was clear: herein lies wisdom and strength.

Demetrius and Juliana had been invited by one of his Roman clients to the celebration of the acquisition of some new Greek manuscripts for the Bibliothecae Ulpiae. The treasures on display had come from a generous benefactor in Alexandria, and were some beautifully copied manuscripts of Homer. As Father and daughter stood admiring the manuscripts and their surroundings, a man in his late thirties approached and introduced himself.

31

"I am M. Suplicius Garbo, the sub-librarian for Greek manuscripts, and I welcome you to our library. It is, as you must know, the finest library in the world."

"Really?" responded Demetrius, seeking to conceal his real feeling. He knew that the library of Alexandria was unrivaled, anywhere in the world, with the possible exception of that at Pergamum. He thought at once of an effective rhetorical strategy. He could ask, "Do you think Galen would agree?" Galen, the famous writer on anatomy, physiology and philosophy, was born and raised in Pergamum. He later studied in Alexandria, and knew both libraries well. Now he lived in Rome, under the special favor of the Emperor, so he would also know the Bibliothecae Ulpiae. He would know from experience what others could only guess: that Rome, for all its wealth, power and conquest could not equal that great center of Greek culture. But Demetrius refused to be drawn. "This is a most impressive place." he replied, in a matter-of-fact tone.

"I hear you are from Alexandria, which also boasts a fine library," continued Garbo.

"We are very proud of it, and it houses many fine volumes."

"And what writers do you especially admire, for we could show you the works of any here," said Garbo, turning toward Juliana.

"This Homer is very fine indeed," she replied, "I believe I have seen it before in Alexandria."

"Yes, but now it is here," continued Garbo, "And all things good and beautiful eventually find their way to Rome. Observe that fine script and those beautifully formed letters. Have you ever seen anything so beautiful? This is truly the perfect setting for such a manuscript."

"I knew the scribe who copied this text," stated Juliana, "a splendid man of letters, who taught me when I first began to learn the copyist's trade."

"You copy, then?" asked Garbo.

"I do, and I am eager to learn all I can about the art of copying." She caught herself, and said no more, perhaps because the sense of Demetrius' hand on her elbow reminded her of the need for caution. She must say nothing of her Christian interest, nor of her learning at the Roman Church's scriptorium. Justin and Marcus, and the whole Roman Church could be put in jeopardy. And a man like Garbo, so obviously full of himself and zealous for the Roman way, might easily find it to his advantage to become hostile to the church. "Yes, I copy all sorts of texts."

Turning to Demetrius Garbo exclaimed. "We could employ your daughter here as a copyist, and she would be herself a great adornment for this place. May I ask, is she spoken for?"

"Juliana will speak for herself. In any case we are here only a short time, and must return to Alexandria." Both Demetrius and Juliana were shocked and embarrassed by Garbo's boldness, but would hardly reveal their sentiments. His assumption that whatever Rome wants Rome conquers, whether it is land or manuscripts or women, seemed to them revolting, and left an awful pit in their stomachs. The relentlessness of the conqueror, his voracious appetite, his ruthless methods, his heartlessness, his arrogance, all masking a deep insecurity, made them nauseated.

"Tell me more about this splendid library," said Demetrius, confident that Garbo would talk on about his little world and himself. "In what Greek writers are you especially strong?"

"We have the great philosophers, Plato and Aristotle, of course, and indeed all of the Greek writers whose busts adorn our library walls, as you can see. There is Sophocles, and there Demosthenes. But we also have more recent writers, as well as sacred texts. We have that translation of the Jews, done in your city by the seventy scribes, and there are texts of newer cults and superstitions." The last word, *superstitio*, which Garbo pronounced with unmistakable contempt, told the Alexandrian visitors that their instincts to be cautious were right on the mark. The Romans used the term *superstitio* to refer to cultic practices that were foreign, and did not conform to the established *religio*, or Roman religious custom. Such superstitious cults, which had found their way to Rome, were an effrontery to the Roman social and religious order. Christians and Jews did not participate in banquets or games because they were essentially religious events. And had not Roman writers of previous generations

33

dubbed Christianity *superstitio?* Pliny had called it "a depraved superstition carried to extravagant lengths." Tacitus had called Christians a "deadly superstition," and accused them of "crimes against humanity," in the reign of Nero. Suetonius had labeled them "a new and mischievous superstition." And if the thinkers had formed these views, what of the populace? Christians were called "Atheists" because they did not worship the Roman gods; they were termed "cannibals" because they "ate the body and blood" of their founder; they were deemed "incestuous" because they married those whom they called "brother" and "sister."

"Ah, Garbo!" The loud and jovial voice of their host, Gaius, echoing through the library was most welcome. "So you have met my guests from Alexandria, Demetrius and Juliana. I trust you have not troubled them with too much detail." Then turning to Demetrius he confided, "His learning is vast, but so is his capacity for talk."

"Indeed," said Demetrius.

"And isn't this a splendid Homer?" Gaius went on, "I suspect you have some rather fine manuscripts in your famous library in Alexandria. Have you seen many of them?"

"Juliana has, she has seen this one, in fact, and studied under the copyist for a time. Anaximines of Alexandria was his name, and he worked closely with the grammarian Phrynicus. They were both dedicated to the revival of Attic literature and style, and would be pleased to know that you hold this copy of Homer in such high esteem. They did much to revive the interest in classical learning among us. Even in Alexandria, it is a struggle to keep to the best standards."

Demetrius knew that talk of culture and style was safe, and would avoid potential clash or embarrassment. Eastern Christians could not be too cautious in the capital, but especially in this setting talk of the great classic civilization, which the libraries had been built to honor and preserve, would be agreeable and welcome. As soon as it was convenient, he and Juliana would politely retire to their villa on the outskirts of the city.

CHAPTER 8

Eleutherus had been Bishop in Rome for five years. During that time the church had known relative peace and tranquility, despite outbreaks of persecution of Christians in several provinces of the Empire. In general the church had flourished during the reign of Marcus Aurelius. Eleutherus himself was a tall stately man, but kindly and approachable, and offered wise counsel. He had come from the East, like so many in the Roman Church leadership of his day, having been born in Nicapolis. A champion of apostolic faith, he was on very close terms with Irenaeus, Bishop of Lyons, who had been in Rome on church business during the great persecution in Gaul. They had consulted and agreed on the need to expose and overthrow the Gnostic errors of such popular teachers as Valentinus, Basilides, and Marcion. These men had visited Rome, where their teaching was having a serious impact on the church, and the firm stand of Eleutherus was an encouragement to young Christians like Justin, Marcus and Rufus.

But sometimes Eleutherus was difficult to read. He had been less decisive with the Montanists, or at least, so it seemed. The movement had begun when a Phrygian named Montanus had been seized by the Spirit, and together with two prophetesses, Prisca and Maxamilla, began to utter prophecies which they claimed to be direct utterances of the Paraclete or Holy Spirit. They spoke their prophecies in the first person singular, predicted that the end of the world was at hand, and spoke of the imminent millennial reign of Christ on the Earth. They believed that Christ would descend to earth in Phrygia, and there begin his reign. Those who rejected this prophecy said the Montanists, blasphemed against the Holy Spirit. Churches in Asia Minor were split down the middle by the teaching, and some churches,

35

like the one at Thyatira, were entirely won over to it. Most of the great church centers refused to recognize the movement. In Rome Eleutherus had deliberated long and heard both sides with care. This was characteristic of him. He refused to draw hasty conclusions. But to some this looked like wavering. Both sides had made strong appeal to him, and he read and thought and prayed while some grew impatient. In the end he decided against the movement, but it left some with the impression that he tolerated heresy.

Justin knew he could count on his bishop to listen, but he was not quite sure how he might respond in the end. After all, he thought, a few differences between Eastern and Western manuscripts, while not insignificant, were hardly worth troubling a bishop whose life was full of pressing matters before the church. Still, Justin felt himself in a dilemma, so it was to his bishop, wise, kindly, approachable, and a great supporter of the scriptorium that he turned for pastoral and practical help.

"Justin, God bless you! It is so good to see you again, and so soon. I trust all goes well with the copying and our visitors. And have you caught up on your sleep?"

To the last question Justin nodded assent, but that was only half-true. Then he went straight to the point.

"The visitors from Alexandria are most delightful, but they are the reason I have come to see you."

"Oh, really, Justin. Is anything wrong?"

"Not exactly wrong," said Justin, "But a question has arisen as I have begun copying Juliana's beautiful codex of the Gospel of St. Mark, and I have come to seek your advice."

"My advice, Justin? But you are the expert, and on any matters of copying and texts I would be seeking you for help. What could the trouble be?"

"Bishop," said Justin, as he removed the small codex from his satchel and untied the leather thongs, "Look at how this manuscript begins and ends. Do you see here? At the beginning it lacks the words "the Son of God" and at the end, do you see, well, there really is no end; it simply stops with the report that they were afraid. I have noticed some other differences as well, in phraseology and style, but here is my dilemma. Do I simply copy what is here, though it is different from all the texts we have received here in Rome, or do I add the things to it which we know from our tradition? If we retain the copy here in Rome, we introduce doubt as to the nature of the text of St. Mark. If we do not retain it, but return the copy with the exemplar to Juliana, she will likely feel we do not value her text. I think she means for us to keep the copy once it is made. Do we keep it, so as not to offend, or do we hide it, or destroy it once she has returned to Alexandria? And how can we be absolutely sure that in these particulars Rome is right and Alexandria is wrong?"

With the last sentence the Bishop sat upright and seemed visibly moved. Perhaps, thought Justin, he should not have said that bit, but there it was. He had said it, and he needed to know. If his bishop could not advise him, who could?

"Justin, my Son, my fellow-worker in the Lord" said Eleutherus, communicating that sense of collegiality and cooperation, and above all Christian love which his fellow Christians had grown to value these five years, "Thank you for speaking your mind. No one wishes more to be faithful to the teaching of the Gospel as actually written than you do, and so I understand your dilemma. You know that for a short time as a young man I worked with your father in the copyist's trade, and that I am no stranger to these issues. I have lost sleep over a reading in a text, which I remembered to be different from another. How distinctly I remember it now, as if it were yesterday. Did Mark write *agapa* or *tima* when he quoted from the middle of the prophecy of Isaiah? I spent a sleepless night on that one, I looked up all the codices and rolls I could lay my hands on, and determined to find others and check them as opportunity allowed. I finally had to decide, and came down on the side of *agapa*, but to this day I have some lingering doubts. It is a small point, and really a matter of flavoring of two synonyms, for *love* and *honor*. But I do know what you are facing, on points that are far more serious. Let me see this again. Yes, well these two you have pointed out to me (He handled the codex with reverence and care) these two look to me like they could be accidental omissions. What Juliana, and for all we

37

know, the whole Alexandrine church, has been reading is a defective, but faithfully copied Gospel of St. Mark."

Justin looked up from the codex, and there stood Eleutherus, still pondering the ending of the manuscript. His comments had been freeing. He had lived up to his name, which meant "free" in Greek. Justin had found an ally, "So what shall I do?" he queried.

"I am not just sure what to do," said the bishop. "We obviously do not want to communicate disapproval of this beloved text, or arouse suspicion, or cause tension between us and the visitors, or between the churches. But obviously you cannot ignore the problem. Perhaps this is what you could do. Choose some insignificant, but real difference, like the one that robbed me of sleep long ago, some difference in style that does not alter the sense or the teaching, and lightly raise the question with Juliana in passing. Simply observe as an interesting sidelight that we know a different word. See how she reacts. If she recoils at the thought that her copy may have any mistakes, however slight, then drop the subject. But if I judge aright, she is practiced at the copyist's trade, and knows all about variants and will be positively engaged by your observation. But remember to keep your tone very low-key. Give no cause for alarm or offense."

Justin could tell that the Bishop, weighed down with the increasing troubles that beset the Roman Church, had been delighted to journey back in his mind to that simpler day when sleep could be lost over a minor variant reading. It had evoked a sense of nostalgia, and the mention of Justin's father had only deepened their bond. Eleutherus was to him a wise father, and a sure guide, with whom he could share almost anything. But there were limits, of course. A fledgling affection for Juliana, which it was hopeless to suppress, was something he must keep to himself, at least for now. It must remain his secret. Nothing in any case could come of his feeling. The visitors were to be gone in less than a month, and he would probably never see Juliana again. Certainly he should not trouble his bishop with the thought that he might lose his chief scribe to Alexandria some day. And in any case, he had no indication that Juliana

38

would ever reciprocate affection. He would be a fool to say anything.

"Have you anything else to tell me?" asked the Bishop.

"Nothing, really," replied Justin. They exchanged the kiss of peace, and Justin found himself alone with his thoughts amid the bustling Roman streets in the brilliant noonday sun.

CHAPTER 9

The hours had seemed to fly by. What Justin had expected would be a one-hour conference with his bishop had turned into almost three hours of rich mutual encouragement. They had both lost track of the time. Though Justin had valued the time with his bishop, he suddenly realized that he would be late for his visitors at the scriptorium. He hated being late, and now the thought of Juliana, her servants and Marcus waiting for him outside his door made him run the last mile of the hilly journey home. By the time he reached the brow of the last hill, exhausted and breathless, he could see the little band he had expected waiting at his door.

"I am so sorry to be late," he panted as he approached. None of the party seemed upset, and Justin sought to keep his composure.

"It is quite all right," said Juliana.

"But it doesn't leave Marcus much time before he leaves for the sheep-fold, I am sorry, indeed!" he exclaimed, as he pressed the key in the door. "Now if you will excuse me for just a minute..." and he slipped inside and shut the door. He caught his breath and walked past his room into the scriptorium. Reaching into his satchel he took out Juliana's precious codex, and placed it in what was now its customary resting-place. She did not know that he had taken it across the city to show his bishop the readings that had concerned him so. What would she have thought? There was no time to ponder that now. He returned to the door and bade them enter.

James, the manservant left almost at once to fetch some supplies at the nearby market while Rhoda, the maidservant, stood by, wandering into the small rear garden to sit and contemplate, ready at the call of her mistress. Justin sat down

41

and went straight to work. He picked up the copying at Mark's account of the baptism of Jesus. By now he was breathing normally, and his eyes fell on the words of the divine voice: "Thou art my beloved son, in thee I am well pleased." At least that is what he saw on the page of Juliana's codex. But what he found himself writing, almost by instinct, was the words familiar to him from his copies of St. Luke's account, and from the second Psalm, so frequently chanted in their public worship and private prayers: "Thou art my son, my beloved, this day have I begotten thee." Had it been his flustered state, his fatigue, his thoughts still distracted by the wonderful conference with the bishop? Whatever the cause, he found himself about to alter the text unintentionally - or was it entirely unintentionally? He put down the reed-pen and rubbed his eyes. Looking up he could see that Juliana was intently watching every stroke. He carefully penned "...in thee I am well-pleased."

The text had been much debated in recent days among the Roman Christians. Rufus had often cited the Markan form in heated debate with heretics who claimed that Jesus was adopted as God's Son and Messiah at his baptism. In more measured tones Justin and Marcus had done the same. But here Justin had found himself about to write the words that would play into the hands of the heretics, even though they were words of the beloved psalm, and used by his namesake, Justin Martyr as the voice at the baptism. But no, he must write what was there in the exemplar. He was to be a faithful copyist, and guard against all the forces, conscious or unconscious to the contrary.

Just as Justin took up the pen to proceed, the door flung open and in walked Rufus, now freed from house arrest.

"Rufus!" exclaimed Justin and Marcus in unison. And then an uneasy silence descended on the scriptorium. After what seemed to Justin a very long time, he said in a voice that communicated and heightened tension,

"Rufus, may I introduce Juliana, a scribe from Alexandria, who is on a short visit with her father here in Rome. Our bishop has asked us if we would show her our scriptorium and our methods of copying."

42

"But you didn't...." said Rufus, and then turning to Juliana he said in a quizzical voice, "I did not know that there were *women* scribes."

"We have several in Alexandria, and I know of a number in other churches. We are especially valued for fine copying and accuracy."

Re-fixing his gaze on Justin and Marcus, Rufus complained, "You did not tell me she was a woman. Now I do not want to be disrespectful of our visitor, but I am a bit puzzled. You said nothing about her being a woman when you visited, and I feel excluded, left out. You have not been entirely honest with me. You know what I think. I think the church is sitting increasingly loose to the teaching of the Apostle Paul: 'I permit no woman to teach or to have authority over men. She is to keep silent.' If we keep going in the permissive direction of many churches today, before too long we will have prophetesses, like Prisca and Maxamilla, and we might as well give in to the Montanists and their chaos."

Turning to Juliana, no stranger to insult and rebuff, he said, "I am sorry to speak thus, but it is all important to speak the truth!"

"Speak the truth in love," she said, "Or so I read in all my manuscripts of the Apostle."

Justin was charmed and surprised by her reply. Pleased by her ready wit and wisdom, he suddenly realized that Juliana might be one who cared about manuscript difference. Was she, perhaps, practiced in thinking out variations and weighing alternatives? She was not just a young girl with a sentimental attachment to her one beautiful copy of Mark. She must have some experience, possibly much experience, in the art and science of copying. But what would come of all this now? She could hardly be expected to feel welcome in the scriptorium after this encounter. Justin's heart sank.

"If you will excuse me," said Rufus, "I must be off." He turned and walked out the door. Marcus followed him, no doubt to calm and mediate, if at all possible. "Marcus the mediator," they sometimes called him.

James was still at the market and Rhoda still in the garden. Justin and Juliana were alone in the scriptorium. But in a moment the servants would return, and Justin knew that this might be the last he would see of her, except, perhaps in the Sunday Eucharist, for a moment of talk.

"Juliana, I am so sorry about all this," he said, "And I can't imagine you will want to come any more."

"You have been most kind, Justin, and I am grateful," she said as she moved toward the table where her manuscript lay open. But I do not want to be the cause of tension between you and your friend."

She closed the codex and stared down at it. He wished he could have said something that would be right, but no words seemed to fit the occasion. In a moment she would be gone.

"Juliana," he said, not knowing quite what to say next. Perhaps he just wished to pronounce the name aloud, with her there. It was better than simply whispering it to himself.

She turned her head, throwing back her long black hair, and gazed fully upon him with her deep, penetrating brown eyes.

"Men!" she said in full voice, "And especially Roman men; all they want is to take, to control, to conquer! I went the other day with my father the Bibliothecae Ulpiae. There I met M. Suplicius Garbo, the sub-librarian. All he could think about was Roman conquest. 'The best library in the world indeed!' Has he no knowledge of Alexandria or Pergamum? The arrogance! All he could think of was conquest: of lands, of treasures, of manuscripts. He even tried to conquer me in the short conversation. Is that all Roman men can think of: conquering lands and manuscripts and women?"

She looked down again to the codex, and started to tie the thongs.

"Women also conquer." said Justin.

She made no reply, which was just as well, since Justin did not want to have to explain what he meant. He had the sinking feeling that the association was over. Then a thought flashed through his head. Why not mention the differences in their manuscripts. He had nothing to lose. She had given some

44

indication that she cared about variations and the issues in copying texts that gripped him too. It was worth a try.

"Juliana," said Justin, "I am sorry it has come to this, as I had meant to tell you something I have discovered. In reading your lovely manuscript of St. Mark I have found some major differences between your manuscript and ours. I do not say that yours are wrong and ours are right. I just want to get to the bottom of it, and to come to conviction about what Mark really wrote in his Gospel. I need your help, Juliana. You would not have to come here. I could come to you, and bring my text and we could compare. Juliana, I need...to know."

She stood silent and pensive, and if he was not mistaken, a bit tearful, but fully self-controlled.

"Differences?" she asked, "What differences?"

"At the beginning and the end, your St. Mark has significant omissions."

"Omissions? What omissions? Well... I don't know... I need time to think. This is Friday, and I will see you at the worship service on Sunday. We can talk after that... perhaps."

James returned and the visitors left. Justin collapsed into his chair and cried. His were tears of exhaustion and pain and hope.

CHAPTER 10

The assembly of Christians for worship on the Lord's Day was the center of life of the Roman church. It had always been so for as long as anyone could remember. Justin Martyr, writing when Justin the scribe was still a small boy, had given a vivid description of the service:

"And on the day which is called the day of the sun there is an assembly of all those who live in the towns or in the country and the memoirs of the apostles or the writings of the prophets are read for as long as time permits. Then the reader ceases, and the president speaks, admonishing and exhorting us to imitate these excellent examples. Then we all rise together and pray and, as we said before, when we have completed our prayer, bread is brought, and wine and water, and the president in like manner offers prayers and thanksgivings according to his ability, and the people assent with Amen; And there is a distribution and partaking by all of that over which thanks has been given, and to those who are absent a portion is sent by the deacons. And those who are prosperous and willing give what each thinks fit, and what is collected is deposited with the president, who gives aid to orphans and widows and to those who are in want on account of illness or any other cause, and to those also who are in prison, and, to strangers from abroad, and, in a word, cares for all who are in need."

On this particular Sunday in late summer in A.D. 179 the President of the assembly was, as often, Bishop Eleutherus, and the Lector or reader was Justin. It was the custom of the reader to arrive first and to make sure all was in order for the service of worship. So Justin found himself awake before dawn and out in the early morning light for the three-mile journey into the city. The assembly took place in a large house which stood near to the

47

bishop's dwelling, and which had recently been given to the church for the purpose of worship. As Justin arrived and found the place in the Gospel of Mark from which he would be reading, he was distracted with thoughts of the events of the past week. The return from Gaul, the encounters with Juliana, the discovery of significant differences in the Roman and Alexandrian texts of Mark, the scene caused by Rufus in the scriptorium filled his mind. He was aware of his anxiety and anticipation over meeting Juliana and her father after the worship and vowed to himself, all in vain, not to be distracted.

"The assembly is for worship, for the hearing the word of God, and for receiving the bread and wine, as the Lord himself commanded," said Justin to himself.

The office of reader was very important, and Justin was one of several in the church. To the reader was entrusted not only the reading of the Old Testament and the writings of the Apostles, but also the skillful exposition and explanation of the text, its meaning and import. He was thus considered an evangelist, reading and expounding the scriptures to the people. His reading would include long portions of the Gospel, which, with other Apostolic writings, had come to be considered "scripture" like the Old Testament. So Justin felt the great importance of his office, and combined with his duty as scribe, this made him a significant leader in the Roman church. The previous week another of the readers had finished reading the Gospel of Luke, and Justin therefore would begin with St. Mark's Gospel, the very text he had been pondering on the previous days. Many would rejoice to see Justin again after his long absence, and would be eager for the report from Irenaeus and the churches in Gaul, which the bishop had asked him to give to the assembly. As people began to arrive, Justin asked God that he might read the text of Mark with the same confidence and assurance and skill as always, despite his newfound questions about its text, and his special reasons to be distracted.

After an opening hymn, and a prayer by the bishop Justin began,

"The beginning of the Gospel of Jesus Christ, the Son of God..."

He said the last phrase with emphasis. He knew it must be the right reading, and he wanted all of the two hundred people in the assembly to be sure of it too. Yet among those two hundred assembled would be two at least who did not know these words. Justin's eyes were glued to the page, but on the occasion when he looked up, he found himself scanning the assembly to catch sight of Juliana. This is just what he told himself he must not do. So he disciplined himself to look only at the book as he read.

The reading lasted for about half an hour, halting after the confession of Peter, "You are the Christ." He found himself tempted to add from the more familiar account in Matthew, "The Son of the Living God." But if he had felt this strong urge here, would it not have been possible, even likely that one of his predecessors, a pious reader and scribe like himself, to have added the words, "the Son of God" at the beginning?

There was no time for these thoughts now. He must expound the sense of the text, and so he exhorted the assembly to trust in Jesus Christ as the Son of God, the Messiah, who had come to save the world. He went on at the Bishop's invitation to tell of the strength and courage of the Christians in Lyons, and to read special greetings from their beloved friend, Bishop Irenaeus. All the while he scanned the congregation, but Juliana was nowhere to be seen. He began to worry that the tense encounter in the scriptorium on the Friday had meant that she had come to feel unwelcome in the Roman church. She had said she would see him there at the assembly, and that the door was left open for further meetings. He felt he had forgiven Rufus and would seek him out in the coming week. He was not sure what he would say to the bishop if the matter came up, regarding either the release of Rufus or the absence of Demetrius and Juliana. If only she had come, as she said she would! Now he was left with a host of textual questions, an awkward situation to explain, and a heavy heart.

All too quickly the worship ended, and the bishop's question came,

"I was surprised not to see our visitors from Alexandria. How are they getting on? And did you manage to raise those questions about the textual differences?"

"We did explore them a bit, " said Justin, in a matter-of-fact way, "and I hope to speak some more of these matters this week." He felt his wise old bishop must surely have detected some strain, some hesitation, some sadness, but Eleutherus made no comment. The Bishop changed the subject, "Oh, I hear Rufus has been released. I think he fears an encounter with me. Will you give him this letter and urge him not to be afraid of coming to see me. He is a beloved brother in the Lord, and needs our encouragement. This will help him to gain self-control."

As always, Eleutherus had put him at ease and had lightened the load. But heavy load it remained as Justin dragged his feet for the three miles back to his abode. But there at his door was a letter. It was from Juliana. His heart raced as he read it.

"Juliana to Justin, greetings in Christ. Please forgive the outburst, 'I said I shall take heed unto my ways, that I offend not with my tongue.' Father has had to be out of town, but we will return tomorrow. Are you still willing to come and bring your copy of St. Mark? James will call for you at midday. Grace and peace."

There was no denying what his heart was telling him. Justin found himself captivated by the beautiful and cultured scribe from Alexandria, and his hopes of deepening that friendship were not in vain.

CHAPTER 11

It was not going to be easy to find Rufus, but Justin knew he must. It was important to ease the tension between them, and in any case, there was a letter to deliver from the bishop. He knew that this meant making his way to the place where Rufus lived, down by the docks on the Tiber, and seeking him out. Rufus worked as a dockhand, and also in his father's fishing trade. He and his six brothers were all at one time involved in the family business, and also in other rough-and-tumble employ as they might find when the fish weren't running. Two of the older brothers had joined the army. Rufus, the youngest, had often thought of doing the same. But his father's pleas, and especially his conversion to Christianity had worked against it. Some Christians refused to join the army, since it might mean worshiping the emperor.

Rufus's house was in a narrow street that sloped down to the riverfront. The street always smelled of dead fish, and was littered with nets and gear for the fishing trade. On some days the smell was almost overpowering to the visitor, and this sunny, hot, late summer day was one of them. Enduring the stench, Justin made his way to the door he thought belonged to Rufus's house. He knocked and waited. He had come early in the morning, so as to complete his errand and be back by noon when James was due to fetch him. Even the briefest conversation with Rufus would help to clear the air, he thought. He had about an hour before he would have to return. He knocked again, but there was no reply. He had been there twice before to visit Rufus, and felt sure that he had come to the right door. He even remembered the markings and hardware. But there was just enough uncertainty in his mind that he felt he could not leave the bishop's letter. This should be delivered to Rufus in person.

51

After waiting five minutes, and knocking again, he decided that a look along the riverside might be more productive.

As he turned to walk down to the river, Justin noticed an old fisherman coming up the lane. His skin was wrinkled and darkened from years in the sun, and his eyes, a deep-sea blue, twinkled like the sea reflecting the morning sun.

"You won't find them there," he said.

"So I noticed," said Justin, grateful that the old man stated the obvious. But then he asked, "This is the house of Rufus?"

The old man stopped and stared straight at Justin, "Yes, that it is, but they're never there, not the young one nor the father, nor the brothers, except only for sleep."

"Do you know where I might find Rufus?" asked Justin.

"Try the boats down there, and to the left," said the old man still gazing quizzically at Justin. He turned to go on, and then spun round and stared again, and shook his head,

"Strange folk, that lot," he mused. "All went kind of funny when the father taught the boys to read. Fishermen don't need to read. What's the good of books for them? Stuffs their heads full of crazy ideas, philosophies and that sort of thing. None of it ever helped to catch one fish. You can hear them at the nets some days, they go on for hours about Plato and Pythagorus, and Virgil, and all kinds of superstitions I can't remember the names of now, something about Mithras and Chrestus and all that stuff. Best get on with tides and currents, I say."

He started to move on and then wheeled round again, and offered further comment:

"That eldest one, Blastus, he went off to the legions, and found himself serving Caesar in the East. Every time he returns he has some new idea more fantastic than the last. This time it was all about Mithras slaying the bull. He talked about it to everyone, and got lots of folks upset. I remember one night coming by here after setting out my nets, and I could hear them all shouting and pounding their fists on the table - and on each other I shouldn't wonder - it's those books, I tell you. That's the trouble. A lot of nonsense, if you ask me."

Justin, eager to be off, nodded, and moved down the lane. Once more the old man wheeled around, and offered his last shot:

"If you want my word on it, I would not like to be them when Neptune comes into harbor and drops his anchor!"

At the bottom of the lane, Justin spied a cluster of boats on the left at the quay. They seemed worn and tattered, with lines all tangled and nets draped clumsily everywhere. The few men milling about appeared to be at work, but none seemed connected to another, a collection of individuals rather than a community. For a moment Justin felt that the scene was a kind of parable of the Roman world of his day, all busy but none sharing a common goal. How unlike this was the Church, where all worked for the common good to glorify Christ. "I go a fishing," said Peter in the gospel. Had he meant that it was back to the old ways, back to the life he knew before he met Jesus? That is what came to Justin's mind as he approached the boats looking for Rufus.

And there he was, fixing some small part on the rigging of his boat, while chatting with one of the other hands. As Justin approached and called out, Rufus turned around.

"Oh, Justin, I am sorry for the other day, and my unkind remarks. I hope you can find a way to forgive..."

"Rufus," said Justin, "The lady has seen much of the world, and I know she does not hold anything against you. True, it was rather rude, but we must not let these things stand in the way. Now here is a letter the bishop has asked me to deliver personally."

The mention of the lady and the bishop, and the rude remarks of Rufus made all his mates seem united in interest where just two minutes before they had been in separate worlds. Justin realized that he had said too much, perhaps, and that his audience might include those hostile to the Christian faith. So he said no more except to urge Rufus to return and work as soon as he could. "You are still on the team, and we need you, Rufus," he said as he gave him the letter and began to move away.

Rufus climbed out of the boat and started to follow Justin, while all the men listened eagerly for any further scraps of what sounded like a most interesting story. But they were unable to catch what passed between the two in whispers as they walked.

"You really do mean it?" asked Rufus with transparent sincerity. "You still do want me at the scriptorium and part of the scribal team? Really, I am sorry. I was out of line, and I do want any honored guest, any brother, yes, and even sister in Christ to feel welcome. I should keep my views to myself. You do forgive..."

"Yes, yes, yes, Rufus, and seventy times seven and then seven, if that's what it must be. The master makes it clear. Now when can you come?"

"I'm tied up here for a day or two more, but then I'll be back. Now wait, what does the bishop say?" Rufus hastily opened the letter, written in a book hand. "He wants to see me. Justin, I think he is angry...angry about the arrest, and then, what if he hears of my behavior in the scriptorium? It's a fearful prospect, but I shall have to face him sooner or later."

"Rufus," said Justin, "Bishop Eleutherus is the kindest of men, and he loves you very dearly. He is not to be feared. Go as soon as you can. He wants to hear from you what has happened, but he will think no ill of you. He will probably admonish you not to put yourself or the church at risk, but he will be gentle, you can count on it."

"Thank you, brother," said Rufus with a relieved smile, and he returned to his work. Justin quickened his pace as he walked up the hill and headed home. He had no time to lose, and he was eager for the approaching encounter.

CHAPTER 12

Juliana sat in the bright sunlight of the late morning reading her precious codex of the Gospel according to St. Mark. The house where she and her father were lodging belonged to Gaius, a prosperous Roman merchant who had invited Demetrius to Rome to discuss a business venture in shipping. Gaius' household had many servants of gracious demeanor, and between them and her own servants Rhoda and James, Juliana was well looked after. Her time was really her own to wander in the gardens or along the porticos, or to sit and ponder the gospel which she loved. The fragrances of the garden, the music played by one of the servants on an awakened lute or harp, the delicious meals, the stimulating dinner guests, all made this lodging place idyllic.

In the gospel story Juliana had reached the record of Jesus' triumphal entry into Jerusalem and the debates and questions that followed. The parable of the wicked tenants and the question of tribute to Caesar, discussions of the Resurrection and of the Great Commandment seemed especially poignant when read in the imperial city. Then came the question of lordship. Jesus quoted Psalm 110:1, that favorite text of the earliest Christians,

The Lord said to my Lord, sit at my right hand until I make your enemies your footstool.

Juliana knew the psalm so well, having often sung it in the worship of the Alexandrian church. But as she read her gospel codex, one word stood out for her in a new way. Her copy of Mark read "under your feet" *hupokato* rather than "your footstool" *hupopodion*. It was a small variation, a small difference between the beloved psalm and the beloved Gospel. She had read the gospel words many times before, and not been struck. Now the difference jumped off the page at her. Had it been the haunting words of Justin, "Juliana, I have found some major differences between your manuscript and ours." What did Justin's codex read, she thought to herself? Little wonder that her heart leapt when just at that very moment Rhoda appeared at the door and announced,

"Justin has come to see you, my lady."

"Do show him in, Rhoda, and fetch him something to eat and drink."

So the scribes sat together and talked.

"The Lord bless you, Justin, Thank you for overlooking my outburst and coming to see me."

"Mine was the fault, Juliana, mine the insensitivity, and thank you for inviting me."

Justin shifted uneasily in his seat, and spoke with anxious voice. He knew that within a matter of a week or two she would be gone. It was likely that he would never see her again. But there was no fooling himself. She had spoken to his heart, and he was captivated. Her voice was like a call from deep within, or far away or long ago. Having once heard it he must hear it again and again. The differences in text only served to underline their oneness in spirit. Yes, it was vitally important for him to be assured as to the beginning of the Gospel according to St. Mark. But it was equally as pressing to answer the call that he had heard, and to enter ever more deeply into that relationship with Juliana. These two weeks would be critically important. Carpentry could wait; the scriptorium could wait; correspondence could wait. He had to be where Juliana was. He caught himself. She was not, after all, the pearl of great price. But she ran a close second.

"Justin," she said thoughtfully, "My father tells me that we must leave in five days' time. Things have not gone well in Alexandria since we have been away. A messenger just arrived from there has told us of trouble in the shipyard, and only my father will be able to sort it out. I'm sorry that this will mean less time for us to compare texts, and I am sorry for myself, but that's as it must be."

Justin's looked down for a moment. Then he said with understanding,

"I am sorry about this, " he said, "but let us get down to the work and see how far we get. I suggest we start from the beginning."

"That will be fine, Justin," she said agreeably, "But first let me ask you how your copy of St. Mark reads here, in this place where I have been reading."

Justin moved alongside her and opened his own codex, which he had brought, the church's exemplar from the scriptorium. They sat together, with the light pouring in on the texts, as Justin found the place. He read out loud,

"The Lord said to my Lord, sit at my right hand until
I make your enemies your footstool."

"Yes, you see that," Juliana exclaimed," That is the familiar wording of the Psalm, the one we love and sing all the time, but look what my codex reads! My codex reads 'under your feet' rather than 'footstool.' I suppose it means the same thing, and it is a small point, but I wonder which St. Mark originally wrote.

"I have never seen that reading before," said Justin, as he leaned even closer to her, to inspect her codex. "As you say, it means about the same thing, and yet it is curious. I suppose if I had to guess, I would say that your codex records what Mark originally wrote. I have found myself time and again citing the Greek Old Testament of the Psalms, and having to correct myself, when copying the gospel or an epistle. The familiar words will always win out in the end, so I have to be on guard all the time."

Just then a gentle knock and the opening door brought Rhoda and some welcome refreshment.

"I have brought you some fresh bread and some nectar," said the maidservant.

"Oh, thank you," said Juliana as she reached for the cup.

"Will you have some nectar, Justin?" she said, turning to her guest.

"Nectar?" he replied, unable to hide the concern in his voice.

"Yes," she continued, almost playfully, "It is James' specialty. He works hard to blend the nectar of different fruits, and concocts the most wonderful flavors, and rich textures."

"You drink nectar?" Justin persisted.

"It is a favorite among Alexandrians," said Juliana.

"But it is the drink of the gods, and..."

"We know that an idol is nothing in the world, as St. Paul says." Juliana knew that she was right in her reply, not to mention being quick, and yet she knew that she was up against a sensitive conscience. After all, for the Roman Christian the challenge of idolatry was supremely real, at any moment an issue of life and death. The interesting questions of Christian liberty, discussed in Alexandria in the schools and the markets, had an especially sharp edge in Rome. Surrounded by the Pagan cults, confronted by the claims of Divine emperors, viewed as the enemies of the human race, and followers of strange superstition, the Roman Christian daily felt the challenge. Association with any pagan practice put one on the thin edge of the wedge. Today it was nectar at a party. Tomorrow it would be incense on the altar of the emperor. There could be no compromise.

Justin knew that he was alone with someone he could trust, and did not wish to offend. No one would know if he drank the nectar. Perhaps in the end no one would care. Perhaps, in any case, the Roman Christians made too much of their scruples. But then again, was he just rationalizing, was he merely bending over backwards to please one whom he desired so much to impress? Was he not in danger, this very afternoon, of casting aside all his scruples about food, indeed about the text of the gospel, and about who knows what else, for a woman he had only just met, a woman he would soon see no more? He could, of course, drink the nectar, and make nothing of it, and then steadfastly resist any compromise on the text. But somehow he felt that the two issues were related. To drink was to compromise. He might as well remove the words "The Son of God" from the first line of the Gospel according to St. Mark. He must stand his ground, and hope that she would understand and respect him for it.

"I thank you, indeed," he replied, only not very convincingly, "But in Rome drinking nectar is considered a compromise to the religion of idols, and so for conscience' sake..."

"Oh, I'm sorry, I quite understand." She replied, "Rhoda, will you fetch some wine?" Juliana hesitated. "You don't have scruples about wine, do you?"

"No, indeed." he replied, unable to detect whether there was some annoyance lingering beneath her kindness. He would simply assume there was not. But the whole exchange left him a little uneasy. Could he ever really be at home in the world of cultured Alexandrian Christianity? He was not himself uncultured, in a way. But her world had a style and a flare and a freedom that now seemed beyond his reach, and even his imagination. And if he felt the challenge of culture on the level of liquid refreshment, he wondered what he faced as he and his newfound friend sat down to spend several hours comparing their texts.

CHAPTER 13

Rhoda stood silently by the door before leaving, her eyes fixed on the couple that stood by the window, bathed in light. Juliana and Justin seemed so compatible, perfectly suited to one another. Could this be the person for whom she had prayed so long? She had recently sat with Juliana through all the turmoil and tears over Hermas, and was glad to see the last of him. Now here was someone with like interests and zeal, a Christian gentleman of some stature, and unmistakable affection and respect for her. How good it would be, thought Rhoda, if this could develop into something life-long.

But, of course, it was not her place to say anything. She was only a servant. A trusted and loved servant, to be sure, but a servant. Hers was a happy and secure life, and no servant could have been treated better. And hers was a willing and joyful service, a true *areskeia*, in which servitude was almost lost in friendship. Nonetheless, she knew it would be wrong to say anything unless asked. Still, she could not help thinking and longing and hoping, even though she knew that it was nearly hopeless. In five days time Juliana would return with her father to Alexandria and she and Justin would develop separate lives worlds apart. This beautiful friendship, like the spring narcissus or summer rose, would fade and die in a matter of days.

With this sad and melancholy thought Rhoda lingered at the door, and then just outside it for as long as she dared, listening to the rich conversation.

"Here at the very beginning of St. Mark," said Justin, "as I have already explained, there is a striking difference. Your manuscript does not have the words "the Son of God." I wonder, Juliana, have you ever seen a manuscript of Mark that has the words?"

"Yes, I have, Justin," she replied, "in Jerusalem."

"You have been to Jerusalem?" He said in astonishment.

"Justin, I have traveled a lot with my father, wherever his business takes him. I have been the length and breadth of the Empire, and that is how I come to be here. I love travel, and wherever I go I always try to find out who is copying Christian scriptures and seek to learn whatever I can from them. And so it was that Father and I found ourselves in Caeserea about three years ago. I made inquiry about local copyists. Someone in the church there told me about an old hermit who lived near Jerusalem."

"But I thought there was not one stone left on another, even as the Lord predicted, " interrupted Justin.

"It is true, and it moved me deeply to see the City of God, the ancient center of my people in ruin."

"You're Jewish?" said Justin, hoping to conceal any element of surprise. He certainly did not share the anti-Judaic feeling of some of the Roman Christians of his day.

"You're surprised?" She replied.

"Delighted!" he said, "Always a privilege to share the faith with one of God's ancient people whom he foreknew."

"My mother was Jewish," Juliana continued, "From one of the Alexandrian Jewish families. For generations we have studied God's law, and now the Gospel. My mother became a Christian shortly before she met my father, but she continued to keep all the Jewish feasts and customs. I first learned my love of the scriptures from her, and from my great uncle who was a Rabbi. I have always loved the gospel, but I have also loved the law. But now, about Jerusalem..."

"Yes," said Justin, who was looking intently at her beautiful, penetrating eyes,

"The old hermit, who was not easy to find, and still more difficult to draw into conversation, allowed us to see his copy of the Gospel of Mark. And his copy began like yours, "The beginning of the Gospel of Jesus Christ, the Son of God." I thought that the addition was fitting and true, but also added for the sake of reverence by himself or some other holy man. But now I find that you have the wording also, and at the opposite end of the empire! Perhaps that is what St. Mark wrote."

Justin was surprised that she so readily accepted a reading not found in her precious codex. Would she be so agreeable at other points where he had found some difference? She continued without a pause.

"That reminds me of the way that St. Matthew begins his Gospel. Let me have a look here. Yes...You see... no, not at the very beginning, further in. There it is. 'Now the birth of Jesus Christ took place in this way.' That is what your codex reads, and most of ours in Alexandria also read this way. But did you know that there is another way of reading it? Instead of 'birth' a number of old copies read 'beginning.' That is what the old hermit's codex read, and it made me think."

"That reading would alarm some people around here, you know," Justin interrupted. "Some would think it played right into the hands of those who believed that the birth of Jesus Christ was his beginning. We are having to battle hard against this heresy right now."

"But you know, Justin, I thought of this too, and I went on wrestling with this text, and thinking about it. You can see where the change could have slipped in by accident, since the words for birth and beginning in our language differ by only one extra letter (*genesis* and *gennesis*). But then I thought of something else. What if Matthew, who is writing to Jewish people mostly, wanted to make his readers remember Genesis, the first book of Moses, and to make his whole gospel a new interpretation of Moses, as given by Jesus Christ. This would be one way of preparing his readers. I really was thrilled by this thought, for it has helped me to see that in order to understand this birth you must go back to the beginning, and in order to understand the beginning you must go back to this birth. "

Justin was captivated and silently nodded approval.

"And now, back to St. Mark," she said.

Rhoda had slipped outside the door, which she left ajar. She felt she could eavesdrop on this conversation no longer in good conscience, although every word, so thoughtful and so considerate, was a thing of beauty to her. Their differences in

63

culture, background and text seemed only to work toward a deepening friendship. As she walked down the long corridor, she found herself in prayer that the association might continue, "O Lord, may this friendship flourish, despite the distance and the differences!" And she went to fetch more refreshments, which would enable her to snatch a further fragment of the most remarkable conversation between the scribes.

CHAPTER 14

From all the way down the hall Rhoda could hear the laughter, and as she got closer to the door, she could detect that it was provoked by Juliana's description of Anaximenes of Alexandria. He was an aged and eccentric Alexandrian scholar and scribe with great amounts of white hair flopping into his eyes. Schooled in the best classical methods, and won to Christian faith in mid-life, he was arguably the most learned scribe of his day in the Alexandrian church. Many were the tales of Anaximines, of his teaching under the table to eager students perched wherever they could, of his midnight walks through the city, unpredictably and sometimes scantily clad, of his playful and penetrating questions about the gospel and culture. Now in his eighties, he was a living legend in Alexandria.

"If you asked him a question, you could not predict the tone of the answer." said Juliana. "Sometimes he would purr like a kitten. Sometimes he would roar like a lion. Always his answer was worth the wait and the risk. Yes, I was one of those students who sat on the floor waiting for brilliance to emanate from beneath the table. And though a bit afraid, we were never disappointed. 'Translate, translate,' he would say in a roar, and then repeat it in a whisper. 'You must translate the Gospel, or people will not respond.' At first we did not understand, for the Gospel was written in Greek, and we were all Greek speakers. This was not like your situation, where you have to put the Gospel in Latin or people will not understand. The same is true in our countryside, or in Edessa, or in many other outposts, where Greek is not spoken. But in Alexandria? I didn't get it. Why translate here? Everybody knew Greek. So why all this fuss about translation?"

"That does seem curious," replied Justin, having recovered his composure.

"It took me a while, but I finally saw what he was trying to tell us. You see, the Greek of the Gospel according to St. Mark is a very crude and colloquial Greek, which sounds quite jagged and unappealing to the cultured people of Alexandria. We do not want our learned folk to laugh at the Gospel, to scorn before they have had a chance to listen. So some of our scribes have worked hard to translate the Gospel of Mark from poorer colloquial Greek into polished Greek, which conforms more nearly to the style of the great ancient writers, Plato, Demosthenes, etc. Now you can just imagine how this kind of expression will have struck our learned people of Alexandria, who delight in polished Greek. "It reads here in your codex, 'And immediately many were gathered together.' But my manuscript does not have the 'immediately.' You see, this is a word that Mark uses all the time. Just count the number of times we have already had it. No Greek stylist would tolerate this, and so, in the interest of winning a hearing for the gospel among our cultured set, Anaximines and other learned scribes have left the word 'immediately' out here and in other places. We translate the gospel in this way into the learned cultural language of Alexandria. It is just a stylistic change. It doesn't change the sense or meaning. It merely makes the gospel more accessible to our people. In fact, we have done this little piece of stylistic polishing in a number of places where the word occurs."

"But that changes what Mark actually wrote," protested Justin. "This may be an important thing to do for your immediate culture, I do not doubt, a worthy evangelistic enterprise, perhaps, but do you see the danger? Once we start changing the Greek text of the Gospel, for whatever worthy reason, there is no stopping us. The next generation in Alexandria, or another culture like mine will mistake your "translation" for the original Mark. Before many years are past, or many generations, we will have departed, first here and there, and then everywhere, from the original Mark, or Matthew or Paul, or Psalm or any of our scriptures. So you see, a small,

66

laudable stylistic change can be the beginning of a dangerous slide."

"Justin, Justin," she retorted, "You make too much of this, I think. Of course, we need to copy with care, and accurately. But we also need to translate, and make the scriptures available to our people. Don't you ever explain in other words what you read to your congregation?"

"Yes I do, but..."

"That's just what I'm saying." She went on, "This is what we are doing, but as our people are a very literate set, we need to do our translation in a written rather than just an oral way, and in Greek, rather than in another language."

Rhoda could sense that she had come in on a crucial moment for the whole enterprise of text comparison. Just the tone of the dialogue told her that the two scribes had found themselves to be worlds apart. She feared what this might mean for their developing friendship. She set the drinks on the table and slowly moved toward the door. Again, lingering just outside she could catch the continuing thread of conversation and sense the building tension.

"We too are faced with challenges as we copy, and seek to make the Gospel as clear as possible for our people," said Justin. "Some of us have especially felt the challenge from the heretical teachers who would separate Jesus and Christ. They try to persuade all in the church that Jesus became Christ at his baptism, and that the Christ left Jesus at his crucifixion. One of their favorite verses is from the Psalm found in Matthew and Mark, "My God, My God, why hast thou forsaken me." Believe me, they have given us in the church leadership in Rome a hard time indeed. My bishop has lost more than one night's sleep over the separationists and their teaching about Jesus Christ. Among some of our faithful church people there has begun to circulate a new way of reading the Psalm in St. Mark's account of the crucifixion. They say and write, "My God, My God, why hast thou persecuted me." Some believe this is what St. Mark wrote. But none of us in the leadership are allowing it, even though it would be very helpful as a way of avoiding the danger which the original reading of the Psalm and of St. Mark places

67

us in. It would be very useful against this rather nasty piece of heresy, but we refuse to use it. We want to read the gospel the way it was written. And I take comfort from the Psalm I was singing over just this morning: 'I cleave to thy testimonies, O Lord, let me not be put to shame!"

"But you are talking about substance, and I am talking about style," said Juliana. "No one in the Alexandrian church would tolerate an intentional change in the actual substance of the Gospel. We are only interested in stylistic improvement, you understand."

"O, I understand, Juliana, at least I am trying to, but then, where does style end and substance begin? Take this matter of 'immediately' How do you know that it is not more than a mere connector, a kind of alternative for "and" or "you see" or "you know" for St. Mark? How do you know that in some places, especially early on in his Gospel, Mark is not trying to give us a vivid impression of the feverish pace of the ministry of Jesus? Reading these early chapters of Mark always leaves me a little breathless..." said Justin, a little breathless himself.

"I too feel that way when I read the first part of St. Mark, and I don't get the same feeling from Matthew of Luke, whose gospels often do not have the 'immediately' where they tell the same stories as Mark. But I still feel that many places where it occurs lose nothing by harmless stylistic improvement." So Juliana continued to stand her ground.

And Justin stood his, "Harmless, Juliana?"

Rhoda so wished she could have caught the expressions on their faces. The tones sounded respectful enough, but the distance and the tension were apparent. She lingered a bit longer to hear more.

"Yes, Justin, and here is another example in the same place." Juliana spoke with knowledge and conviction, but Rhoda sensed also, with real caring for the one for whom this was all new. "My Mark wrote, 'It was reported that he was at home,' speaking of Jesus' hometown ministry. I observe that your text reads, literally, 'into home.' We all know that this is increasingly everyday, common speech in the Greek world, but by any classical stylistic standards it is impossible and not a little

68

offensive. You should have heard Anaximines on this point! He thundered. I have seen your reading, in Alexandrian manuscripts, and this is an issue in a number of places in St. Mark. Look carefully at it. Where you have the preposition into you must have some idea of motion. 'He had come into his home' would be fine, but not, "he was into his home.' Surely you can see this is awkward Greek. The workmen and dockhands in my father's firm love St. Mark for this very reason. The Jesus it portrays speaks their way. But it won't do for the cultured people who are making their way into the church, and finding in Jesus Christ a philosophy they can really live by. And here is another example..."

"Wait a minute," said Justin, feeling at this point a bit overwhelmed. "Didn't St. Paul make clear that not many wise, or mighty or noble were called to Christian belief? By doing such a cultural upgrade of the Gospel are we not departing from the spirit, if not the letter of the Apostolic teaching? Is it not essential that we leave the gospel the way it is, a stumbling block to the Jews and folly to the Greeks, that it may continue in its purity to be the power and the wisdom of God?"

This was Justin's best shot, and he knew it. Juliana knew it too, and Rhoda sensed that his answer had restored a balance to a conversation that Juliana so fully controlled. Rhonda could feel the silence that followed. No easy answer would do, not even from so skillful an interlocutor as Juliana. No tone in her voice, no special plea for her situation, and the opportunity of winning the cultured, no facial or body language, however compelling or alluring, could silence the power of his questions and the depth of his convictions.

"One other example," she went on, almost as if she had not heard, though somehow he knew that she had. "Here in the same sentence we read, "And again he entered into Capernaum..." We had a long discussion in the scriptorium, after one of Anaximenes' lectures as to whether Jesus was really entering Capernaum again, or whether we were dealing with another stylistic quirk of Mark, edited out without a loss of the essential message of the gospel. Now let me see what your manuscript reads. Interesting! It does not have the word again, but many manuscripts I have seen have it. This is a strange thing. I fully expected yours to have it. In several other places in St. Mark we have felt obliged, in the interest of commending the Gospel to our neighbors to leave out this irritating and superfluous mannerism of St. Mark."

"Irritating and superfluous, Juliana?" He retorted with pathos, "Nothing in the sacred Gospel could ever be irritating or superfluous. Every word shines with holy radiance, and should be faithfully preserved."

Just then they were interrupted by James, who looked disapprovingly at the eavesdropping Rhoda as he pushed past her and announced, "Juliana, your father must see you at once. It appears we are leaving sooner than we thought, and he needs your help."

She looked at Justin as she rose to show him to the door. "You must come to Alexandria some time and see what we see, and face what we face. You would be our guest, and we could show you our scriptorium. Our scribes could probably be much more convincing than I."

"But not more captivating." There. He had said it. And why not? He probably would never see her again, and given the textual discoveries of the past few hours, that was probably for the better. But he could no longer leave what he felt unsaid. She could not be allowed to return to Alexandria without some indication of his love for her. Some day, perhaps, he would find his way to Alexandria, perhaps as the courier for Bishop Eleutherus. Then *he* would be the visitor with the interesting new readings, preserved against the pressure of odd and eccentric sounding heresies. *He* would come across as the one who preserved the scriptures against the corrupters, without and within. *He* would be admired and emulated, yes, and loved for who he was and what he had done. He would be the scribe from far-off Rome whom Juliana was proud to know as her friend and...

"If there is time tomorrow I will send James to fetch you." She said as he tucked his codex under his arm and moved toward the door.

70

"I do hope this is not the last I will see of you on this visit," he said.

"So do I," she said, "I don't think I have ever had so engaging a conversation about the text, and I am grateful for it. I shall go on thinking about what you have said. And now, if you will excuse me...."

Justin walked the better part of the mile in the direction of his home, lost in a mass of thoughts and emotions. At one and the same moment he wished she had never come and he longed to hold her in his embrace. He felt more firm in his conviction that the Gospel must be preserved as it is, but secretly lured by her concern to commend it to the learned people of the world in their day. He walked on, almost dazed, and found that his feet had taken him not to his own home, but to the house of his dear friend, Marcus the shepherd.

CHAPTER 15

Marcus had been struggling for most of the morning to free a sheep that had wandered into some thick brambles, and as Justin approached he could see that his friend was frustrated.

"Justin, how are you!" he exclaimed, looking up with a sense of exasperation. "I have been by to see you several times, and have worried about you since the scene with Rufus in the scriptorium. Are you all right?"

"Oh, yes, I have been to see Rufus, and we have talked...here, can I help with this sheep?" Justin knelt down to assist Marcus who kept talking,

"Yes, thank you so much, would you hold this leg. There. If I can just slip this bit round through there like that, without hurting this little fellow. Right, I think that has it. We will have him completely free in a moment."

The young sheep was soon on his feet and bounding around the fold, as Marcus and Justin sat down to rest on the stone wall.

"That's the third time this week that this little fellow has gotten himself into trouble," said Marcus, catching his breath. "Yesterday he wandered into a gully and couldn't get out. It took me several hours. Then last Monday he had wandered a mile away, and I just found him minutes before the wolf did. Well did the prophet Isaiah liken us to sheep. 'All we like sheep have gone astray, we have turned everyone to his own way....'

"How right you are, Marcus, " said the still dazed Justin, "how right you are."

"You have not gone astray," asked Marcus, "I mean in some major way, have you, my brother?'

"Rufus would think that I have, I dare say."

"Because you entertained a woman scribe, and showed her how we copy, and enjoyed her company, Justin?" asked the shepherd-scribe.

"Marcus...Marcus, it's more than that." said Justin staring at the ground.

"What do you mean?" asked Marcus, with the caring of a true shepherd in his tone.

"It's Juliana, Marcus. I am totally captivated by her. From the first day I laid my eyes on her I have felt drawn to her. But now she has completely won my heart. I think of her all the time, and long to be with her, and would seize the first opportunity I could to ask her to be my wife. I have never felt this way before about anyone, and am quite overwhelmed by it."

"I can only admire your choice, and say that I am pleased for you," interrupted Marcus.

"But Marcus, she leaves for Alexandria soon, maybe tomorrow, and I shall probably never see her again, and that is probably just as well."

"Just as well?" asked Marcus somewhat puzzled.

"Indeed, for you see," Justin went on, "She must live there in Alexandria, and I must live here in Rome. Her father could not part with her, and my Bishop depends upon me."

"But he would certainly understand. There is no more sympathetic man in all the world, and he loves you dearly. And, after all, it was he who introduced you to Juliana. I suspect he is not so foolish as not to have entertained the notion that the association might reach beyond the work of copying." Marcus looked straight at Justin who was gazing off at the distance, as if lost in another world. "Have you said anything to the Bishop about this?"

"No, Marcus, but I think he suspects something," said Justin, his attention somewhat retrieved from another world. "He really does depend on my help, above all in the scriptorium, and in so many other ways, and he is not getting any younger. To leave him would be like leaving my own father, in a time of need."

"Justin, he would be especially saddened to sense that he had kept you from your heart's desire," said Marcus in an earnest

74

tone, "and also dismayed if he ever found out that you had kept it from him. You must tell him, if you feel you can."

"Yes, but I think he already knows, and I almost said something to him at our last meeting, but then I didn't."

"Why not?" Marcus asked as he leapt off the wall to catch the young sheep before it ran into its fourth disaster of the week. Returning with the sheep in his arms, he sat back on the wall and repeated, "Why not? Why not tell the Bishop?"

"But there is no point now. It is hopeless," retorted Justin, with a slight tenseness in his voice. "Hopeless! She leaves in a day or two, never perhaps to be seen again."

"But there are letters, Justin, and you could be a courier to Alexandria, and see her again in the service of your Bishop. I feel sure he would allow this, and even encourage it."

"Marcus, you are so good and kind, but it is more complicated than that." said Justin in a plaintive tone.

"Complicated?"

"Yes, Marcus," said Justin, now staring him full in the face, completely retrieved from the far-off place to which his thoughts had wandered. "You see, there is a world of difference between Rome and Alexandria. I tell you it is more than miles that separate us. To be sure between our church and theirs there are vast differences."

"But diversity is good and healthy," said Marcus, still determined to be helpful.

"Truly there is a great gulf fixed," said Justin.

"What do you mean?" asked his shepherd friend.

"Marcus, I am facing a very great challenge indeed, and make no mistake, it is a great challenge to the whole church. Remember how I pointed out to you the difference in the way Juliana's Gospel of St. Mark begins and ends? Well, Marcus, there are many more differences than that. I have spent the last two days at the estate where Juliana is lodging, in close comparison of our texts..."

"That must have been very pleasant," interrupted Marcus.

"And very revealing. Marcus, there are many differences in our texts, large and small. Now at first I deemed that this must be due to the inevitable mistakes to which we copyists and scribes are prone in our profession. No matter how careful a scribe is, he cannot be perfect, and errors will creep in. That cannot be helped. But in Alexandria, Marcus, in Alexandria, so Juliana tells me, they intentionally alter the text, and laud themselves for doing so!"

"It cannot be, Justin," said the incredulous Marcus.

"It is true, Marcus. Now Juliana insists that it is only in matters of style that the Alexandrian scribes do this, and for the laudable aim of commending the Gospel to their cultured friends, who would be offended by some of the colloquial Greek of the evangelists, especially of St. Mark. So, for instance, we noticed how her St. Mark is missing the word *immediately* several times in the first part, whereas our St. Mark has them all. She claims that according to the best of attic tastes, currently in fashion in her fair city, such a recurrent mannerism is irritating. Fine for dockhands, but not good for the academy. She claims that the word is just a stylistic connector in St. Mark, and the narrative loses nothing by a few eliminations for the sake of polish, and helps to pave the way for the Gospel among the cultured. She quotes her teacher, Anaximenes of Alexandria, a brilliant if eccentric convert to the faith, who thinks this is a matter of translation. 'Translate, translate!' she imitates his very tone, and Marcus, it would be a great deal easier for me if she did not throw her hair back in the way she does, and penetrate so with her beautiful brown eyes. But that woman haunts, arrests, and captivates. My heart is at her mercy!"

"Justin!" Marcus exclaimed, suddenly realizing the full weight of the dilemma his friend was facing. The two sat silently for a few moments. Then Marcus asked,

"Do you think she regards you in the same way?"

"I don't know, brother," he replied, "She is so very difficult to read. She gives the impression of enjoying my company, and even the scene in the scriptorium did not put her off. She called for me. She wrote and asked me to come. But then, it all may be her own curiosity about the text, or a splendid Eastern courtesy and no more. The only way that I will ever know for sure is to tell her plainly how I feel. I must talk to her as freely as I am talking to you now, and tell her both of my affection and

76

of my textual dilemma. I know she is aware of the latter, but she may not sense the former. I must tell her, and I probably only have tomorrow, and then she is gone."

"Then tell her, man. You have nothing to lose by it, and perhaps all to gain." Marcus spoke with caring and conviction, and Justin knew that this was the right thing to do. Why bother the bishop with details of a relationship that might not even exist? Why continue to imagine what she might feel, or second-guess her motives and her tone. Justin determined he would see her and ask her, if there was a moment alone together. On the other hand, he thought, why not declare himself within earshot of her servant Rhoda? She seemed to Justin to be in sympathy with his visits, and singularly kind to him. Though but a servant, she might champion his cause if the opportunity presented itself.

"I think her maidservant suspects something is afoot," said Justin.

"Really?" asked Marcus, intrigued by this wrinkle in the developing plot.

"Yes," Justin replied, "She lingers after bringing refreshment, and enters the room with great frequency. I think she suspects...and hopes, if I am not mistaken. But even if I am bold to speak, and my declaration receives a warm response, and I have the maidservant's counsel to my aid, that is not the great obstacle. The distance of our homes...and of our texts, this is the real challenge, Marcus, not to mention that she is wealthy and cultured!"

"And she has not given any hint of how she feels?" asked Marcus?

"Oh, yes, she feels very strongly about the need to translate...and change the text if necessary."

"No, no!" exclaimed the exasperated Marcus, "How she feels about you."

"I simply can't tell, Marcus, but this I do know, that I am committed to the faithful copying of the text, whether it helps or hurts my cause, and my heart. Only this will mean the faithful preservation of the Gospel, and nothing is more important than that."

Marcus sat puzzled, and said nothing for a few minutes. Then he said with all the earnestness he could muster, "Justin, you must tell her. Reveal to her your heart. Tell her in a way that fully discloses your dilemma. You have been our strong leader for a number of years, and I know you have the strength to do this. That is, I know that the Lord will give you the strength. Tell her. At least then you will know. And you will have made a clear and heartfelt statement of your principles as well. Go and tell her. You have no time to lose."

"Marcus, you are right," replied Justin, after a moment of quiet. "Thank you so much for your help. I shall go tomorrow, and if I have missed her, I shall find a way to get to Alexandria, and find her there and tell her."

"And ask her to be your wife?" asked Marcus.

"If all the world were mine I would give it for her hand in marriage, for her lifelong friendship, for her magnificent self. But there is something more precious than all the world, and that is the Gospel and its faithful preservation. No person or thing is so dear to me that I would compromise the Gospel."

Justin's dilemma had now come home to Marcus with its full force. No true friend could offer easy answers or cheap consolation. But the promise of fervent prayer and a listening ear, as well as the renewed counsel to speak to Juliana, seemed to Justin to lighten the load, and strengthen his resolve. As he walked home quietly in the sunset, he began to whisper to himself the words of Psalm 84:10-12

"For the Lord God is both sun and shield
He will give grace and glory
No good thing will the Lord withhold
From those who walk with integrity
O Lord God of hosts
Blessed is the man that putteth his trust in thee."

CHAPTER 16

In the dusk of a warm late-Summer evening, Justin could just make out the presence of two figures at his doorstep. As he approached them it became clear that one was Rufus. The other was a tall figure he could not identify. There was no mistaking Rufus, however, with his stocky build, red hair and ruddy complexion.

The sight of Rufus at the door of the scriptorium dredged up a mass of conflicting emotions in Justin. The last time Rufus had been to this place he had reacted violently to Juliana's presence, and had caused much difficulty. Of course, Justin had been to see him, and all was forgiven. But the sight of Rufus, here at the Scriptorium, and as it happened on the eve of Juliana's departure, made him feel some slight resentment toward his colleague. It also made him aware of how difficult and unproductive these days since his return from Lyons had been. He had done no copying work for his own church. He had done almost no carpentry. He had been totally sidetracked, and that by someone he would probably never see again. Perhaps, he thought, Rufus was right after all. Maybe women were just a snare, and the work of the gospel called for all the caution that St. Paul had imposed on himself and urged on the Corinthians. Had Justin been the fool in allowing his heart to be so overtaken? Had he not better stick to the task at hand of copying with faithfulness and preserving the text? But no, he thought to himself. The events of the past month were powerful and positive and good, yes good, and from God, and something deep inside him would not allow him to deny that. He would continue to hold Juliana in his heart, and if opportunity came for a continued letters, or perhaps, a journey to Alexandria, he could not refuse it.... and should not. Nevertheless, he was not happy with his continued resentment of his friend and colleague, Rufus, and it reminded him of how far he still had to go in his growth in Grace.

Drawing nearer, Justin was now able to recognize the other figure who stood by his door. It was Florinus. This tall white-haired figure with striking features, fair complexion and high cheekbones was a leader of the Roman church who had caused quite a stir in recent years. He was well known for his loud and eloquent voice, and also for his peculiar views. He had had the rare privilege, like Irenaeus, his junior, of sitting at the feet of Polycarp in lower Asia, and hearing stories and teachings which the old sage had heard from the Apostles. He therefore was in touch with the very source of Christian faith. Yet in later life he had begun expounding odd views, at variance with anything found in the Scriptures or the teaching of the church. He had begun to teach that God was the author of evil. More recently his status as a Presbyter had been questioned in the church by his teaching of certain doctrines that sounded very much like the teaching of the Gnostic Valentinus. Irenaeus had mentioned something about this to Justin during his recent visit to Gaul. Now here was Florinus, in the company of Rufus at Justin's doorstep. What, thought Justin, could be the purpose of their visit? And how was he, over-tired by the events of the past month, going to muster the acumen required of anyone who would engage with Florinus? And how had it happened that he should now be in the company of Rufus?

Justin did not need to spend long wondering. Rufus greeted him warmly.

"Justin, I'm glad you're here. We had almost given up and gone away."

Despite himself, Justin wished that they had.

"Rufus, how are you?" Justin said warmly, extending his hand, and before Rufus had any opportunity of explanation or introduction, he turned to Florinus and said, "Florinus, may the Lord be with you. It has been some time since we have seen each other. I hope you are keeping well and keeping the faith of the Church."

"Indeed I am, and advancing it," was the reply.

"Come in, then, both of you," said Justin with as much genuineness and enthusiasm as his tired mind could muster.

Inside the house Justin poured drinks and sat round the table with his two visitors. "Now tell me, my brothers, the purpose of your visit."

Rufus spoke quickly, "Florinus and I have been engaging in a debate for some time about the true teaching of the church. We have come to an impasse, and he agreed to come with me to see you, on the chance that you might be able to help."

"I agreed," said Florinus, "but unwillingly, Rufus. It was part of our bargain, our wager, and I think it a very clever trick. Nonetheless," said the senior man, turning to Justin, "I know you to be a highly-respected reader and scribe, with the confidence of our bishop Eleutherus, and the admiration of my life-long friend Irenaeus. I am confident that there are places where we will disagree, but I am willing to discuss and debate."

"Well, you have caught me at a very tired moment, but I am glad to give you an hour, and if this will not suffice, then we can arrange for further discussion some other time."

Justin's voice sounded sincere and confident now. "Tell me what you have been debating about."

"The Ogdoad," burst in Rufus, with unmistakable pugnacity in his tone.

"The what?" replied Justin, feigning ignorance of a term he knew all too well. The very mention of the term caused him dismay.

"Yes," said Florinus in his deep stentorian voice, "The Ogdoad....The unnamable parent that emanated from the heights: the light of the fullness; the eternal light of the aeons: the light in silence - in forthcoming and the parent's silence - the light in word and truth: the light of the incorruptibilities: the inaccessible light: the light that has emanated forever, belonging to the aeons of the ineffable, traceless and unproclaimable parent: the eternity of aeons: the self-originate, self-radiation and alien; the inexplicable power of the ineffable parent. Three powers emanated from it: namely the father, the mother and the son...."

"Stop," cried Rufus at the mention of the mother. "This abominable error ought not even to be heard!"

81

"Yet even the great Irenaeus hears these things, in order to discern them, to expose them, to overthrow them, Rufus," said Justin, "Let Florinus continue."

And then the voice of Florinus changed, and he spoke in a whisper, as if in a trance, his eyes gazing upward and his hands outstretched in adoration and praise.

O Iesseus!
Oeouooua!
In very truth
O Iesseus-Mazareus-Iessedekeus
O living water
O child of the child
O name of all glories
In very truth
O eternal being!
In very truth

Florinus's voice could not be heard. His lips moved and his face looked heavenward. His breathing was heavy, and his eyes filled with tears. A few words were discernible, "...parent, father-mother...in very truth...ineffable...."

"Are we thinking and discussing," broke in Rufus, "Or are we compelled to be swept away by a trance of gnosis." Rufus' loud protest broke the spell, and Florinus returned from his flight of praise. He fixed his deep blue eyes on Justin, and said, "I have come to know the mystery, and true gnosis."

Justin knew that in his state of total fatigue he could not do justice to this challenge. He must be fresh to meet this most formidable threat to the church he loved and the gospel he believed. But he wished to be cordial and respectful, so he turned to Florinus and asked,

"Where did you come upon these new beliefs which you now hold?"

"In Egypt," was his reply.

The mention of Egypt was entirely disarming to Justin. The Egyptian visitor, the Egyptian manuscripts, with their peculiar textual readings, and the desire, in spite of his misgivings, to

82

visit Egypt were quite unnerving. These had worked upon his conscious and subconscious mind in such a way that when Florinus noted that he had found his Gnostic views in Egypt, Justin felt a kind of paralysis of heart and mind. He must go, but he dare not go. It was plain to him that he could not think clearly, and the conversation would have to be postponed.

The guests agreed to return in the morning. But Justin could hear them arguing loudly as they left the house and the fading sound of their debate lasted for several minutes, until all was silent.

CHAPTER 17

An early bed meant an early start for Justin. An extra long time in prayer, in the Psalms, and in meditating on the gospel was an absolute necessity for the morning that lay ahead. He felt much refreshed by sleep, and much encouraged by his reading of the Psalms:

O think upon thy servant, as concerning thy word:
Wherein thou hast caused me to put my trust.
The same is my comfort in my trouble:
For thy word hath quickened me.

And of the Gospel:

Beware of false prophets who come to you in sheep's clothing but inwardly they are ravenous wolves. You will know them by their fruits.

Florinus was impressive indeed. His standing as a presbyter in the church had given him a position from which to influence many young Roman Christians. Indeed, Justin knew of several who were being drawn in the direction of this gnostic teaching. Even Rufus' intensity of opposition had alarmed Justin. Was the great vocal and volatile young champion of the truth in danger of being swept away? So Justin was aware that much was at stake in these conversations. He was considered a champion of the church's faith, and as a student of Irenaeus, he was increasingly being asked to give judgment, and indicate the way the Bishop of Lyons might decide. A rumor that he had not stood up well in open debate with Florinus might harm him and the church. He must remember to stand on the deposit of faith he had been given, rely on the scriptures as an apostolic and authoritative witness to Jesus Christ, both God and man. And he must remain courteous. He must, in the words of the Apostle, let his speech be "always gracious, seasoned with salt." As with his faithful copying, so with his defense of the faith, he believed that he was standing in the gap.

The arrival of Rufus and Florinus, and the polite preliminaries passed only too quickly, and the debate was joined.

"Thank you for understanding and being willing to return today," said Justin. "You must tell me about this system of gnosis which you have come to embrace."

Florinus stood to his full stature and stretched out his hand. "The beginnings of the heavens and the earth were like this: From the Parent of eternity emanated Barbelo, the second principle and from this came forth the ten aeons. The last of the aeons is Sophia."

"Parent, Barbelo, aeons Sophia, emanations, What is this dark speech?" Rufus protested.

"Let him continue," said Justin, "even dark speech can illumine."

"Gnosis falsely so-called," muttered Rufus under his breath. Justin chided, seeking to draw out the old man who seemed to be straying from the faith of the church.

"You speak of the Parent of eternity, what do you mean? I do not know this name from the sacred writings, the prophets or the apostles."

"We have heard the word of prophecy, and we have the word made more sure, as even Peter has said," exclaimed Florinus.

Justin looked intently at him and said,

"But I do not find what you are saying in the scripture, so I cannot take it as the faith once for all delivered to the saints. For in the scriptures alone - the writings of Moses and the prophets, and in the Psalms, in the four Gospels and in the letters of Paul and Peter and James, and the other apostles, who first followed our Lord Jesus Christ - has the truth been delivered to us as a sacred deposit. We preserve and copy it faithfully. We study it carefully and teach it to our children, that they might know it and find life in him to whom it bears witness, even Jesus Christ. But I too have interrupted you and not allowed you to speak. Tell me of the 'Sophia,' the wisdom of which you speak, for we speak of wisdom also, as St. Paul has said."

Florinus seemed pleased with the courtesy offered by his host, and he continued: "I have learned from a great master the words spoken by our Mother Sophia:

"I am the first and the last. I am the honored one and the scorned one. I am the whore and the holy one. I am the wife and the virgin. I am the mother and the daughter. I am she whose wedding is great and I have not taken a husband. I am knowledge and ignorance. I am shameless; I am ashamed. I am strength. I am fear. I am foolish. I am wise. I am godless, and I am the one whose God is great..."

Rufus could stand this no longer. "Stop," he cried with red, indignant face. "A motley garment, sown out of a heap of miserable rags! Listen if you will," he said as he turned to Justin, "But I will no longer endure this blasphemous talk of female gods and demi-gods. I trust when you have listened you will confute, as does our brother Irenaeus; confute and do not spare him, lest we all be swept away, and all is lost."

So Rufus departed, and Justin and Florinus sat alone in silence. At last Florinus broke the spell,

"Do you condemn me too, with the crueler condemnation of a pretending listener and learner?"

"My friend is a creature of impulse, true-hearted but volatile. Rufus is a volcano, more powerful than Vesuvius, and we have learned to live with his outbursts. I willingly took you in and wished to hear you out that I might judge for myself according to the truth. I owe you at least a listening ear. Did you not once know my father, the martyr who copied for our church? Were you not on close terms with him some years ago? And did you not know the great martyr, Justin, after whom I have been called, and our dear mentor Irenaeus? Did you not once cherish friendship with him, in your younger years, when at the feet of

Polycarp you learned the oracles of the Lord and the words of the apostles? Did you not then embrace the faith of the church which now you seem to alter and distort? Yes Florinus, think of your glorious heritage and training! So many of us who are younger in Christ and in age would give all we had for the privilege that was yours...a privilege which now you turn your back upon. But for your privilege alone I owe you at least my ear. But I cannot consent with my heart and mind. And my spirit pleads with yours to return to what is yours of old, that faith of John, and Polycarp, and Justin and Irenaeus, and do not be lured by this novelty called "gnosis."

Justin's appeal to the man seemed to work what no appeal to the mind could have done. For a moment Florinus was arrested, pensive, even a bit uncertain. But he regathered his composure.

"If anyone could convince me, it would be our great friend, the Bishop of Lyons, but even his letters, firm and friendly as they are, now have a hollow ring. I must seek gnosis. I have heard the voice of Sophia and she has bade me come, and I cannot turn back."

Florinus arose and moved toward the door to leave. "I thank you for your time and your ear," he said. He started to open the door, and Justin rose to bid him farewell. The elder man stopped in the half-opened door, and the sunlight caught him on one side. There he stood, half darkness, half-light.

"There is one question I wanted to ask you," said Florinus, almost in a whisper.

"What is that?" asked Justin.

"I mentioned a bargain I made with Rufus. It concerns a debate about the right reading at the beginning of St. John's Gospel. The evangelist writes of a birth 'not of blood, nor of the will of the flesh, nor of the will of man, but of God.' Tell me, of which birth does he speak? Of the birth of Jesus (*egenethe*) or of the birth of his followers (*egenethesan*)."

"Florinus," said Justin, "You know the debate between us, and that I have received the singular reading, which refers to Jesus, the Word made flesh. You know that even in the church there are those who take the reference to believers, though they do not follow the Gnostic views you espouse. I copy what I

88

receive, and seek to do so faithfully, and the singular reference to Jesus is what I have received. But wherein lies the bargain?"

"I agreed to come," said Florinus, now in a fuller voice, "If he would seriously consider this reading we espouse, and even some of your teachers espouse. Rufus thinks that our people have corrupted the text to read the plural, but I believe that the change was made from plural to singular, to refer to Christ. I suspect that the change was made by one of your scribes some time ago. I see that Rufus is not interested in serious discussion, but only in condemning what he does not understand."

"Florinus," said Justin earnestly," I have seen copies of St. John which read as you read them. And I have often thought about this matter. But our gospels in this church all read the singular, which speaks of Jesus' miraculous birth, and this is how I take it. Yes, I will discuss this with you some time, and I would be pleased to see your copies of St. John. But for now, and since our texts read as they do, I stand where I stand."

"And I stand where I stand, and bid you good day."

CHAPTER 18

The noonday sun poured in through Justin's door. Florinus was gone. Rufus was gone. By now Juliana was gone. For the first time in weeks Justin saw time stretching before him without a new crisis. The whirlwind of the past weeks was enough for him to think through, and sort out, for some time to come. Now he might be able to catch up on his carpentry. And then there was the gospel manuscript he had been copying for the new congregation out on the Appian Way. He had finished Matthew, John, and Luke, and had started in on Mark. Perhaps he could even finish it by the Lord's day, so that they could have it for their celebration. He was determined to make that his aim. Bishop Eleutherus was visiting there that coming Sunday, and while he felt no pressure from the Bishop or anyone else to finish the gospels book for that occasion, he rather delighted himself in setting his own goal. He sat staring at the sunlit doorway and the trees and flowers bathed in the sunlight against the brilliant blue sky.

Just then Justin sensed the presence of a shadow. It was strange, for there was no cloud in the sky. He had caught the import of Florinus' parting remarks in that strange interchange about the bargain with Rufus. The full weight of the words hit Justin in the stomach. "I believe that the change was made from the plural to the singular. I suspect that the change was made by one of your scribes some time ago." Did Florinus mean to imply that Justin's father had sanctioned, or even made the change himself? It is true that this particular reference in St. John's gospel had been fiercely debated in recent years. Gnostics had accused church leaders of the change, and some of the young churchmen had returned the charge, although Justin knew of no official sanction for it. Had Rufus made such a charge in the

91

heat of debate? Whatever the circumstances of charge and counter-charge, it now left Justin feeling a bit ill to think that Florinus would imply that his father had been privy to the tampering with the sacred text. Perhaps, he thought, Florinus had not meant that at all. Perhaps Justin was weaving all of this in his head, and imputing to Florinus a motive and idea not his own.

Then Justin thought of the differences in text he had observed between his codex and Juliana's. How did these come to be? Which text was original? Which words did Mark write? Who was preserving the true reading? Was everybody copying a text somewhat true, somewhat corrupt? He had learned from Juliana of some motives for changes in the text, even laudable motives like the desire to commend the gospel to cultured neighbors. But he knew that these changes corrupted the text. He also recalled that when he had recently checked his own copying of St. Luke for the new congregation, he had found five unintentional errors: two omissions, and three repeats. Had he not checked his own work but simply let the copying stand, new errors, albeit unintentional, would have crept into the stream of texts. Future copyists would then have been as puzzled and perplexed about Justin's copies as he now was about others. He saw his life work, which he had taken over from his father, to be the faithful copying of the text as he received it. But now he had added a new complication, and he could no longer ignore it. How was he to know that the text he was faithfully copying was the original text? He could now no longer assume that the text of the gospels as it was known in Rome was the purest text. Was there a way of finding out which codices best represented what Mark or John or Luke or Matthew or Paul had written? He was confident that God had preserved the sacred words in the church. But in which copies? Which church could lay claim to be the most faithful in handing on the words of the Lord and his followers? He sat paralyzed for a few minutes, in the grip of a seemingly unanswerable question.

Just then a cloud really did move across the sky and darken the little group of houses, and Justin's doorway. This broke the spell, and he moved into the scriptorium room and began copying St. Mark again.

It felt good to be back at the work. He resumed his copying with the story of the healing of the demoniac, copying what was before him, and feeling more strongly than ever his conviction to copy what he had received. He marveled at the story of the healing power of Jesus, in the face of tremendous spiritual oppression. Moving on to the next section, he began copying the story of the raising of Jairus' daughter. The story was fresh in his mind from his recent copying of St. Luke's account. But suddenly he stopped. He had copied this story before, from this manuscript, most recently for the church in Lyons. But it struck him that the name of the ruler, Jairus, was missing in his copy. He knew it was in Luke, and he remembered seeing it in St. Mark's gospel. But it was not in his copy. Had he just not noticed before? Had the events of the past few weeks made him more aware of the omission? Never before had the thought crossed his mind that his copy might be in error, and he was faithfully re-producing that error. What, thought Justin, would Juliana's copy read? Would the name Jairus be in it?

"A simple, unimportant difference, " he muttered to himself. But all the turmoil of the past three weeks came home to him. He knew he could never escape the questions raised by Juliana's visit and Florinus' question and his own desire to produce a text faithful to what the Apostles had written. He had started on a journey and there was no turning back. Where would it lead?

CHAPTER 19

It had rained all night. At midmorning the torrents were still running off to the sides of the well-drained Appian Way. Justin and Marcus sat huddled together with two other passengers as their raeda, a sturdy four-wheeled carriage drawn by two horses made its way south. The cover which protected the travelers from most of the wet flapped in the heavy winds. Through the rear opening Justin spotted the house where he had been just three days before, and where he had presented the finished gospels codex to the new congregation. Marcus was asleep next to him and did not awaken, even with a heavy nudge. Justin's mind raced with the events of the past days. What had just passed and what was about to take place seemed like a dream.

Several days of uninterrupted copying had enabled Justin to complete and check the Gospel of Mark. He had worked efficiently, remarkably untroubled by the questionings that had arisen in the weeks before. Once or twice he stopped to wonder at a reading, but pushed on to the finish. The congregation had been overjoyed and the Bishop very pleased. At the feast following the service the Bishop had cornered Justin, and after congratulating him for his work had turned to another matter. Would he be willing, in company with Marcus, to deliver some letters to several churches in the East: Corinth, Antioch, Caeserea, Jerusalem, Alexandria? The Bishop was willing to spare him, though he knew he might be gone for some time. Some merchants from the Roman congregation would include them in their retinue. The letters must not simply be sent. They needed to be entrusted to someone who would guard them and see that they were delivered, and who would return with letters from these churches. But it must be someone who could speak for the Roman Church and fairly represent her position on any

95

number of issues. Justin and his friend Marcus were the Bishop's choice.

The overland trip to Puteoli on the coast would take them along the Appian Way to Sinuessa and thence over the Domitian road, and so bring them to the place where they would board a ship for Corinth. Except for his recent journey to Lyons, Justin had never been outside of Italy, and the prospect of an errand in the East on his Bishop's business filled him with awe and wonder. He would visit churches in cities which were only romantic names to him: Corinth, where Paul had preached, and to which he had written two pastoral letters; Antioch, famous as an early missionary center; Caeserea, known for its school and its copyists; Jerusalem. Jerusalem! The holy city, where Jesus preached, and died and rose, the city of the Great King. Then there was Alexandria, and all that it had come to mean for Justin in the past few weeks. Famous for culture and learning, and for its school and scribes, the city where Juliana lived. Perhaps he would see her again. Perhaps he would find some answers to his vexed questions about readings. Perhaps there would be more puzzles.

Suddenly the raeda lunged to one side, sending a spray of rainwater into the carriage. Justin bent forward to protect the satchel on his lap which contained his precious gospel codex. The wet spray jostled Marcus out of his sleep. He looked at Justin and asked, "Where are we?"

"Appian Way," he replied, "We've just passed the new church." Justin then wondered how wise it had been to share this information, not knowing who the others in the carriage might be. Marcus dozed again, and Justin tried to brush himself off, avoiding the eyes of the other travelers. He looked out the back of the raeda at the receding countryside. The storm began to clear and there were patches of sun. Justin wondered who these other passengers were. He knew they would join a merchant and his party at Puteoli who were part of their congregation at Rome, but he and Marcus had had to hire the carriage that would take them there. There was no telling whether the other travelers, a well-dressed man and his wife in their fifties, would be friendly or hostile to the church. Even in a time of relative peace the threat of persecution was real. He had learned this afresh in Lyons.

"My name is Albinus, and this is my wife Sabina," said the man in a soft and cultured voice.

"Justin, and my sleeping friend Marcus," replied the scribe, no longer able to ignore his fellow traveler.

"What's your trade?" asked the man.

Almost instinctively Justin replied, "books, manuscripts, codices...that kind of thing." But he felt he should rather have spoken of carpentry.

"How interesting," said the stranger, "I too deal in books, in a way, and have a great interest in them. Have you any with you?"

Justin knew he could not lie, but he dared not expose the codex to a Roman stranger. Then he thought of a legitimate excuse. "As it is raining, I'd best not take it out now, if you understand."

"I do," said the gentleman.

Endeavoring to shift the conversation to the subject of Albinus and his work, he asked, "And what is your employ?"

"Skins, I deal in skins. All sorts of animal hides, and especially leather. This is where my interest in books comes from. I began to sell leather skins for covers and tongs to libraries wishing to preserve Papyri and parchments. Then I began to supply mambrana for manuscripts. I am just now headed for the East, to Pergamum, where they have a booming trade in leather rolls and codices. 'Diphthera,' as they call them. I am going to discuss the supply of skins for their use."

Justin prayed that the rain would continue, so that he would not be forced to show his codex, but the view from the rear of the raeda told him that the answer would be "no." The sun was now shining in the distance, revealing a landscape all green with red poppies in the foreground and the blue mountains rising in the distance. Justin pointed to the landscape and said to his traveling companions, "Beautiful, isn't it?" Flora and fauna seemed a safer subject.

"A rich soil, fortunate in sweet moisture, abounding in verdure, a level richly fertile such as we often look down on in a mountain nook, where from the rocks above the streams run down, bringing fertile earth - - such a soil will make strong vines flowing with the wealth of the grape....So wrote Virgil." said the stranger.

A man of culture and learning, thought Justin to himself. His wife Sabina then spoke for the first time.

"You mentioned a new church."

Justin's heart sank. There was no hiding and no escape. Was he safe? Was his codex safe? In any case the time for candor had come. He nudged Marcus, to awaken his sole human support at that moment, and he opened his eyes.

"Yes, we belong to the Roman Christian congregation," he said in a matter-of-fact tone.

"I have been curious to know more about the Christian way," continued Sabina with apparent sincerity and interest. "I have a friend who has joined you, and she has been telling me about your *chrestus*, or is it *christus*, or whatever. It is hard for me to understand how one crucified for sedition in Jerusalem can save people from sin and death, but this is what she claims. She is so sincere and kind and she really believes it. Albinus has seen and read some of their books, their gospels, I think they call them, and I have asked him to find me one, haven't I, dear?"

"Yes, my dear, " said Albinus dutifully.

Justin breathed a sigh of relief, opened his satchel, and took out his treasure.

"You will enjoy this," he said. Albinus and Sabina poured over the codex with interest and delight as the raeda bounced along the Appian Way.

98

CHAPTER 20

The three-day journey down the Appian Way and the Domitian road went swiftly and pleasantly, filled with conversation about books and ideas, and punctuated with outbreaks by Albinus from Virgil, whose works he appeared to have memorized:

> Perpetual spring our happy climate sees.
> Twice breed the cattle, and twice bear the trees.
> And summer suns recede by slow degrees.

The summer sun was receding slowly as the raeda carrying the four Roman travelers reached Puteoli.

"Where are you lodging tonight?" asked Albinus.

"We don't know," replied Marcus. "And you?"

Sabina sat forward and said, with a note of concern in her voice, "We sent ahead, and will stay with fellow merchants in the leather trade. Lodging ought not to be left to chance. We would offer you hospitality, but it is not ours to give. I hope you find somewhere decent. In general, stay away from the inns."

Justin and Marcus looked at each other. They knew the reputation of inns, nurseries of sin! They could, of course stay up all night until their ship was ready to board the following day. But the streets would be even more dangerous in a strange port city, which collected rabble from all over the empire. The brigand, the mob, the pirate were not uncommon in such a place, and only too eager to prey on the innocent traveler. An inn, if it was not too wretched, was their best hope. There was the Christian community, but no introduction had been given, and they might cause more problems than they solved by trying to locate it. This was admittedly a poor piece of planning, but in the rush to catch their ship, such a detail was easily missed.

"I'm afraid it must be some inn for the night," said Marcus.

"Oh, dear!" sighed Sabina, "Do be careful of yourselves, won't you?"

"The Lord will watch over us," said Marcus. Then he added, "But we will proceed cautiously. Do you know Puteoli, and could you recommend any place?"

Albinus and Sabina both shook their heads. "Many times I have been through this seaport, but never have I had to seek lodging in an inn," said Albinus. "Nor would I want to!"

The raeda came to a stop in a square just as farmers and merchants were dismantling their stalls for the day. The travelers alighted, paid the driver, and collected their luggage. There were warm and polite farewells, with promises to be in touch when next in Rome, and one or two further lines from Virgil. Then Justin and Marcus found themselves in a thinning market crowd, in the twilight faced with a search for suitable lodging.

"Better a place that is lighted and open, than a hole in a back alley," said Marcus. They looked around the square, but nothing appeared to be a hostelry. They took the broadest of streets leading from the marketplace. There they saw, on their right, a sign over a doorway, quite visible still. "The Elephant" was the name, and on the sign was a painting of an elephant, struggling in the coils of a serpent, and being defended by a pygmy.

The two travelers plucked up their courage and entered beneath the sign. The noise inside was deafening. In one corner there were rowdy sailors made more rowdy with drink. In another, three suspicious characters sat huddled, as if to plot, who knows what mischief. A thinly clad dancer sang loudly to the clientele. To the two Christian scribes the whole place reeked of sin. They made their way toward the innkeeper, and asked if there was a spare room. The keeper looked them up and down, eyed their luggage, glanced at the silent little man standing beside him, and returned his gaze to the travelers.

"One room left," said the innkeeper, speaking loudly in order to be heard over the commotion. He glanced again at the little man, and gave him a nod. Without a word the man moved toward the side door and motioned to Justin and Marcus to follow. Down a dark corridor he limped visibly. At the very end was a small room with a bed big enough for one and a table with an oil lamp. Without a word the little man left them there and returned toward the noisy parlor.

It was a dirty, dark, dank hole of a place, no doubt infested with fleas and lice. Justin closed the door, and they agreed on a plan for the night. They would spell each other. One would keep guard while the other slept. They were safe here, or at least they assumed so, and it was only for one night. Justin slept first while Marcus read his copy of St. John, trying to ignore the incessant noise of drunkenness. At one point a man's blood-curdling scream startled Marcus and even woke Justin. It was followed by the sounds of crashing and banging and more screams. After midnight the noise began to dwindle, and Justin's watch offered more opportunity for quiet contemplation. What would the next days bring? It was now mid-September, and while the sea-lanes were open until November 11, travel became increasingly risky. What dangers awaited them? Was all of the great sea no safer than the "Elephant?" They must throw themselves upon the Lord for help. The Sixty-second Psalm came to his mind and to his lips:

"My soul truly waiteth upon God
For of him cometh my salvation
He verily is my strength and my salvation
He is my defense, so that I shall not greatly fall".

The light began to filter in through the narrow window, and after a while stirrings could be heard in the corridor. A man and woman began arguing and calling each other foul names, and a bell rang to indicate that the world was waking up.

"Today we sail for Corinth," said Justin to himself, and then added in his prayer, "save us and help us, O Lord!" He woke Marcus, and the scribes, after paying more than they wanted, or should have, set off for the wharf.

101

CHAPTER 21

Puteoli harbor was a crossroads of the world. Bathed in sunlight and bustling with ships and seafarers, dockhands and customs officials, and all the people and things that made travel by sea possible and problematic. The quayside was never silent in the busy months; there was loading and unloading, fitting and fixing, customs and clearance. The skipper, the sailmaker, the oarsman and the cook, the dockhand and the pirate all mixed and mingled and went about their business, giving each other moral support...or immoral support.

Justin and Marcus knew they must find the captain of the *Neptune*, a merchant ship bound for Corinth. They were to sail in company with a certain Lucius, a prosperous member of the Roman congregation who had underwritten the expense of their passage, and had promised to look after them, at least for the first part of the journey. The two scribes made their way down the busy wharf, amid the heavy stench of rotting fish parts, and the loud sounds of rowdy sailors, and they inquired for the *Neptune*. At last they came upon her, a moderate sized merchant vessel, capable of hauling a mixed cargo and at least fifty passengers, as well as captain and crew.

"Is this the *Neptune*, bound for Corinth?" called Justin to a burly hand on deck.

"*Neptune* she is, and a sturdy ship she is," said the sailor, and then added, "only one of her kind!" Justin and Marcus wondered what he might have been referring to. Justin called back, "We're in the company of Lucius of Rome."

"Then climb aboard. He's just gone off to fetch his family, but should return soon. You may wait for him up here if you like. Will be safer, I think."

Justin wondered what mischief could possibly befall them in the sunlit morning in the view of many people, but he refused to let his mind explore the possibilities. He and Marcus boarded and joined the hand on deck, who relished a break from his work and a chance to talk.

"Only one of her kind, this ship," he said in a friendly tone. "And I been with her now fifteen years and wouldn't sail with another. Rather do farming, I would, than sail with any other captain. It's him you see, that makes this ship the only one that's like her on the sea. The captain, old Jason, he's the finest ever sailed. He does it all. Oh he lets us help, and there's plenty to do, but he does all the steering and navigating and piloting, and none there is that's like him. You see, he's blind. Hasn't seen at all in ten years or more, and all the time I've known him he's been blind, or near blind. And yet he steers and pilots in and out of every harbor on this great sea as though he knew every inch. He navigates as if he had an inner compass, and inner instruments for telling all the stars. He smells a storm a good three days away, and knows just where we are, and where best to head, and just how long we're likely to be laid up. He knows the crew and all the things on board. He senses when a rope is out of place, or when a sail is loose, or torn or has been mis-stowed. He sees things clear where sighted men are blind. That's Old Jason, and I wouldn't sail with anybody else. And when he's done at sea, then I'm done too."

Justin, a bit alarmed at the prospect of a blind captain, asked in as assured a voice as he could muster, "But how does he do it?"

"He seems to have been blessed with inner sight. As if old Neptune smiled upon him for the naming of the ship, or for his crying out for mercy to the gods. I don't know, but I've seen it time and time again, and marvel how he knows his way around. He knows the rocks and reefs. He knows the time it takes from port to port. He knows the danger spots where pirates lurk. He feels the tides, as if they ebbed and flowed like blood in his veins. He'll keep you safe, Old Jason, and you'll wish you had him back when you've trusted yourself to someone else upon these waters."

Just then a man appeared on deck, and moved slowly toward the sailor and the scribes.

"And here he is," said the sailor proudly, "Checking everything in the way that he does. I never cease to be amazed." Then calling to his captain he exclaimed. "Two passengers for Corinth, Captain." Facing in their direction as if he saw them clearly, he called, "Welcome to the *Neptune*. We should have pleasant passage. Perhaps but one brief storm, but not too much for this sturdy craft." As he moved his way slowly toward them, he added, "Where are you from?"

"Rome," said Justin.

"The eternal city, the center of the world. If I could not be at sea, I'd want to be in Rome. For all that could charm and fascinate a man is there. And where are you bound?"

"Alexandria," said Justin, "with stops along the way." He suddenly began to stiffen. Here was a man with inner sight. How much should he be allowed to learn about the two scribes, their faith and their errand? Great captain though he was, could he be trusted as a friend of the Church? Anyone who roamed the seas as long, as thoroughly and as knowingly as Jason must have encountered Christians. Anyone with inner eyes like Jason must surely have his mind well formed about the Christ and his Church. It seemed best to avoid the captain and go about one's business quietly, and pray for a speedy passage to Corinth.

The conversation was interrupted by the arrival of fresh cargo and several extra passengers. The Captain continued his rounds of the deck, and Justin and Marcus were left to wonder in silence what it would be like to sail with a blind captain. Should they trust the word of the crewman? Were they really on the safest of ships? Besides the party from the Roman Church, were there any friends aboard? They stared through the rigging at the bustle on the dock below.

Then suddenly from behind them came a loud voice with a familiar ring. "We meet again, good friends!" It was Albinus.

Justin and Marcus felt relief. It was not that they feared or mistrusted the Captain or anyone else on this very strange ship. But to them Albinus seemed to be a familiar and friendly face. And although it meant an extra week of incessant talk, and more

105

lines from Virgil than they had the appetite for, they greeted him as if they had come upon a long-lost friend.

CHAPTER 22

The passage down the coast and through the Sicilian straits was swift and pleasant, and confirmed everything the deckhand had said about his captain. Lucius and his family proved pleasant company for Justin and Marcus, and Albinus and Sabina were pleased to be included in their fellowship. Wherever possible, Albinus would spice the conversations with lines from his beloved Virgil. At one point Marcus turned to Justin and said, "There's a model to us. We should know *our* sacred text off by heart."

Justin agreed. After they rounded the straits the sky began to become gray and cloudy, and the surf rose up, so that the ship began to rock. The captain seemed attuned to the change, and by instinct set the sails and changed the course a bit more to the southeast. This meant six, rather than five days out, but not a soul on board doubted that the captain knew what he was doing.

The sun was now only partly visible in the sky. The edge of the disc appeared and the center was covered by clouds. Albinus looked up from the cluster of passengers on the deck, and declaimed:

> "The sun too, alike when rising and when sinking under the waves will give tokens: tokens most sure attend the sun, both those he brings each dawn and those he shows when the stars arise. When hidden in the cloud, he has chequered with spots his early dawn, and is shrunk back in the center of his disc. Beware of showers; for from the deep the South wind is sweeping, foe to tree and crop and herd."

And sure enough, the words had scarcely escaped his lips, when the first drops were felt, and all but captain and crew went

107

scrambling for shelter. Justin and Marcus huddled beneath a tarp which promised to keep them dry, but from which they could look out the stern and have Old Jason clearly in view. He seemed to feel the oncoming storm, and braced himself as an Olympic athlete would prepare himself for the contest. He steered the ship to and fro in rhyme with the waves, so that she seemed to dance in tune with the billowing sea. The wind blew stronger and the waves larger with every passing hour. Justin recited to himself the lines of Psalm 107:

They that go down to the sea in ships,
and occupy their business in great waters;
These men see the works of the Lord,
and his wonders in the deep.
For at thy word the stormy wind ariseth,
which lifteth up the waves thereof.
They are carried up to the heaven, and down again
into the deep;
their soul melteth away because of the trouble.
They reel to and fro, and stagger like a drunken man,
and are at their wits end.
So when they cried unto the Lord in their trouble,
he delivered them out of their distress.
For he maketh the storm to cease,
so that the waves thereof are still.
Then they are glad because they are at rest;
and so he bringeth them unto the haven where they would
be.
O that men would therefore praise the Lord for his goodness;
and declare the wonders that he doeth for the children of
men!

The words were a comfort to Justin's fearful heart. Did not God save St. Paul from shipwreck on this very sea? Did not Jesus still the storm on the Sea of Galilee? Is he not the Lord of sea and sky and land and all there is? Was he not preserving them now with the provision of Old Jason, who seemed untroubled by the storm he could not see? He stood there, at the

108

tiller, a brave and admirable figure, a Cyrus of the seas, leading a straight path for God's little flock.

The storm grew intense, and Justin and Marcus took shelter below. Albinus was too sick to quote whatever passage of Virgil might have befitted the occasion. And all that afternoon and evening the winds blew and the ship reeled and rocked. More and more the water seeped in from every crack, till all were damp. Justin feared for his fragile treasure, hidden in the satchel beneath his coat. Such weather is no friend to the codex! Many hours had gone into its making. And it bore with it the hope for Justin of an anchor to hold his ship fast amid the torrents of other readings and ways of treating the text. He prayed that God in his mercy would preserve it.

And then the storm began to subside. The water still seeped through from the deck, but the worst seemed to have passed. Albinus looked up at Justin, somewhat improved, took out a fine dry piece of leather, and said as he handed it to the scribe, "Perhaps this will help you keep your precious codex dry."

Justin was touched by the gesture of friendship and respect. He smiled at the merchant who by now had recovered sufficiently from his seasickness to launch forth with a few more lines:

"Thus Neptune speaks, and swifter than his words he calms

The swollen seas, puts to flight the gathered clouds, and brings back the sun."

"You live by your book, don't you," said Justin to Albinus, "and I live by mine: Jesus said, 'Take heart, it is I, have no fear.' And he got into the boat with them. And the wind ceased. And they were utterly astounded."

"Jesus calmed the raging of the sea, and he calms the raging of our hearts." Justin could hardly believe his boldness, but it had been evoked by Albinus' kindness. And Justin knew that there was a time to keep silent and a time to speak.

In the morning the sun came out and the ship and its passengers began to dry. They learned to their horror that the ship's carpenter had been swept overboard in the raging storm. So for the last three days of the pleasant run into Corinth, Justin found himself at work at his old trade, mending spars and planks that had been broken in the storm. The rich ornamentation on the high prow had been damaged on the port side, and Justin especially delighted to spend a whole day piecing and carving to make it once more match the starboard. While he carried out this tedious but rewarding task, he entrusted his gospel codex to Albinus, who was eager to learn more about the Christian way. He wished especially to understand how well it fit with Virgil's vision of life. So while Albinus read and kept Marcus busy with questions and quotations from Virgil, Justin applied his skill with wood, and lifted his heart to God in prayer and praise, and enjoyed the constant wash of sea spray in his face. It made him glad to be of use. And he loved the smell and feel of wood. It made him remember the wood that had set him free, and the waters in which he had been cleansed.

CHAPTER 23

Old Jason proved as skilful in the harbor as he had been in the storm. And he was as ready to praise skill as to display it. Running his fingers along the repair work that Justin had done on the prow, and smelling the fresh wood with the sensitivity of a wine taster he beamed his approval and asked the scribe to consider signing on as ships carpenter. Justin basked in the glow of praise, and said, "Thank you, but I am on an errand for another master."

"I quite understand, but it's his gain and my loss. If ever you complete that errand, you are welcome aboard the *Neptune*. The gods have looked with favor on our ship."

The Captain returned to piloting the vessel up the Gulf of Corinth. All along the narrow gulf there was a heavy traffic of ships of all sizes and descriptions. Old Jason seemed to know most of them, but for a few, the newer ones; he needed the aid of his trusted mate. There was a massive grain ship from Alexandria, headed home from its business in Rome. There were various craft with exotic names: *Acturariae, Curcurus, Horiola.* There was the light fast-sailing *Lembulus* with its sharp prow, the *Lusoria* or pleasure yacht, the *Monoxyla*, a vessel made out of one piece of wood, the *Myopara*, a small practical craft. An old ship of the Phoenician type sailed by, and Albinus pointed and proclaimed, "*cumbae instabilis*! unsteady Barques that take up ballast in a tossing sea." A vessel with five banks of oars nearly ran into the *Neptune*, and would have done considerable damage, had not Old Jason sensed the danger and changed his course. Fishing skiffs and floating debris made the whole passage a challenge, even for the pilot who could see. And in among the busy waters no doubt lurked a pirate or two,

111

waiting for night to fall, or a heavy fog to roll in, letting them do their work unseen by all but a captain with inner sight.

The port town of Lechaeum, a short distance from Corinth, and connected to the city by long walls was full of ships from Spain, Italy and Sicily. The wharf was crowded so the anchor kept the *Neptune* in the harbor and a skiff was lowered to transport goods and people. The mate whose name they still did not know joined the little group of friends, and resumed his friendly chat begun in Puteoli, as if it had not been interrupted at all by six days on the stormy seas.

"Ah, Corinth! The sailor's favorite port. O that we might stay here many days. Old Jason knows we like it here and says, 'Just make sure you don't come back drunk or broke,' no questions asked. There's everything in Corinth man could want. I won't elaborate, for there are ladies in our company. But what a city! And we've three days here."

The mate had been looking at the wharf, overstuffed with ships, but turned to Justin and asked, "So it's the East, and Alexandria, that you'll be making for?" And then not stopping long enough for a reply he said. "Be careful what you bring with you. The customs house is full of men angling to get rich at the travelers' expense. The ones at Corinth are the worst of all. Purloin your bags, they will, and take what fancies them. They'll take it all, they will, so travel light."

A fear crept over Justin's heart and mind as he stood in the warm Corinthian sun with the little party of travelers. Would they confiscate his codex? Some library might pay a goodly sum for such a text, Christian though it was, and put it in the section with magical and superstitious books. He'd heard of it happening before with collections of St. Paul's writings and Gospel codices, and even full collections of the Christian sacred writings. But then Sabina, now almost recovered from her seasickness, but still looking ghostly white spoke up.

"They can't purloin the bags of a matron. No Roman official, no matter how greedy and devious, would dare. I'll take your codex and it will be safe, and then return it to you in the city."

Justin thanked the Lord for the generosity of his newfound friend, and knew that he could trust her, but before he had a chance to speak she added, "Or you can let me hold it till you find secure lodging. Corinth is a worse place than Putioli on that score."

"Oh, we're provided for here," he said with confidence. "The Bishop will keep us for the week that we're in Corinth, but I am very grateful for your kindness." Justin handed Sabina the codex, and she hid it in her bags. Marcus then produced his own copy of St. John, entrusting it to the Roman matron.

The skiff, or *scapha*, as it was called, was lowered, with the passengers, Then came the luggage. Sabina's bag, with its peculiar treasure, suddenly slipped from the hands of the crewman and fell into the water. Justin and Marcus found their hearts in their boots. Some quick work on the part of an oarsman recovered the bag. But what of the contents? Would they not be soaked through and through? What of the precious papyrus codices? Sabina nearly fainted with shock, and Albinus tried his best to comfort her. The Roman couple both turned to the scribes at the same time and said, "I am so sorry." Then Albinus added, "The leather of that case is the very best, and probably has kept the water out. But I am sorry for the fright."

Upon inspection, it became clear that only an edge of Justin's codex had been dampened. But the fright had been bad enough. When the *scapha* finally reached the customs house, and the officials took their daily loot, the scribes agreed to meet Albinus and Sabina at their lodgings in the city that evening. As the two friends walked toward the city of Corinth in the hot sun, they were both quiet for a time. Then Marcus spoke:

"Justin, I have been wondering about the events of the past two weeks, and of all the misfortunes that could have befallen us and our gospel books. And I am amazed that Albinus seems to know the whole of Virgil by heart. Why shouldn't we take to learn by heart a much more sacred text, our own gospels? What if our books were lost, or stolen by pirates or ruined in a storm? What if persecution caused the confiscation of all our books, as has happened in one or two places? Then the only way we would know our sacred texts, as we have received them, is through

113

what we stored up in our heads. Juliana and her Alexandrian friends have their own texts which they have received, and in some instances changed. We could, of course, copy them, but they would not be the same. But we believe that we have received the gospels as they were written. We need to preserve that form of the word delivered to us. If Albinus can memorize Rome's great poet for an earthly reason, how much more shouldn't we know word for word the sacred text for a heavenly cause?"

Justin was pleased by the suggestion, and the friends agreed upon a pact to memorize one story or section a day, Justin in Mark, Marcus in John. By mid- afternoon they had found the bishop's house and were warmly welcomed into the Corinthian fellowship.

CHAPTER 24

Corinth was a teeming emporium. The mate of the *Neptune* was right. All that a man's heart desired could be bought there. Situated on an isthmus, between the Saronic and Corinthian gulfs, it could boast two harbors. The one was a key to Rome and the West, the other a gateway to the East. From all over the Empire, and beyond, merchants brought their wares to be sold. Populated by Roman freedmen, whose status was just above that of slaves, it was an essentially Roman city. Latin was its official language, and it had strong ties to the capital. An efficient Roman administration, a fresh water supply, control of the Isthmian games, just below the Olympian in importance, all insured its continuing prosperity.

Justin and Marcus walked through the Corinthian streets toward the market square in the mid-afternoon sun. They were looking for a house, just off the square where Albinus and Sabina were lodging. It was the house of a bookseller. There they would retrieve their copies of John and of Mark from Sabina. As they made their way toward the marketplace, they could hear the noise of buying and selling. Loud shouts of hawkers, and the bleating, mooing, braying and neighing of penned-up animals filled the air. The Market was crowded with people, all eager for gain or troubled by loss. No sooner had the scribes entered the marketplace than they were approached by a surly little man who asked, "Would you like to have a woman with whom to spend the night?" They shook their heads and went on. An angry man, who had drunk too much wine, was arguing with his wife, and fell back on Marcus, nearly knocking him over. He turned to Marcus and scowled angrily, "Will you watch where you are going!"

As the scribes picked their way through the sea of people and booths, a noise began to make itself heard over the general bustle of the market. They were moving in the direction from which it came, and it got louder. Then they came out on a clearing near the center of the market, and saw the cause of the noise. A man was on a platform calling out in a very loud voice, as about fifty people stood around him. With him were three people in their late teens, with their hands tied. The three faces looked very similar, and very sad. Justin and Marcus knew they had come upon the slave market of Corinth, or at least, one of them.

Justin and Marcus were arrested by what they saw, even though they had seen slave markets before. Many times they had passed them in Rome or elsewhere in Italy. It was a fact of life in their world. But something was different about the scene today. Perhaps it was the prominence of its position in the market. Maybe it was the fast and shrill voice of the seller. It dawned on Justin that the three young people for sale were from the same family.

"Siblings?" Justin said, as he turned to his companion.

"It looks that way to me," said Marcus.

"Listen," said Justin, " he is trying to sell them separately. This means that they may never see one another again."

Both scribes stood frozen, simultaneously struck by the full weight of the scene, as the traffic in human life continued. The seller and crowd were unmoved by the anguish of the two young men and the one young woman who stood on display, half-naked in the Corinthian sun. Seized by pirates and chained in the hull of some rat-infested ship, they had endured days of starvation and abuse before being brought to this scene of humiliation and heartbreak. And now sale and separation seemed inevitable. Bids began to be made for the woman, who would be used as a domestic or a concubine or a prostitute. The seller seemed disappointed at the crowd, whose offers were not very generous.

Justin noticed that standing next to him was a distinguished-looking man in a toga, who stood in silence. He stepped forward to join the crowd of bidders and called in a loud voice, "I will give you a thousand Drachma for all three!" The crowd turned to

116

face him in stunned silence. The auctioneer, so surprised at the offer, was speechless for a moment. The man repeated, with great volume and passion. "A million sestertii for all three!"

"Sold!" said the hawker, beaming with delight at the sale. It was far more than he expected, even if they had been sold separately. The distinguished gentleman stepped up on the platform and moved to hand over the money and claim his property. He looked the three young people in the eyes and whispered a word to them. Then he turned to the crowd and cried. "They are now mine, and I have set them free!" Suddenly not a voice could be heard in the crowd around the platform. The man released the three from their bonds and moved off the stage with them. The crowd made way for the four as they passed out of sight.

"And now for the next slave!" shouted the auctioneer, with as much self-confidence as he could muster. The crowd began to thin out. Justin and Marcus stood together, still awed by what they had seen. Who the man was, or why he had done what he did they might never know. Was this his habit, or was he just moved by the moment? The scribes walked slowly toward the street where they would retrieve their books. Both were speechless.

Once beyond the marketplace and headed down a quieter street, Justin turned to Marcus and said, "That was a wonderful thing we have just seen. But you know that is what our Lord Jesus Christ has done for us. We were slaves, enslaved to sin, 'sold under sin,' as St. Paul says in his letter to our church. But Jesus Christ, by his death on the cross, has paid the price to set us free. We did not earn it or deserve it, any more than those young people had earned or deserved the grace and favor of that Roman gentleman who bought them. But now they are free, and so are we. 'We were bought with a price.' as St. Paul put it in his letter to the church in this city, bought with a price!"

The scribes arrived at the door of a rather large villa, and were shown in by a slave. In the main room Albinus and Sabina greeted them warmly, Albinus, after another citation from Virgil, introduced them to their host, Heliodorus, the bookseller.

"And I see you have some fine papyrus codices!" Heliodorus exclaimed. Sabina has been keeping them for you, despite my pleas to consider a sale. Of course, they are yours, but would you entertain a deal of some kind, a bargain we might strike...."

"O cursed lust for gold," said Albinus in a firm but friendly tone, "to what dost not thou drive the hearts of men."

"Just expressing interest, my friend," said Heliodorus, and then he turned to Justin, who was taking his copy of the Gospels from Sabina, and thanking her profusely. "I did not know that your Jesus was angry!" he exclaimed.

"Angry?" asked Justin, a bit puzzled.

"Yes," replied Heliodorus, "Sabina kindly showed me your codex, and I turned to St. Mark near the beginning. I began to read, and came upon the story of the leper. Now I have seen this story several times, and in fact I have a copy in my salesroom now, albeit under the heading of superstition. But all the copies I have read say that Jesus was moved with compassion. Yours reads that he was angry. What do you think this Mark wrote? I do not want to be rude. I'm just curious."

Justin thought, and prayed quickly for wisdom. It was one thing to have a common ground in the Lord when discussing differences in their copies. It was quite another to speak about such matters with an unbeliever. He had, in fact, noticed the reading, "He was moved with compassion," in Juliana's copy of St. Mark, but had not given it further thought. What was he to say now?

"I have seen that reading myself, and have wondered at it. In any case, we must return to our lodgings. We are expected for dinner."

Heliodorus invited the scribes to come back and look at his collection, and Albinus bade them farewell with a line from the *Aeneid*.

CHAPTER 25

"The Bishop has come home ill and gone to bed."

These were the first words that Justin and Marcus heard as they entered the bishop's house at sunset. The young man said them in a whisper, which reflected the hush that had fallen over the whole house.

"I am very sorry to hear this," said Justin, "We will pray to the Lord for his quick recovery."

"It is really bad this time. Last time he was this ill, he nearly died. We thought the Lord had taken him at one point. But he was spared, and we were spared, for without him we would be in great sorrow, and great danger." The deacon paused, and seemed to check himself from further comment. Instead he introduced himself. "My name is Christophilos, and I am the deacon and secretary to the bishop. My whole life is dedicated to serving the Lord by serving my bishop, Dionysius."

Justin continued the conversation in a whisper as Christophilos led them into a side room.

"I remember well your bishop's visit to Rome. It was some years ago, during the days of Soter. I remember that your bishop had written a letter, which proved exceedingly helpful on a number of points, and our Soter, of blessed memory, asked me to pen his reply. He encouraged us in our gifts to the needy brethren, and shared with us your custom of reading the scriptures on the Day of the Lord. But what really left a lasting impression on me, was the warning he gave about those who tamper with the Scriptures of the Lord. I shall never forget it, for it has confirmed me in my own faith and work."

"And what is that work?" whispered Christophilos.

"We are scribes in the Roman Church," said Marcus. And now we are on an errand for our bishop, Eleutherus, to take

119

letters to churches in the East. And we have some for your own bishop. I do hope he will be well enough to receive them in person and reply!"

"Please keep your voice down, " said the deacon.

"Forgive me," said Justin. "I remember your bishop's letters and his visit. What a princely figure he was. And it was my privilege to attend his meetings with our Bishop Soter, and with my teacher, Irenaeus. I was a kind of notetaker for my bishop, and the whole of the discussions over several days, indeed maybe a week, was the best education I ever had. They conferred mainly about the rising threat of the school of Valentinus, and of the Gnostics, and about Marcion and his influence. Many of the faithful were being tempted and others were completely carried away by these teachers and their practices. Our Soter was standing firm in the faith, as does our dear Eleutherus today. But what a help it was to have the wise counsel of the bishop most highly esteemed of any in the world. He was a giant. Or rather, I should say he was a David, for he was small in stature, and frail in health. But he slew giants with the smooth stone of Jesus Christ, the living stone."

Marcus nudged Justin with his elbow, to remind him to remain quiet. Justin went on,

"I do so hope he will recover. He is a great man, and his letters and visit are still talked about to this day, you know."

"Yes," said Christophilos, "He does write many letters, or rather, he dictates them and I write them out. There were letters to the churches at Athens and Lacedaemonia. There was a long letter to Bishop Pinytus of Cnossos. Others were written to churches further afield, to Nichomedia, the chief city of Bythinia, and to Philip, the Bishop of Gortyn in Crete. These letters were full of apostolic teaching and wise counsel, and it was a privilege to be the copyist. I always made copies before sending them, and have a complete collection, which I often steal a few minutes to ponder. And what has really troubled him recently is that some have taken to tampering with his own letters. I have actually seen some altered copies, and I know they were falsified, for I took them in dictation myself from the

120

Bishop. Imagine what his sway must be that some would find it to their advantage to change his letters."

Justin concurred, "Yes, he is renowned, indeed, and I know how much we depend upon his counsel. For shortly after his visit our dear Sootier died, and Eleutherus became Bishop. Now Eleutherus has proven himself to be a strong and godly leader. Indeed I have never met a more godly man. But in the early days of his office, he looked to your bishop for encouragement and strength, and was not disappointed."

Christophilos continued, "In recent years Dionysius has taken to visiting churches in person, partly to verify the contents of his letters, and partly to strengthen the brethren in the church far and wide. There have been several synods in which he has been prominent. And we had just returned this day from Athens, where he had been preaching, and refuting the Marcionites, but he took ill on the voyage. I fear he will not be at the next synod, which meets soon in Hierapolis. May God spare his life!"

"And his church," said Marcus.

CHAPTER 26

"Just in here is the library and scriptorium," said Christophilos proudly, as he led Justin and Marcus to a room at the corner of the house. "Let me light these lamps...there...and here are the copies we are making. On that table is a package of new codices, and letters, which were given to us by one of the brethren from Carthage, who had come to observe our synod, and deliver an opinion from his bishop. I have not even had a chance to look at them. We can do that later. But here are our copy things. Make yourselves at home, brothers, and I will return when I have made sure all is well with our dear Bishop Dionysius."

Justin and Marcus stood in front of the copying table. A codex was open to the Gospel of Mark, to the middle of the gospel, and a marginal note caught their eyes. Beside the quotation from Isaiah, "This people honor me with their lips, but their heart is far from me," was written the word "love."

"Look, Marcus," said Justin; "here is the alternate reading in the word from Isaiah. Bishop Eleutherus told me one time how he had wondered over this variation. In this manuscript we have both of the readings."

"This people love me with their lips?" mused Marcus." This is not in our Mark, if I remember, nor for that matter, in Isaiah, who wrote, "They draw near to me with their lips...""

"I do say, Marcus, your knowledge of Scripture, both of old and new, is remarkable. I will benefit more from our pact than you will. I suspect you know most of it by heart." Justin's tone was admiring, but betrayed a bit of envy too.

"I have worked at it over the years. I discovered at an early age that my memory was very good. It probably was aided in my tender years with the task of having to remember the names

123

of sheep. On my father's farm, as you know, we named them all. As far as I could tell, it just made it harder when it came time for slaughter. But that's as it was. In any case, I found I had a good memory, and when I became a Christian, I simply applied my God-given skill to this greatest of treasures. It has been a great blessing in times of crisis and need."

"And it has helped to make you the rock that you are, so that we weaker fellows can lean on you," said Justin.

"Hardly weaker!" exclaimed Marcus in a voice that might easily have woken the Bishop, had it not been drowned out by a hard and persistent knocking on the door of the house. Christophilos ran down the stairs at once, and unbolted the door. Justin and Marcus looked on from the doorway of the Scriptorium. There stood a corpulent middle-aged man, who appeared almost breathless, as if he had been running. As he caught his breath he stammered out in a loud voice,

"I must see them at once!"

"See what?" asked Christophilos in a whisper, "And please keep your voice down, our Bishop is not well, and must have his sleep."

"The letters!" he exclaimed, still in too loud a voice.

"What letters?"

"The letters from Carthage, the letters you brought back from the Synod. The satchel of letters I delivered to you. I fear one of my private letters has been mixed in with them, and I must have it now."

"I am sure we can look through...." But Christophilos had no time to finish, for the man now regaining his strength and breath pushed passed him exclaiming, "Now!"

"I must ask you, please to keep your voice...."

The man moved toward Justin and Marcus in the doorway,

"You have them," he insisted, glaring at the two Roman scribes, and then asked, "have you seen them?"

"Seen what?" asked both scribes softly, and at the same time.

"The letters! My letters! The ones with the codex, and the letters from our bishop. I need to see them at once. They must be in here," With his big body he pushed past the scribes and into

124

the scriptorium, like a dog on a scent. He lunged for the satchel and began to pry it open.

"I beg you," said Christophilos, "Keep your voice low, sit down, and explain to us your business, and we will help you in any way we can."

"I do not need your help," said the man in a pugnacious tone as he tore open the satchel and began rummaging through its contents.

"Just who are you, and what is your business? Do you have some letter of introduction from your bishop?" inquired Christophilos.

"My Bishop!" exclaimed the man. And then he checked himself. His sudden appearance and wild behavior could only have aroused suspicions in the three men in the room, and his unchecked hostility toward his bishop, wherever he was from, plagued the scribes and deacon with questions and suspicions.

"Here it is!" he exclaimed as he removed one papyrus sheet, and then a second from the pile, now scattered on the table, and tore them in pieces.

"And I must have this too," he insisted, as he picked up the codex that had been included with the letters.

"I am afraid I cannot let you take that." said Christophilos, with exasperation. At that moment the deacon realized that to wrest the codex from the stranger would mean a scuffle, and more noise than would be conducive to the bishop's recovery. Enough clamor had already been made to waken and disturb the sick bishop. So he asked Justin and Marcus to stand back just as they were about to seize him. The man backed up to the doorway of the scriptorium, pulled out a small knife which had been hidden in his cloak and said, now in a whisper.

"And don't any of you follow me, or you shall feel this."

The man hurried to the door of the bishop's house. Soon he would disappear in the night, and none of the startled company would have any idea what lay behind this bizarre visit. But at the doorway he stumbled and fell over, writhing in pain as he clutched the codex and the knife to his chest. Justin, Marcus and Christophilos hurried to the doorway, but by the time they reached the mysterious stranger, he was struggling for breath.

He cried out and then lay still. Looking up into the eyes of Marcus, who had come to his aid before the other two, he said in a quiet, but desperate tone, as he released the codex from his dying grip.

"I beg you, give this to Tatian."

CHAPTER 27

"Tatian?"

All three men said it at the same time in a bewildered whisper. Then after a minute of silence Christophilos said, "Well I must go and see whether any of this has disturbed the Bishop. Please stay here and I will be right back, and we can decide what to do."

Christophilos was back in no time with a comforting report. The bishop was sleeping soundly and peacefully.

"Now, what to do," he said as if the journey upstairs and down had cleared his mind. "I think we must inform the powers that be and tell them as best we can what happened, arranging for a decent burial for this fellow. We must assume that he was a Christian...of some sort...and arrange for Christian burial. As to the codex and the torn letters, here is what I suggest: we should keep them here for a few days, until the bishop is well enough to render his judgment. Then we will lay the whole matter before him. I have always known his judgment on complicated matters to be full of wisdom. He has the Wisdom of Solomon, and so I think we should await his ruling."

"As to the letters," said Justin, "it would be helpful to the bishop, and to us, if we tried to piece together the fragments of papyrus, and get some sense of what this poor man was up to. We might discover his connection with Tatian, or some possible motive for this bizarre behavior." Then turning to Christophilos he added, "Do you think we could do that?"

"I think it could only help," he said. "We should also look at the codex for other clues. Perhaps we should read through the other letters as well. Here is how we should proceed: if the two of you will work to piece together the letters, I shall send for the local magistrate and report the incident. When I return, we can look over the codex and other papers together. Then I think we need some sleep. And I understand you have business to do with the church in Athens?"

"Yes," said Justin and Marcus at the same time. They were both transfixed by the clarity of Christophilos' mind and the reasonableness of his plan.

"The bishop will need absolute quiet for several days. Why don't you take the isthmian road to Athens, do your business and return. By then, God be pleased, our Dionysius will have regained health and strength, and we can take the time we need with him to sort out this awkward matter about Tatian. And now, brothers, come in. I will be off. Gather the fragments and get to work. I expect to be back within the hour. I would not like to leave the bishop for any longer."

The Roman scribes set to work gathering up the fragments of papyrus that lay scattered on the ground, and began assembling their puzzle on the table. The texture of one sheet was slightly different than the other, and with the aid of all the lamps available they had no difficulty sorting them into two piles. Then began the tedious task of fitting the pieces together. Marcus began to feel a mounting headache, so Justin urged him to sit.

"No, brother, I should do my share of the hard work," he said. And then he added, "Justin, I am amazed at how clear-headed Christophilos has remained through all the commotion. He can't be any older than you, and is probably younger, late twenties, maybe thirty, I should have thought. Where do you suppose he gets such strength and stability?"

"Dionysius," said Justin. "It must be association with this the greatest living bishop in the church. I imagine that in time our Eleutherus will attain that position, but today pride of place goes to the Bishop of Corinth. No doubt, the bishop will have been shrewd in his selection, and the deacon has probably been in his bishop's service for ten years, like a son with the father, laboring in the gospel. I do look forward to meeting this giant."

Justin had just finished assembling the fragments of one letter, and stopped to read it before proceeding to the next. One or two letters had been damaged in the tearing, but most was still clear, and Justin read aloud, though stumbling, and softly:

"Nerus to his most esteemed Tatian greeting. Many here oppose the four into one, and are seeking to destroy all copies, alleging corruption, heresy, and destruction of the true way of God. The bishop is in league with them, so I am leaving them and coming to you, to remain your bondservant forever. They have given in to the way of the Devil, and have wine at Eucharist and women in their company. Some even partake of meat (no doubt offered to idols). O for a life of *encrateia*, of true self-control. I am bringing the last remaining copy...."

With these words the letter ended. So Justin scrambled to assemble the second. He too was now fighting a headache, but Marcus had recovered sufficiently to take over while his friend rested. The piecing together of the second fragment was especially tedious, for it had been badly torn and mangled. But slowly it came together. As the last piece was finally set in its place the door opened, and Christophilos entered.

"All will be well," he re-assured. "I shall wrap the body for tonight, and the officials will be by in the morning, and give leave for its proper burial. We will see to all that. And I have arranged for one of our merchants, Appolonarius, to come mid-morning and take you to Athens. And now tell me, what have you discovered?"

Christophilos looked at the first page, shaking his head as he read. Then Marcus read the second page of the letter

So fierce is the opposition here in some quarters that your followers have taken cover and meet in secret. I have disguised my own allegiance thus far, and will be able to accompany a friend to the synod in Athens, where I may have success in escaping to the East, and to come to you. O joy! True follower of God, Hail and farewell.

"Well," said Christophilos. "That explains a lot. At the synod in Athens there was considerable talk about Tatian's 'four into one,' his Diatessaron. Some were fiercely opposed, while others saw in it no great threat to the Church. Our own bishop is committed to the four Gospels, as I know yours is, but is not opposed to the gospel reaching the barbarians in this other form, as long as it does not become the official version of the Church."

"In Rome," said Justin, "we are committed to the four gospels. I can still hear my teacher Irenaeus saying, 'Just as there are four winds, and four corners of the earth, so there are four gospels, and those who oppose this form of the truth are vain, unlearned and audacious.'"

Christophilos nodded a tired agreement and added, "All this we must lay before the bishop when he is well. But for now, we must get some sleep. Tomorrow you have a journey to Athens, and I have the care of a sick bishop, the arranging of a Christian burial, and the reading of the Latin Diatessaron."

CHAPTER 28

"Ah, there you are, Justin," said Marcus as he found him in the library of the Christian school at Athens. "We had better hurry or we will miss the lecture."

"What a library!" exclaimed Justin, as they walked down the hall to the lecture room where some thirty students were listening to Athanagoras hold forth.

"Whereas you got lost in the library," said Marcus, "I got lost in the city where there are more gods than men! What a challenge these Athenians face if they wish to remain true to Christ. All the competing philosophies and religions seem more tightly packed together than in Rome. I'm sure we have them all, but they have more room to spread out. Here the air is thick with them, and it has been so since the days of Pericles."

The teacher's stentorian voice could be heard down the hall, and it suited his stately appearance. A distinguished man in his sixties with white hair and luminous face, he filled the room with his presence and his words. Justin and Marcus quickly took the last available seats.

"And we welcome our visitors from Rome!" exclaimed the great Christian orator. "And now for the question to be addressed today: the charge that Christians are atheists. When I took my deputation to speak before the Emperor as an ambassador of Christ, I thought very carefully about how to establish common ground. It would take more than hailing the Emperor and his son as real philosophers, seekers of the truth, although like St. Paul in this city, or before Agrippa, I tried my best at this. But I knew that the truth of our Gospel would commend itself the better if I established that we were agreed with the Philosophers and poets, that there is but one God. The Prophets of Israel were clearer than all on this point. So I said something along these lines: We are not Atheists, as we are accused of being, but Plato himself has written 'To find out the maker and Father of this universe is difficult, and when found it is impossible to declare him to all.' So Plato conceives of one uncreated and eternal God. And if he recognizes others as well, such as the sun, the moon and the stars, and yet he recognizes them as created, 'gods, offspring of gods of whom I am the Maker, and the Father of works which are indissoluble apart from my will, but whatever is compounded can be dissolved...' and so Plato goes on in his *Timaeus*. It is a most interesting work, and you should get to know it well if you are to engage philosophers with the gospel. So I tried to establish this common ground, and then went on to argue that if Plato is not an Atheist for conceiving of one uncreated God, the Framer of the universe, neither are we atheists who acknowledge and firmly hold that He is God who has framed all things by the Logos, and holds them together by his Spirit.

"I then turned to Aristotle, who speaks of God as a kind of compound living creature."

There seemed to be a special attentiveness in the room as the teacher went on, picking up speed as he spoke, so as not to miss anything in the hour allotted for the session.

"I well remember asking myself how best to tackle this question when addressing the Emperor. Of course I should quote the poets, as St. Paul did, 'in him we live and move and have our being,' or 'We are indeed his offspring.' But also some more puzzling and enigmatic words of Euripides, 'If Zeus indeed does reign in heaven above, he ought not on the righteous ills to send.' But such questioning does not make the poet an atheist! No the poets believed in the one god indeed. So Sophocles could write: "There is one God, in truth there is but one, who made the heavens and the broad earth beneath." Yes, there is much in the old poets and philosophers that will help us to establish that there is but one God, and that we are not atheists for rejecting the gods of human creation, any more than were these writers of old."

"Then, when we have established this truth, on the grounds that they will receive, namely their philosophers and poets, we

132

then show that this truth, of the one true, living God is more ancient, more movingly set forth in the Hebrew prophets. Isaiah, toward the end of his prophecy is full of wonderful words, which can move the heart of any listener with an open mind: 'I am God, the first and the last, and beside me there is no other God.' Or again, 'Heaven is my throne, and the earth is the footstool of my feet. What house will you build for me, or what is the place of my rest?' The Psalms also speak movingly of the one true and living God. "Our God is in heaven, he hath done whatsoever pleaseth him. Their idols are silver and gold, even the works of men's hands."

"Having established the truth that there is but one true God, as the poets and the philosophers and the prophets all declare, you need to go on to show how it is that their 'idols of silver and gold' are indeed 'the works of men's hands.' Point out the absurdities of the heathen gods. It was actually quite an intense moment when I held forth thus: 'How Kronos, for instance, mutilated his father and hurled him down from his chariot, and how he murdered his children, and swallowed the males of them, and how Zeus bound his father, and cast him down to Tartarus, as did Ouranos also to his sons, and fought with the Titans for the government, and how he persecuted his mother Rhea when she refused to wed him, and she, becoming a she-dragon, and he himself being changed into a dragon, bound her with what is called the Herculean knot, and accomplished his purpose of which the rod of Hermes is the symbol; And again, how he violated his daughter Persephone, in this case also assuming the form of a dragon, and became the father of Dionysius.' As I spoke these things, these absurdities, plainly the room was silent. All were attending with great care. I knew not what the Emperor thought, or his son, or any in his retinue, and I knew not whether my life was safe henceforth. But I spoke the truth, and all could hear it. For I had read these things, and studied them, and knew the ground on which I stood. And I believe that all knew that we were not in fact atheists, but truly did worship the living God.

"Appeal always to men's reason, to their sense of the truth and of the light, and you cannot go wrong. They may persecute you or dismiss you, but they cannot confound you, for you worship him whose word is very truth."

The hour had sped quickly and the lecture was over. A few questions addressed minor points, and one or two students seemed troubled by the existence of evil in a world God had created. The gathering broke up, and the great apologist moved through the crowd and greeted Justin and Marcus,

"So you are the scribes from Rome."

"Yes," they said. "And we thank you for your faithful witness to the truth. We bring you greetings, and a letter from our Bishop, Eleutherus."

"We hear your copy work is going well," said Athenagoras.

Justin beamed with pleasure that their reputation as scribes had reached this far. "I am surprised that you have heard of our work," he said.

"Oh, yes," said the Athenagoras. "Why, just last week a young scribe from Alexandria, a woman in her twenties, was here. She spoke very highly of your scriptorium and of you."

Justin's heart leapt. All the way back to Corinth he was silent and a bit dreamy. And Marcus was kind enough to allow his friend to be lost for a while in his daydreams.

CHAPTER 29

"Good news!" said Christophilos as Justin and Marcus arrived at the bishop's house in Corinth. "The Bishop is better, and you will be able to see him tomorrow. He has taken food and drink, and is even able to sit in his chair and dictate some letters. You know how he loves to write letters. This is a sure sign of returning health. Thanks be to God."

"We rejoice in the Lord with you!" exclaimed both visitors in unison.

"And how was your visit to Athens?"

"We heard Athenagoras hold forth on answering the charge of Atheism. A most impressive witness for the Gospel," said Marcus.

"And we saw their library at the academy," recounted Justin. "I had but an hour there, and could have spent days. In any case I am glad to return, to hear of the Bishop's recovery, and to have news from you of the manuscript."

"Oh, yes, Justin, the manuscript," Christophilos said shyly. "Well, I have done some reading and checking, but my Latin is not excellent. I have always been more at home in Greek. But come in here and see what I have found."

Christophilos led the scribes through to the scriptorium, and took them to the table where the Latin harmony of the Gospels lay side by side with the official Greek Gospels codex of the Corinthian church.

"Look here," said Christophilos. "Here at the beginning of the Gospel story, if we compare the note about Anna, we see that the Latin work says that she lived for seven years with her husband as a virgin. Now this is just the sort of thing we might expect from Tatian and his followers. And look here in Matthew, where Jesus is talking about marriage, the word from

135

Genesis,' Therefore a man shall leave his father and his mother, and shall be joined to his wife,' well these words are not spoken by God but by Adam, so it gives the impression that marriage is a human rather than a divine institution. As for references to wine, I noted that the story of the wedding at Cana does not have the expression, 'and when men have drunk freely'. And at the crucifixion Jesus is offered 'vinegar and gall,' rather than 'wine and gall.' Now what do you make of all that?"

"It looks like the influence of Tatian to me," said Justin, "And this fellow was eager to get into Tatian's hands a copy of the harmony current among his followers in Carthage. We in Rome are aware of these developments. You see, some years ago, in the last year of Soter, we began to hear from the increasing numbers of Latin-speaking Christians in the newer churches round the city that they wanted to be able to read and hear the gospel in their own language. We were supportive of this concern, but felt that the four Greek gospels as they stood were sacred, and ought not to be translated. We did, however, agree to the production, under the Bishop's watchful eye, of a kind of Latin gospel compendium, that would provide the story in the language of these congregations. Not long afterwards we learned that Tatian had begun championing this kind of harmony, and we learned that he was compiling one. As a pupil of Justin Martyr, he had a kind of credibility among us, although he had left for the East after Justin's death. So we became concerned in the church, lest the "four into one' should displace the sacred four, inspired by God. We were further concerned when Tatian emerged as leader of the Encritites, and espoused all kinds of ascetical views. We dealt with this personally, as our third scribe is very much given to this view. A delightful brother he is, but he has to be carefully looked after. I think his own preference would be for the harmony, and for just the sort of readings you have shown us. Though mind you, we know he would not willingly alter a text."

"I do believe the Bishop will be very eager to hear all of this tomorrow," said Christophilos. "And I am sure he will know just what to do."

136

Marcus then added thoughtfully, "You know, that last curious change from wine to vinegar, well, it may be that this reading, whoever has translated it, for whatever purpose, may not be a willful change, so much as a conformity to the Old Testament. You know that in the Psalm, the sixty-ninth, about the suffering of the Christ, there are the words, "They gave me gall to eat, and when I was thirsty, they gave me vinegar to drink." Now we know that in Rome, for a good many years, some of our churches have been singing the Psalms in Latin, and that they took over their translation from the Jews, who were probably using them in that language before Peter and Paul came to Rome. If vinegar is what was found in the Psalm, and if this is fulfilled in the sufferings of Christ, then it is understandable that this reading, rather than the 'wine' would get into the gospel account. Of course, with the Encritites there would be all the more reason to go for this reading. I'm sure that some of these changes you have showed us are willful on the part of these folk, and are to be resisted, but we must be careful not to be too hard on them. I feel this is the position our own bishop would take."

"Yes, and our Dionysius as well," said Christophilos. "No doubt some of this is translation, some willful alteration."

"And how to distinguish between the two?" said Justin, deep in thought. "That is the great question we face. Whenever we translate the gospel or epistle, into Latin or Syriac, as I hear they are doing, or even from Greek into a better style of Greek, you are in danger of altering the text. How then will the next generation know what the apostles actually wrote? So the text moves ever farther away from the original. To do such translation, to make the Gospel available to more people, is a good and necessary thing, for the gospel must reach to the ends of the earth. But what are our controls? How do we preserve for all time, till the Lord comes in glory, the gospel as it was written? I have struggled with this question very much these past few months."

"And we have too," said Christophilos. "Last year we had a visit from an Alexandrian scribe, a young woman, very learned and able. Juliana was her name. She left quite an impression, and not a few of our young men applied to be the Bishop's next envoy to Alexandria, I tell you."

Justin's heart raced, and his eye caught Marcus' who gave him a look of deep sympathy and understanding. "Yes, she visited us recently as well. She seems to have visited a lot of churches."

"She was very articulate and convincing on the matter of translation," said the Corinthian scribe, "and she spoke of efforts to make the gospel more available to the cultured people in her city. A laudable effort indeed. But I see the problem it creates, if you want to preserve the Greek text as the apostles wrote it. You have somehow to indicate that the translation, albeit in Greek, is just that, and not to be confused with the original. True it is that no cultured Greek from Alexandria, or anywhere else, would be drawn to faith in Christ by the poor style of St. Mark's gospel."

"Unless the Holy Spirit overrules," said Marcus.

"You yourselves are going to Alexandria?' inquired Christophilos.

"Among other places," replied Justin.

"And so you will probably encounter Juliana and her teacher Anaximines."

"I imagine so," said Justin, still in as matter-of-fact a tone as he could muster. The conversation was left there, as Christophilos offered some bread and wine before they turned in for the night. "I'm afraid our Corinthian wine may disappoint our Roman brethren," he said with a twinkle in his eye.

"It will be fine, I am sure," said Marcus. "I doubt that you would serve us vinegar."

CHAPTER 30

A slender sickly figure sat in a chair in the sunlight at the corner of his bedroom. His face looked pale and drawn, and his eyes weak. He looked like a man who had been through a tremendous storm and had barely lived to tell the tale. His frail body shook slightly, and as his visitors entered he stood with some difficulty, being steadied by his deacon.

"Justin and Marcus, scribes from the Roman church," announced Christophilos.

"So pleased to see you, may the Lord be with you," he said, stretching forth his frail hand, pure skin and bone, "And how is our dear Eleutherus?" Without leaving time for a reply, his eyes caught Justin's and he said, "Oh, I remember you from the days of our visit with Soter, of blessed memory. You were the scribe and secretary for our conference, where we discussed the Gnostics, and Easter, and Montanus and a whole host of other issues. And I well remember those hours spent with Irenaeus, now preserving the faith in Gaul. He was the most intelligent man, and the most gracious, I have ever known. What a privilege it was for you to learn the gospel at his feet."

"Yes indeed," said Justin.

"And I hear you have been to Athens to hear Athenagoras and deliver letters." The illness had done nothing to lessen the bishop's acumen. He seemed to know everything about everyone in the church in the Roman world. "I have always been delighted with his lectures. I especially love the way he speaks of God as a divine musician. I can still hear him, "If the world is an instrument in tune, and moving in well-measured time, I adore the being who gave its harmony, and strikes its notes, and sings the accordant strain, and not the instrument." Now there's a winsome word at which even an emperor would stop and think!"

Christophilos helped the bishop to find his chair, for he was showing signs of weakness, but only in body. So he went on, "And my deacon tells me that you have come into the possession of a document, due to the unfortunate end of one of the Encritites from Carthage. He has told me of its peculiar readings, and of the link with Tatian, and I think the picture he has of what has happened is correct. These are not easy times for the church, for there are great challenges from within and from without. But here is what I ask you to do. Tell me, are you going to Antioch?"

"We are, indeed," replied Justin, "on our way to Alexandria."

"Please, if you would, take the Latin harmony and the letter in your possession, and show it to Theophilus, who is the bishop there. He is the wisest man in the Eastern Church, and while I do not always understand him, I respect him greatly. He will know what to do. He has not been opposed to the harmony, the Diatessaron, as much as some of us, though I understand him also to be a great champion of the four gospels. You may, in fact, leave the things with him in good conscience. He does see Tatian from time to time, and is the only one among us who can really communicate with him at all, if even he can any more. In any case, he will take over the matter for you. Before you leave this city I will dictate a letter by our dear Christophilos, and signed with my own hand, that will spell out the matter to him. And will you also take another letter which I have for him?'

Justin and Marcus were amazed at the mental energy and clarity of this very sick man, and Justin quickly replied, "By all means we will, and we will pray for you, that you make full recovery."

"Not so much for me," said the ailing Bishop, "Not so much for me as for the church. For if I die, I will go to be with the Lord, and God will raise up others, like your own Eleutherus, or Irenaeus, or Theophilus, to stand in our stead and to write catholic letters and to strengthen the church. For so he raised up Quadratus, after the dreadful persecution in Athens, in which many fell away and denied the Lord Christ. But that great Bishop brought the church of Athens back to the Lord, so that today it is the shining light that it is, a Gospel beacon, shining to

140

the four corners of the world. Yes, do pray for me, but most of all pray for the church."

With this last word Dionysius fell into a slumber, and the scribes made their exit. They both knew that they had been in the presence of a giant of faith, a holy man of God. Christophilos joined them after a few minutes, and re-assured them that the Bishop was sleeping soundly.

"What a remarkable man!" said Justin.

"So he is," replied Christophilos thoughtfully." Just this morning I was penning the letter he wrote to the Cnossians, and to their Bishop Pinytus. That bishop has been proclaiming the virtues of celibacy, as a sign of true Christian maturity. He urged him to remember that most people are weak, and we must not lay on them burdens too heavy to bear. The letter was a model of wisdom and tact, and shows what wide influence he has to be able thus to address a church and its bishop."

"Would you like us to deliver that letter as well?" asked Marcus.

"Thank you very much for offering, but it has already been dispatched. Our youngest courier took it on his way to Alexandria. The Bishop saw to it that the youngest should go, and not the three so eager to make the visit to Alexandria for other reasons, if you know what I mean."

"I think I do," said Justin, hoping not to give any impression of the anxiety that was on his heart. Then he quickly added, "How will Bishop Pinytus take to another bishop, even one so eminent as your own, writing directives to him and to his diocese, as Dionysius has done?"

"Oh, I can tell you, he will not like it. To a similar letter our bishop wrote two years ago we received a frank reply from him which basically said, 'Feed your own flock and mind your own business.' But the plain fact of the matter is that our Bishop is respected the world over, wherever there is a church. To his great wisdom he can add the claim of Apostolic foundation for our see, and so the younger bishops simply must listen. Only your bishop, by virtue the Apostolic foundation of Rome, is on the same level. Why even in Jerusalem they will listen to

Dionysius. May God be pleased to grant him many years longer as a wise ruler of the church!"

Justin and Marcus thanked Christophilos for his kindness, and after some time in prayer and worship, they found themselves in the mid-morning bustle of the Corinthian street, to visit Albinus and Sabina, and to see again the Christian books in the 'superstition' section of the bookshop of Heliodorus.

CHAPTER 31

In the harbor of Cenchreae Justin and Marcus found the ship they had hired to take them to Ephesus. That city would provide access to the various churches in Asia Minor for which they were bearing letters. The merchant ship they found was a large, leaky and loaded craft called a *navicularia*. It promised to get them across the Aegean Sea, provided there were no severe storms or other mishaps, but the captain and crew were reluctant to say how long the voyage would take, especially at this increasingly precarious time of the year. Having no special links with merchants in Corinth, the scribes were forced to hire a vessel and take their chances. They had hoped that Heliodorus or Albinus and Sabina might help, but all their links were with landed merchants. So it was off to sea with a pack of strangers in a singularly unpromising craft, with no mate boasting of the captain's skill, as the mate of the *Neptune* had done with Old Jason.

"Give me the blind captain and the sound craft any day of the week." said Marcus to Justin as the ship pulled away from the wharf. "Yes," said Justin, "This *navicularia*, as I think it is called, should serve well to increase our trust in the saving power of God!"

"And what is that unpleasant stench?" said Justin to his friend, commenting on a pungent odor that reminded them of rotting fish. Then he added in a whisper, "Not much respect for the captain or discipline among the crew. May the Lord preserve us!"

Not wishing to be overheard or singled out the scribes changed the subject.

"I must say, I have grown fond of Albinus and Sabina," said Marcus.

"To be sure!" exclaimed Justin. "Wasn't he remarkable yesterday, when Heliodorus, still greedy for our manuscripts, to build up his 'superstitio' corner, made that rude remark about Christian scribes altering our texts and bishops encouraging it. What nonsense! But our objection would hardly have held any weight for him. How wonderful it was that Albinus sprang to our defense, with Sabina chiming in with her own witness. He was full of praise for a faith he only half understands, but one I think he is being drawn to. And he peppered his arguments with quotations from Virgil, as ever. Of course, Heliodorus had no answer, only a slanderous report, second hand, that gives us a bad name. And how marvelous it was when Albinus challenged him to name one place where he had evidence of corruption at the hands of a church scribe. The bookseller was speechless. Oh, he mumbled something about the cry from the cross, but hadn't got his facts straight, "My power, My power, you have forsaken me!" But did he understand this to be original? No, it is clearly one of those attempts of those who oppose the essential unity of Jesus Christ. It has not been handed down to us. None of the churches, from the time of the apostles has received such a saying. It was so heartening that Albinus would not let him off, but insisted, 'How do you know this has come from the church or one of her scribes, and not from some Gnostic, or other deviation?' We could not have made a better defense of the Gospel. When we return to Rome, I have little doubt we will see more of those two, and likely within the fellowship of the church."

"I shouldn't be surprised myself," mused Marcus, who was staring at the open sea, as their creaking craft made its way into the deep water, and the sea traffic began to thin out. Before long only a few sails could be seen on the horizon. The weather was very fine with a light prevailing wind that promised to carry them swiftly across to Ephesus.

But as the day wore on, the scribes began to sense some anxiety among the crew. Those who had gone about their tasks in a rather lachadaisical fashion began to be more alert and attentive. The presence of a captain barking strange orders in rapid succession signaled that something was not right. Then it

144

dawned on Justin what was happening. They were being pursued by another ship, which was quickly gaining on them.

"Pirates?" Marcus whispered to his friend.

"I fear so."

Both scribes knew what this meant. In a vessel like this it spelt almost certain capture, perhaps bloodshed, imprisonment, torture, slavery, and confiscation of belongings. The manuscripts, the letters, all seemed doomed. The sleek pirate ship bore down on the slow merchant-man with furious pace, and the end seemed but hours away. A feverish desperation now overtook the crew. The captain seemed hopelessly adrift in his depression. He had already given up. In less than two hours the pirates were alongside, and boarded brandishing swords and knives, and screaming threats, some in vulgar Greek, and some in an unknown tongue. Several of the crew on board the *navicularia* were slashed and bleeding, and one or two were dead. The capture was complete in minutes.

While they were still on deck, the pirate captain suddenly appeared, a fierce, black-bearded man of immense size, almost a giant. He stepped onto the deck and stood. Then almost at once, he fainted. Two of his mates propped him against a mast, and used some smelling substance to refresh him. The scribes could not tell what had caused the fainting. Had he been stabbed by one of the merchant crewmen? Had he slipped and fallen? What would be their fate in the hands of a captainless band of cutthroats?

Before the captain had fully revived the prisoners were sent below and their possessions seized. It was all Justin could do to restrain himself as his satchel was pulled from him. He valued his codex as much as his life, and he had only begun memorizing it. Now it was gone, together with Marcus' copy of John. Huddled tightly together with strangers, many of them now sea-sick or panic-stricken, Justin's composure began to erode. He began to feel ill himself, and he could tell that Marcus felt the same. To quiet his soul he recited to himself a Psalm:

"The Lord is my light and my salvation

Whom then shall I fear?

The Lord is the strength of my life,

145

Of whom then shall I be afraid?"

But even this hardly held back the encroaching panic, and for what seemed like a long time the boat rolled aimlessly on the sea. The prisoners could hear above them the noise of their captors, now as revelry, now as argument. Then suddenly a crewman appeared at the hatch and shouted. The captain wished to see the Romans Marcus and Justin! A fear bordering on panic gripped both scribes, but they found themselves obeying orders, and standing on deck before the big, black-bearded captain.

"Are these your things, and are you Justin and Marcus from Rome?" He bellowed.

"Yes," answered the trembling scribes in unison.

"Transfer them to my boat. They will go with me to Crete." Said the captain, but this time he seemed more angry at the crew than at the captives.

The same gruff crewman who had called them took the scribes to the small pirate craft and sent them below. He practically pushed Marcus down the ladder with the sinister comment, "And don't try anything. The captain plans to fetch a handsome sum for slaves like you."

For a long time the scribes sat in silence, interrupted by each scribe in his turn whispering incredulously, "Crete!" Then Justin spoke.

"I thought the Romans had rid the sea of pirates."

"Apparently not, my brother," replied Marcus.

Justin felt that any conversation was better than sitting in silent fear, so he continued, "Was it not right around these waters that Julius Caesar himself was captured by pirates? And when they demanded twenty talents for his ransom, he laughed at them for not knowing who their captive was. Of his own accord he agreed to give them fifty! Then after his release he immediately manned vessels, captured the pirates and crucified them, as Plutarch tells us in his Lives of the Caesars."

"Justin, Justin," said a weary Marcus, "do not tell me of Plutarch and Caesar and crucifixions. Rather speak to me of Moses, who relates how Joseph, sold into slavery, and then thrust into prison was raised up by the Lord. Remember how he eventually welcomed his own brothers who had sold him. We must make his words our own, since we will need them; "You meant it for evil, but God meant it for good."

"But Marcus," cried Justin, his voice now breaking, "How can God bring good out of this?"

"As the Lord lives, he can," replied Marcus in quiet confidence, "For God works all things together for good for those who love him."

For some time both men were silent, praying not to be overcome by fear. Then Justin said, "Lord, I believe, help my unbelief."

CHAPTER 32

The beautiful bright almost blinding blue of the Aegean sea lifted the spirits of the scribes as they threaded their way past islands all green and dotted with clusters of bone-white houses which sparkled in the autumn sun. Justin and Marcus had never seen such brilliant blues, such breathtaking sea vistas, such enchanting coves. A passing shower drenched them. It lasted but a few minutes, and served only to polish the scenes that paraded before them as the Myoparo, the small piratical craft in which they sailed, headed for Crete.

The scribes had been tied up on deck, and the captain and two crewmen went about their business. All the remaining crew had been left with the prize ship, which would slink its way into some contraband cove. Justin and Marcus wondered why they had been singled out. They both dozed , and were awakened by the sense that the sun had gone and they were in the shade. The shadow was cast by the immense captain standing in front of them.

"So you are Justin and Marcus from Rome."

The scribes were surprised by his friendly tone and replied together, "Yes we are."

The big pirate looked fore and aft, and noted that the crew were out of earshot, so he continued in soft voice. "I am Aulynchus, and I hail from Cnossus in Crete. I have read the things in your bags, and this is why I have taken you with me. You see, I have been a pirate now for many years, but with each passing year I hate this work more and more. I am not cut out for it. Did you see that when I first came aboard your ship., I fainted? It is the sight of blood that I can't stand, and I faint when I see it."

The incredulous Marcus asked, "Then why are you still a pirate?"

"My mother made me go to sea." Aulynchus replied, now taking the scribes into his confidence. "Yes, my mother made me go to sea to be a pirate. So here I am with a cutthroat crew. It's a terrible life, I tell you, but my mother makes me go on with it. I do wish they wouldn't be so violent when they come on board! I do not like this work. Oh to be a farmer or a baker or just live a quiet life! Oh that I could have been a philosopher or a poet, but there's no money in it, and mother wants the money. I will need to sell you as slaves to get money, or mother will be angry. But I took you on board my ship because I found in your satchels some interesting works of philosophy, and I'm desperate for good conversation. I haven't had any cultured talk in months. This lot are wholly ignorant."

"I see," said Justin, emboldened by these revelations, "So you will first use us for talk, and then sell us for booty."

"No, no," cried Aulynchus, "I don't want to sell you. But I don't know what to do, for if I return to mother empty-handed....well....it is best not to do that." He shook his head and walked away from the dumbfounded scribes to take the tiller for a while.

A sense of relief had begun to settle in. There was very little chance of further pirate activity, with a crew of only two, and a captain singularly uninterested in such pursuits. He had caught his prize, and would be able to hand the booty from the captured craft to his mother, Perhaps he would regale her with tales of the adventures he so disliked. It was not absolutely necessary to sell the scribes, although they would fetch a handsome price. But as he steered his craft through the Greek islands, his mind seemed more on the philosophies they had spawned than on the prizes they might yield or the money they might pay. Leaving the tiller to a mate he made his way toward the scribes again, still half lost in his thoughts.

"I have decided I cannot sell you. You are correct that it would be wrong. And what I want is not money but conversation. Tell me, you are from Rome?" With this remark Aulynchus untied the ropes and set Justin and Marcus free.

150

"Indeed we are," replied Marcus.

"And what is your work?" asked the captain.

"Carpentry and sheep-farming," was the reply.

"Again, I do apologize for the fright, and inconvenience, and as soon as we have called in Cnossus, I can take you where you wanted to go. I am so sorry. As I said, I wish I were a philosopher and not a pirate."

"And what is your philosophy?" asked Justin, seeking to be cheerful and pleasant, and finding the view before him tended toward a happy mood.

"A Cynic, I tell you, I'm a Cynic," was the captain's reply. "Ever heard of the Cynics and the teachings of Diogenes?"

"Yes, we know them," said Justin, and then Marcus added, "All philosophies find their way to Rome."

Aulynchus went on, "Well, as I said, my mother made me go to sea, and signed me on a pirate vessel when I was only fourteen. Before that my uncle had taught me to read and write, and told me all the myths and leant me his copy of Plato and nudged me in that direction. But when my mother found out, she determined that I would be in a trade that made some money, so it was off to sea, and I very well had better not come back empty-handed. So I learned the seafaring arts and the pirates' trade, and I hated it. And you can see why. I hate violence and faint at the sight of blood. But, of course, once I was at sea, my mother could not check up on me. About four years after I went to sea, our craft sprung a terrible leak, and we were laid up in Athens many days. There it was that I really learned philosophy. For there was in that city, at that time a noted Cynic, Perigrinus by name, a very wise and powerful man."

"Yes, we have heard of him," said Justin rather coyly. "I think they call him Perigrinus Proteus, after the ancient sea god who changed his form all the time."

"So he was called by his critics, and they also said other things that were slanderous, like the lie that he killed his father, and exploited his students, and other such nonsense."

"Was it not he who threw himself upon the Olympic flame some years ago?" asked Justin.

Aulynchus seemed to take Justin's question as a challenge, and replied, "That he did, and a heroic end to a splendid life, it was! For a while he had been a wandering prophet of the Christian sect, and for this he was persecuted and nearly martyred. But later he read the writings of Diogenes and others, and adopted a philosophy of simplicity and indifference. This is what he was teaching when I sat at his feet for those two weeks. Those were the most wonderful two weeks of my life. But I have never told my mother about all this, so if you meet her, please do not say a word about it. Yes, you are right about his end. He did throw himself on the Olympian flame, and I was there when he did it. It was the most moving spectacle I have ever witnessed. You see he came to have an indifference for all the riches and pleasures of the world. He called his pupils to renounce all that was unnecessary to existence, and to despise even life and death. This was his ultimate act of faith and devotion. He owned nothing, loved nothing, feared nothing. He even quoted that sophist on the cross, whom some call the Christ, who had taught that we not even fear God! 'Do not fear him who can cast both body and soul into hell.'

"But Jesus never said that, " protested Justin, "Peregrinus got it all wrong. I don't know what manuscripts he was working with, but there is a line missing. What Jesus actually said was, 'fear him who can throw both body and soul in hell.'" Then Justin realized he had given away his true identity. By instinct he found himself defending the true text. This made him both glad and nervous. So to remove all doubt and tension he added, "You have seen our manuscripts and know that we believe, Jesus is the Christ, the one sent from God. He is the Philosopher we follow, and we believe he is God."

"A crucified man?" objected the captain, now fully engaged. "How can he be God? Peregrinus followed this Jesus for a while until he found the way of the cynic. But how can one who hung upon a tree be God, and Lord and Savior as you claim?"

"There is an old saying in the Scriptures of Jews, which we read as well," Justin answered, "that says that everyone who hangs upon a tree is accursed of God. And when Jesus hung upon the tree, the cross, he took the curse of our sins, and brought us back to God. This is what we believe."

The captain stood in silent thought looking out at the sea. After a while he spoke. "You speak with force and conviction and this has much appeal, but I still choose to go the way of the cynic, which calls us to own nothing, to love nothing, to fear nothing."

Boldly and straightforwardly Justin looked Aulynchus in the eye and said, "But my friend, you do not live by your philosophy."

"What do you mean?" protested the Pirate indignantly.

"You fear your mother," Justin replied.

As the ship glided through the sea, and into the setting sun the splashing waves seemed to punctuate Justin's unanswerable charge.

CHAPTER 33

Marcus lay half-asleep in the hold of the Moyopara, sensing that something was different. As he found himself awake he realized that the ship was not moving, and he could hear a familiar sound: the bleating of sheep. As he poked his head through the hatch he saw in the dawning light a field covered with sheep. The ship was tied up inside a little cove, beyond which stretched miles of black sandy beach. He turned his head to the sound of the captain's voice.

"This is Kallite, and it is one of my favorite places. Myths and legends abound, the people are friendly, and the wine is very tasty!"

"For a man who renounces everything you do enjoy life," said Marcus playfully.

"You know, I am indebted to your friend. What he said made me angry for a while, but you know, he is right. I do fear my mother. No more! I will never go to sea as a pirate again. But I want you two to come and support me when I announce this to her." He offered Marcus a sip of his drink.

"Thank you, kindly, but I think I will wait a while."

The ship's crew began to ready the craft for the long day's sail to Crete. Justin remained asleep below, and didn't stir until they were under way.

"Good Morning, Marcus," he called to his friend.

"Oh, Justin," replied Marcus, "you slept through the blackest beaches, the friendliest people and the best wines of Kallite!"

"Really? But I slept soundly, and have awakened with a clear head. I suspect I shall need it in the next few days."

"What do you mean, Justin?"

"Marcus, I woke up with an anxious thought about the coming encounter with Aulynchus' mother. To him we have

155

become friends and philosophers. To her we are booty. She is sure to want him to sell us and our treasures, for what money she can get."

"I fear you may be right, Justin, but he is determined that not only shall we meet her, but that we shall support him in his determination to quit the pirates trade in defiance of her."

"This makes us all the more vulnerable," said Justin.

"We must pray against it, but also formulate a strategy. We need to be able to have some independent refuge, some separate connection. If only we had letters or some connection with the church here," said Marcus, rather anxiously.

"Very wise, Marcus." Justin was now wide-awake. "What we will do is claim a link with Pinytus, and the church here. No harm in trying. Perhaps they can give us sanctuary, and even passage to Ephesus. Pinytus is a powerful man, it seems, judging from his rather bold response to Dionysius of Corinth, who is clearly the Bishop of greatest stature in Greece, or perhaps anywhere. It would be best, however to find out discretely from Aulynchus whether he knows of him, and how his mother may react to this plan. I will try to do this when he seeks out philosophical conversation."

About midday the expected conversation began. The pirate, hungry for philosophical talk, approached the scribes, and asked, "So have you read the works of Diogenes?"

"A bit of them, " replied Marcus. "I believe Justin has read more."

"Indeed I have," said Justin, "but it was some years ago."

"And what did you think of it?"

"In the end I found it rather negative and unappealing, although one had to admire the rigor of his thought. And I have a question for you."

"Yes, " replied the captain, raising an eyebrow and shifting his big bearded head to one side.

Justin continued his friendly inquiry, "Do you happen to know a man on your island named Pinytus?"

"Of course, I know him. Everyone on Crete knows Pinytus. But I also know him because he is a distant cousin. Even mother has a sort of respect for him...as much as she has for anyone. He is a powerful leader of the church in our town, and follows through on his philosophy with vigor. Any who fall under his strict discipline must beware. He is pretty severe. We don't know all that goes on, but in Cnossus people talk, and the word gets round. You do not trifle with Pinytus."

"Well," said Justin, pleased that he had struck on a possible plan of escape, "we must see him when we get there. We must see him at once, and report to him from our church and from other churches. We must see him even before we see your mother. If we do, I think we may be able to help you."

"Mother will want to see me right away, and will ask whether I have brought any prizes. She will demand an account, and it is then that I must stand up to her. I need you two with me."

Justin continued to be firm. "We may be of no help to you, but only two extra people whom you refuse to sell as slaves. But if we have seen and recruited Pinytus, I do believe we have a chance of helping you, and we would really like to."

The pirate pondered the request. "He is not always easy to find. Perhaps he has gone to Gortyn on business. He could be visiting another church or hidden away studying his sacred books, or just not interested in meeting strangers from Rome."

"Well this is the chance we take. At least we must try," replied the scribe.

"You do not realize the danger that this puts me in. If mother ever found out that I visited Pinytus, or anyone else, for that matter, before finding her, and giving her a full report, she would be very angry. I think we want to avoid making her angry."

"Then let us go to find Pinytus while you go to your mother, and we can meet you later, and go together to see her."

"It sounds very dangerous to me, Justin," said the pirate, almost shaking, "but if you insist, I suppose I shall have to go along with it. Now tell me more of your impressions of Diogenes."

A long conversation followed that did not end until the island of Crete was in sight.

157

CHAPTER 34

To their great surprise and relief, the man who answered the door when Justin and Marcus knocked was none other than Pinytus himself. An older man with a very weathered and wrinkled face, but with a contagious smile, he opened the door wide and exclaimed, "Hello, strangers. What is it that you wish?"

"We are looking for a man named Pinytus. We were told that he lodged here," said Justin.

"I am the very man whom you seek," the man replied.

"And are you the Bishop of the church here in Cnossus?" asked Marcus.

"That I am," he said, with a tone of curiosity, even concern in his voice. "Who are you and what is your business?"

"We are Justin and Marcus, scribes of the church in Rome, and we bring you greetings from our Bishop Eleutherus, and from the church in our city," said Justin.

"Well," said the old man, still looking somewhat surprised, but now with delight, "I was not expecting...I mean. To what do I owe this pleasure, this honor, that the church in Rome should send envoys to me? Is there some letter, or some new discussion, perhaps on discipline, or some other matter on which I am known to have strong views...Well, whatever your business, my brothers in the Lord, you are welcome. Do come in. Do you need lodging, food and drink, or anything else? We are honored to have you."

The scribes entered, greeting the old Cnossian leader with a holy kiss, and then took the chairs offered.

"Our business in this city is of a quite unexpected nature," Justin continued. "We are on an errand, delivering letters to several churches from our bishop. We were, in fact, on our way to Ephesus and Asia when we were captured by pirates."

"Heaven has preserved you! You have lived to tell the tale! It is a wonder you are not in the salt mines, or rowing as galley slaves!" exclaimed Pinytus.

"Indeed, and God be praised!" replied Justin," but the pirate who captured us took a liking to us, and has brought us here, en route to our freedom. He is a man known to you, I believe, a distant relative, who has allowed us to come find you. Aulynchus is his name."

"Aulynchus a pirate? I always worried a bit over him. But a pirate? What would his mother think? She is a distinguished, I say rather, a formidable lady in this city, and while not a Christian has been kind to some of our people."

Pinytus sat in shock and amazement as the scribes told their tale of the reluctant pirate who really wished to be a philosopher, under the spell of Peregrinus, and living in dread of his mother.

"Unbelievable!" exclaimed the Bishop. "But now that you tell me all this, it does seem credible. There have always been puzzling things about the mother and the lad, though hardly a lad now in his thirties...or is he nearly forty? And as to your desire that I should appeal to her for his freedom from the pirate's trade, I suppose I can try, but she is known to be unbending. She's been that way since we played together as children. Tomorrow we will go together to the house, and I will see what I can do. I've sensed that she has softened a bit in the last few years." Then changing his tone, Pinytus asked, "Now tell me of your travels, of the churches you have visited, and are yet to visit ... er ... if we can get you off this Island."

"We began at Corinth," said Justin.

He could not continue, for Pinytus interrupted, "I suppose you will have met the formidable bishop there, Dionysius?"

"We did indeed, and a very impressive man he is," replied Justin.

"True, said Pinytus, as he poured a little wine for the two scribes. Lifting one eyebrow, he continued, "A great letter writer he is, and gives his opinions on all kinds of matters, and writes to churches all over the Greek world. And these are open letters, to

160

be read in congregations, like Ignatius or Clement, or one of the Apostles. So if a bishop takes issue with some of his ideas, he may have elements of his congregation to contend with."

"I do not understand," said Justin, though he understood only too well.

"Why, not long ago, we received a letter. That is, I did, but it was to be read publicly, in the congregation, urging me not to put too heavy a burden on the brethren, especially as regards those repenting of sexual sin. Well, in this instance I felt compelled to write him back and to say that we exercise godly discipline here. We have had to. You notice that no deacon answered the door. Well, just last week my trusted deacon sinned with one of the young women in the congregation. So you see the difficulty we face. And so when I wrote Dionysius, I tried, gently but firmly to let him know where we stand. I went on to say that while I admire and esteem him greatly, and I do indeed, he should mind his own business, tend his own flock, and provide them with more solid food, and not just a milky diet. In general, I think many of the churches are becoming too lax, both in doctrine and in matters of morality, as befits the gospel."

"In some places that may be so," replied Justin. "But did not even our Lord, in the Gospel of St. John, forgive the offending woman with that merciful and wise admonition, 'Neither do I condemn you, go and sin no more?'"

"I too have heard of that story," Pinytus retorted, "but it is not in our copies of St. John, nor in any copies I have ever read. Recently I was in Alexandria, and I looked at their copies of St. John, since this story is often held up to me as a model. But it was nowhere to be found in their copies."

"We have always known it in St. John," replied Justin, "and I know that the Alexandrians have manuscripts which differ from ours in other ways. But we believe that it belongs where we have it. Why it is not in St. John in the East is a puzzle, and I shall certainly look at the copies of the gospel wherever we go."

Sensing a stalemate, the bishop and the scribes turned their talk to other matters, and found that it was late in the evening before they finally slept, after singing a psalm:

Behold what a good and pleasant thing it is,
for Brethren to dwell together in unity!

As they turned in for the first comfortable night they had had since leaving Corinth, Marcus remarked to Justin, "Well, brother, even if we cannot agree with him, or indeed with these easterners on whether this important passage belongs in the writings of St. John, we must admire him. He is battling hard to keep a firm standard in the church, against all pressures to be lax."

"Yes, my friend," mused Justin. "And he will have an especially difficult time here. For you recall the words St. Paul wrote to Titus, citing Epimenides:

"Cretans are always liars, evil beasts, lazy gluttons."

"Tomorrow may prove for us how St. Paul could come to quote this proverb," said Marcus. "We had better get a good night's sleep."

CHAPTER 35

Selene sat on the porch of her seaside house in Cnossus brooding over her son's rather unproductive venture. Her stony square face stared blankly at the ship-filled harbor and the blue sea beyond. Beside her sat a large, fierce, hairy dog, whose face bore a striking resemblance to that of the owner. Besides his occasional growl, the only sound was the stiffening breeze, playing through the trees beside the house. The calm but eerie silence was broken by the approach of the visitor.

Selene looked up and exclaimed with a note of astonishment, "Ah! Pinytus! Why it has been some time since we have seen each other. Tell me, how is your little flock?" Her condescending tone could hardly be mistaken.

"Well, indeed, and hardly little any more, my dear Selene," the Bishop replied.

"And to what do we owe the pleasure of your visit?" Selene carried on without a smile.

"Do you remember the last time we met?" he asked.

"Indeed I do, though it must have been a year or more ago. I do thank you for your help in securing the release for my friend. I do hope she wrote a proper letter of thanks."

"She did not, and neither did you, dear Selene, but never mind about that. I now come to ask a favor of you."

"What could I possibly do for you, Pinytus? I am an old lady with one unpromising son, and you are the leader of, as you say, a growing flock of sheep."

He still could feel the sting in her tone, and no real remorse for failing to render thanks, but he pressed his case.

"Yes, Selene, it is precisely on behalf of your son that I have come to visit you today." Pinytus paused, and the silence that followed made the wind in the trees sound almost a roar.

163

"I would prefer not even to mention Aulynchus. His most recent venture was a miserable failure," she said.

"And what sort of a venture was that?" asked Pinytus.

"Oh," she replied, "you know he has been involved as a sea merchant for some years."

"But Selene," he replied, "you never told me he was a pirate!"

"And what makes you think he is a pirate?" she snapped back, obviously annoyed at being discovered in her deceit. The dog sensed the tension, curled his lip and gave a rather sinister growl.

"He told me himself, Selene, and asked that I appeal to you for his release from this sinful work."

"The coward!" she shouted. The dog added a loud bark, and stood up to protect his mistress. She turned to him, and said, "It is all right, Gullius, he will not hurt us." Then recovering her composure, she asked angrily, "And where is he now?"

"Oh, I'm sure he is somewhere in this city. You saw him just yesterday, did you not?" The bishop carried on in measured tone, not wishing to lose the advantage the surprise had won him, "And I ask you to release him from the dreadful work to which you have consigned him all these years."

"Let the coward speak for himself!" she shot back. This time the dog was silent.

"He will, and so will his friends, who have accompanied him here." The Bishop went on, wishing to have the whole tale told, and to take full advantage of the revelation. "You know, do you not, that piracy is outlawed in the empire? While Crete is out of the way, and still a haunt for such scoundrels, the authorities are not unaware of goings on here. If this story were known, it would be not only his life, but yours that would be in danger."

"How dare you threaten me!" she said through her teeth.

"This is not a threat, but a warning. He means to be free, and has appealed to me for support. I have no desire that this story become public, nor do you. Of course, he wishes to have it all behind him too."

"And then what will the lazy coward do with his life? Sit and read? You know his uncle tried to ruin him years ago. I will not hear of it. How do you propose that this no-good son of mine will make any money, and support me in my old age?"

"There are many things he could do," said Pinytus. "He could become a respectable merchant captain with his skill at sea."

"There's no money in it," she replied. "He might be able to work in the meat market." She knew this suggestion would gall Pinytus, because of the inevitable association with idol-worship.

"He can't," said Pinytus.

"And why not, Bishop? Oh yes, I remember, you do not approve. No wonder the world persecutes you and your flock. You're a pack of atheists!"

"Selene, that is not it at all. We are used to this insult, but the plain fact is that he can not work in the meat market because he faints at the sight of blood."

Taken aback by this further revelation about her son, she gasped (and the dog growled again). "So he's no good even as a pirate. No wonder he's always come back so empty-handed. He's useless, I tell you, and when I see him I'll..."

"Not so fast with the threats, Selene," Pinytus went on, "You will remember that your friend's release was conditional. It was on my word that she would behave herself that she was set free. Well, I have had to invoke special grace upon myself to keep things as they are. She has... well, I had better not elaborate, but the situation is rather awkward. I am not at liberty to expand upon it. But your co-operation in the matter of Aulynchus secures my continued protection of her, uh, within limits, of course."

"I demand to know what she has done!" said Selene.

"Then ask her yourself," he replied.

In the long silence that followed Selene glared at Pinytus. The breeze had died down and all was calm. Finally she said, "Right, you have won, as you always do, but you must promise to find Aulynchus some employment that will earn him, and me, some money."

The Bishop promised to do his best, and set off to find the reluctant pirate and his two friends. To everyone's relief, the matter was settled, though not without lots of fuming and

165

growling, and the following day Aulynchus set off for Ephesus with the scribes, and his small crew, to fulfill the promise he had made to them. When he returned to Cnossus, he would never go to sea as a pirate again.

CHAPTER 36

"Land Ho!" cried a mate as the coastline near Ephesus in Asia Minor was revealed by a flash of lightning across the pre-dawn sky.

"Marcus," said Justin, "that must be the beach where St. Paul bade farewell to the Ephesian elders."

"And a sacred spot it is," replied Marcus, his words punctuated by the delayed thunderclap.

By the time the sun had risen, the small pirate craft, now traveling as a merchant vessel, found its way into port, and the scribes felt somewhat saddened to say goodbye to Aulynchus.

"But it is not really goodbye!" exclaimed the big black-bearded seaman. "I propose to take you to Antioch, when you are ready to go there."

"That really is kind," said Justin, "but it could be more than a week, as we have some business here, and some letters to deliver in the Lychus valley and Phrygia."

"That won't bother me. You see there is a noted cynic philosopher here in Ephesus, and I have always wanted to meet him. I now have all the time in the world, and a bit of money." And then he added in a whisper, "You see I never gave it all to mother." He then continued in normal voice, "The crew will love the time off here, and we will be ready to go when you are. Only don't be much more than a week, for it is now almost November, and the sea lanes will be closed in three weeks time."

With this happy arrangement secured, Justin and Marcus, set off to find the Ephesian church, with Aulynchus adding a parting warning, "Be careful in Phrygia...a place of desperate brigands and wild religious cults!"

The deacon who answered the door was overjoyed to see Justin and Marcus. "We have been expecting you! But visitors from Corinth told us that you had left there some days ago. So we have been worried that some evil had befallen you."

"And well you should have worried," said Marcus. "For we have had quite a time of it. Captured by pirates, and taken to Crete. But God had mercy on us, and spared our lives, and he used the great Pinytus, that champion of the faith, to secure our release. Believe me, it is quite a tale."

"God be praised!" exclaimed the deacon. "Now come and meet the bishop. I believe you have some letters for him, and he is eager to see you. Did you know that a great friend of your church is visiting here in these days?"

"And who is that?" asked Justin.

"Hegesippus, the collector of the old traditions of the church, from the days of our Lord and the Apostles until now."

"Hegesippus, here in Ephesus? How good it will be to see him! For some years he was with us at Rome, you know, collecting and compiling lists of all the bishops, from the earliest times, and showing that the tradition of our faith has been the same from the beginning, and had been faithfully handed down." Justin's tone was respectful, for he had always stood a bit in awe of Hegesippus.

Marcus added, with the same tone of respect, "No one in the church knows so well the early Jewish traditions and interpretations. And none is a more staunch defender of the Faith of the Church."

"Well," continued the deacon, "he is here, and you may be able to see him, if we can pry him away from conversation with Polycrates." Then the deacon said in a whisper, as he led the scribes down the hall, "He's likely to be our next bishop, you know, but don't tell anyone I told you. They have been in conference all of yesterday and again today. Polycrates is concerned to get all he can in defense of his views on Easter." Then the deacon checked himself, for he remembered that the Roman church had a different view about when to celebrate Easter. "Mind you, " he added, "we are grateful for your Bishop Eleutherus, who disagrees with us, but allows us to go our own way, and celebrate the fourteenth day, rather than always on a

168

Sunday. We hope your church will always be as flexible in this matter. The Lord's Passover is for us the greatest of feasts!"

"The greatest of feasts indeed!" said Justin.

"Here we are," said the deacon, as the door opened, and revealed a small room with four men sitting around a table.

The deacon started to make introductions. The saintly old man sprang to his feet when he caught sight of the scribes and exclaimed, "Justin, Marcus, the Lord be praised! How wonderful to see you both. Is our Eleutherus well? And how are the brethren at Rome?"

Extending the kiss of peace, they both gave greeting, and Hegesippus introduced them to the others in the room. "This is the Bishop of Ephesus, a staunch defender of the Faith, and Polycrates, his special scribe and envoy, and this is the young man, Timothy, who serves me as once the first Timothy served the Apostle Paul."

"We have been discussing the celebration of Easter," said Hegesippus, as he placed his hand on a pile of five large books which were sitting on the table. "Much that I have collected here, from all the early traditions, from East and West, point, in my view, to the fourteenth day. But I am well aware that the Roman Church sees things in a different light. Several of us are meeting here to solidify our minds, so that we might be clear in our conscience and strong in our unity. We expect Melito of Sardis to arrive at any moment, and he knows more about the Lord's Passover than any of us."

"We are honored to be here," said Justin, "and do not wish to disturb you in your conference. But as you know, while we observe a different custom, and value the Sunday celebration, our Eleutherus is a man of peace and wishes churches to be free to choose in the matter."

"Free, indeed!" exclaimed Hegesippus. "For that is the meaning of his name." Justin and Marcus felt proud to be scribes to such a church with such a bishop.

"We pray that it may ever be so," Hegesippus went on, "but we fear it may not be."

Then Polycrates added, "God spare us! What if someone like that young Victor were to become bishop in Rome? He is faithful, promising and intelligent, but he drives a hard line on the question of Easter. Who knows what he might do?"

"Never mind that," said the bishop. "Eleutherus is young and healthy, our fellowship with Rome is strong, and God will preserve us in unity."

Hegesippus again spoke, "Yes, and even if we disagree, and even hurt one another in such matters, though pray God we do not, there is always a spirit of forgiveness with the Lord. For did he not say, even when they were crucifying him, 'Father, forgive them, for they know not what they do'?"

"So tradition has it," said Polycrates. "But we do not have this line in our copies of the Gospel of St. Luke." He opened his gospel codex to the end of St. Luke, and pointed to the place where the saying should have been. Hegesippus, Timothy, the Bishop and the scribes all stood pouring over the text.

The Bishop went on, "I have heard some say that Jesus did not, and would not have said this, especially of the Jewish people, for it is evident both from the destruction of the temple, and of Jerusalem, and from the terrible war which some of our number remember well, that God has not forgiven them for what they have done."

"But how wrong they are!" exclaimed Hegesippus. "How wrong they are. God has not forsaken his ancient people whom he foreknew, as the blessed Apostle Paul has said in his letter to the Romans. And in any case, Jesus was speaking of all who crucified him, and not just of the Jews. He was speaking of Pilate and the centurion and the soldiers. And indeed it was our Lord's word and example that was to be followed shortly thereafter by the blessed first martyr Stephen, and then by James the Just, who also prayed thus for those who stoned him, saying, 'Father, forgive them, for they know not what they do.' I have no doubt that the words were spoken by our Lord and recorded by St. Luke, and that some, of hatred and malice, have removed them from our sacred writings."

Hegesippus spoke with an authority no one could gainsay. His hand was still on the pile of five large notebooks, the fruit of a lifetime of collecting. His eyes were looking up as if to

170

heaven. His was a word no one could contradict. All stood in silence.

The silence was broken by the appearance at the door of a distinguished man with a dark face and a shock of white hair.

"Melito!" exclaimed Hegesippus, as his gaze returned from heaven to earth.

CHAPTER 37

A long discussion about the date for celebration of Easter lasted well into the evening. The company sang the Psalms together: "When Israel came out of Egypt...Not unto us, O Lord...I Love thee, Lord...Praise the Lord, all ye nations...O give thanks unto the Lord for he is gracious," and entering into the spirit of the great feast on the other side of the year, they turned in to bed.

The following morning, Marcus awoke feeling ill. As the day wore on, it was determined that he and Justin could not journey on to Hierapolis, Sardis and Pergamum. After another day, in which Marcus did not improve, it was decided that Justin should visit the churches in these cities and return to his companion before they set off for Antioch. Justin was torn. He did not wish to leave his ailing friend, but the trusted physician in the congregation, who had recently been baptized, re-assured him that Marcus was in no danger.

"It would be a mistake to travel, however, under these conditions. Perhaps in a week or two he will be fit to move on. We shall look after him, giving him the warmest hospitality, as also the holy apostle has urged us. And you may expect him to be fully up to the next stage of your long journey when you return."

Melito then spoke, "I have business in Hierapolis, before returning to Sardis, and I would be honored to have your company that far. I am afraid you are on your own after that. But before we leave Ephesus, Hegesippus and I must visit an aged lady, and we would be pleased to have you join us."

"An aged lady?" asked Justin, in a tone of voice that bespoke his pleasure at being asked to accompany Melito on both the visit and on the journey.

"Yes," said Melito, "for many years there has lived in this city a certain Julia. She is now over one hundred years old, in good health and sound mind. Hegesippus desires to meet her, and record what she can tell him. You see, her father was scribe to the Apostle John, and helped him with his Gospel. She herself knew the Apostle when she was ten or so, and remembers him to this day. Here is a piece of living tradition soon to be taken from us."

Justin made his way with Melito and Hegesippus to a small house in a winding Ephesian street. They were greeted at the door by an aged woman, frail and bent over. They sat together, and after Melito explained their errand she looked up at the three men, and spoke.

"Yes, I remember the Apostle John." Her voice was high-pitched and scratchy. "My father was his scribe, and he would often bring me with him when he attended the Apostle. I remember the hours he spent taking down every word the Apostle spoke, carefully checking his phrases, reading them back to him, correcting a word here and there as the great Apostle desired. I remember especially the voice of that holy man, who lived more in heaven than on earth, as he pronounced with deep solemnity those great words, 'I am the bread of life...I am the light of the world... I am the door...I am the way.' I can still hear them ringing in my ear as if it was yesterday. His was a voice from heaven. He lived so completely in the presence of God. He loved little children, and would sometimes stop his dictation, look at me, smile, and say, 'little children, love one another.' I tell you, it was the greatest thing I have ever heard. When he began to speak, you forgot that John was there, and you saw Jesus."

The three visitors sat in silent awe. The only movement was that of Hegesippus, as he wrote down quickly, seeking to keep up with the holy narrative. Julia continued, in a different more melancholy tone,

"And I have seen all that he predicted come to pass. 'If they persecute me, they will persecute you...In the world you shall have tribulation.' Yes I have seen this, as the world, which neither sees nor knows the Father has persecuted the church. My own younger brother perished some years ago in a fiery trial."

174

"As did my father," said Justin.

"But we are his witnesses," Julia went on, "for Jesus said, 'as the Father has sent me, even so I send you.' He is the true light, the true Logos, the true bread, the true lamb, who takes away the sin of the world."

Again the silence prevailed. Now no one spoke for several minutes. Julia continued, "And I remember, when the Apostle was telling of the death of Jesus. I remember how he raised his voice, for he always spoke in the kindliest whisper. But I remember him saying in a loud voice, almost a shout, *tetelestai!* The shout of triumph, that Jesus' work was finished, and that triumphal note was so loud, so sure, so final, so strong, that I still hear it ringing in my ears today, as vividly as if the Apostle had just pronounced it. And then I think of the solemnity with which he said the word *peace* when recounting the sayings of our Lord. Nor can I forget the tears that flowed as he recounted the words of the great prayer of Jesus, 'That they all may be one, as thou, Father, art in me and I in thee, that they may all be perfectly one, that the world may know, and see, and believe the love with which thou hast loved me.'

Justin knew the prayer of Jesus before his crucifixion by heart, and knew that her version of it was slightly different from any known version. He knew that hers was the living oracle, and neither he nor the two giants of the Church whom he had accompanied on the visit would dare to correct the words the way she phrased them. He rather basked in the glow of a living touch with the words of Jesus and his aged apostle, and thanked the Lord for the word as it had been written.

For several hours Julia spoke and Hegesippus wrote. The aura of the room was something Justin would remember as long as he lived. The woman who had known the disciple whom Jesus loved, the collector of all the traditions from the times of the apostles, the strong defender of the faith from the great city of Sardis, all in one room. This was the very last of the living tradition, and Justin knew himself to be part of a holy moment. The slightly different wording, which had caused him some disquiet, seemed not to matter so much now. What he had witnessed on that day was something no one in the church would

175

ever witness again. What must surely have been the very last oral tradition had been handed on.

CHAPTER 38

That bothersome insomnia which sometimes plagued Justin had returned, and he lay half-awake in a dark room, forgetting for a moment where he was. Then his mind was flooded with the impressions of the past day, and he began to turn over in his mind the different reactions which sleep had brought up from his subconscious. It all now seemed clear, and formidable: how after breakfast Melito had announced that they would be traveling together in company with Hegesippus and the Bishop of Ephesus, and after spending the night at Tralles, would move on to Hierapolis. There the Bishop, Claudius Apollonarius, was convening a meeting of the bishops in Asia to determine a response to the New Prophecy, which had overtaken Phrygia and was making itself felt in Asia and in the church throughout the Empire. Melito's silence bespoke the compromising position in which he found himself, for he too was a prophet, and in his great Pascal Homily had spoken directly to his people as the voice of God. Hegesippus, filled with questions about the New Prophecy, and its founder, Montanus, had called forth from the Ephesian Bishop new information in tones of unmistakable censure:

"They speak directly from the Holy Spirit, they disrupt services with their ecstasies, they forbid marriage, their fasting is taken to extremes, they condemn the use of wine, even at the Lord's table, and they exhort their people to seek out martyrdom!"

"But do they teach anything heretical about Jesus Christ?" asked Justin.

"Here they seem to be sound, to a point, " replied the Bishop, slightly annoyed that he had been checked in his condemnation. "And how do you receive this teaching in Rome?" he asked, knowing full well how awkward the question would be for Justin.

"Eleutherus has weighed the matter very carefully, for some time, and I know he seeks peace in the church," was his reply.

For a while the party was silent as their carriage moved along the valley of the Meander, past Magnesia, with the mountains rising on one side, and the fertile valleys, smelling of fresh-mown grass stretching out on the other. To Justin, now awakened, it all felt so strange. Marcus lay sick in Ephesus. He was traveling with distinguished leaders to an important meeting, where he might have to speak for Rome. He so wished his friend had been able to come!

Justin turned to thoughts of the advance of the Gospel. He mused how this must have been the route by which some traveler, perhaps Tychicus, had carried the gospel to Collossae, and Laeodicea and Hierapolis, over a century and a quarter ago, having heard it fresh from the Apostle Paul in Ephesus. Now he and his companions were to find themselves in the city where Papias had taught the truth for so many years, within the memory of many who still lived and worshipped there. But these musings could not quell the sense of a great responsibility, which was being thrust upon him, a responsibility that only became clear in the lonely hours of the morning. Before over twenty Asian bishops, he would be asked to speak for the Church of Rome, indeed for the whole Western Church, about the New Prophecy.

His concentrated thought was interrupted by the sound of a large pot breaking in the kitchen, not far from the room where he lodged. Justin arose and dressed, singing psalms over to himself, "In thee, O Lord, have I put my trust. Let me never be put to confusion. But deliver me in thy righteousness..." Then he made his way to the kitchen, where a woman of about sixty was cleaning up the last shards of the broken pot. Justin could see the first light of morning through the kitchen window.

"Oh!" the woman started when she saw him. "I'm sorry to have disturbed your sleep. I get clumsier all the time. This is the second pot I have broken this week!"

"I was already awake," replied Justin.

"You must be the visitor from Rome. They told me about you," she said as she threw out the bits of pottery, with a broad smile and a laugh. "My name is Fortunata, and, as they say here in Tralles, welcome to the 'first of the Greeks' but I like to say we are 'first in hospitality.' And what is your name?"

"Justin," was the reply. But before he could say more she went on, "Justin, is it? From Rome? We get them from every church in the empire, being located here on this main route, but we haven't had anyone from Rome recently. You are traveling with some great men, so you must be going to the council at Hierapolis. We have had several bishops through in the past week, all headed in that direction. They are all concerned about the new prophecy coming out of Pepuza. That's all they talked about when they were here. I'm not a busybody, mind you, but I couldn't help overhearing them while I was serving meals."

"Yes, indeed," said Justin, determined that if he simply sat and listened he might learn things he could not get elsewhere. "Listen and learn," he remembered his father tell him when he was a boy.

"Yes, it is such a pity, you know. That young Maxamilla. She has been here a number of times. Her husband is from here, and when she left him with the two children, they moved back here to be with his parents. We see the children in the market all the time with their grandmother. The boy is very promising and bright, but the girl is not right. She hardly ever speaks, and will not look at you. I think she must miss her mother awfully. She must be ashamed of what little she understands. But Maxamilla found herself 'speaking by the Holy Spirit,' as they say, and off she went with that Montanus. She used to visit here often, when she passed this way on mission, but now we hardly ever see her. And the last time, I tell you, she was worse than ever, if you know what I mean."

Justin simply nodded assent, so as not to stop the flow of information.

"Oh, all that fasting and ecstasy, and who knows what else. I mean, I don't mean to judge, her or anyone, but it's gotten people in these parts in an uproar, and I guess whole towns in Phrygia

179

have gone over to the New Prophecy, and they even call Pepuza 'the New Jerusalem.' Now isn't that something!"

"Do you think she has gone mad?" asked Justin.

"Not mad, exactly, but deluded, and the power of being a prophetess has gone to her head." Fortunata's tone bespoke a real caring, even an affection for Maxamilla, but also an exasperation. And Justin knew from those in Rome who had been influenced by the New Prophecy that they were among the most lovable and appealing people in the church. He thought of several of his friends, who were still friends, who had begun to prophesy in this way. And he was absolutely sure that his bishop was right to weigh the matter carefully, and not to be too harsh with them. But this only made the task that lay before Justin all the more delicate and demanding.

"And what do you make of the New Prophecy of Phrygia?" Fortunata asked Justin with a broad smile.

"Our bishop, Eleutherus, is committed to peace, freedom, and welcome in the Church," was his reply. But he knew that although the bishops assembled in Hierapolis would be eager to know the judgment of the Roman bishop, this was less important to her. It was on him that her gaze was fixed. At that moment he felt as though the gaze of all Asia was fixed upon him.

"Offer them peace and call them to be faithful to the Lord and his apostles" was his reply.

"I hope it works," said Fortunata. She returned to washing the unbroken pots, muttering audibly, "Pepuza, the New Jerusalem, indeed!"

CHAPTER 39

The next few days were a whirlwind. By the time the party from Ephesus had arrived in Hierapolis, the council of Asian bishops had already begun. The Bishop of Ephesus counted twenty-five others, and he was the twenty-sixth. As they entered the room, the convener, Claudius Apollinarius, called attention to them:

"We are honored to have our brother from Ephesus, and with him Melito of Sardis and Hegesippus, our great collector of apostolic history." Then noticing another man with them he added, "And please introduce your companion."

In a deep and reverent voice Melito said, "The Lord in his goodness has sent to us Justin, a scribe and reader of the Church in Rome, who brings letters and greetings from our brother in Christ, Eleutherus."

"I bring you greetings from our Bishop and our church, and I am honored to be with you all." Justin was awestruck at the occasion. The faces that looked upon him with welcome and applause showed all the marks of suffering for Christ, and the glory that comes through it.

Without hesitation Apollinarius continued, "We are here, as you know, to come to a common mind and policy concerning the New Prophecy, which is sweeping through Phrygia and beyond. Many of our people are being carried away, and some of us believe that this is a very dangerous heresy indeed. Montanus and his followers, especially Priscilla and Maxamilla, his prophetesses, speak words they claim to be directly from the Holy Spirit. They limit marriage, forbid wine, call for great fasts, and believe that the end of the world is near. They have proclaimed Pepuza, their chief city to be the New Jerusalem. We in Asia must stand together against this false teaching. What encouragement do we have from our brethren in Christ at Rome?"

The dreaded moment had arrived. All eyes were on Justin. He spoke in a slow and measured tone. "I trust that all I say will fairly represent our church, our bishop, Eleutherus, and indeed, many of the churches in the West in close communion with us. As you know, Irenaeus, my own teacher, now Bishop of Lyons, with whom I visited not three months ago, has thought much about the New Prophecy. And he is one of your own, as was Justin Martyr before him, after whom my father named me. They were from your very cities, and have understood the kind of challenges you face. Our own Bishop, Eleutherus, has thought and prayed much about the Prophecy and Montanus, and while not fully embracing it, and certainly not its excesses, he is reluctant to condemn. For they worship Christ as we do, both God and man. They hold to the scriptures of the Old covenant, and the scriptures of the Lord, as we do. Our bishop does not push prophecy, but neither does he prevent it. We do not condemn what God has not condemned, and we do not bless what God has not blessed."

Apollinarius interrupted, "But they change and embellish the scriptures of the Lord, as also Marcion and the other heretics have done."

"They do?" asked an incredulous Justin in a more confident tone.

"Yes," said the presiding bishop. "They add extra lines about the Holy Spirit in the Acts of the Apostles, in order to push their insistence that prophecy is still in their mouths. Why, here in the Acts, in Peter's Pentecost speech, they change the words of the Joel quotation to say that it is their own sons and daughters who will prophesy. They add that no one could withstand Stephen because of the Holy Spirit that was in him. They add of the Apostolic injunction to the gentiles at the end of the Jerusalem council 'being borne along by the Spirit.' Moreover, when they tell of Judas and Silas, the prophets, they add that these were filled with the Holy Spirit. All this and more they add to the sacred writings."

182

"They may indeed have these readings, and use them," said Justin, "but they did not create them. For these expressions in the Acts we have in our copies in the Roman Church. Thus they were read in the days of my father, who copied them from a papyrus codex of Acts, dating back, we believe, to the time of St. Luke himself!"

The company was silent, and this line was pursued no further. One of the bishops stood up to speak, and asked Justin, "May I ask, does your church approve of women preaching and prophesying? Do you have women acting as readers and scribes?"

While Justin could answer the question truthfully in the negative, he felt a special sting in the last word. He felt a surge of emotion, deep within, an overwhelming desire to spring to the aid of a loved-one whose honor had been offended. Suddenly, all the feeling for Juliana, which he had so far kept in check, clamored for expression. He paused and pursed his lips, saying quietly to himself, "The fruit of the Spirit is self-control." Then he spoke slowly and quietly, "Not at this moment, but we have had them, and we welcome them if they are of the truth, as did all the churches of St. Paul, when they welcomed Priscilla and Aquila, and the four daughters of Philip who prophesied."

"We are in the habit of saying Aquila and Priscilla, as we read the names in our copies of the Acts of the Apostles," replied the bishop. Despite his wise reply, Justin was caught off guard. For he had seen this order of the names, but it was not to be found in the official copies of the Acts which he had received from his father. "Yes," he replied, "I have seen this order, but it is not what we have received in the Acts, and so we speak of Priscilla first."

Justin's answer was received with respect, but the whole exchange had brought vividly before his mind both his growing love for Juliana, and his dilemma about different readings in the manuscripts of the gospels and epistles. Was the gap widening between the churches? Would they stand together on the great matters of Christian faith and practice, based upon a common scripture, which differed only on minor points, or was the scripture they had received substantially different in the different

183

churches? The assembly recessed, and Justin found himself cordially welcomed by all. Apollinarius of Heirapolis was a formidable speaker, and a fierce defender of the truth, but in private conversation he was the kindest of men. He greeted Justin warmly, and spoke with love and admiration of Eleutherus and Irenaeus and many others in the Roman Church. For all the debate, Justin sensed an overriding unity.

The conference would last several days. Before a decision was finally reached, which would not have been all to the liking of Justin and Melito, these two took their leave of the council, and of Hegesippus, who was to return to Ephesus, and they made their way through Philadelphia toward Sardis. In that city Justin would bid farewell to Melito and move on to Pergamum, and after delivering letters from his bishop would rejoin his friend in Ephesus. For a while they journeyed in silence.

As they sped on their way together toward Philadelphia, the city where the Lord had promised an open door of opportunity, Justin sensed the privilege of being in the presence of a holy man. He also knew that he and Melito were of the same mind on the new prophecy from Phrygia. This came home all the more to him, as they were praying together in their lodgings, as guests of a member of the Philadelphian Church. Melito began praying to God, and then broke into prophecy himself:

> Who will contend against me? Let him stand before me.
> It is I who delivered the condemned. It is I who gave life to the dead.
> It is I who raised up the buried. Who will argue with me?
> It is I, says Christ, who destroyed death.
> It is I who triumphed over the enemy,
> And trod down Hades, and bound the strong man.
> And have snatched mankind up to the heights of heaven,
> It is I, says Christ.
> So then, come here all you families of men,
> Weighed down with your sins.

And receive pardon for your misdeeds, for I am your pardon.
I am the Passover which brings salvation.
I am the Lamb slain for you.
I am your lustral bath. I am your life. I am your resurrection.
I am your light, I am your salvation, I am your king.
It is I who bring you up to the heights of heaven.
It is I who will give you the resurrection there.
I will show you the eternal Father.
I will raise you up with my own right hand.

Prayer in the Spirit was followed by sleep, which was interrupted by a sound of commotion. At first the two travelers thought that they were experiencing an earth tremor, for these were plentiful in and around Philadelphia. But as they awoke and opened the window, what they saw was a large woman, preaching and prophesying and baptizing in the river nearby with a large crowd of people gathered for the all-night vigil. She shouted, she sang, she cast out demons, and she made the crowd to laugh and cheer and sigh and weep, with her many stories of the ministry and marvels of Thecla, the legendary Phrygian woman who followed St. Paul in his journeys.

"Yours is the true prophecy," said an exasperated Justin to a tired Melito. "It weaves together what God has revealed in his word, not what man, or woman, has contrived through her imagination."

CHAPTER 40

The name Pergamum had always held a magical spell for Justin. Here was one of the great centers of culture and learning. Here had been founded the greatest library in the world, except for the one in Alexandria alone. Here had been developed and marketed the Parchment, that durable hide on which the best of manuscripts were copied, the best of texts preserved. Papyrus was more practical for Christian use, and more accessible. But some day the gospels and Paul might find their way onto this more durable substance, especially if more cultured people were won to the faith. Pergamum was one of the cities, like Sardis, Philadelphia, and Ephesus, to which the Lord had sent the letters in John's Revelation. Justin had often wondered about the picture of Pergamum, as the Lord saw it: the place where Satan dwells, the place of the Nicolatians, the place where Balaam still tempted Christians to idolatry and immorality. Here, if anywhere, Justin felt the need for faithfulness to the words of Him who has the sharp, two-edged sword. And as he approached the city, he meditated on the Lord's promise of the hidden manna, the white stone, the new name.

As Justin stood outside the city, he saw the spectacle of a prosperous Hellenistic center. The public buildings were laid out in terraces on the hillside. They culminated in the palace and fortifications of the Acropolis. There stood her famous library, built and beloved by her philosopher-kings. Justin stopped on the road to stare. This was one of the most beautiful cities. He longed to see its library, yet he had little time to spare. He must return to Ephesus in haste, and depart for Antioch with his friend, now, he prayed, fully recovered. He calculated that he could spare one day extra, and return in time, completing his voyage before the sea lanes closed for the winter. He hoped to gain access to the library. This would be possible if he could make contact again with his newfound friend, Albinus, who had come to Pergamum on business. Although the library was connected to the temple of Athena, Justin felt that in the company of such a host he would be respected and safe within its walls. With the Lord's watching eye he would be safe, even in this city where the imperial cult had begun, and where, as the Lord had warned, "Satan dwells."

"How wonderful to see you again!" exclaimed Albinus. As Justin had hoped, his friend, the merchant of fine leather, and his wife, Sabina, were there at Pergamum. As Albinus showed Justin his splendid lodgings, he went on to boast about the city. He recalled the lines of Virgil's *Aeneid*, which had made the link with Pergamum and Troy, which lay in ruins just a few miles away: "You remember, my friend, how Old Troy, that old Pergamum, was destroyed by the treachery of the giant horse sent by the Greeks, and how our Aeneas was given the solemn charge:

> Troy falls from her lofty height
> All claims are paid to king and country;
> If Pergamum's towers could be saved by strength of hand,
> By mine, too had they been saved.
> Troy commits to thee her holy things and household gods;
> Take them to share thy fortunes:
> Seek for them the city- the mighty city which,
> When thou hast wandered over the deep,
> Thou shalt at last establish!

Then, looking intently at Justin, Albinus added in solemn tone, "Latium is the newborn Troy, Pergamum newborn is Rome!"

Justin tilted his head, and with a blend of confidence and respect replied, "But here we have no abiding city, we seek one to come!"

188

The leatherseller had come to respect his Christian friend deeply, and almost to relish the dialogue in which a word from scripture would return to match and spar and mingle with a word from Virgil. Nor had the poet of the empire lost anything of its spell for the man who had learned his works by heart. But a new love grew up along side the other, and Albinus now knew he was incomplete without this other voice.

"I cannot deny the wisdom of your words, and I long to know your poets as I know my own. Where may I procure a copy of their writings, of Moses and the law, of the Gospels and the letters?"

"Most of our copies belong to congregations," said Justin, "but when we are both back in Rome, I shall see that you have one, so that you and Sabina may come to know the Lord Jesus Christ of whom it speaks, and recite his wisdom, alongside the wisdom you already know."

"Thank you kindly," said Albinus. "And now, would you care to see the great library here?" Justin agreed, and they were quickly up the steps and in the main reading room. Albinus found a man of about sixty, who was re-arranging some old rolls on their shelves.

"This is Telephus," he whispered to Justin, "Now librarian here, but once the teacher of the Emperor Lucius Verus, and the author of five books on Attic Syntax."

"O Telephus!" called Albinus, "this is Justin, from Rome, a Christian scholar, and a great friend. Have you any books of the Jews or of the sect of Christians we may look at?"

Justin was rather fearful of public exposure, but somehow felt that he was safe as Albinus' guest.

"Oh!" said Telephus, who still seemed half lost in his pile of scrolls. "Oh, Oh, yes... Christians, yes. We have a few, but just now Galen is consulting them. There are five, and he can't be looking at them all at once. Come with me."

Galen. That most highly respected philosopher-physician of the empire, and attending physician to the Emperor Marcus Aurelius: the very name inspired his contemporaries with awe, and Justin himself felt this as he stood before the great man.

"Galen, I am sorry to trouble you, but I believe that you will be interested to meet Justin. He is a Christian scholar..."

"A scribe," said Justin with a respectful bow.

"A Christian scribe from Rome, who might be useful in your research on the Christian philosophy. And I believe you have already met Albinus."

"Yes, " said Galen, "I have been reading these books, especially those of Moses, which both Jews and Christians believe, and I have wondered about the teaching that your God created the world out of nothing. Did not Plato teach in the *Timaeus* that the creator, or fashioner or Demiurge of existing matter is a wise and providential craftsman, who takes matter, as a potter takes clay, and fashions it into an object of form and beauty? The creator is the maker and the modeler, who brings order out of disorder."

Justin replied, albeit with some trepidation, "We believe that The Creator is before all things, and uncreated, who by his word brought into being all that exists. Moses begins his account of creation thus: 'In the beginning God created the heavens and the earth.' What God created he then afterwards formed and shaped and ordered. 'Nothing can come out of what does not exist', said Aristotle. Nothing can ever be created by divine power out of nothing, said Lucretius, and so I must say, with respect, that your view is abhorrent to anyone of learning and culture." Galen spoke in a firm but friendly tone.

"With man it is impossible," replied Justin, "but not with God. It may seem foolish to you. But the foolishness of God is wiser than men, and the weakness of God is stronger than men."

Galen seemed impressed with Justin's reply, but unmoved in his conviction, and turned to the codices that lay before them. How these books had got into this library, and what their text, at least in St. Mark might tell Justin were questions that played on the scribe's mind. But a yet more pressing question was how to make a better, more convincing answer to the men of learning like the giant who stood before him, interested but unconvinced. Perhaps Theophilus of Antioch would have some answers to this question, as well as to the question about Tatian.

190

The time in the library went quickly, and Justin found himself speeding back to Ephesus, via Smyrna, another of the seven churches of Revelation. In Ephesus he found Marcus fully recovered, overjoyed to see him, and waiting with some news.

"Justin, I am so sorry you did not come a few hours earlier. Juliana was here, but has just left for Alexandria."

Justin's heart raced, "And did she..."

"Yes, Justin, she was so sorry to miss you, and she greatly looks forward to your visit. But we must hurry. Our ship leaves for Antioch tomorrow morning early. You must tell me about your tour round the churches. The two scribes shared fellowship and sang psalms till late into the night.

CHAPTER 41

"The waves raised by the north wind are large and rapid as possible. But as soon as the wind subsides they disperse and become calm, and the surface is almost instantly without a swell; but it is not so when the south and southwest wind blow, which if not very high, made the swell continue longer, and when the wind ceases to be felt, the sea continues for a long time tempestuous." The words of Aulus Gellius, in the Attic Nights, which recently had charmed and informed the citizens of the Empire, gave the scribes, setting out in late October on the great sea, reason to pause and pray, as they boarded their friend's now respectable vessel, which would carry them past Rhodes and Cyprus to Antioch. It was a southwest wind that caused the ship to roll up and down, back and forth throughout the voyage of four days. But while the passage was somewhat boisterous, it was not stormy, and provided a safe and pleasant journey for the scribes. Indeed, the swell was such that it created a rocking motion for Justin, who, exhausted from his travels and experiences since midsummer, slept for almost the whole voyage. Philosophical talk with Aulynchus was left to Marcus, while Justin spent three days in the belly of a ship.

"Miletus!" exclaimed Aulynchus as he pointed to the coastline of Asia.

"Yes," said Marcus, "and the place is important for us as the scene of St. Paul's farewell to the Ephesian elders, which we read about in the Acts of the Apostles."

"Did you say the Acts of Paul and Thecla?" asked the captain.

"No," said Marcus, "I refer not to legends but to history."

"Well," said Aulynchus, "Miletus is a wonderful place. In its most prosperous days it was the home of the first Greek philosophers: Thales, Anaximander and Anaximines. Oh what a sacred place it must be that from here should come forth such giants in human thought and divine speculation."

"And tell me, " Marcus went on, "How did you come to be a philosopher... a Cynic? Was it largely the influence of Peregrinus?"

"Not entirely," replied Aulynchus in a friendly tone, but slightly annoyed that this shepherd from Rome should think of him as a mindless sheep, simply following some powerful leader. "I did my own reading and thought my way into the position, slowly but surely. I will say that at an important moment in the journey Peregrinus had a strong influence on my thinking. But you see, no two cynics think alike. We are an independent lot. I think that is what makes it so attractive to so many.."

"Then what do Cynics believe?" asked Marcus.

"You see my cloak, my wallet, my staff," replied Aulynchus in lively tone, "these are the signs of a man who has sought to free himself from the yearning for fame and riches and pleasure, and all the shackles that would bind a man. We Cynics unite in denouncing the values and conventions of this world. For we believe that people value the wrong things. A treasure is sold for a trifle, a trifle for a treasure. So we strive to live according to nature, and while our actions may seem shocking, and unconventional and "doggish," as they would say, yet in this way we may dramatize our teachings and awake the sleeper."

"What sort of actions would these be, these actions which shock?" asked Marcus.

"On one of the ships I captured in the pirate's trade the captain had a splendid cloak, and I so admired it that I took it for myself. I did not sell it and bring the handsome sum to mother, but took it for myself. It became a part of me, and a symbol of my status as a dog of the sea. But then I thought of the other dog I was meant to be, the "doggish" philosopher, the Cynic. I was to be free from desire and anger and fear and grief. I was to be free from city and state and the moral conventions of men. I was to be free of possessions and the love of money or things, and so, on a crowded wharf, on a market day, in the sight of friends and strangers, I burned my splendid cloak. I thereby declared, by my action, that I was free of this and all possessions. I suppose it was my response to Peregrinus having burnt himself on the Olympic flame. Who knows? Who cares? But I would burn this ship if it stood between me and true freedom."

"I trust you won't until we're safely to Antioch!" retorted Marcus with a laugh.

"Don't you worry, I need it for my new found life, to be a dog of the sea in a different way, a Cynic who wanders from port to port, stealing men's complacency and giving them their freedom. That's the sort of pirate I want to be!"

As the two men stood on the deck of the ship, with the setting sun behind them, Marcus felt real affection and admiration for the big black-bearded seaman. Their talk went on late into the night, interrupted only once by questions from a mate about equipment and rations. Otherwise the mates went about their work conscious that the captain was engaged in the real business of life, and therefore ought not to be disturbed.

Ships found it best to sail at night and rest in the day. Although Marcus longed for sleep, he could not bring the conversation to an end. Aulynchus' endless variations of the Cynic way began to be rather tiresome. Then, suddenly Marcus found himself wide awake. Perhaps, he thought, it was the sea-spray in his face, as a large wave tossed its edges onto the deck. But no, it was the question Aulynchus asked.

"Tell me, What do you make of this manuscript?" From his bag the Cynic brought out a small papyrus codex. But he stepped back to the place just at the foot of the main mast, so that he might protect the document from the spray and show it to Marcus by the light of the lantern.

"What is this, and where did you get it?" asked Marcus.

"The man with whom I stayed in Ephesus gave it to me. He had made several copies. He called it the Gospel of Thomas, and said it was the sayings of Jesus. He told me that it had been written up by an old friend of his some fifty years ago, collecting oral and written traditions of Jesus. He claimed that Jesus was the true Cynic. I have been reading it carefully, as you know I care about all philosophies, and especially those that claim to be Cynic."

"And what do you make of it?" asked Marcus as he stared at the crude codex, written in a severe documentary hand, with the strange sayings of Jesus.

"Well," said Aulynchus, "There are some striking sayings here. But where are the actions? Here is the saying 'Jesus said, I will destroy this house and no one will be able to build it again.' Now I distinctly remember hearing Peregrinus say that although he abandoned Christian faith, he admired the great action of Jesus cleansing the temple of the impure money-changers. Yes, that made him very like a Cynic. But even more dramatic is the action of his own self-sacrifice, the death on the cross, which you Christians say saved the world. But I do not find it in this Thomas. Here is a collection of sayings, some striking, some insipid, but where is the action in the story? Whoever this figure is, he is no Cynic!"

Aulynchus' diatribe gave Marcus a moment to glance at the codex. His eye caught the very end, "Simon Peter said, 'Let Mary leave us, because women are not worthy of life.' Jesus said. 'Look, I shall lead her so that I will make her male in order that she also may become a living spirit, resembling you males. For every woman who makes herself male will enter the kingdom of heaven."

Marcus thought for a moment. Then he read the words aloud. He looked Aulynchus in the face and replied. "Whoever this figure is, he is not Jesus!"

The sailor gave the document to the scribe, and they mused on for a while about its strange picture of Jesus as the ship pushed on in the night. "Can one be a Cynic and a Christian?" asked Aulynchus.

Marcus replied thoughtfully, "If anyone can tell us, my friend, you will be that man."

"And I have the time and the money, now that I am free." said the seaman, "And I will stay with you... that is, if I may...until I sort this out."

"Why not?" replied Marcus.

CHAPTER 42

It took the better part of the day for the scribes and their companion to walk from the port to the city. The autumn weather was fine, but they were fairly tired as they neared Antioch.

"Have you been here before?" Marcus asked Aulynchus.

"Oh, yes," he replied, "Several times in my former employ. And I remember one day like this one, not too many years ago, when I stayed several days. The air was as clear as today, or even clearer, do you see that mountain over there?"

He pointed to Mount Casius to the southwest of the city. "On that fine day I walked to the top of that mountain, and from it I could see all the way to Cyprus. It was a great day, for I sat and read Diogenes, looking up, from time to time, and contemplating the wisdom on these pages as I looked at the splendor of the vista laid out before me. I wish you had time to do this while you are here, and to sit there and read your books of the words and deeds of Jesus, your gospels, as you call them. But I know you are in a great hurry to get your business done. By the way, who is it that you are visiting in Antioch?'

"Theophilus, " replied Justin. "He is the bishop of the church here, and like your Pinytus of Cnossus a very learned man. We have letters for him and questions to ask him." Justin decided to remain vague regarding the exact nature of their business, for although Aulynchus was now their friend and helper, he was not really one with them in faith, and the matters they were concerned with were very delicate. They walked on in silence, hoping to find the bishop's house before sunset. Someone at the church in Ephesus had given them some fairly clear directions: a side lane off the main thoroughfare.

The main highway into Antioch was a grand Roman Road that ran right through the center of the city. It had all the feel of Roman imperium and Greek culture about it. It was a great colonnaded street that ran for two miles, and paved, for a good part of the way with granite, by the emperor Antoninus Pius. The strong, clear breeze blew up the valley of the Orontes, from off the Mediterranean sea, with a steady, almost relentless force that reminded Marcus of the Greek culture and the Roman legions, which had left such an indelible imprint on this street, as it seemed, on the whole world.

The change of atmosphere, which greeted the travelers as they turned down the side street, in search of the Bishop's house, was very marked. Here the houses were bunched altogether, and leaned toward one another across the narrow lane. Indeed the inhabitants of a house might borrow oil or grain or wine from their neighbor across the street without leaving the house. They would simply reach out the window and touch their neighbor's hand, or even his house. The air was close, and there was no breeze. In the early evening several men sat outside their houses on the front stoops, and loudly exchanged stories old and new. If the high street had been the world of cosmopolitan Rome, the side street was a Syrian village. Marcus, Justin and Aulynchus heard people speaking loudly in a language they could not understand. And while Rome had offered the scribes all kinds of opportunity to meet the world, with all its variety, and if piracy had given Aulynchus his own sort of worldwide exposure, all three knew themselves to be in a strange and foreign land, the land of the East.

The young man who met them at the door of the bishop's modest dwelling confirmed their first impression.

"Greetings in Christ Jesus, I am Serapion, deacon to Bishop Theophilus, and I bid you welcome." His accent, demeanor, courtesy and bearing were all of another world. He ushered the scribes to a small, well-furnished room and made full inquiry about their church, their business, their friend, and their length of stay. On learning that their visit would have to be short (for the sea-lanes were now all but closed) Serapion drew himself up,

198

heaved a sigh of disappointment, but then recovered himself. Cheerfully he announced,

"You have come just in time, for tonight is the Bishop's banquet, and I am sure he would want you all three to attend. Some have had to refuse his invitation, and he will be delighted to include two visitors from Rome and." He cast his gaze at the big black-bearded seaman,

"Crete"

"Ah, yes, Crete, and how is our brother Pinytus, that champion of the true faith of the Gospel?"

"Quite well indeed," replied Aulynchus, playing along admirably.

Marcus interrupted, "And tell me about your Bishop's banquet."

"Yes," said Serapion, "Twice a year our bishop, Theophilus holds a banquet here at his house. At his table are assembled a number of people, old and young. Some are long-time followers of Christ, others new to the church, still others exploring, or even skeptical. They are people with whom the bishop has been in conversation about some aspect of the Gospel. Tonight you shall dine with us, and in the course of the meal each man will speak in turn, telling his story. The rule laid down by the bishop is that all must speak and none may judge or criticize another. So it is that we listen and learn. And our Bishop Theophilus is the best listener."

In no time the sun had set and the scribes and Aulynchus were ushered into the banquet room. Before them was a table covered with bread, and over much of the bread all kinds of dishes of meat and fruit and grain, and a great jar of wine. The smell was wonderful and almost overpowering, and around the room were eight other people, seated on benches. At the head was the Bishop, a man of great age and dignity, who rose to greet the visitors.

"We are honored to have guests from Rome and Crete, and we welcome you to this banquet." Wine was poured, and a great blessing was offered, 'Blessed art Thou, O Lord, God of our fathers.' and then the Bishop spoke. "I am Theophilus, and I am a Christian. I was born in the East in the region between the

199

Rivers, the Tigris and the Euphrates, and grew up in a pagan house. I was slow to learn, but when I could read, I came upon a copy of the books of Moses, which were a schoolmaster who brought me to Christ. With him I have been these many years. To him I owe my life, and all that I am. For him I live today, and he has graciously entrusted me with upholding the Christian gospel in these parts. I have contended with teachers like Hermogenes and Marcion and have spent much time in recent years in the study of the early record of this world, laid down by Moses. I greatly enjoy the opportunity to discuss these things with inquiring minds, and I look forward to hearing the stories of those whom God in his wisdom has brought to this banquet." He turned to the young man on his right, and urged him to begin his story.

"I am Bardaisan, from Edessa." said a young man with a dark face, flashing eyes and a marvelously musical voice.

CHAPTER 43

I am the son of the River, the river Disan.
I am the friend of the king, the mighty Abgar.
I am strong with the bow, sharp with the arrow.
I am the child of the stars, the hosts of heaven.
I am the voice of the Savior, the living Christ
I am the priest of the Father, a royal priesthood.
I am the man in white raiment,
Made white in the blood of the Lamb.
The Lamb was slain and we are free.
The Ancient of Eternity was a boy.
The child of the virgin was the Highest.
So the Soul may escape from its prison,
Freed from the strife of the Powers,
And life may be lived in God.
So rejoice, O Sun, thou Father of life.
Rejoice. O Moon, thou Mother of all.
Together you renew the universe.
And I am caught up in the ecstasies!

The music of Bardaisan's voice arrested the attention of all.
Justin glanced at Marcus, and Marcus at Justin, but the rules of
the dinner forbade any comment, even with the eyebrows. More
wine was poured, accompanied by more dipping in the dishes,
and the next speaker began:
"I am Marcus, a shepherd from Rome, and I serve Jesus
Christ, the good shepherd of the sheep. But I did not always do
so. Not so long ago I went astray, like the one sheep that
wandered from the other ninety-nine. I went astray, I turned to
my own way. I rejected the Lord of life. But the Good Shepherd
in his mercy left the ninety-nine in the wilderness, and found me

and laid me on his shoulders, and brought me home. It cost him dearly to save my life. I was that sheep straying, but now I have been returned to the flock by the Shepherd of my soul, and to him belongs all the thanks and the glory and the praise."

The tender strength of Marcus' words brought great silence and thoughtfulness to the assembled band of men. They began to sip and dip again, at the Bishop's bidding, and he gave the nod to the next in order, his good friend Autolychus.

"My name is Autolychus, and I prize my friendship with Theophilus, the Bishop of this church. We often talk late into the night, and while I do not accept the doctrine he teaches, I am drawn by the kindly spirit with which he invites me to investigate divine things. For myself, I am a lover of the ancient wisdom of the Greeks, of Homer and Hesiod, of Aeschylus, Sophocles and Euripides, of the great histories of Herodotus and Thucydides. And I love the other philosophers, Plato and Aristotle, and especially Diogenes. They tell me timeless truths about the world and about the gods, about our life and about our fate. They are the stars by which I navigate the sea of life in my little ship."

All were listening intently, but Aulynchus was spellbound. The man with the similar sounding name had praised his philosophy and illustrated from the seafarer's life. Faith had spoken to faith.

Next was Justin, who told his story briefly but from the heart:

"My name is Justin, and like my friend Marcus, I am from Rome. I grew up in a household that honored Jesus Christ as savior. My father was the scribe for the Church of Rome, and he faithfully copied the gospels and other writings of the scriptures, both old and new, for use in our worship. Like my father before me I am a carpenter by trade, honored to work at the woodbench like my Lord Jesus. But my father perished in a fierce persecution some fourteen years ago. And now I carry on his work, and am in the service of my bishop, the godly Eleutherus of Rome."

With more wine and more dipping the storytelling went on. At the far end of the table sat the deacon, Serapion, whose deep

202

brown eyes, and jet-black hair complemented the majestic tone of his youthful voice.

"Serapion is my name. I am a deacon of this church, and my hope is that all my life I may be granted the privilege of spreading and defending the faith of Christ crucified and risen."

His words were few but powerful. Marcus could not help wondering whether here was a future Bishop of Antioch! The meal continued. After a brief silence, the next speaker began.

"I am Ben Jacob of Berytus, I am a Jewish Christian, of the remnant of the tribe of Judah. I study Torah, Nabiim, Kitubim and the scriptures of Jeshuah ha Meshiah. In my city, famous for its commerce and its wines, I live among that colony of Jews who worship Jesus. We talk much with those of our people who do not. We have much to learn from the Rabbis, and we want them to consider the Messiah, who is Jesus. Sometimes I fear the talk is bitter, but we seek to love even those who count us enemies, for so the savior commanded us. We sometimes fail. We have in our church library a precious treasure, a copy of the Hebrew Matthew. You who are scribes may someday want to visit us and see it. In it are hidden many secrets, which I must not tell tonight, but may yet tell, for as one of the Rabbis says, "When wine goes in, secrets come out."

The mention of the Hebrew Matthew made the hearts of Justin and Marcus leap and their minds race. They had always known Matthew in Greek. Was there more of a tale to be told, raising yet more questions about the text and its original form? The meal continued, all now feeling slightly mellow, nearly ready for Ben Jacob's secrets.

"I am Macrinius," the next speaker bellowed in raspy voice, a sharp contrast to the melodious stories already shared. "I follow Tatian and the ways of the Encritite. We believe in one narrative gospel, the Diatessaron, rather than four separate ones. And we believe that the Kingdom of God is for those who practice *encriteia*, or self-control. As you see, I have been content with the water, and respect the Bishop for serving it. I eat no meat, and eschew the company of women. Thus I will attain to life. Tatian could not come and has sent me in his stead, with warmest greetings to all, and especially to Bishop Theophilus."

This naturally unattractive man had nonetheless something of an admirable quality to him. None could doubt his sincerity. None could challenge his rigor. In any case challenge was not the tone of the evening.

The next to speak was Aulynchus, who told of his life as a reluctant pirate, and of his recent deliverance. He quoted somewhat from Diogenes, offering a deep nod of gratitude and fellowship to Autolychus.

The last to speak faced an audience full of food and merry with wine (with the exception of Macrinius). "Maxamin is my name, and I am the keeper of the sacred books, and the secretary to Bishop Theophilus, in whose service, and at whose command I would gladly spend my life, as unto the Lord."

So the stories had been told, and the feast went on as each speaker had the right to ask a question of one other, but only in the most respectful tone. "So tell me more of your love for Diogenes," the pirate asked the pagan. "Are there other churches with a Hebrew Matthew?" Marcus asked Ben Jacob. "On what grounds may we forbid marriage?" Justin asked Macrinius. All the questions engaged critically with another view, but all did so respectfully. At the end Theophilus asked Autolychus,

"I ask you, with all respect, my friend, what did it profit Homer to compose the Trojan wars, or Orpheus to posit three hundred and sixty-five gods, only in the end to reject them for one God? What good did it do Epicurus to maintain that there is no providence? What did Plato's system of culture profit him?"

Suddenly there was tension in the air, till all realized that this kind of banter, albeit in a kindly spirit, was the stuff of the strong friendship between philosopher and bishop. The questions went on late into the night, and the discussion turned to the subject of creation. What Theoliphus said gave great encouragement to Justin, who was still smarting from his encounter with Galen in the library at Pergamum. The Bishop of Antioch spoke with commanding authority:

"The prophets have taught that God made all things out of nothing, for nothing was coeval with God: But he being his own

204

place, and wanting nothing, and existing before the ages, willed to make man by whom he might be known...The sacred scripture teaches at the outset that matter from which God made and fashioned the world, was in some manner created, being produced by God."

Autolychus retorted, as in a great athletic contest, and Theophilus came back with loving and firm support from Moses and the prophets, "far more ancient than your philosophers..." Late into the night they argued, with an occasional aside, in rhyme from Bardaisan, and others joined in the debate. In the early hours of the morning the banquet broke up in cordial laughter. As the scribes returned to their lodging for the night, Marcus said to Justin, " Now there is a model for you. Oh that we might defend the truth from error in a way that is more like the games than the wars!"

CHAPTER 44

Marcus and Justin had only the morning to spare in Antioch. They would go together to see the Bishop and deliver the letters, and then Marcus would stay on to talk about the codex meant for Tatian while Justin looked at the scriptures and other writings in the church's possession. By midday they were to meet Aulynchus and walk into the setting sun, reaching the harbor well after dark. But the more they pondered the plan, the more it became clear that there would not be time for it all. So another scheme was devised. They found that Ben Jacob was on his way to Jerusalem, and would be delighted to have Marcus' company. The overland journey would be swift in the horse-drawn vehicle which the Jew from Berytus had hired. And Marcus might learn some of the secrets of which Ben Jacob had spoken at the banquet.

Justin and Aulynchus would make their way by sea to Caeserea. Here the scribe would deliver letters and confer, and they would meet in five days' time. This might also give Justin some time with the scribes of Caeserea. Aulynchus knew of a cynic philosopher in that city, so he greeted the plan with enthusiasm. Then it would be once more to sea, this time for Alexandria. There was no time to lose. It was now November 4th. In a week's time the sea-lanes would be closed, and they would have to stay the winter in Alexandria. This was a long time to be away from Rome, but not a wholly unpleasant prospect, from Justin's point of view.

"Good morning, and may God be with you, my Roman friends," said the ever-encouraging Theophilus. "I was so pleased that you both could be with us last evening, and that your friend came too. He and my old friend Autolychus had much in common. Perhaps they will see more of each other at some point. Perhaps the evening was an instrument of Almighty God to bring each, in his own way, to trust in him. In any case, tell me news of Rome and of our dear Eleutherus."

Justin presented the letters, and spoke of the concern over the teachings of Marcion and Valentinus. He brought special greetings from Irenaeus of Lyons, noting how much that bishop had been helped by the treatise Theophilus had written against the teaching of Marcion. The Old Testament was indeed the divine revelation, and it was evident to those in the Roman circle that Theophilus' heavy dependence on the old scriptures was judicious.

"For myself I was very much helped when you cited the prophecy of Isaiah to affirm that God is the creator of all." Justin's voice was full of feeling: "Thus saith the Lord God who established the heavens, and founded the earth and all that is therein, and giveth breath unto the people upon it, and spirit to them that walk therein. This is the Lord your God" (Isa.42: 5) Then recovering his composure a bit, he continued, "When I was in Pergamum, I went to the library. There I happened to meet the famous Galen, that philosopher and physician to the Emperor. He was exploring the few Christian and Jewish books in that great library, for he wished to discover our doctrine of creation. He said that our view that God created the world out of nothing is abhorrent to anyone of learning and culture. I tried to answer, with gentleness and reverence, but felt I was no match for this man of letters. But now you have restored my confidence as well as my conviction."

"Everything that came to be in him was life," said Theophilus, "For even the heretics affirm this truth from St. John." They conferred on other matters, and Justin departed, with a holy kiss, and many words of thanks to God and to the Bishop. Marcus then settled in to discuss the matter of Tatian and the mystery codex, which had come into their hands in Corinth.

"This is a most interesting development," said the Bishop. "I tell you, I know Tatian. That is, I met him a few years ago, but I can hardly say I really know him. You see, he is an elusive fellow with a great following. I met him two years ago when I went east to the area of the Tigris and Euphrates, where the race of man began, for I had some family business to conduct in those parts. There I met up with some Encritites, and Tatian was with them. I found him a most intelligent and appealing man, but as I say, elusive. One never quite knows whether one has actually met Tatian, I mean the real man. In any case, his followers were fiercely loyal to him, and as you know, many of the churches in the East are now favoring his Diatessaron over the Four Gospels. On my return, I stopped in Edessa, and there I found a new and growing Christian community, under the blessing and protection of the king, who is Bardaisan's friend Abgar. The king, as you know, is a Christian, and has done much to abolish disgusting pagan practices like ritual mutilation. But the church in Edessa has also gone in favor of the Diatessaron. I do not say that this makes them heretics. But we know that God has inspired four gospels, and these we read. I have tried to stay in touch with Tatian. I have asked him to visit me when he is here. Yet despite the fact that he has come to Antioch several times, he has avoided me. He always communicates through an emissary. Macrinius, who was at our banquet, was one of many. I tell you, Marcus, Tatian is a mystery."

"The scribe was silent for a moment, and then asked, "So what do you think I should do with this document, entrusted to me with a man's dying breath?"

"If you leave it with me," said the Bishop, "I will see to it that it is delivered to Tatian. Perhaps I will be able to do that myself. Perhaps it will be the means whereby I make contact with him again, we shall see."

"You will note," said Marcus somewhat shyly, "There are a number of readings which the Encritite would choose if he did not invent. You see here, about Anna, living with her husband as a virgin, and you see here, how Adam, not God speaks the words about a man leaving his Father and Mother in marriage, and in the wedding at Cana of Galilee, "When men have freely drunk" is removed. And look here where vinegar, not wine is offered to our Lord on the cross."

"All the marks of an Encritite, it seems," mused the Bishop. "But let me take it and I shall see what I can do. I do wish this

Tatian and his followers were more reachable and more reasonable. Do pray for me in this effort."

The Bishop and the scribe sang some psalms together, and Marcus stood up to leave. Then something moved him to ask, "Oh, Bishop, can you tell me something about Bardaisan?"

"Ah, yes, Bardaisan." The bishop stood thoughtfully, as if weighing how much to say. "Bardaisan...is...well, perhaps the most brilliant and imaginative man I have ever met. He is a recent convert to the faith of Christ, and has come here on business. The way he sings his devotion to Christ is captivating. He was born among pagan astrologers. We share a fascination for genealogy and the study of local customs and tales. With the right guidance and teaching, he could prove in time to be one of the great leaders of the Syrian church." The Bishop then stopped, and after a pause continued excitedly,

"By the way, did you say you were going to Caeserea?"

"Justin and Aulynchus are, this very afternoon." replied a curious Marcus.

"Well I know that Bardaisan had to go there next on business. Is there a chance he could travel in their company?"

"I don't see why not!" exclaimed Marcus. "Since I am going with Ben Jacob to Jerusalem, and then meeting my friends in Caeserea, Bardaisan can have my place in the ship's company."

So the plan was fixed. Marcus headed for Jerusalem, Justin for Caeserea Maratima, both with the promise of a most interesting week.

CHAPTER 45

The bustling, man-made harbor of Caeserea was filled with sea craft of all sizes, making preparations for their last voyage before winter. Some appeared to have already begun the preparations for a long winter stay. The Myoparo which had been the nautical home for the scribes, their captain and the two crew, and most recently Bardaisan, was waiting to set sail. All that was needed was the arrival of Marcus from Jerusalem. Aulynchus was growing more impatient with every hour. His stoical self-control was beginning to fray at the edges and he paced up and down the deck, eyeing with suspicion the stiffening breeze and the ominous clouds in the distance. The mood of the two crewmen was sullen, and echoed the threat of the distant clouds.

At last Marcus arrived at the designated place. Justin was shocked to see that he was unshaven and weary, and hastily welcomed him on board. The anchor was weighed the sails were hoisted, and the Myoparo headed into the rolling sea for Alexandria. In two days the sea-lanes would be officially closed. It felt to the scribes as though they had already closed.

"My brother, you look very worn," said Justin to his friend once they had cleared the jetties.

"Yes," said Marcus, "I am exhausted. There was very little time in Jerusalem, and we were nearly killed by brigands at one point, but God had mercy on us. Thankfully, the highway was crowded and the driver was well-armed, but Ben Jacob and I reached the Holy City, what is left of it, rather shaken but thankful."

"I do regret not having seen Jerusalem myself, and traveled where our Lord had traveled, " said Justin.

"Yes," replied Marcus, standing back to avoid the sea-spray, "But two wars with the Romans have left the land of the Jews pretty devastated. Still it was a thrill to see where the Lord Jesus Christ had lived, and Ben Jacob proved a wonderful guide. 'Look, over there is the Mount of Olives' he would say. 'Beyond that point is the Sea of Galilee, where Yeshuah walked on the water, and called the fishermen to be his followers.' Wonderful indeed!"

"And did Ben Jacob reveal any of his secrets?" asked Justin.

"Oh, yes...secrets." mused a half-drenched Marcus. "Well, I learned no secrets, but we talked a good deal about them. I asked him about the secrets, and he replied, with the raising of an eyebrow, 'The secrets of the kingdom of God were told by our Lord to the crowd in parables; without a parable he told them nothing. This was to fulfill what had been spoken through Asaph the prophet: I will open my mouth to speak in parables; I will proclaim what has been hidden from the foundation of the world.'

The sea was kicking up even more, but Marcus went on with his tale, speaking more loudly to be heard in the heavy breeze: "Well, Justin, I knew I had heard the Hebrew Matthew, even if I had not seen it. And I said to him, "I have never heard that scripture attributed to the prophet Asaph, and our copies of St. Matthew end with the word "from the foundation." and do not add the word *kosmou*, or world, as it appears at the beginning of the seventy-eighth psalm." A lively discussion followed, and it was apparent that Ben Jacob knew the whole of his Hebrew Matthew by heart. I think he said his form of it was a scroll and not a codex, in conformity to the old Jewish ways. He was most insistent that his way of reading it was the way that St. Matthew had dictated it, and he was most kind to translate it into Greek for me. I knew I was in the presence of a man of great learning..."

But just as Marcus finished the word of praise, the scribes were interrupted by the sound of shouting at the other end of the deck.

212

"I have had enough, and I will not go to Alexandria!" exclaimed one of the two mates, and the other chimed in, with irrepeatable epithets, "I demand that we go to Crete."

"We are going to Alexandria!" shouted Aulynchus into the full-blown gale.

"We have had enough." retorted the first mate, "We are sick of waiting around while you talk to philosophers and these friends of yours spend time with their cults. We want to go home for the winter, and will not spend several more months of this in Alexandria."

Aulynchus now set aside all reserve and spoke his full mind in his full voice. "You will do as you are told now! We have no time to lose. Keep the course for Alexandria." And turning to the other mate he barked through his teeth. "Aloft, and trim the topsail, so that we are not blown over in the gale!"

At this the second mate drew a sword, and waved it at Aulynchus. "It is our ship now, and we are once again pirates! You and those despicable cultists will do as we say or we will feed you to the fish."

"Mutiny!" cried the first mate. "I am now the captain, and you will do as I say."

The ship was now reeling heavily back and forth, and being blown at the sea. The sails would have to be trimmed at once.

"You go aloft and trim the sail!" shouted the first mate to Marcus. Fear fell upon him and caused a kind of paralysis in the already exhausted scribe.

"Do you hear me, go aloft and trim the sails. I've killed many men in my days as pirate, and I'll kill another if I have to." But Marcus could not move. The armed seaman ran toward the scribe with his sword raised. Justin gasped. But the ship reeled to the port and the mate lost his balance. Before Justin or Marcus knew what was happening, Aulynchus lifted the stumbling mate by the collar and leg and threw him out over the side. Losing no time the gigantic black-bearded captain rushed to the other mate, lifted him as well and tossed him into the sea. Then turning to the dumbstruck scribes he exclaimed. "We'll see who will be food for the fish!"

Without delay Aulynchus climbed the rigging and cut the ropes of the topsail, relieving the heavy pressure of the wind on the ship. But his knife slipped and slit his arm, and when he saw the blood, he fell to the deck. Justin and Marcus staggered to revive him, splashing him with the water that was now washing the deck. Gradually Aulynchus came to and thanked the scribes for their help, and for bandaging his wound. He staggered to the tiller and gradually took control of the Myoparo. Three days of heavy wind and sea passed slowly, as Justin and Marcus learned new nautical skills by doing. But they were glad at last to see the lighthouse at the entrance to the harbor at Alexandria. Someone had told them that it was one of the wonders of the world. It certainly was a wonderful sight to the scribes. Justin heard a tired Marcus singing the Psalm that had sustained them in the last crisis at sea:

> The Lord is my Light and my Salvation
> Whom then shall I fear?
> The Lord is the strength of my life
> Of whom, then, shall I be afraid?

And then Justin remembered the haunting phrase he had several times heard from the lips of Bardaisan: "The fear of the Lord, which delivers us from all fear."

CHAPTER 46

Aulynchus had been patient with the scribes, and their bungling efforts at seamanship. As the ship came to anchor in the crowded harbor of Alexandria, the captain spoke to the scribes, appreciative of their indispensable help, but eager to take the time himself getting things back in order on his damaged boat. Justin and Marcus were left to prepare some light meal below, and then returned to wait on deck for Aulynchus to be ready for them to row in together to the cultural capital of the Hellenistic world.

The city of Alexandria was built around its harbor, and as Justin and Marcus stood on deck on a sunny November afternoon, they began to take in the sight that was before them, the city where they would be lodging for the winter months.

"That building there, catching the sun must be the palace area," noted Marcus, pointing to a stately building, "and in the center there is the monumental theater."

"Yes," replied Justin, "and with it the Caesareum, in all its glory, and all its shame...for it is the focus of the imperial cult, the worship of the emperor!"

"That must be the library," said Marcus, "And it is supposed to be the greatest library in the world, a treasure-house of learning."

"So they say," replied Justin, in a tone that indicated that his mind was elsewhere.

"You never told me about your time with Bardaisan and your stay in Caesarea." Marcus said to his weary, storm-worn, distracted friend.

"Ah, yes, Bardaisan. Well, he is a shining light indeed, burning more brightly for the Lord than ever that lighthouse could shine. I do not always understand what he is saying, but then, he does come from a wholly different world. He pleaded with me, if ever we were in Edessa to allow him and his King Abgar to show us hospitality. I hope some day to be able to do that. We shall have quite a tale to tell if ever we do."

"It would be quite something to meet a Christian king!" exclaimed Marcus. "Now tell me about Caesarea."

"Well, Marcus," said Justin with a sigh, "It was a remarkable time. The church there seems to be disciplined in its life, and truly engaged in refuting the Gnostics. They have a fine scriptorium. Probably not as advanced as the one we will find here, but more elaborate than our own. I visited their scribes and saw their work progressing. One of them, a man named Titus, showed me round, and took special care to share both his time and his convictions with me. He was just beginning a copy of St. Mark for a new church in the region, and was eager to compare his text with my own codex. Marcus, I tell you, what I saw amazed me. In the story about Jesus healing many people and casting out demons, where Mark wrote that Jesus would not permit the demons to speak because they knew him, Titus added the words "to be Christ." I saw him write these words, and noted that they were not in the codex from which he was copying! I was dumbfounded. When I regained my composure, I pointed out to him that he had added the words, although they were not in the church's copy. 'Oh,' he said, trying to hide his embarrassment, 'but that is, of course, what is meant.' Then sensing that I was neither pleased nor convinced, he added '...yes...well...I have seen a copy of St. Mark that includes the phrase...in Jerusalem, no less (and he gave reverential accent to the name of the Holy City, as if that, too, justified the change). I showed him my own St. Mark, of the Roman church, but it seemed to carry no weight. He looked me in the eye, and said, with a sense of assured triumph, 'And is not this what St. Luke reads... they knew him to be Christ.' So, Marcus, there was no dissuading him. And there will be no dissuading any scribe who wishes to alter the text to make it say what they know, or feel it means, with or without the blessing or knowledge of his bishop.'

"Or *her* bishop" mused Marcus, but then he was sorry he had said it. The awkward silence that followed only increased his regret. "I am sorry, Justin, I should not have said it. James is right, no man can tame the tongue. Please, I beg you, my brother, forgive me."

"Oh, no, Marcus, it is quite all right. You have borne with me well, and I suspect there is much more to come. What they do here in Alexandria with the copying of texts, albeit in the interest of commending the Gospel of Christ to the cultured, will test to the limit our conviction to hand on faithfully, to the very jot and tittle, the gospels, the acts, the epistles, the revelation, as we have received them. Here we are in this harbor, having journeyed these last two months, our copies of St. Mark and St. John in our satchels. We have seen them safe through storm and customs, through drenching and pirates. They have been saved from brigands and greedy merchants, and we still hold them uncorrupted. Now here we begin another stage of the journey, and before us lies a far more serious challenge. Will we be able to resist the Alexandrian pressure for change, in order to commend the very gospel we and they proclaim?"

"Indeed," replied Marcus, "but in one particular you are in error."

"What is that?" asked Justin.

"I no longer possess my copy of St. John!"

Justin gasped.

"It was stolen just outside Jerusalem."

"How? By whom?" shot back Justin.

"I do not know, my brother, but you are not to worry. I had committed it all to memory before the theft. And they have not stolen my memory! I shall write it down when we reach our lodgings. Oh, by the way, who did you say was to be our host here in Alexandria?"

"A man about my age named Clement. You may have met him in Rome. He left for Alexandria about the time you came to work with me at the scriptorium. Clearly one of the most intelligent believers I have ever met. He is as brilliant as Irenaeus."

Justin stood in silent admiration of his friend, who had memorized far more than he did. Then he noticed that

217

Aulynchus had lowered the small boat and was signaling to his friends to climb in.

"Now for Alexandria and its many challenges" said Justin as he stepped awkwardly into the dinghy.

CHAPTER 47

"Is this the house of Clement?"

The tired storm-drenched scribes had found their way to the house where their bishop had arranged lodging for them, and the man who opened the door greeted them warmly, if a bit formally:

"It is, or rather, to be more precise, it is the house of Titus Flavius Clemens, teacher in the Alexandrian Catechetical School." and then he added, "But you won't find him here."

"Oh?" said a bewildered Justin, in no mood for one more puzzle or challenge, and still trying to regain the sense of terra firma.

"No, he is away today, with our teacher, attending the institution of the new Bishop."

"New Bishop?" asked Justin, "And what of Agrippinus?"

"Oh, he died two weeks ago, went to receive his crown of glory, and the twelve city pastors have elected Julian to succeed him." Then changing his tone, and looking the scribes up and down he asked, "And who are you?"

"Justin and Marcus, scribes of the Church of Rome, on errand for our Bishop Eleutherus. He told us we would find lodging here."

With this news the man's face fell, and his voice took on a more plaintive tone. "Yes, we have been expecting you, and we are glad you have arrived safely. We had news that you had been captured by pirates, and were delayed in other ways. In fact, I think the sea-lanes are now closed, so this is the last day you could have come, at least by sea. There is the overland route through the Sinai desert, but it is not recommended. In any case, come in, and may I fetch you some refreshment, some wine, or perhaps some nectar."

"Wine would be welcome, indeed" said both scribes in unison. Justin remembered a previous conversation with an Alexandrian about nectar.

Justin and Marcus sat in the small outer room of the house of Clement while their host went to fetch refreshment. As they sat in silence, the news of the Bishop's death began to play on Justin's mind. He was Juliana's uncle. What did this mean for her future status or connection in the church? What sort of changes might this mean for the policies or procedures of the church, especially as regards copying the sacred text? Would there now be a greater discipline imposed, resulting in a greater accuracy in copying the text, or would an even fuller freedom prevail in an attempt to commend the Christian gospel to the cultured Alexandrian Greeks? He had been briefed by his bishop concerning the kind of church he would find in Alexandria. Was this now to be a very different church? His questionings were interrupted by the return of their host, with wine, speaking as he entered the room.

"My name is Nicolaus, and I hail from Sparta in Greece. I have been here in Alexandria for three months, and have enjoyed the hospitality of Clement. But he warned me that when the scribes arrived from Rome, I should have to find lodging elsewhere. So you see, I am both joyed and saddened to see you both."

"And what is your business here in Alexandria?" asked Marcus.

"I am here studying at the catechetical school, under the great teacher Pantaenus. I am a new Christian, having come to faith about two years ago. I came here to study the Christian way and to learn all I could about the Lord Jesus Christ, and how to commend him to my friends."

"And who are these friends?" asked Justin.

"The Spartans, and a very tough group of men they are." Nicolaus began to speak with more vigor. "Before I became a Christian I was a runner. I ran in the Olympic games. I trained hard. I pummeled my body and my mind. I set out to win, and I won. In our whole set of friends, winning was everything, and everything was to be sacrificed for the fading crown. But then

220

an old man in Sparta told me of an unfading crown of glory. He told me of the Lord Jesus Christ, who would award the crown on the last day to all who had remained faithful to the last. I determined to know him, to follow him, to run for him. My friends ridiculed me, but I pressed on. I joined the church in Sparta and began running errands for my bishop all over Greece. Whenever a letter had to be delivered or a codex taken to another church, I was the courier. I grew to love the words of the prophet Habbakuk, "Write the vision, make it plain, so he who runs may read it. If it is slow, wait for it. It will surely come it will not delay. Behold, he whose soul is not upright in him shall fail, but the just shall live by my faith."

"My faith?" thought Justin, who had never heard the text in this form. But he decided not to pursue the question. Instead he queried, "Did you meet Bishop Dionysius of Corinth in the course of your errands?"

"Indeed I did, and I think you will agree with me that he is the greatest bishop of them all!"

"With the possible exception of our own," replied Justin.

"It was actually through Dionysius that I found my way to Alexandria. You see, I had delivered a letter to him from my bishop, and he kindly asked me to run back the reply. It took him several days to think out exactly what he wished to say. During that time he and his deacon Christophilos offered me warm hospitality."

"A splendid man is that Christophilos," chimed in Marcus.

"Yes, and I found myself growing in grace just by association with those two. When the letter was complete, the Bishop read it over aloud to me before sending me off. In it he offered to my church the most tremendous challenge. He called us to remain firm in the true gospel, the orthodox faith, and also to keep peace and unity. At that moment I felt a great challenge. Here was a prize harder to obtain than an Olympic laurel. For some churches keep the faith intact but sacrifice unity to do it. Other churches strive for peace, but in so doing are tempted to compromise the gospel, the orthodox faith, as Dionysius calls it. But we are called to champion both, to hold the truth in love. Now there's a prize worth running for. When I asked that grand

221

old bishop where I might best go to train for this great challenge, he urged me to come here and study under Pantaenus. So here I am, reading and running. In fact, tomorrow I am off with letters to churches further up the Nile valley. But I'll be back in a week, and so may enjoy further conversation with you."

"Tell us more about this catechetical school here in Alexandria." Justin asked.

"As I mentioned, Pantaenus is the chief teacher, and he is assisted by your host Clement. Pantaenus is a man of great faith and learning, and Clement, though only about your age, seems to know everything about everything, both sacred and secular. Then there is Anaximines. He is a wise old eccentric teacher who first frightens, but then entertains and charms, and last of all challenges his students."

"Yes," said Justin, "We heard about him from one of your scribes who visited us in Rome."

"That must have been Juliana," said Nicolaus. "She has visited all over the world with her father, and has had many visitors...mostly men...if you know what I mean."

"Yes," replied Marcus, and quickly added a question so as to spare his friend further discussion in this direction, "And how many scribes have you here?"

"There are five, three men and two women," replied Nicholas, "and they are all students in the catechetical school. You will meet them all, I am sure, though Juliana is away right now. She has a place in Oxyrynchus up the Nile. I will see her in a few days, and would be glad to convey your greetings."

"Thank you kindly," said Justin in as plain and matter-of-fact a tone as he could muster.

"She is due to return very soon, and to resume her studies and copying here. But just now she is mourning the death of her uncle, the Bishop, and has gone to the country for peace and quiet. I am sure she will be glad to hear you have come. She spoke with warmth and feeling about the very interesting conversations you had together in Rome about differences in methods and readings between our churches."

Then, as if some forgotten task had suddenly been remembered Nicolaus, stood up and announced, "Now, if you will excuse me, I have something I must attend to. The room where you are staying is just in there, and I will remove my belongings when I return. May the Lord bless you both richly during your stay in Alexandria."

Nicolaus departed and the scribes found themselves sitting together in silent exhaustion in the house of Clement in the capital city of Hellenistic culture.

CHAPTER 48

The small classroom of the Alexandrian catechetical school was a buzz of conversation. It was full of students who eagerly awaited the arrival of the teacher, Pantaenus. Justin's mind raced with thoughts of the preceding day. He thought of the engaging encounter with Nicolaus the Spartan runner, and his news of the new bishop, Julian. He had news of Juliana, now in the country but soon to return. There was the excitement generated by the catechetical school and the quest for learning in this center of learning. And then there was more.

After Justin and Marcus had found some dinner in Clement's stores, they noticed on his table a codex of the four gospels. When they opened it, several things intrigued them. The first thing was the order. Whereas they knew the order in Rome: Matthew, John, Luke, Mark, this codex had Matthew, Mark, Luke and John. Then there was the format. The codex was copied in a very neat hand, more like a work of literature than an everyday document. The first letter of each page was slightly enlarged, as well as the first letter of each new section. Justin carefully turned to the end of St. Mark's gospel. He was not surprised to find that it ended with the words "for they were afraid," just as Juliana's copy had done. Turning to the beginning of that gospel, he noticed that this codex too lacked the words "The Son of God." However, in the margin, written in another hand, in characteristic abbreviations, were the words, "The Son of God." Had Clement himself made the addition? Were they added because they were found in some other copy known to the Alexandrians? Was this codex even copied in Alexandria, or had it been brought from some other church in the empire? Marcus asked to have a look, and he turned to the Gospel of St. John. Here his scripture memory paid off, for he noticed a number of small differences between this copy of St. John and the one in his head. Most of the changes seemed to be in the interest of slightly better style. Just as he was looking for the long passage about the woman taken in adultery, Nicolaus entered, and the scribes had to close the book. By the time their friend had departed it was late in the evening. Clement's codex would have to wait for another day.

In the morning the scribes found that their host, Clement had returned and was preparing breakfast. He was a tall man, about Justin's age and already balding. He was full of questions for the scribes, about where they had been and whom they had seen. He was especially eager for news of Dionysius, Melito and Theophilus, all of whom he had met in his travels. He wanted news of Irenaeus, and of the Roman brethren. It struck the scribes that the reason Clement knew so much was that he was always asking questions. It was also clear that Clement really cared about people. His penetrating gaze and pertinent questions made it clear that he had a sincere interest and sympathy. He expressed his pleasure that he was to be the scribes' host for the next few months and he expected that the association would be mutually beneficial.

"Didn't we meet in Rome?" asked Clement, as he looked quizzically at Justin. "I think it was in the last year of Soter, when I passed through Rome on my quest for the best teaching and the best teacher."

"Yes," said Justin, "I do remember, it was in the company of Hegesippus, who was then staying with us. I remember you asking him all kinds of questions about the early days of the church in Jerusalem."

"And I am still full of questions," said Clement, "though I have found the best of teachers. This Pantaenus is remarkable. I call him the Sicilian bee, for he has gone from place to place, collecting the pure prophetic and apostolic nectars, and has finally settled here. From him more than from all have I learned the godly art of interpreting the scriptures in their true deep and spiritual sense. You will see when you hear him lecture. He is matchless as a teacher of divine wisdom. Well, after all my travels I tracked him down here, in his Egyptian lair, where he

226

had been called after laboring as a missionary in India. And I tell you, they have needed him here. For he was first trained in the philosophy of the Stoics, and the practical, down-to-earth character of this philosophy, which he has not lost in coming to Christ, is much needed in this land of the Gnostics."

More questions followed after this praise of Pantaenus, concerning Eleutherus and Irenaeus and the Gnostic movements in Rome, the Basilideans and the Valentinians, and Marcion. Justin and Marcus were relieved when breakfast was done, with its friendly but penetrating examination, and they were out the door with Clement on their way to the catechetical school. Then Clement turned to Justin and said,

"Oh, I almost forgot to give these to you. Here are two letters, one from your bishop and one from Irenaeus."

Justin took the letters and opened the first immediately. It brought warm greetings from Rome for him and Marcus, and an expression of concern on the news that they had been subjected to storms and pirates. There was praise for the report of his faithful witness at the Phrygian synod, and an assurance of daily prayers as they made their way among the Egyptians.

In the lecture hall Justin sat in the corner, where he had a private opportunity to open the larger letter from Irenaeus. It also expressed both concern and prayers for safe travel. And then it continued:

"I am sending you the enclosed section of the book I am writing in an attempt to expose and overthrow the Gnostic sects which abound here, and everywhere, and threaten to distort and destroy the true faith of the church, which we have held from the beginning. Please let me know, when it is convenient, perhaps on your return to Rome, whether I really understand the Valentinians and other Gnostic groups. Do the Egyptians have a different form of this myth? What are the methods they use to win new converts? Who are their main teachers?

"My dear brother in the Lord, I do pray for you and Marcus, and commend you to the Lord, and to the word of his grace. Greet the brethren in Christ Jesus who are in Egypt. The grace of our Lord Jesus Christ be with you always."

227

Justin began to take a look at the codex, but found that the commotion of the crowded room kept him from concentrating. He slipped outside for a moment in the garden behind the lecture room. Refreshed by the quiet and the breeze, he opened the book near the beginning and began to read about a certain Marcus the Magician:

"He devotes himself to women, especially to those who are rich and beautiful. He teaches them incantations to be said over cups of wine, induces them to prophesy, and whips them into a frensy. They then reward him not only with money, but with their own selves. One of our deacons took Marcus into his house. The man's wife, who was very beautiful, was taken in by Marcus, and fell prey to his charms. She was only won back to the faith of the church, and restored to her husband with much difficulty."

Justin remembered that Irenaeus had mentioned Marcus the Magician to him when he was in Lyons during the summer. But this was the description of a heretical leader local to Gaul. He searched to find some more general description of the Gnostic myth. His eye fell on another paragraph that ran thus:

"A multitude of Gnostics have sprung up, and have been manifested like mushrooms growing out of the ground. I now proceed to describe the principal opinions held by them. Some of them, then, assume the existence of a certain unaging Aeon, which they call Barbeloth, existing within a virgin spirit. In that place, they say, there exists a certain unnamable parent, and it willed to show itself forth to this Barbeloth. And this thought emanated and stood at rest in its presence, and made a request of it, to have prior acquaintance. And when prior acquaintance, too, had emanated, and these, moreover, had made a request, incorruptibility emanated, and then eternal life. Barbeloth rejoiced in these, and gazing at the magnitude, it (Barbeloth) took pleasure in the act of conception and became pregnant, and in respect of this (magnitude) begot light similar to it (the parent). They declare that this was the beginning both of the light and of the begetting of the entirety; and that the parent, beholding this light, anointed it with its own kindness until it became perfect."

228

Justin's mind was spinning, but he determined to read on...

"Moreover, they maintain that this was the Christ, who, again, according to them, made a request that it be given a coactor, namely intellect. And intellect emanated. Moreover, besides these, the Parent sent forth the word (or verbal discourse). Then the following joined as consorts: Thinking and the Word (verbal discourse); incorruptibility and the anointed (Christ); eternal life and will; intellect and prior acquaintance. These, then, glorified the great light and Barbeloth."

Justin suddenly sensed that he was not alone in the garden. He looked up, his mind dizzied by Irenaeus' description of the Gnostic myth. At the other end of the garden sat a familiar figure. It was Rhoda, the maidservant to Juliana.

CHAPTER 49

Pantaenus had begun to lecture. The room was crowded with people. As Justin stood at the doorway he could see that Marcus had saved a seat for him, but he would have to squeeze his way along the back of the room to reach it. Another latecomer stood beside him, also looking for somewhere to sit. The students were listening with rapt attention to the teacher, as he explained "spiritual exegesis" of the scriptures. "You must look for the true meaning of the scripture, which everywhere points to Christ." The man standing next to Justin whispered to him, "Remarkable!"

"Yes," replied Justin quickly, wishing not to miss a word.

The stranger went on, still looking to spy a seat, "He speaks as one who has authority, and not as the scribes."

Justin muttered to himself angrily, "Is this what they mean by 'spiritual exegesis?' " And then, chiding himself for his negative reaction to someone who could not have known he was a scribe, he squeezed his way across the back of the room to his seat, scraping a prickly cactus plant someone had placed in the corner. He noticed that his arm was bleeding, and gave thanks that this was not the lecture to which he had invited Aulynchus. The speaker continued, arresting the attention of all, including Justin:

"In the nineteenth Psalm we find the most beautiful statement, which surely points to Jesus Christ. 'In them hath he set a tabernacle for the sun; which cometh forth as a bridegroom out of his chamber, and rejoiceth as a giant to run his course.' Now we know it to be true of prophecy that for the most part it utters its sayings indefinitely as to time, using the present sometimes for the future, sometimes for the past. So here we may see clearly, by the principle of spiritual exegesis, that Christ

231

and his church are foreshown in the history of creation and paradise."

Like everyone else in the room Justin was spellbound by the wonderful unfolding of the Psalms which seemed everywhere to speak of Christ. But he could not concentrate. He had just seen Rhoda. That meant Juliana was somewhere nearby, perhaps in this very room! Looking out over the crowd of about twenty men and ten women, he moved his eyes slowly from one to the next. There she was, with her unmistakable flowing hair and striking bright brown eyes. He had just time to catch his composure when Pantaenus stopped and announced a short break. As the crowd moved out toward the courtyard and garden, Justin and Juliana caught each other's eye.

"Juliana!"

"Justin, greetings in the name of Christ, and welcome to Alexandria. Clement told me you had arrived with Marcus. And what is this I hear about pirates?" Her tone was animated and caring.

For a fleeting moment Justin felt the temptation to embellish the story, to make it sound more heroic. But then he realized that she already would have had some report from Marcus in Ephesus. And in any case, a pirate turned philosopher was much more interesting than the normal, predictable tales of bloodshed, imprisonment, floggings, slave markets, galley ships, and futile attempts at escape.

"Pirates, indeed, but God had mercy on us, and our pirate has turned Cynic philosopher, has brought us here, and will probably be in our company before long. Have you ever met a real pirate, Juliana?"

"Oh, yes, I did once. A cutthroat band attempted to overtake my father's vessel. But we were so well armed that they were all repelled, except a few who were taken prisoner. I guess the word gets around in that underworld, and pirates always steer clear of ships owned by Demetrius of Alexandria."

"I am sorry to hear about your uncle, Bishop Agripinus." continued Justin, sensing that any further adventure stories could be matched by one who could also match his textual readings.

The next few months in Alexandria would be as challenging to his mind as to his heart.

"He has gained the crown of life," said Juliana, "I will miss him, but I know that God has raised up a faithful man in Julian. And I know him to be a great supporter of this school, and of the scriptorium."

"So when do I get to visit your famous scriptorium?" asked Justin.

"You may come this afternoon, if you like. It would be an honor to show you what we do, and to introduce you to our band of scribes. And I think Anaximines will be there!"

"Anaximines!" exclaimed Justin, his enthusiasm mixed with curiosity, and not a little trepidation. The thought of finally meeting the eccentric scribe and scholar from Alexandria, of hearing his shouts and whispers, of observing his students as they dutifully upgraded the style of the gospels, in order to commend the faith to their cultured friends -- all this filled him with a sense of excitement, of awe, of resolve.

"Does he like to debate?" asked Justin.

"He will enjoy wrestling with the challenging issues we have discussed. I told him of our conversations in Rome, and he listened with great care and thoughtfulness. He was intrigued to know you were coming here to Alexandria." Juliana turned and caught Pantaenus out of the corner of her eye. "Pantaenus," she called.

"Why, Juliana, I am glad to see you back in Alexandria. I was saddened at your uncle's death, but rejoice that he is with Jesus. And how is your father? Are you here for awhile, or do you have to return to Oxyrynchus? And…"

Juliana had to interrupt Pantaenus, who was buzzing like a bee.

"Pantaenus, I want to introduce Justin and his friend Marcus, who are scribes of the Roman church, and here on an errand for Bishop Eleutherus."

"So you are Justin and Marcus. Welcome to Alexandria. You have the finest host in Clement. He will look after you well. And I am pleased to see that you have made the acquaintance of Juliana."

"We met when she visited Rome," said Justin. And then he added, "And I am fascinated by your 'spiritual exegesis' of the Psalms. You truly bring out the deep meaning of the text, and show how all inspired scripture points to Jesus Christ."

"You know, Justin," Pantaenus went on. "I did not always see it this way. I think it began to dawn on me when I was in India, on a mission to preach Christ. I found there some Christians who had the Gospel of Matthew in Hebrew characters, as they had received it from the Apostle Bartholomew, who preached the gospel there. Their preaching of the good news drew heavily on Genesis, Exodus and the Psalms, and they began to discover Christ everywhere in the scriptures of the Jews. So I determined to seek him there myself. I have found him in the sacred text. And you will find him too."

"Did you ever know Justin, the philosopher-martyr?" asked Justin. "My father knew him well, and named me after him."

"I did meet him once," said Pantaenus, "And I think his writings have helped me to understand the spiritual exegesis of the scriptures. How I love that splendid passage in his dialogue with the Jew Trypho where Justin recounts the many names for Jesus Christ found in the scripture. Jesus is called the Angel of the Great Counsel. He is called a man by Ezekiel, and one like a Son of Man by Daniel. David calls him Christ and God who is to be worshipped. Solomon calls him wisdom. Moses names him Joseph and Judah and a star. To Zechariah he is the East. And for Isaiah Christ has many names: Israel and a rod and a flower, Son of God and stone and a cornerstone. Indeed many call him a stone – all these great names from the prophets prefigure him who was to come. Indeed he has now been born, and suffered and ascended into heaven and is coming again.

"See how wonderfully Justin opens up before our eyes the treasures of the scripture, which point to Christ!"

The ringing of a bell recalled the students to their seats, but not before Juliana had again invited Justin and Marcus to visit the scriptorium.

"James will call for you at the house of Clement, and you shall have the opportunity to observe our scribes at work."

234

On their walk back to their lodgings Justin whispered to Marcus, "I think I am very much encouraged."

Marcus thought to himself, "I hope it is not in vain."

CHAPTER 50

The Scriptorium of the Alexandrian church was as different from its Roman counterpart as a factory is from a cottage industry. Justin was impressed with the scale and the style from the moment James escorted him and Marcus into the room. It was light and spacious, and there were chairs arranged around a central reading desk. The scribes were ready to begin work. They would take dictation from a reader sitting at the central table. Juliana rose to greet her friends, and to introduce them to her scribal comrades.

"This is Ariston, the newest member of our band, and here is Taesion. She has an extraordinarily beautiful hand, and is known for her accuracy. She often works as one of our correctors of finished manuscripts. Now this next chair is usually occupied by Leonidus, but he is away just now, for his wife has recently given birth to a little boy. Next is my place. And this one over here belongs to our esteemed senior colleague, Anaximines, who I believe is reading under the table. Anaximines!" called Juliana, pleased that her tale of this eccentric but lovable old scholar had been confirmed on the spot. "Anaximines!"

"Quiet!" came a roar from under the table. Out crawled an old man of medium height, with scruffy clothes. His hair was bushy, white and uncombed, and his eyebrows so covered his eyes that there was no telling their color. He was poring over a copy of Homer's *Odyssey*, while waiting for the copy work to begin.

"Quiet," Anaximines whispered, and then in a louder voice he declaimed "Hear again the story of the wooden horse." He had been bent over with his head in the book, but he stood erect and read:

"But come now and change your theme, and sing of the building of the horse of wood, which Epeius made with Athena's help, the horse which once Odysseus led up into the citadel as a thing of guile, when he had filled it with the men who sacked Ileum, no less. If you indeed tell me this tale rightly, I will declare to all mankind that the god has with a ready heart granted you the gift of divine song."

Then, looking at Juliana, Anaximines queried, "And who are these visitors to our Scriptorium?"

"Justin and Marcus, scribes from the church in Rome." said Juliana proudly.

"Rome?" Anaximines replied, "The other see of St. Mark. Yes, Juliana has told me of your interesting conversations. I think we may learn much from each other."

"I trust so, and be mutually encouraged by one another's faith." Justin added.

Just then the door opened and in walked a man in his forties, dignified and well groomed.

"Good," said Anaximines, "With Castor here we may begin our copying. To your books, oh scribes."

Castor took his place at the central desk from which he was to read. Anaximines moved over behind his desk, to read and listen. Justin and Marcus took seats by the entrance and waited to see how the Alexandrians copied their texts. They were especially eager to see what part Anaximines would play.

"Today we continue copying the Gospel according to St. John," said Castor in a loud, clear voice. We ended yesterday with the witness of John the Baptist to Jesus, where he says, "And I saw and bear witness that this is the elect of God."

Marcus whispered to Justin, "The Son of God is what all our manuscripts read. Think what the adoptionist heretics could do with this one!"

The animated Castor went on in measured pace:

"The next day again John stood and two of his disciples, and seeing Jesus walking he said..."

"Wait!" rang the booming voice of Anaximines. "The word *again* in this place will not be pleasing to those who value good Greek. I am quite sure Phrynichus would condemn it. If you

238

intend these copies to be read by the cultured, you had best drop the *again*."

Castor began afresh: "The next day John stood..."

But Anaximines interrupted again: "Now here you may polish the style a bit by eliminating the article before the proper name. Read *Johannes* rather than *ho Johannes*. I think in these unofficial copies for the private use of your cultured friends, who love to read the great writers, the name without the article will commend our gospel. You see here in Homer it is always *Odysseus* and seldom *ho Odysseus*. Or Plato, in the apology always has *Socrates*, never *ho Socrates*. Even the sacred text, translated here in Alexandria, reads *Mouses*, not *ho Mouses*."

Juliania interrupted, "But Aneximines, does not Demosthenes, in the Philippics, sometimes read *Philippos*, sometimes *ho Philippos*?"

In the silent tension that followed, Justin felt great admiration for the woman who stood up to her teacher. Marcus whispered, "No mindless sheep, that one!"

"Yes," Aneximines mumbled, still chewing his reed-pen, "And what do you make of it?"

Juliana retorted, "Oh, some manuscripts have the article, while others do not. But which are right? That is the question!"

The copying went on. Justin listened with increasing discomfort, Marcus carefully noted down the differences from the copy of St. John he had committed to memory.

Castor continued: "The next day John stood...and two of his disciples...And he looked at Jesus as he walked...and said...'Behold the Lamb of God.'

The reader seemed relieved that Anaximines had let him finish the sentence. In the pause left for the copyists to catch up with the reader Marcus whispered to Justin, "The Lamb of God, who takes away the sins of the world."

"The two disciples of his heard him say this... and they followed Jesus," continued the voice of Castor. But Anaximines interrupted again, now muttering thoughtfully, having ceased his chewing.

239

"The phrase, 'the two disciples of his' is acceptable, though you could improve things by eliminating the possessive, but why not write the more pleasing 'his two disciples'? "

Castor started once more,"And Jesus turned and saw them following him and said to them, 'Whom do you seek?' And they said to him, 'Rabbi,' which being interpreted is 'master,' where are you staying?"

The reader had gotten through two whole sentences without being interrupted by the stylist of the Alexandrian church. But the reprieve was not to last. Anaximines was mumbling and chewing once again, and still very on guard for an infelicitous phrase. Castor went on:

"He said to them, 'Come and see.' Therefore they went..."

"Therefore?" rang the voice of Anaximines. "Cut down on the *therefores* and other such particles. It makes the style more terse and rich, like that of the great writers!"

The copyists dutifully changed the text in accordance with the better style, and the copying went on with about one correction for every sentence, coming now with a shout, now with a whisper from the beloved and eccentric scholar. Marcus could tell that Justin was in some turmoil. He knew his friend to be committed to the faithful preservation of the gospel text, regardless of all pressures to change it.

The session lasted for two hours, after which someone served refreshments. Nectar was offered, but there were other choices as well. The scribes talked about methods of copying. The Alexandrians had many questions for the Romans. But the Roman had questions also.

"You say that these copies are intended for private use." Justin said to Juliana.

"Oh, yes, each of us is making a copy of the spiritual gospel, the Gospel according to St. John, for a friend who has an eye for good Greek, like that of the classic writers. We would never make such alterations in the copies to be read in public worship, and in the official teaching and work of the church. We would be as scrupulous and accurate as you are in your copying, Justin."

240

"And who is your copy for?" asked Justin, now much reassured by her comment.

"For a dear friend named Pollux," she replied. "He is part of a group of friends in the town of Oxyrynchus, up the Nile valley, where we have a second home. This group meets together to read and discuss books. Some of us are lovers of literature, others professional scholars, like Pollux. If you are in Egypt for a while, you must come and visit us in Oxyrynchus. I am returning there next week, and will be there for several weeks. You would be most welcome. We could provide hospitality for both you and Marcus. James would gladly bring a carriage and fetch you both. Or one of my friends could bring you in his boat. I tell you, Oxyrynchus is a wonderful place!"

Juliana's words were a healing balm to Justin's ailing heart. He had been troubled by the wholesale alteration of the text of scripture, but was somewhat relieved to know that these copies were private and not official. Nonetheless, what was to prevent some later generation from treating them as authoritative? Indeed, there was no preventing this from happening anywhere in the church. Yet for the moment this cloud was brightened by the kind invitation that promised to draw him more fully into Juliana's world.

"By the way, Justin," Juliana added in a whisper, "If you happen to be talking to Anaximines, do not mention that my copy of St. John is to be a gift for Pollux. You see, this distinguished scholar crosses verbal swords with Phrynichus, who was Anaximines' teacher. And as you can see, our dear friend here in the school and scriptorium has the profoundest respect for his teacher."

"So I noticed," replied Justin. "And as for your invitation, Marcus and I would be most pleased to come. I think we would be ready to leave by this time next week. Thank you indeed for your kind welcome."

Justin and Marcus took their leave of the Alexandrian scriptorium at sunset, and walked in silence to the house of Clement. Before reaching the house Marcus spoke.

"That can't have been an easy afternoon for you, my brother."

241

"It left me both discouraged and encouraged." said Justin. "It was heartening for me that Juliana has invited us to Oxyrynchus. I am encouraged to think that she desires to deepen our association. But Marcus, as for the copying, I believe that today we have come face to face with the Trojan horse!"

CHAPTER 51

Justin was sick. He had taken ill and gone to bed after returning to the house of Clement. All night he lay with aching head and uneasy stomach. About dawn he finally fell asleep, and he slept the whole of the following day. With Clement away on business, Marcus was left alone for the morning with the first opportunity to explore the codex which he had seen upon their arrival. At noon he would have to walk alone to the house of the new bishop Julian, to deliver letters, and confer about matters of concern to the Roman and Egyptian churches. This pre-arranged appointment was one Justin would not be able to keep.

The codex belonging to Clement was revealing. Marcus found that it lacked the long passage about the woman taken in adultery, the section they had discussed with Pinytus of Cnossus. Further, he noticed that the sentence before the place where the story should have been, offered the interesting variation "the prophet" rather than "a prophet."

Marcus then turned to the beginning of the Gospel according to St. John, and began to compare the codex to the text of the stolen manuscript he had committed to memory. While turning the pages he thought about what might have become of his codex. Would it someday appear in the shop of a bookseller like Heliodorus of Corinth? Perhaps it was sitting on the "cults" shelf of some bookseller in Jerusalem or Caeserea or Antioch, or even in Rome. In any case, the complete text was in his head. So with a blend of confidence and curiosity he began to read, "In the beginning was the word, and the word was with God and the word was God. He was in the beginning with God..."

The beginning of St. John's Gospel was the heart of the Christian faith for Marcus. These words were his constant companion. He said them over to himself as he began each day.

He meditated on them often. They had been for him a source of strength in time of weakness, a path to faith in times of doubt, and a place to stand in the midst of controversy. Almost every line had some association for Marcus. He never read the words, "The light shines in the darkness and the darkness has never put it out" without thinking of his shepherd-father, on some Italic hill, tending the sheep with his sons, and looking up to the starlit sky, and reciting the words with reverence and awe. How he missed his father, there in far-away Egypt, and determined to write him another letter, if possible that very day.

Marcus came upon the words, "All things came into being through him, and without him nothing came into being." Here the codex owned by Clement read *nothing(ouden)*. He knew this reading and had used it often. But he had memorized another form of words: *not one thing(oude hen)*. This word made him think of Heracleon, and of their long and lively debates. Heracleon had come to Rome when Marcus was a boy, and had for some years been a disciple and intimate friend of Valentinus, the leader of the Gnostics there. Marcus met him one day in a market, and they discovered a mutual love for the Gospel of John. Despite his heretical views, Marcus found Heracleon to be the most appealing and impressive of men. He was the sort of person who drew people to himself. Marcus would meet with him to discuss interpretations of the Gospel of John. Their weekly meetings would go on for about six months, and then, suddenly, Heracleon would disappear. It was rumored that he had gone to Sicily, or to Puteoli, in which places he had disciples. Then he would appear again, and the discussions would resume, almost as if there had been no break. Around the time that Soter died and Eleutherus became Bishop, Heracleon left Rome, and had never returned. After about a year Marcus made discrete inquiry concerning him. The most reliable report was that he had moved to Egypt, where he was attracting a large following as one of the chief successors to Valentinus. So Marcus wondered to himself, as he came upon this line in Clement's copy of John, whether he might run into his friend again while in Egypt, and what that meeting might be like, now that Heracleon was a most distinguished leader of the Gnostics.

Marcus remembered well the debate that had arisen over these words during their long conversations in Rome:

"And without him nothing came into being," said Heracleon, and then he added in his authoritative and appealing voice, "...Nothing, that is, of the things in the cosmos and in the creation."

"So, then," Marcus asked, "Nothing exists that he did not create?"

" 'All things' means the world and all that is in it," continued Heracleon. "But this excludes the things that are different from the world and the things that are therein. Neither the aeon nor what was in the aeon came into being through the Logos, for that came into being before the Logos."

"Not one thing!" Marcus insisted, drawing on the reading he knew would make his point most strongly.

"Nothing!" retorted Heracleon with a twinkle in his eye, but a note of steely determination in his voice, making all the more questionable Heracleon's insistence of "Nothing...except, of course, some things!"

So they had agreed to disagree, and still remain friends. Both men knew both readings, and neither accused the other or his group of inventing a reading for convenience in debate. But now, thought Marcus with a sigh, such generosity was all but gone in discussions between Orthodox and Gnostic. The battle was inevitably and irreversibly underway.

Marcus found that the hours had flown by, and it was time to leave for the conference with Bishop Julian. After checking on Justin, whom he found asleep, he walked quickly to the bishop's house, through a crowded market, and down a narrow lane where he was nearly crushed by a camel.

"I am sorry your friend is not well," said the bishop. "We have had letters from your Bishop Eleutherus, and I understand you have other things to give us."

Julian was a pleasant man, and a champion of Orthodox faith. He and Marcus talked about the Roman church, the growing reputation of Irenaeus, and the spread of the Gnostic heresies.

"They are especially vigorous and aggressive here in Egypt," said the concerned bishop. "I think the teaching of Pantaenus and Clement in our catechetical school will do much to strengthen our people in the face of this challenge."

"Tell me more of the Gnostics here, and of their leaders," asked the curious Marcus.

"There are as many versions of the Gnostic myth as there are Gnostic teachers, " said Julian with a note of exasperation. "What troubles me," he went on, "is the new Gnostic enclaves, the new communities that have sprung up in places round the country. Perhaps the most worrisome is a community in the Fayum which they call "the House of Valentine," named after the great leader of the Gnostics. It doesn't help that Imperial policy has threaten whole area with ruin, and the House of Valentine, for all its strangeness, has become a source of life and strength to the surrounding neighborhood. But what troubles me, Marcus, is that two of our most promising young leaders have gone there, partly out of curiosity, and have not returned."

"And who are the leaders of this House of Valentine?" asked Marcus.

"Well, I am not sure," replied the new bishop, "and I do not know an easy way of finding out, without risking yet another of our people. They are in touch with one of the chief Gnostic teachers in Alexandria, a certain Heracleon."

Marcus' heart raced, but he said nothing. He wished no suspicion whatever toward Rome from the Alexandrians. In any case he doubted that his private friendship would be of much value now that Heracleon was one of the chief Valentinian Gnostics in Egypt.

After Psalms and prayers Marcus returned to the house of Clement, to find Justin still asleep and a letter from Juliana, addressed to his friend, and docketed from Oxyrynchus. She had already left, and was urging them to visit:

"My friend Diodorus has a boat made of willow wood; it is a handsome and sturdy craft, and he will send his servant down the Nile to bring you in it to Oxyrhynchus. My father Demetrius and I will be honored to have you and Marcus as our guests. Greetings in Christ Jesus our Lord."

246

Marcus knew that the letter would encourage his friend, who was beginning to recover.

CHAPTER 52

On the third day Justin's health began to improve, but he still slept most of the day. In the meantime, Marcus continued to read and ponder the codex in the house of Clement. Their host had returned, but his story about the book had not really offered any new light on some of its puzzling readings.

"Oh, yes," the affable Alexandrian said, "That codex was given to me by someone in Ephesus a few years ago. I do not remember his name (how memory fails us, even in youth!). He had found it among the possessions of his deceased brother, who had attached a note to it, claiming that he had borrowed it from someone in Alexandria, and that it should be returned to that city."

"Do we know where it was copied and by whom?" asked Marcus.

"I am afraid I cannot tell you," said Clement, "But it does read very much like some of our own codices of the gospels. I suspect it was copied here, sometime in the last fifty years. Perhaps it was copied in Philadelphia or Oxyrhynchus or one of the other larger towns on the Nile, where they have a scriptorium. I sometimes read it for my own meditation, as I believe it to be both accurate and elegant."

The mention of elegance reminded Marcus of the importance of the cultured and the beautiful in Alexandria. Then he remembered the plan he had privately devised for his day, so he bid Clement farewell, entrusting to him the care of his recovering friend, and slipped out the door into an overcast day and a busy street.

The plan was to try to find Heracleon, his old friend from Roman days. Now that the man had become one of the most respected Gnostic teachers in Egypt, Marcus felt a little awkward about his secret quest. He had never talked about his conversations with his friend from the marketplace, and had only mentioned once to Justin, in an offhand remark, that he had stumbled upon Heracleon in the market. Now going in secret to search him out, Marcus felt a bit guilty. Yet he mused to himself that the contact might even prove useful. If relations continued friendly between them, he might be able to track down some of the missing brethren who had gone to the "House of Valentine."

Of course, five years and newfound prestige may well have altered the Gnostic teacher, so that friendship was now impossible with a scribe of the Roman church. But Marcus' curiosity got the better of him, and he determined to make discrete enquiry in places where he was told the Gnostics congregated. Clement had supplied this information with detailed description and entertaining comment, but with no knowledge of his guest's intention. Marcus made his way to a small market square on the edge of the city, and asked at the booth of a leatherseller:

"Heracleon?" replied the sunbaked old merchant, "I do not follow this teaching, but his followers come here. That woman over there is one of them."

The man pointed to a woman behind a stall where beet roots were sold, and the scribe meandered unsuspiciously in her direction.

"So it's Heracleon you're looking for," replied the woman, looking Marcus up and down, as if to size him up. "And what do you want with him?" she continued in suspicious tone, as if to ask, "Are you friend or foe?"

"We are old friends." replied Marcus.

She paused, still inspecting him carefully. "Well, he lives round that corner, the third door down. Ah...is he expecting you?"

"No," Replied Marcus, feeling rather under examination.

"Well, I don't think you should stay long. He has many visitors, and tires easily."

Marcus moved in the direction the woman had indicated, still sensing her suspicious, even accusing gaze. He knocked at the door which opened to reveal his old friend, little changed from their last meeting.

"Marcus!" Heracleon exclaimed. "I never thought I would see you here in Alexandria!"

"Nor did I," replied the scribe.

"And are you still studying St. John?" Heracleon went on, smiling and grasping his hand, obviously delighted at the surprise visit.

"Studying, memorizing and meditating on it," he replied, "And you?"

Heracleon showed his old friend in, and led him to a chair, pouring some wine without asking whether his guest desired it, and continued his animated speech.

"I am studying and also writing, as I have learned more and more the true meaning of the text. I have just this morning been writing down my meditations on the story of the woman of Samaria at Jacob's well. You see what she says to Jesus when he talks of living water? She says, 'Sir, give me this water that I may not thirst, nor come here to draw.' Its true interpretation is this: Insipid, temporary and unsatisfying was that life and its glory, for it was worldly. Why even the cattle of Jacob drank from it! But the water which the Savior gives is from his spirit and his power."

Marcus could take no exception to this teaching. It all sounded very much like the kind of "spiritual exegesis" he had been hearing from Clement and Pantaenus and the other Alexandrian teachers. But then Heracleon went on:

"So Jesus said to her, 'Go, call your husband and come here.'

And she answered, 'I have no husband.' And Jesus said to her, 'you are right in saying, 'I have no husband' for you have had five husbands, and he whom you now have is not your husband; this you said truly.' Its true interpretation is this: The husband of the Samaritan woman mentioned by Jesus is her Pleroma, so that, coming with him to the Savior, she may obtain from him power and union and the mingling with her Pleroma. For he was not speaking about her earthly husband and telling her to call him, for he knew quite well that she had no lawful husband. In the world the woman had no husband, for her husband was in the

251

aeon. And by the six husbands there is indicated all the material evil with which she was intertwined and with which she consorted when she debauched herself, contrary to reason, and when she was insulted, rejected and abandoned by them, that is, by the six husbands."

Marcus began to feel very uncomfortable. For although he admired Heracleon as a friend, he could never accept the Gnostic myth which so clearly informed his reading of every phrase in St. John. He found himself yet more uncomfortable as Heracleon went on to explain the difference between Mt. Gerazim and Jerusalem.

"This mountain (Gerazim) represents the devil or his world, since the devil was one part of the whole of matter, but the world is the total mountain of evil, a deserted dwelling-place of beasts, to which all who lived before the law and all the Gentiles render worship. Now the mountain is the creation which the Gentiles worship, but Jerusalem represents the creation or the creator whom the Jews worship. But the pneumatics, those who are spiritual, worship neither the creation nor the Demiurge, but the Father of truth. So Jesus accepts the Samaritan woman as one already faithful and to be counted with those who worship the truth."

Heracleon had lost nothing of the charm which had arrested Marcus in the days of their Roman association. But Marcus knew that the doctrine which he was expounding through his use of the Gospel of St. John was so completely at odds with what was taught by the apostles and their successors, and still held by the great churches of Marcus's day. So the scribe was saddened to think that there might be occasional, friendly conversation between them, but there could never be real fellowship.

There was a knock at the door. A visitor from the house of Valentine interrupted their private conversation.

"My teacher has sent me with a question about the parable of the hidden treasure" said a rustic fellow in broken Greek.

Heracleon answered him quickly and sent him off, so as to continue to expound the Gospel of John to his friend. But Marcus knew that he had already spent more time in the company of Heracleon, the noted Gnostic teacher, than was wise,

252

appropriate or wholesome, so he made for the door. But on departing he could not resist one more question.

"Have *you* been to the House of Valentine?"

"I have not!" exclaimed Heracleon, and then he added, "And I am not sure I want to go. They send their emissaries for advice, but are reported to be a very closed group. Perhaps some day I must go. But I prefer the freedom I enjoy here in Alexandria, where I can read and meditate and teach, and I am not too closely tied to any one group. But if I were to journey to the Fayum, to the House of Valentine, well, I tell you, I might be constrained to stay on. I might never come back."

With this word the old friends bade each other a cordial goodbye. Marcus walked home, his mind filled with questions. Is it really possible to be friends with a Gnostic, even one so attractive as Heracleon? What are the limits of "spiritual exegesis?" What is the secret of the House of Valentine?

CHAPTER 53

Clement was sorry to bid farewell to his Roman guests. They had provided pleasant company and useful information. But the time had come for them to meet their escort for the journey up the Nile River. He was Valerius Diodorus, scholar at the Alexandrian library, and compiler of an interpretation of problems in the twelve orators. Juliana had made arrangements for him to bring them to Oxyrhynchus, since he was making the boat-journey himself. As the three men made their way to the library, to find this scholar, with whom Clement had had some dealings, the Alexandrian said:

"So you are going up the Nile past the towns where the crocodile is worshipped to the city named after the fish."

"Yes," replied Justin," and I understand that this fish-city has a very lively intellectual life. Juliana told me that it is the home of Diodorus and his father Polydukes, or Pollux, for whom she has made a copy of St. John in polished style. She also mentioned Harpocration, author of the lexicon to the twelve Orators. So our minds should be kept sharp."

"And I trust your bodies kept safe," said Clement, and then he added, "Oh, the Nile is well traveled, and the towns well policed, but one does hear of mysterious goings-on, especially in the cities around the Fayum. I trust that the Lord will preserve you."

Valerius Diodorus was waiting at the library for Clement and his guests, and when the introductions had been made, and farewells bidden, with Christian restraint in the presence of an unbeliever, the scribes followed Diodorus through the city to the waterside. There they found a small riverboat of willow-wood, together with a boatman. The boat was twelve cubits in size,

255

weather-beaten, but appeared sturdy, and was equipped with two oars, a sail, and a rudder.

"Quite a handsome craft," said Justin as they approached the boat and its toothless boatman.

"Yes," replied Diodorus, "It has served me well these six years, since I bought it from Apollonius, son of Serapion and Tanechotis. But I paid too much for it: two hundred silver drachmas! And I have had to repair it several times, as well as pay the boatman. Then turning to the man who was by this time loading the scribes' satchels into the storage chest, he said, "This is Zeno, my faithful boatman."

The sturdy Egyptian nodded to the scribes, and continued preparing the boat. Justin surveyed the water's edge, and noticed an abundance of tall reed-like plants growing in the shallows,

"That is an interesting plant with the triangular stalk and fluted flower." he remarked.

"That is the papyrus," said Zeno. And then Diodorus continued, as if he was concerned to be the supplier of information, rather than his boatman, "From this we manufacture our papyrus leaves that are made into books."

Zeno chimed in again, without lifting his eyes off the oar which he was securing in place, "And the manufacture is strictly regulated, and taxed by the Romans, you can be sure."

Diodorus, frowning, now continued loudly as he reached for a book in his bag. "As it happens, I have with me a roll of Pliny's *Natural History*, which I have obtained for a friend in Oxyrhynchus, and I was just reading his description a few days ago...let me see...yes here it is...'Papyrus grows either in the marshes of Egypt or in the sluggish waters of the river Nile."

The scribes nodded, the boatman shifted impatiently, and Diodorus went on with the reading of Pliny.

"It has no seed..."

"It has a seed," muttered the frustrated Zeno, "a tiny one.'

"It has no seed," Diodorus continued, as if he had not heard the boatman, "and is of no use except that the flowers are made into wreaths for the statues of the gods."

Zeno had had enough, and abruptly pushed the boat off the land with a pole. The undaunted Diodorus sat down and continued with the section that he knew would be of special interest to his traveling companions:

"The process of making paper from papyrus is to split it with a needle into very thin strips made as broad as possible, the best quality being in the center of the plant, and so on in the order of its splitting up. The first quality used to be called 'hieratic paper' and was in early times devoted solely to books connected with religion, but in a spirit of flattery it was given the name of Augustus, just as the second best was called 'Livia paper' after his consort, and thus the name 'hieratic' came down to the third class. The next quality has been given the name 'amphitheater paper' from the place of its manufacture."

Diodorus looked up, now conscious of motion on the river, and explained to the scribes, "The place of its manufacture is the amphitheater in Alexandria." Then he carried on with his reading.

"This paper was taken over by the clever workshop of Fannius at Rome."

Just then the boat struck some object in the river, and began to leak. Pliny was quickly stowed in the bag, and the boatman scrambled to do some temporary repairs. Justin observed that Zeno appeared relieved by the crisis, which called for the undivided attention to an area where he had special expertise and control. He even wondered whether the mishap had been engineered! Marcus whispered to his friend, as Zeno and Diodorus stuffed the leak with a cloth, "It should be an amusing week. I wonder who will win."

When calm had been restored, and all had taken their seats, Justin said to Diodorus. "That was of great interest to us. We are scribes, who use the papyrus codices all the time."

So the scholar from the Alexandrian museum opened his Pliny again, while Zeno inspected his rudder with a quite audible groan, and began sailing up the river in the setting sun.

"All these various kinds of paper are made upon a table, moistened with Nile water -- a liquid which, when in a muddy state, has the peculiar qualities of glue."

Zeno muttered under his breath, "The Nile mud is not glue. That shows you what Romans know."

Diodorus appeared not to hear him, but read on. "This table being first inclined, the leaves of papyrus are laid on it lengthwise, as long, indeed, as the papyrus will admit of, the jagged edges being cut off at either end; after which a cross layer is placed over it. When this is done, the leaves are pressed together, and then dried in the sun; after which they are united to one another, the best sheets being always taken first, and the inferior ones added afterwards. There are never more than twenty of these sheets to a roll."

So up the Nile they went, four men in a boat: a scholar, two scribes and a boatman. Sailing all day, and staying in inns at night, their journey took the better part of a week. For Justin and Marcus it was a new adventure, an introduction to the mysteries of Egypt, and a taste of things to come.

CHAPTER 54

The predictably rowdy life of inns along the Nile was relieved by one pleasant evening on a country farm near Tebtunis. The farm was owned by a wine merchant, Apollonios, whose vineyard supplied the scribes and scholars of Oxyrhynchus with the best drink in the Nile valley. The food was equal in quality to the drink, and the scribes were grateful for the warm hospitality. Their fears of taking some pagan oath were allayed, and they found themselves in the most agreeable and tolerant company. A legendary welcome always awaited any friend of Diodorus on the estate of Apollonios. For this vinteur-scholar loved to collect and share fine books and fine wines.

The good talk and cheer only improved as the evening went on, and Apollonios pleaded with his guests to stay on several days.

"We really must push on to Oxyrhynchus," said Diodorus. "Father is expecting us, and I have some important letters for him."

"And how is Pollux?" asked the host.

"When last I saw him, two weeks ago, he was very well indeed. You know that they have been considering him for the Chair of Rhetoric at Athens! I have here with me a letter that may confirm the appointment."

"Open it!" exclaimed Apollonios.

"I have never opened my father's mail, unless specifically requested to do so by him," protested the shocked Diodorus.

"I am quite sure he would not mind," replied Apollonios in the most agreeable tone. "But have it your way, and leave us all in the most horrible suspense. Why even my slaves, who are waiting on our table will want to hear the news, and will rejoice if Pollux has defeated Phrynichus for the chair."

"You shall be the first in Tebtunis to know, my good friend," said Diodorus, "And now, tell me, what is this splendid wine you have served us."

"This is from the Thasian grapes," said Apollonios, "and, if I say so myself, it is one of the best wines we have produced in the last ten years. I have saved it for a special evening, and here we are."

"Yes," continued Diodorus, reaching into his satchel, "And I believe Pliny speaks very approvingly of the Thasian grapes...look here he says..."

Zeno groaned, and muttered under his breath, "Pliny again!"And wine was served all round.

Diodorus continued, as if he had not heard his boatman, "Here is what Pliny says about foreign wines, 'The wines held in highest esteem subsequent to the great vintages of the Homeric age about which we have spoken above were those of Thasos, Chios, and of the latter the wine called Ariusian. To these the authority of the eminent physician Erasistratus, about four hundred and fifty years after the foundation of Rome, added Lesbian."

"I hate Rome!" exclaimed Zeno more audibly, as he downed another cup of wine.

Diodorus continued reading Pliny, "At the present time the most popular of all is the wine of Clazomenae, now that they have begun to flavor it sparingly with sea-water. The wine of Lesbos by dint of its own nature smacks of the sea....Next after these in esteem are the wines Sicyon, Cyprus, Telmesus, Tripoli, Beirut, Tyre and Sebennys. This last is grown in Egypt, being made from three famous kinds of grapes that grow there, the Thasian, the shoot grape and the pine-tree grape."

"I am surprised," interrupted Apollonios. "That Pliny rates the wines of Egypt so low."

"Well, he died a hundred years ago, " replied Diodorus, "so things may have changed considerably between his time and ours. Indeed, judging from this wine you have served us, things have changed!"

Again Zeno interrupted, now quite audibly, "The Romans oppressed us then, and they are oppressing us now: the taxes! the slavery! the massacres! "Pulling a coin from his pocket he flashed it in the light of the lamp. The image was of the Emperor Hadrian standing on a crocodile, holding a spear downward. "The Romans think that this depicts the subjugation of Egypt. But for us it has a different meaning: the Emperor is Horus taking on Seth, thus defeating Seth and all outsiders!"

Justin caught Marcus' eye. Both feared that with more wine the boatman might turn to violence against the first Romans he could find. But fortunately the wine put him to sleep, and Diodorus continued to regale the company with more of Pliny's comments on wine, read from the splendid roll intended for some scholar's library at Oxyrhynchus:

"Wines are of four colors, white, brown, blood-red and black. Psithian and black psithian are kinds of raisin-wine with a peculiar flavor which is not that of wine....Next after the raisin wine of Crete those of Cilicia and of Africa are held in esteem."

Marcus whispered to Justin, "That Cretan stuff must have been what Pinytus served us."

Apollonios, taking advantage of the pause caused by the scribe's comment, interrupted,

"Diodorus, my dear friend, enough of Pliny! Tell us of yourself, tell us of our friends. How is Harpocration? Give me news of Demetrius the bookseller. I have asked him for a good copy of Homer's *Odyssey*. I fear he has forgotten the request. Remind him that I will pay a good sum for it. And what of Apollonides? He has several of my books, and I hope to retrieve them, when I next come to Oxyrhynchus. Seleucus is also a good friend, and will no doubt take good care of the books I have lent him, especially the Hesiod. Above all, tell me about Juliana. I am so glad you have included her in the Attic Club. Such an attractive and intelligent woman!"

Then, turning to Justin and Marcus, before Diodorus could report on this catalogue of learned friends, Apollonios added, "Do you know Juliana?"

261

"As a matter of fact," said Marcus (to deliver Justin from having to do the talking), "we are to be her guests in Oxyrhynchus."

"Ah," replied Apollonios, "More men to visit Juliana! Many have come, but all have come away, how shall I say, empty-handed, unsuccessful...if you know what I mean. You are of the same sect, uh, Christians, I presume. No one who does not share her belief has any chance of winning her heart."

"We are," replied Justin in a confident voice. "When Juliana visited Rome, she and I discovered a common interest in literary things, and she invited us to come if ever we were in Egypt. We have seen her in Alexandria, and are eager to meet her friends in Oxyrhynchus."

"Well, I wish you well. I once hoped to win her heart, but alas I do not ascribe to her belief. And even if I did, I suspect there would be no chance for me with her."

Justin was quite unnerved that Apollonios somehow knew, or just assumed that he had affection for Juliana. But the conversation returned to books, and stretched on late into the evening. It all was most agreeable, despite the snoring of a boatman, who occasionally cursed the Romans in his sleep.

Justin turned in for a comfortable night, after reciting several psalms, including the One Hundred and Fourth. He was delighted to sing the lines to himself:

The earth is filled with the fruit of thy works.
He bringeth forth grass for the cattle,
And green herbs for the service of men;
That he may bring food out of the earth,
And wine that maketh glad the heart of man;
And oil to make him a cheerful countenance,
And bread to strengthen man's heart.

CHAPTER 55

"Ha! Here is our little river, the Bahr Joseph," exclaimed Diodorus as the boatman, still suffering the effects of too much drink, and of a stern rebuke from his employer, rowed the last few miles to Oxyrhynchus. The Joseph Canal brought the boat with its four occupants to a prosperous town on the edge of the desert west of the Nile. Here they could see the desert, with its "little oasis," and beyond that the Libyan hills.

The willow-wood boat creaked as it bumped the bank of the placid canal. The old craft seemed especially overloaded at the end of its journey. In Tebtunis Apollonios had added to the weight of four passengers, a crate of books for Harpocration and friends, and a crate of his best wine for the feast. Diodorus continued:

"Here is our Oxyrhynchus, a flourishing town of fifteen thousand or so, all of whom pack the theater on public holidays. And oh what pitiful performances the mimes are, these plays of Charition. It's a take-off on Euripides' *Iphigenia in Taurus*. Along the coast of the barbarian country the pretty Charition is captured, and due to be sacrificed by the native kings to Selene. But her brother and a party of Greeks rescue her in the nick of time, by intoxicating the jailers. All this happens amid the beat of drums, the stammering of barbarians, the vulgar gagging of the clown, and the coarse laughter of the spectators. A pretty low sort of entertainment. What would Euripides have thought! But enough of this. We must get you to your lodgings. You are being given hospitality by a certain Paulus, one of the scribes who copies documents for Juliana's Christian group."

Diodorus set off to find his father and deliver the important letter from Athens, but not before extracting from the repentant Zeno the promise to apologize to the Roman scribes and tame his tongue. Yet no sooner had the learned Diodorus disappeared, but

263

Zeno began chattering at the scribes, while securing the boat and stowing the gear.

"He talks a good line, and can dress it in fine speech, but they feel the same way we do. We all hate the Romans, their oppression and their taxes! He has the advantage of all that learning. His father paid for it, of course. Pollux has lots of money, and he spends much of it on books and learning. He is a master with words, that Pollux, and I'll bet you he ends up in Athens. But you should hear them when they get together. They can really wax eloquent against the Romans. You should ask Pollux to tell you about all the terms of abuse he's found for tax collectors. He really makes them laugh. I don't know what half the words mean, but I'd use them too if I was as clever. I tell you, I would. "

Just then Justin was heartened to see Juliana's servant James appear in view. The scribes took their leave of the still-muttering boatman, and were taken to Juliana's house on the edge of the city. As James led them through the streets, he pointed out with some pride the different regions of the well-kept town. " Here is the Cretan section, and there the dwelling of the Jews. The gooseherds are round there, and down that street are the shepherds." He stopped an extra moment for Marcus to have a look. "Just round there is the cobblers' market quarter. I love coming here to Oxyrhynchus with Juliana. It's the place I really consider home."

When Juliana greeted the scribes she seemed different to them, Her hair was up in a bun, and her speech seemed more formal. She seemed almost in a rush and took them at once to the Scriptorium. There they would meet their host Paulus and the other local scribes.

"You are fortunate, my friends," said Juliana, " since all three of our scribes are here today. We may be able to repay you the favor you have shown to us." Juliana's genuine enthusiasm was heightened as they neared the scriptorium, and she added, "Oh, yes, and I almost forgot to tell you. The day after tomorrow, in the evening, we have the meeting of our club, of which Diodorus has no doubt told you. We read and discuss all the great writers, and tomorrow it is Pollux's turn to lead the conversation on one of Sophocles' plays, *The Searchers*, it is called. Please say you both can be with us. I do want you to meet my friends." And then she added in a whisper,

"It is wonderful to me to see the way they will listen when I tell them our Christian story, when it comes up naturally in the conversation. Pollux will usually ask, 'And what does our Juliana have to say?' I am honored as they listen to my relating the themes of the work being discussed to the good news of God in Jesus Christ.' Oh, dear Pollux," she exclaimed. "I do hope he has had good news from Athens!"

"Did you give him the copy of St. John that you were making in Alexandria," asked Justin, "The one in...uh...the polished style?" Justin's hesitation betrayed his dilemma: a deep uncertainty about the enterprise, coupled with his great fondness for Juliana."

"I did," she replied, "And he seemed charmed by the gift. I did not tell him, and nor must you, that my coach in the work was a student of Phrynichus, his chief rival for the chair at Athens!"

Entering the scriptorium, Justin and Marcus found three scribes at work with copy tablets on their laps. Juliana made the introductions. The first scribe was their host, Paulus. He was nearly finished with a copy of St. Matthew. Justin looked over his shoulder and saw that he was copying the story of the woman anointing Jesus' body for burial: "She poured it on his head as he was at table. When they saw this, the disciples said indignantly..."

Juliana interrupted, "Come and meet the others." The other scribes had by this time looked up, but the copyist of Matthew continued at his task.

"Here is Malichus," said Juliana, with a tone of respect. "He has been copying here for over thirty years, and his father did so before him." Then turning to Malichus, she said, "Justin is a scribe from Rome, and like you, has followed his father in the work."

"May God bless you and keep you both," said Malichus.

Justin noticed a set of worn papyrus sheets in the old scribe's hand. "May I see these?" he asked.

Handing them to the Roman visitor, Malichus continued. "I received these from my father. They contain the whole of the Gospel of St. John, but they have been worn by constant use and handling. I am now making a fresh copy, so as not to damage these treasures any further. My Father told me that they were copied in the time of Hadrian, and may have been copied from the original manuscript of the Apostle." Then he added rather nervously, "You are a scribe yourself, so I know you will handle them with care."

Marcus and Justin studied the pages that were open. It was the story of the trial of Jesus, and it read, "Again Pilate entered the Praetorium..."

"Well, that's very fine!" exclaimed Marcus, "This old Codex agrees with our own at Rome, and against some of the copies I have seen here in Egypt, which read, 'Pilate entered into the Praetorium again...' In fact, I have seen one or two copies in my travels which omit the word 'again' altogether. This early copy of yours must certainly be right."

"It is in any case what I have received, and will copy faithfully," said Malchios. Juliana was pleased that Justin had heard of scrupulous fidelity in copying from the lips of one of her friends at Oxyrhynchus.

The third copyist was a woman.

"This is Eucharion," said Juliana, pleased to introduce another woman scribe. "She has been working here for many years, copying the Scriptures, both old and new."

Eucharion looked up and said cheerfully, "And I will continue to do so as long as the Lord permits me."

The hand in which she was copying had all the marks of training in the schools. The letters were well-formed capitals, basically bi-linear. Several of the letters were more or less circular in shape: epsilon, theta, omicron and sigma. Letters were completed by the addition of small serifs, that is, small curls at the end of strokes. Some lines extended beyond the column's left margin. Justin was impressed with Eucharion's fine training and deep devotion. Like Malichos, she was copying St. John's narrative of the arrest and trial of Jesus.

Marcus' attention was arrested by the manuscript that lay before him. But he made no comment to Justin until they were alone in the house of Paulus.

"Justin, you must have been pleased and relieved by what you saw today!"

"Yes, Marcus, it gladdened my heart to see the scribes of Oxyrhynchus seeking to copy faithfully what they had received.

And what did you make of that last manuscript that was being copied by the woman Eucharion?"

"Remarkable!" exclaimed Marcus. "Remarkable! Remember how in the Alexandrian scriptorium we watched the production of a better style of Gospel, at the direction of Anaximenes, and on the principles of his teacher Phrynichus (But remember, do not mention the name to Pollux!). Remember how they dropped the article before the names, and removed words like "and" or "again" or "Therefore." Well, this manuscript, which was being copied by Eucharion with such skill and care, kept all these little words. And Justin, best of all, her copy of St. John contained the words of Pilate, 'Behold the man.' So we read in most of our copies in Rome, though I have not yet found them in Egypt. Clement's codex did not contain them. It was a wonder to see here in Egypt this rather pure copy of the Gospel of St. John."

Just then they were interrupted by a knock on the door. It was a Jubilant Juliana with the news that Pollux had been appointed Professor of Rhetoric at Athens. She exclaimed excitedly:

"So our feast will be more than just a book party. It will celebrate our friend's triumph. And to add to the occasion, we shall have visitors from as far away as Rome!"

So the visitors went to bed. But Justin could not sleep. He had seen a side of Juliana which cemented both his affection and his conviction. And he was eager to see how she would commend the good news to her scholarly friends at Oxyrhynchus.

267

CHAPTER 56

Just after mid-day James came to fetch Justin and Marcus at the house of Paulus. The streets of Oxyrhynchus seemed more crowded than usual for that time of day, but they walked past market crowds and playing children to a handsome three-story house on the edge of town. Here Juliana welcomed them, but they ate nothing so as to be prepared for a sumptuous feast at the ninth nour at the home of Harpocration.

Juliana was eager that her Roman friends should join her for the feast, and that they should understand who was to be there and how she would engage with her cultured friends in the hope of sharing with them the Good News of Jesus Christ. An afternoon of conversation in Juliana's walled garden promised to be both enjoyable and instructive.

"We call ourselves 'the ten,' said Juliana, "after the famous ten Attic Orators, and we allow ten members at one time. I am the only woman who is a member, but my mother, Anna, was one of the original founders some years ago. When she went to be with the Lord, several members determined that when I reached twenty I should join them. Three years ago a very aged member, one of the founders, died and I was elected in his place. It is heartening to see how much respect they have for me, and for my beliefs, but so they treated my mother before me. So the ten of us meet several times a year, when we are in Oxyrhynchus together, and we share with each other books we have obtained, and end with a dramatic reading of one of the great plays of antiquity. Tonight we will read together Sophocles' *The Searchers*. Normally we restrict our numbers, but several are away, and Harpocration was very taken by the idea of guests from Rome who care about the life of thought. You see, my friends, the more intellegent Christians they can meet, the better are the chances that they will take the gospel seriously. They were delighted when I brought Clement as a guest about a year ago."

"I can imagine they were," said Justin, "But he is far more learned than either of us! Aren't you taking a bit of a risk?"

"Not at all!" exclaimed Juliana, "Both of you are lovers of books, and careful readers of texts. And Marcus told me of your encounter with Galen in the library at Pergamum! You will do much, just by showing interest, in dispelling the widely-held prejudice that we Christians are anti-intellectual, hold to base supestitions, and use questionable methods."

"Prejudice?" asked Marcus.

"Indeed," said Juliana, "I encounter it all the time, especially in cultured Alexandria. You have probably heard of Celsus, a distinguished philosopher who lives in Alexandria. Well, you should see the things he writes. Here, I have a copy of one of his books. Justin, just read this aloud, and note how he makes sport of us!

Justin read:

"Christians everywhere speak of the tree of life and of the resurrection of the flesh by the tree -- I imagine because their master was nailed to a cross and was a carpenter by trade. So that if he had happened to be thrown off a cliff, or pushed into a pit, or suffocated by strangling, or if he had been a cobbler or a stone-mason or a blacksmith, there would have been a cliff of life above the heavens, or a pit of resurrection or a rope of immortality, or a blessed stone, or an iron of love, or a holy hide of leather. Would not an old woman who sings a story to lull a child to sleep have been ashamed to whisper such tales as these?"

Juliana was fully animated. She said in full voice. "These words make a mockery of the greatest truth! Why should cultured men like Pollux and Harpocration and Diodorus not have the opportunity to hear the truth, and see it lived out?" Then turning to the other scribe, she said, "Marcus, read us this paragraph." So Marcus read:

"In private houses we see wood-workers, cobblers, laundry workers, and the most illiterate and bucolic yokels, who would not dare to say anything at all in front of their elders and intelligent masters. But whenever they get hold of children in private, and

270

some stupid women with them, they let out some astounding statements as, for example, that they must not pay any attention to their fathers and schoolteachers, but must obey them; they say that these talk nonsense and have no understanding, and that in reality they neither know, nor are able to do anything good, but are taken up with mere empty chatter. But they alone, they say, know the right way to live, and if the children would believe them, they would become happy and make their home happy as well."

The scribes could see that Juliana was annoyed at such writings, and the influence they were having. Justin asked, "But your cultured friends, these Pollux and Harpocration, and Diodorus aren't taken in by this stuff, are they?"

"Some of our number still are." answered Juliana, "although they have softened, I think, and I trust in part because of my witness to the truth."

"What did you say to them?" asked Justin.

"In particular, there was one named Seleucus," said Juliana. She pronounced the name with respect, even with admiration, but with a guarded tone. "He was carrying on in one of our meetings of the Ten, one of the first I had attended, about the growth of mindless superstition in our time. He included in the catalogue of cults "the sect of Chrestus," which we know as the church. 'Foolish ideas and questionable practices,' he would say, and 'totally lacking in *arete*, in virtue.' The other men knew of my Christian belief, and wondered how I would respond to Seleucus' charges."

"What *did* you say?" Justin asked.

"I quoted to them from St. Paul's letter to the Philippians, where the Apostle says, 'Finally, brothers, whatever is true, whatever is honorable, whatever is just, whatever is pure, whatever is pleasing, whatever is commendable, if there is any excellence, and if there is anything worthy of praise, think about these things. Keep on doing the things that you have learned and received and heard and seen in me, and the God of peace will be with you.'

"And their reaction?" querried Justin.

"Well," she continued, "I could see how pleased Pollux and Harpocration were, not only that I, so young a member of the Ten, answered so confidently, but also that my answer was on the mark. Even Seleucus was softened when I got to the word *arete*,

271

'excellence,' 'virtue.' They thought that Christians cared nothing for this. But St. Paul shows that we truly do! Seleucus remains something of a skeptic, and none in the group has affirmed Christian faith, but none will criticize Christ or his church in my presence. May God in time turn their respect into conviction."

The Roman scribes were impressed with Juliana's strategy, but wondered about the limits of such engagement with cultured pagans. Justin continued his questioning, "But what of their literature, of Homer and the gods and myths, and of the poets and philosophers? Are they not wrong and offensive in many places? How can you avoid criticizing their beloved literature at some points? And you are surely aware that the best Christian teachers argue that all the good in Homer he got from Moses, who is of much greater antiquity. I remember as a boy hearing the great Justin Martyr argue in this way. So also you will find Athanagoras of Athens and Theophilus of Antioch arguing like this. What about Clement? What would he say?"

"Clement?" replied Juliana, slightly unnerved by the question, but aware that it was a serious issue, and cut to the heart of her attempt to relate the gospel to her cultured friends. "It was actually Clement, and his teacher Pantaenus, who taught me a right use of the literature of the pagans. You see, traveling around to the churches in the empire, I heard the argument time and again that Moses was more ancient than the Greeks, and that all the good they had they stole from him. We spent much time talking over this issue in the school. It was Clement who urged me not to challenge my friends directly with this argument, but rather to follow the method of the blessed Apostle Paul at Athens, and to quote their own poets to make your point. Of course, I would have loved on many occasions to cite some splendid passage from the prophet Isaiah, like this one." She reached for an Isaiah roll, but knew the passage by heart...

Bel bows down, Nebo stoops.
Their idols are on beasts and cattle.
These things you carry are loaded
as burdens on weary animals
They stoop, they bow down together;

They cannot save the burden,
but themselves go into captivity.
Listen to me, O house of Jacob,
All the remnant of the house of Israel,
Who have been borne by me from your birth,
carried from the womb;
Even to your old age I am he,
Even when you turn gray I will carry you.
I have made and I will bear
I will carry and will save.
What a splendid declaration...and it goes on...
For I am God and there is no other;
I am God, and there is no one like me,
declaring the end from the beginning,
and from ancient times things not yet done...

"I love these words, Justin, and so do you, and yet to bring them up as a challenge to their ideas and their literature would be foolish. So, as Clement urged me, I let their own poets do the work. I recently used a passage from Sophocles to say the same thing, and then pointed to the similar wisdom of Isaiah. Sophocles wrote...

One, in truth, One is God
Who made both heaven and the far-stretching earth,
And ocean's blue wave, and the mighty winds;
But many of us mortals, deceived in heart,
Have set up for ourselves, as a consolation in our afflictions,
Images of the gods of stone, or wood, or brass,
Or gold or ivory;
And, appointing to those sacrifices and vain festal assemblages,
Are accustomed thus to practice religion.

"I say," Juliana went on, "Why not let Sophocles do our work for us!"

"Indeed!" said an impressed Justin, "but how did *they* react to this... Pollux and the others?"

"Pollux was very pleased with the citation from Sophocles," Replied Juliana, " He recited the old saying, 'Sophocles is wise, Euripides is wiser, but Socrates is wisest.' I could tell the others were listening intently. And then I read some from Isaiah. They seemed to be ready to hear, prepared by their own poets."

"Juliana," Marcus asked, "Several times you have warned us to say nothing in Pollux's hearing about Anaximenes or his teacher, Phrynichus. We won't mention them, of course, but could you give some explanation?"

Yes," answered Juliana. "You see Anaximenes, my dear eccentric teacher of style in Alexandria, studied in Bithynia with Phrynichus before coming to our city. From this Atticist he learned his rules of Attic style. I love and respect Anaximenes, though I do not always follow him in his judgments. You see Pollux thinks Phrynicus is much too rigid in his definition and application of Attic rules of style. Moeris, another Atticist, is even more rigid. And there are many others who comment on Attic style. I had to work this out for myself, and take my own course on style. Well, when I was in Athens, with my father, some time ago, I heard that Phrynicus was there, and so I tracked him down, and questioned him thoroughlly about Attic style. He was a little surprised to have so many learned questions from an Egyptian girl! But when he learned that I was a friend of Anaximenes, he welcomed me. He was gracious and I learned much from him, although I, too, think his rules on style too rigid. Even the Attic writers sometimes break the rules of Phrynichus! I have not mentioned to Pollux that I sought Phrynichus out, and I doubt that I would ever mention it. But you see, this is a prcatical way in which I rejoice in the liberty of Christ, who is our reconciler. I do not have to be the enemy of Phrynichus to be Pollux's friend."

And so the hours fled by, and the three were off to the house of Harpocration. On the road Marcus whispered to Justin, "I think she knows who she is, and where she is going."

"And so do I," said Justin, "And so do I."

CHAPTER 57

The house of Harpocration was of the same size and scale as that of Juliana, having been produced by the same artisan who lavished care on both, and received a handsome fee for it. The difference was that in the house of Harpocration the garden was smaller and the banqueting room was larger. That room was alive with talk, since most of the guests had arrived. The case of wine sent by Apollonios had already been opened, and the case of books was being brought in. The convivial atmosphere was enhanced by wonderful smells of cooking from the kitchen.

Juliana's enterance commanded the attention of all in the room. She introduced her guests.

"We are honored to have two Roman friends, and we welcome you to the feast of the ten." said Pollux in the authoratative voice one might expect from the new professor of rhetoric at Athens.

"And I understand you are to be congratulated." said Justin with a smile and a bow.

"I thank you kindly," said Pollux, "News does travel fast, and one has no way of controlling its spread or its significance."

Justin, encouraged by the pleasant banter continued, "So also has the news reached us of your work on names. You collect names for everyone and everything, and your *Onomasticon* includes many words used to abuse tax collectors!"

"Thirty-three to be precise," said the delighted greying scholar as he sipped his cup of the finest wine from Tebtunis. "Throat-snatcher, robber, plunderer, embezzeler, sea-serpent, beast of the field, mad-man, violent man, low-life, afflictor of those already overloaded. What did you say, is it adjectives that you prefer, very well, inhuman, offensive, immoderate, sordidly greedy. Are we back to nouns, forcer, seizer, choker, oppressor, persecutor, stripper.   Shall we be more vivid, animals, serpent's coils, shipwreck, and whatever form of insult that is in use!"

"That wasn't thirty-three," said a short, dark-haired, dark-eyed man in the corner.

"Demetrius," said Pollux, and turning to the scribes he continued, "This is Demetrius the Bookseller. We all depend upon him a great deal for books, and he always wants the highest standard."

"And the highest price!" exclaimed another.

"That's Seleucus, the sternest critic in our group. He gives us all a hard time, but we give it right back to him. Seleucus, these are Juliana's guests, Justin and Marcus." The tall young man with a long, thin nose extended a welcoming hand.

"And now for the books," said another, heavy-set man in jovial and expectant voice.

"Apollonides," said Pollux, who was obviously the leader of this band of scholars, "Apollonides, you rush the evening, come and meet Justin and Marcus, and wait your turn for the books. After all, there may or may not be one for you!" And then turning to the host, a most distinguished looking man in his fifties, he said. "Harpocration, may I introduce Juliana's guests, Justin and Marcus from Rome."

"Juliana," said Harpocration, "I understand that your friends are scribes and lovers of books, and belong to your sect of Chrestus, the Christians."

"You are right," she said. "I honestly admit that one of the greatest challenges to thought was my visit to these scribes in Rome last year."

"Let me assure you," said Justin, "we are here more to learn than to teach, and we are honored to be your guests."

"And now," continued Pollux, "Let us learn what is in the box of books sent to Harpocration by Apollonios. Let us explore what treasures he has given us."

Harpocration pried the crate open with care, revealing about ten rolls and one codex. The presence of a codex intrigued the Romans, for they knew that the Jews and the pagans used rolls, whereas the Christians used the book form. Was the Christian custom beginning to catch on?

"Let me see," said Harpocration, as he reached into the case. "Here is a note. Oh, it's a private letter....yes...yes, For Diodorus," He muttered to himself, and read out a few lines, "I cannot, and would not if I could, put any relation of mine in such a position, especially after what I have learned in such cases." He looked quizically at Diodorus and skipped to the end, "I pray your health my lord brother."

Diodorus took the note, and read it in full. "Here is a postscript," he said. "It reads, "Make and send copies of Books 6 and 7 of Hypsicrates' *Characters in Comedy* (or is or *Topics in Comedy, or Men Made Fun of in Comedy*) For Harpocration says they are among Pollion's books. But it is likely that others, too, have got them. He also has his prose epitomes of Thyrsagoras' work *On the Myths of Tragedy.*" He paused, and then he read a further note in another hand, "According to Harpocration, Demetrius the Bookseller has got them. I have instructed Apollonides to send me certain of my own books which you will hear of in good time from Seleucus himself. Should you find any apart from those which I possess, make copies and send them to me. Diodorus and his friends also have some which I haven't got."

He paused and stared at the note, and looking up he said, "There is a further note for Dionysios, but he should read it to himself." So he handed that aged scholar the letter.

More wine was poured and Harpocration began removing the rolls from the case.

"Ah, this one is marked for Juliana. It is a roll of the fifth book of Homer's *Iliad*. There is a note attached, 'I thought you would be especially pleased with the large, careful, even bookhand. This book speaks to the issues we discussed when we last met as a group in Oxyrhynchus." Juliana took the book with care, for it was clearly an old copy. Several others crowded around her to see it.

"Here is another!" cried Harpocration. "Yes!" he continued, "Demosthenes! *On the False Embassy*! And what a fine copy!" The distinguished lexicographer pored over the text, with others looking on.

"Oh, this is fine!" exclaimed Pollux. "Look at the hooks and loops with which the strokes begin and end. This is a book for a scholar of wealth and taste!"

"Like You!" said Diodorus to Harpocration, showing exagerated respect.

"Yes, but it is alas only on loan," replied the scholar. In due course I must return it to Apollonios." He took another sip and reached for another roll. "It's a book of Pindar for Apollonides." This lover of poetry had been silent, but now he read from the old scroll with a voice of beauty and charm, at the place where Pindar praises one of his predecessors:

> But I, while I hear him playing his few notes,
> Playing as I do a babbling art,
> Vie with his lay
> Like a dolphin of the sea,
> Whom the lovely sound of flutes
> Thrilled on the waters of the waveless deep.

"Like a dolphin of the sea, a playful dolphin, that's how Pindar makes me feel," said Apollonides. As this scholar buried himself in the roll of the poet, Harpocration reached for another.

"Here is Plato's *Republic*, Book Ten, and it is for Diodorus."

With excitement the scholar of the Alexandrian library opened the book and began to read out loud from its handsome script. "We have been talking of poetry. Listen to this:

'Let us freely admit that if drama and poetry, written for pleasure can prove to us that they have a place in a well-run society, we will gladly admit them. For we know their fascination only too well ourselves; but it would be wicked to abandon what seemed to be the truth. I expect you feel the fascination of poetry yourself, I asked, and especially when it is Homer exercizing it? And we will listen favorably, as well as gain much, if we find her a source of profit as well as pleasure.'

"Yes, we will gain a lot. But if they fail to make their case, then we shall have to follow the example of the lover who renounces a passion that is doing him no good, however hard it may be to do so."

At this last sentence Diodorus fixed his gaze on Justin, whose heart-secrets had not escaped the notice of the man with whom he had spent a week on the Nile. Justin turned red as the wine. But it was Harpocration to the rescue with another book and a cheerful announcement.

"Seleucus, here is a book for you...a bit of philosophy, the *Protreptics* of Aristotle. I think this belongs to you, and he is returning it." Seleucus took the book and opened to read from the narrow columns written in informal uncial script, with a glance at Diodorus, whom he wished especially to instruct:

"Want of discipline combined with power breeds folly. In a bad state of the soul neither wealth nor strength nor beauty are good things, but the greater the abundance of these qualities, the more do they injure their possessor, if they are unaccompanied by reason."

"Is not a young scholar a dangerous thing?" shot back Diodoruus.

"Enough of this," retorted Harpocration. "We would not want our private quarrel noised as far away as Rome." More wine was poured and more books dispatched. There was a Roll of Thucydides, Book Four, containing a hundred columns. When rolled out it was eight meters long. The scribes admired the script, which was at once mannered and fluent. The letters were a rounded style, often decorated with hooks and loops, and sloping slightly to the left. "This one is for Demetrius, and it is meant for keeping, not for selling!"

Next came the codex, a copy of Xenophon's *Cyropaedia* labled for Didymus. "Where is Didymus?" called out Harpocration.

"He's on official business in the Arsinoite Nome," replied Apollonides.

"Here, give this to Juliana. She will probably see him before any of us." said Diodorus. Justin and Marcus wondered what was implied by that exchange.

Harpocration reached into the almost empty crate. "Now this is for Dionysius. It is an old document on the back of a tax roll -- that should please Pollux!"

"And Zeno!" whispered Marcus.

Harpocration unrolled it and declaimed, "*Hypotheses on Euripides' Alcestis and Aeolus.*"

"I love the *Alcestis*" said Dionysios, as he took the volume. Unrolling it, he sang the closing chorus in raspy voice:

279

Many are the forms of what is unknown.
Much that the gods achieve is surprise
What we look for does not come to pass;
God finds a way for what none foresaw.
Such was the end of this story.

"I love *Alcestis*," Dionysius repeated. "It is a noble idea that one person should die for another!"

"And greater still in history than in myth." said Juliana. At that moment Justin saw what she was trying to achieve. But it was not so different from his conversation with Albinus.

"It is another play that we will have this evening." said Harpocration, removing the last things from the crate. "And what is this? A joke for Pollux? Well that is what it says. Here is a note. It reads, "In anticipation of good news from Athens, I send this gramatical exercise for your correction. Behold the hideous script, the many mistakes in grammar and spelling! hours of fun criticizing and correcting, and tearing out what little hair remains! But lo, this farce has a companion and a splendid one, for one so splendidly honored."

All gathered round to enjoy the fine copy of Book 24 of Homer's *Iliad*.

"And now for the feast!" said Harpocration.

CHAPTER 58

A sumptuous feast of local game hens and vegetables and fruits, prepared by Harpocration's personal cook was followed, as was the custom of "The Ten," by a dramatic reading of Sophocles' play, *The Searchers*. But the dinner conversation had its own delights for the Roman scribes. Seleucus, as critical as ever, remarked:

"Euripides always gives me a headache. No wonder they drove him into exile from Athens! And the *Alcestis* is especially strange, neither tragedy nor comedy. And who ever heard of anyone dying for someone else? We all have to do our own dying!"

"Quite the contrary," retorted Pollux, "Many have died for others, and I take this to be a grand myth." And then he said with the aire of a man whose recent victory had placed him above contradiction, "What does our Juliana think? And do her Roman friends agree?"

All eyes were fixed on the young Alexandrian scholar and scribe. "I think," she said, and then paused deliberately, "I think it is great as myth but even greater as history. For our Apostle Paul writes, 'For scarcely for a righteous man will one die, though perhaps for a good man some will even dare to die. But God commends his love toward us in that while we were yet sinners, Christ died for us."

The long silence that followed was broken by Justin, who said, "Juliana has spoken well for us. We can only add that this is for us the greatest truth, the greatest treasure." He was pleased to be standing with her in their witness to Christ.

Questions followed about Rome, the availability of rolls and codices, the methods of copying and preservation, and it was well into the evening before the table was cleared and the play reading begun.

"Juliana, " said Harpocration, "You and your friends will be our audience. "Pollux, I see you have a copy there. Will you play the part of Apollo? Apollonides, Silenus. Seleucus, will you take the part of Cyllene? Demetrius, will you be Hermes, and use that fine copy you have brought? The rest will be the chorus. Well, then, let us begin.

"The scene of the action is Mount Cyllene in Arcadia. Apollo has lost his cattle; he has sought them vainly in Northern Greece, and has now come to the Peloponnese. He promises a reward to their discoverer. Silenus enters and offers the aid of himself and his sons, the Satyrs, in return for a prize of gold and release from slavery..." He paused and gestured for Pollux to begin.

"APOLLO. To every man and every god proclaims Apollo: if anyone has seen my cattle, near or far, to him I promise a reward. Grievous and heavy pain is in my heart; someone has robbed me of the cows and all my calves and herds of heifers. Not one is left. All are gone unseen, far from the stables: vainly I follow the traces of their stealthy plot. I never should have thought that any god or mortal man would dare to do this deed. Since I have heard the news, distracted with alarm I hunt and search, and make full proclamation to gods and men, that none may be unaware...I follow frantic in pursuit. I visit the tribes...seeking, which man of all the host..."

Pollux waved his arms and contorted his face, causing a roar of laughter, and the audience missed three lines...

"I rush to the fruitful plains of Thessaly, and the wealthy cities of Boeotia, and then..."

More laughter and comment interrupts the declamation of the new Professor of Rhetoric, so that the listening three, now laughing too, can only catch the threads:

"Doric...neighbor, whence...I have come swiftly...and of Cyllene...and to a place...So if any shepherd, farmer, or charcoaler is at hand to hear me, or any nymph-born wild man of the mountains, to one and all I make this proclamation: whoever catches the prey taken from Apollo, earns forthwith the reward that lies ready here."

So the play went on, late into the evening, relating how Selinus and the Satyrs take up the hunt, like dogs on a scent. They hear strange and frightening sounds from the cave of Cyllene, which prove to come from the musical instrument which the infant prodigy, Hermes, has invented by stretching cowhide over a tortise shell. So the thief is detected. Hermes took the hide from cattle he had stolen and slain. The young Hermes then appeases Apollo by giving him the lyre. The Satyrs have their reward.

Well past midnight the party broke up and Justin and Marcus escorted Juliana to her house. As they stood at the door, Justin was bold to state what he had observed.

"Juliana, I noticed that during the play reading a certain sadness crept over you. Did we miss some irreverence in the presentation by your delightful friends?"

"No, it isn't that at all," replied Juliana, "It was just that the play reminded me of my cousin Apion. You see, he has left us and gone to be with the Gnostics, the Valentinians. He and I grew up together and were the best of friends. We shared so much together, and he was always such an encouragement. And when his father, Agrippinus became the Bishop of Alexandria, I saw even more of him, both there and here in the country. For his father was very busy, and his mother very ill, and he came to live with us. For about ten years he was my closest friend. But then he began to talk with the Valentinians. He also began to speak against his father. Young men sometimes do. Perhaps it was his way of trying to assert himself. But it grieved his father. When he left for the House of Valentine it broke his father's heart...and mine too. So you see, when Pollux began to say those words of Apollo, I felt that they were my words.

'So if any shepherd, farmer or charcoaler is at hand to hear me, or any nymph-born wild man of the mountains, to one and all I make this proclamation: whoever catches what has been taken away earns forthwith the reward that lies ready here.'

"How I was caught off guard by these words! What reward would I not give to see Apion restored to the faith of the church, restored as my own dear friend, restored as the son of his godly father! What reward would I not give to bring him back from the house of Valentine."

"But Juliana," said Marcus, "They say the House of Valentine is a strange, mysterious and alluring place. I've heard it said that there is a maze and within the maze there is a book and within the book there is a secret. To find that maze and that book and that secret has enticed many. And I fear what they say of the House of Valentine is true, that you may get in, but you can't get out. We can pray to God that he might bring him back, but I fear that is all anyone can do. But we know that God hears and answers prayer."

In the silence that followed Justin looked up at the brilliant star-studded sky and thought on the eighth Psalm, "When I consider the heavens, the work of thy fingers, the moon and the stars which thou hast ordained, What is man that thou art mindful of him, or the son of man that thou visitedest him?"

They bid each other a somber farewell. As Justin walked to his lodgings with his friend in the quiet of the early morning, a plan began to form in his mind.

284

CHAPTER 59

Marcus slept until midday. When he did awaken, he lay on his bed in the house of Paulus, half asleep, with a sense that something was different. As he came to full awakedness, he realized that the house was very quiet. He pulled on his cloak and went to see whether Justin had slept late too. But Justin was not in his room. All his belongings were removed. And there, on his pillow, was a sealed letter, in Justin's handwriting, for Marcus. The drowsy scribe opened it and read:

"Justin to Marcus, My dear brother in the Lord, I have gone to the Fayum, in search of Apion. I did not want to disturb you, and I knew that if I had, you would try to dissuade me. But this is something I *must* do. I have asked Zeno to take me as far as Tebtunis, and I will make my way from there. Please do not attempt to follow me. I know that there are dangers on the way, and a great mystery surrounding the House of Valentine. But I have heard the cry of Juliana's heart, and I must do what I can to reach Apion and challenge him to return to the truth. Please pray for me. I know that I face danger, but I believe all will be well, and that God will be with me and bless me. You may tell Juliana where I have gone and why. Farewell in our Lord Jesus Christ."

Marcus stood paralyzed as he re-read the letter. He recalled what he had heard of the House of Valentine. He remembered the words he and Justin had heard about this mysterious place several times in their travels, "You can get in; but can you get out?" He remembered his conversation with Bishop Julian in Alexandria, and the bishop's concern over the two men who had gone there. He remembered how even the great Gnostic leader Heracleon had been suspicious about the House of Valentine. He feared for his friend Justin. Had his head been taken captive by his heart? Instictively he returned to his room, put on his clothes and shoes

285

and ran out the door and down to the quay. Zeno and his boat had gone and a few Egyptian boatmen were milling about lazily in the early afternoon.

"Have you seen Zeno?" Marcus asked one of them. His breathless anxiety was a stark contrast to the practically lifeless quay-side mood.

"Left early this morning, with that Roman man. Seemed in a great hurry. It'll do Zeno good to charge a Roman dear."

Marcus knew there was no catching Justin. He also knew that he could not hide the truth from Juliana. But how would he tell her? If he simply showed her the letter, she would know how Justin felt, and why he had gone. But then he mused that Juliana already knew. He deemed that she had invited Justin and himself, fully aware of Justin's feeling for her, and not averse to developing a similar feeling for him. Marcus made his way, now at a walking pace, to Juliana's house.

When James opened the door, he could tell at once that the Roman visitor was agitated.

"Oh come in, and sit down. Are you all right? I shall fetch Juliana. She has been up for several hours. We were not expecting you until later. And where is your friend Justin? Is he not well? I do hope the feast did not cause him to be ill."

"No," replied Justin, and added with confidence. "He is very fit and eager for new tasks." Then realizing he may have said too much, he added, "Yes I would be pleased to see Juliana."

"This way...she is in the garden."

Juliana was reading her codex of the Gospel of St. Mark in the afternoon sun. In another corner Rhoda was working with some of the plants.

"Marcus!" Juliana exclaimed. "Are you by yourself? Is Justin all right? I pray to God that there were no ill effects of the feast."

"No, indeed," said Marcus, as he sat down near Juliana. "No, it was a splendid feast, and we greatly enjoyed ourselves. And how we admired your bold witness to Christ among your friends. But Juliana, I slept until midday. And when I awoke, I found that Justin was gone, and so were his belongings, and I found a note on his bed. I think it best if I let you read it. He has given me permission."

Juliana read in stunned silence. She read and re-read. She began to read some phrases aloud "...I have gone to the Fayum in search of Apion...This is something I *must* do...Dangers on the way...mystery surrounding the House of Valentine...I have heard the cry of Juliana's heart...I must do what I can to reach Apion...God will be with me...You may tell Juliana where I have gone and why..."

"But why?" asked the incredulous Juliana.

"He has heard the cry of your heart." replied Marcus, determined to say nothing beyond what was plainly in the letter.

"He has listened to my heart," said Juliana slowly and softly. Then looking up from the letter and fixing her full and penetrating gaze on Marcus, she said in a quivering voice, but with deep sincerity. "And I have heard his heart."

Rhoda continued to tend the plants as she overheard the conversation, and quietly prayed for Justin and for her beloved Juliana.

She now stood, and Marcus rose too. She handed him back the letter, and continued, "I first heard his heart in the scriptorium in Rome last summer, when Rufus caused that little stir, and we were left alone to talk it out. I told him that I had had it with the Roman men who were always trying to conquer. They conquer lands, and treasures and books. They conquer women! He did not deny it. He knew it was true. He simply answered with a calm, quiet strength, 'Women also conquer.' I knew then how he felt. And from then on I began to feel the same way. You know, Marcus, that many scribes from around the world have visited us in Alexandria, and even here. Many have come to try and win my heart. But I have found none like Justin, not one. How he must love me to be willing to risk his life in the Fayum and endanger his faith in the House of Valentine!"

Juliana's voice began to waver, and she could not hold back the tears. She leaned her head on Marcus' strong shoulder. After a moment she spoke, "You know what they say about the House of Valentine. 'You can get in, but you may not get out!' O Lord, let it not be that I have lost him!"

She sat down again, and Rhoda came over to assist. James was ready with a liquid refreshment, and the two scribes talked and prayed for several hours, in words mixed with fear and joy and friendship.

CHAPTER 60

Justin's boatride down the canal to Tebtunis was a long day's journey, peppered with rude comments about the Romans and their accursed taxes. Justin determined to bear with it in silence, but he almost grumbled when Zeno, now not under the watchful eye of Diodorus, asked an outlandish sum for the portage. It was as if he finally had a chance to get even with Rome, and as far as he was concerned, Justin *was* Rome.

At the water's edge, not far from Tebtunis, on the east end of the Fayum, Zeno docked and began talking to some other boatmen he knew. Justin made his way on foot toward the vineyard of Apollonios, where he knew he would find a welcome. All the way up the path he could hear Zeno and his company heartily singing their drinking song, with its memorable refrain, "aulei moi, aulei moi":

In life these songs I love to sing:
And when I die, set a flute above my head,
Beside my feet a lyre
Play me a song...(aulei moi)
Whoever found the measure of wealth or poverty
Who, I repeat, found out the measure
Of gold among mankind?
For now, he that possesses money
Desires more money still:
And rich though he is
Poor wretch he is tormented like the poor
Play me a song...(aulei moi)

For some time Justin could still hear the boistrous refrain, "aulei moi...aulei moi...aulei moi..." And then it died away.

289

Apollonios was surprised and delighted at the arrival of his unexpected guest.

"Come to stay the night? Why of course! Stay two! Stay a week! Is your friend with you?"

"I have come on my own," replied Justin, as Apollonios poured some wine. "I have some business to take care of in the Fayum."

"Business in the Fayum?" asked the puzzled Apollonios, and then his mood changed from curiosity to renewed glee, and he continued, "Well, we can talk of that later. First tell me. How was the feast? Oh, I so wish I had been there. How I love those gatherings. And we have already heard about Pollux! Splendid news from Athens, don't you think? And how is Harpocration?"

"He loved the books. They all did. How kind of you to send a note for each one, even that disagreeable Seleucus."

"Oh, he is not so bad as he seems," replied Apollonios, "And how is Juliana?" Justin was heartened at the very mention of her name. He felt he must guard his tongue, and not make known the true nature of his errand. But he also felt sure that Apollonios might well give him valuable information about safe conduct in the Fayum. He might also provide some leads to the House of Valentine. After all, as a leading wine merchant, he would know all kinds of people in the region, and hear all kinds of news and gossip. Justin replied:

"I say, that was a splendid copy of Homer's *Iliad*, Book Five that you sent to Juliana."

"A beautiful book for a beautiful woman! Don't you think?" Apollonios queried.

"Yes," said Justin in as matter-of-fact a tone as he could muster.

"And speaking of books," his host went on, "Look at this fine copy of Homer's *Odyssey*, Book Seven, which I have just received from a friend in Alexandria." Apollonios opened the roll, and exclaimed, "look at this elegant script. A beautiful and practiced hand! And look at the serifs adorning the feet of most of the letters."

Justin was re-living the delightful dinner party he had only just left in Oxyrhynchus.

"This one is for me!" said Apollonios excitedly. "And there is another one here, an *Odyssey* Book Six, an older roll, and not so elegant, entrusted to me by a friend, that I might supply corrections." Then he paused, and asked Justin, "Do you ever correct *your* manuscripts?"

"I sometimes do," answered Justin, wondering what the scholar- cum-vinteur was driving at. "On this recent journey I have on occasion noted differences between my texts and those of others, writing them at the margins."

"You see," continued Apollonios, as if he had not really taken in Justin's reply, "You see here I have corrected this mispelling of the word *Athene*, but I made rather a hash of it. I hope my friend won't judge me too severely. And here I added the letter that was wanting. But other than these small mistakes, it is a fine old roll. Listen to this." So Apollonios read to a tired Justin, who struggled to stay awake:

"No, stranger, quickly harken to my words, that with all speed you may win from my father an escort and a return to your land. You will find a handsome grove of Athene close to the road, a grove of poplar trees. In it a spring wells up, and round about is a meadow. There is my father's estate and fruitful vineyard..."

"Don't you see why I love this book!" exclaimed Apollonios, jogging Justin from his near slumber.

"A fruitful vineyard, as far from the city as a man's voice carries when he shouts. Sit down there, and wait for a time, until we come to the city and reach the house of my father. But when you think we have reached the house, then go to the city of the Phaeacians, and ask for the house of my father, great-hearted Alcinous. Easily may it be recognized, and even a child could guide you..."

"I am looking for a house." said Justin, now fully awake. He could not believe he had said plainly what he had hoped to conceal. But Marcus knew, and Juliana knew, why shouldn't Apollonios know; he might even be able to help.

"A house... a house in the Fayum...what house is this?" asked Apollonios.

"Have you heard of the house of Valentine?" asked Justin.

"I have *heard* of it...one hears all kinds of things from visitors to the west, from the divisions of Themistos and Heraclides, and places round Lake Moeris like Theadelphia and Dionysias Euhemeria. I believe the House of Valentine is somewhere near those towns, near to the lake." Then he paused and in more like a whisper he added. "The House of Valentine...Uh...isn't that where Juliana's Cousin...Apion, I think his name is...Isn't that where he has gone? I know that when he left a few months ago, it upset her very much."

"That is right," said Justin, his heart racing.

Apollonios cocked his head to one side, and looking at Justin from the corner of his eye, with the other eye squinting, he said. "So you are on sort of an odyssey too."

"You might say that," replied Justin.

"But mind you," the host continued, "This is the Fayum, not Athene. Here you will find no handsome grove of poplar trees, no springing wells, no meadows. And the vineyards aren't so fruitful, if you ask me. It's only mounds of sand blown round desert lands reclaimed from under water. And be careful how you travel, there are many hazards, human and natural, along the way."

"Yes, it will take more than a child to guide me," agreed Justin.

"I know a man who can help you," said Apollonios in a louder, and more cheerful voice. "He is a small man named Ninnaros, 'the stump-fingered,' they call him, for he is a very small man with very small hands. He is actually the owner of this *Odyssey*, Book Six, and I wonder if you would be kind enough to return it, now that I have corrected it. He would not take you to the house of Valentine, for he speaks of it with fear and suspicion. But he knows a man in the next village who can. I think he is named Heron. He is practically a giant, and fears no one. He has some dealings with the House of Valentine, and he may help you."

"I would be glad to take this *Odyssey* to him," said Justin.

The last bit of wine was downed, amid more warnings about the Fayum, and Apollonios showed Justin to his room. "May you sleep well, my Roman friend." he said and then added,

"She is a lovely woman, and you are a brave and worthy man. I wish you all the best on your odyssey."

292

CHAPTER 61

For what seemed like a very long time, Justin lay on his comfortable but strange bed, half awake, half asleep. "What day is this?" he asked. "What time is it? Where am I, Why am I here? Was it all a dream?"

The shapes and shadows of the darkened room, and the strange and wonderful Egyptian smells, drew his mind to greater alertness. Now it all came flooding back to him. Here he was on the Vineyard of Apollonios in Tebtunis, near the River Nile on the edge of the Fayum. He recalled how just two days ago he and his friend Marcus had been in Oxyrhynchus, about sixty miles upstream, on the Bahr Josef, at a splendid feast with the scribes and scholars of that town. After the feast Juliana had told of her beloved cousin, Apion, who had left the Orthodox faith and had joined the Gnostics in the house of Valentine in the Fayum. The haunting words from Sophocles' play, *The Searchers*, which they had read that evening at the party, rang over and over in his mind, as if she had just said them:

"So if any shepherd, farmer, or charcoaler is at hand to hear me, or any nymph-born wild man of the mountains, to one and all I make this proclamation: whoever finds the one that I have lost, earns forthwith the reward that lies ready here."

So here he was, on his way into the Fayum, in search of Apion in the house of Valentine, the secret enclave named for the great Gnostic teacher. What would the day bring?

Justin's musings were interrupted by sounds in the hall of the still-dark house. Someone was at the door, and had awakened Apollonios.

"I am afraid you must have the wong place." came the voice of Apollonios.

293

"No, it says here, Justin, the Roman," was the official sounding reply. There followed a knock on Justin's door, and his host said in a concerned whisper, "It is someone asking for you."

In the light of the lamp which Apollonios had trimmed Justin could see a tall, officious looking man, who held a note in his hand. "Are you Justin, the Roman?" he asked.

"I am."

"I have a warrent for your arrest," said the man.

"What?" asked both men together. Apollonios added. "Arrest? This cannot be! He has done nothing! He has been here with me since coming to Tebtunis. What is the meaning of this?"

"It says here," the official went on, breaking the seal and reading the note:

"To the *Archephodos*, the head policeman of Tebtunis, send Justin the Roman, on the charge of the murder of Zeno, boatman of Diodorus of Oxyrhynchus."

The incredulous Justin looked at the note, which had been hurriedly folded,, the wet ink offset, producing a mirror image on the back of the sheet.

"This cannot be...I mean I did not..." stammered Justin, and Apollonios picked up the refrain,

"This is impossible," and in more defiant tone he added. "Someone has framed him. He is innocent! You will answer for this."

"I answer to the *Archephodos*!" exclaimed the policeman, pointing to the note. Taking Justin by the arm, he continued. "You get dressed and come with me. I must have all your belongings, as material evidence." He seized Justin's satchel, containing his copy of the Gospel of St. Mark, and other necessities, and led him away.

The jail at Tebtunis was an old barn, a dirty, dark, dingy dungeon of a place. A dead rodent in one corner, and a dreadful odor pervading the whole area made him sick. Another prisoner huddled in the corner.

"You can keep each other company," said the policeman, and then he locked the cell and was gone. Justin spied the other prisoner, who looked a desperate fellow.

"Two years I been here," said the man, in so broken a Greek that Justin had difficulty understanding. "Probably spend the rest of our lives here on bread and water." Justin fought the feeling of panic. He sat down on the narrow bench that was to be his bed, and started reciting a Psalm. "The Lord is my light and my salvation, whom then shall I fear, the Lord is the strength of my life, of whom then shall I be afraid..."

More comment from his cell-mate interrupted his hold on this lifeline. "If the magistrate's away, it may be some time before they examine you. The last man in here with me they sent to the galleys. Not sure he even got a trial. Can't count on it with the Romans. Say, what did you do?"

"I did nothing!" exclaimed Justin to the unpleasant man.

"No, what's the charge?"

"Falsely accused of murder," replied Justin.

"Murder! They like to hang them or behead them for that. He must have provoked you something awful to lead you to do that."

Justin did not answer, but began again with the Psalms, this time, the Sixty-ninth:

Save me O God, for the waters are come in, even unto my soul.
I stick fast in the deep mire, where no ground is;
I am come into deep waters, so that the floods run over me.
I am weary of crying; my throat is dry
My sight faileth me for waiting so long upon God.
They that hate me without a cause are more than the hairs of my head
They that are mine enemies and would destroy me guiltless are mighty...

"No use crying to a God who cannot save," snarled the bitter man, "There is no God."

Quietly Justin whispered to himself, "The fool hath said in his heart there is no God." He continued reciting the psalms, which he knew by heart, until, after an hour, fear and panic notwithstanding, he caught a little sleep. He was awakened by a blood-curdling scream from another part of the barn.

"They torture them sometimes, especially slaves." said the other man, who had not slept. "It helps them to tell the truth."

295

Justin then recalled the words of Peter, the founder of his church, in his first letter:

"But let none of you suffer as a murderer, or a thief, or a wrongdoer, or a mischief-maker; yet if one suffers as a Christian, let him not be ashamed, but under that name let him glorify God."

For Justin here was the worst part of this whole terrible business. "O Lord, If I must suffer," he prayed, "Let it be for the name of Christ."

Then he began doubting. Was this whole scheme of his trip to the Fayum, his quest to retrieve Apion from the house of Valentine, his readiness to take the risks really honoring the Lord? Or was he simply following his romantic inclinations, now out of control? Was he not much too hasty in leaving without talking with his friend Marcus, or taking due time in prayer over the matter? And then he thought of his precious codex, his personal copy of the Gospel of St. Mark, confiscated by the chief of police. Fresh waves of anxiety gripped him as he realized that this copy contained not only the text of the gospel as the church of Rome had received it, but a number of private marginal notes of his own, where he had noticed different readings. He had started writing them as he noticed them, first in Juliana's own copy of Mark, and then from other copies he had seen in Corinth, Ephesus, Antioch and Alexandria. Now these private jottings were loose in the world. In other hands, at other times, they could easily work their way into the body of the text of future copies, which used his as an exemplar. Had he now, quite unwittingly, contributed to the corruption of the text of the Gospel?

Then he remembered that he had memorized most of the text of St. Mark, but had only got as far as the crucifixion; "And the scripture was fulfilled which said, he was numbered with the transgressors." So he realized that if it depended upon him to produce a copy of St. Mark from his memory, it would be even shorter and more defective than Juliana's, which lacked only the last section. He should have finished his memory of Mark, as

Marcus had done with John before his copy was stolen near Jerusalem. Justin hung his head in black despair.

All day and all night Justin refused food and drink, and seemed only semi-conscious. The next morning he was jolted by a policeman calling his name:

"Justin, the Roman, you are called to appear before the magistrate."

"Quickly judged, quickly hanged," said his desparate cell-mate.

After the darkness, the blinding Egyptian light was a further shock to Justin's system. By the time he regained his bearings, he was in a rather simple courtroom, standing before the magistrate, hearing the accusation.

"Justin of Rome, arrested on charge of murder of Zeno, boatman of Diodorus, son of Polydeuces of Alexandria and Oxyrhynchus."

The very mention of Diodorus and Pollux gladdened Justin's fear-gripped heart for a moment.

"Murder?" asked the magistrate, looking the prisoner up and down, "And what evidence is there to condemn this man?" he asked the accuser.

"It was reported, your honor, that he was seen with Zeno, having come down the river with him. Now we know that Zeno was always cursing the Romans and their hated taxes. Several said they saw this man quarreling with Zeno, and that the boatman required an exorbident sum for the trip, which made this Justin, this Roman, very angry. You can see why he would kill him."

The magistrate turned to Justin, "What do you have to say for yourself?"

"I am a Christian, and I worship Jesus Christ as Lord," Justin's calm, steady voice surprised even himself. "He not only commands us not to murder, upholding the old law of Moses, but calls us to love our enemies, and this I have tried to do."

"Christian?" the magistrate queried. The courtroom was silent as all waited for what the magistrate would say next. Suddenly he produced a papyrus sheet and a reed pen and ink and demanded of Justin:

"Here, write on this paper, 'Do not murder'."

Justin dutifully wrote the words *me phoneuses*, "Do not murder."

The magistrate then produced Justin's satchel and removed from it his copy of St. Mark. He opened it to the middle, and placed it next to the papyrus leaf and examined the two in silence. Finally he asked, "Is this your book?"

"It is," replied Justin.

The magistrate continued, "I have inspected it with care. This is his book to be sure, for the handwriting in the margins is his, beyond any doubt. And here is a list of commands, in the middle of the book, given by Jesus, whom this man calls 'Lord,' and the list reads, "Do not commit adultery, do not commit fornication, do not steal." And this man Justin has written in the margin of his book, at this place, "Do not murder." He has not only written it but also underlined it boldly. This man did not commit this crime. And in any case, I have been reading this book carefully, and am fascinated by the character of Jesus, the central figure. Perhaps he *is* the Son of God. Anyone who reads this book and believes in Jesus could not have done this crime."

Turning to Justin the magistrate handed him his codex and his satchel, and said, "You are free to go, and we apologize for the pain and embarrassment this may have caused." The assembled company was astonished.

As Justin left the room to rejoin Apollonios, the magistrate added, " I have just one request. Would you be kind enough to let me know where I can get a copy of that book?"

"I will make you one," said Justin.

CHAPTER 62

The prison had broken Justin's feverish pace, but not his determination. Like an Olympic runner, stumbling near the starting line, he regained his stride, all the more focused on the finish and the prize. As he set off into the Fayum, he went over in his mind the instructions and warnings from Apollonios.

"Stay close to the canal, where it is slightly safer. Do not deviate from the path, and greet no strangers. Especially resist advice to turn off to Crocodilopolis, the city also named for Queen Arsinoe, the chief city of the nome. The men there may be friendly, but the women are beguiling, and the wines are poison."

So with this much for advice, with a refreshing night of sleep at the Vineyard, and with no more than the directions to Theadelphia, where he would inquire after Ninnaros "the stump-fingered," he set out on the twenty-five mile walk along the canal, the Bahr Nezla. The fields round the canal, made fertile by the irrigation system, gave way in the distance to the desert sands. As he walked and breathed the clean air, Justin thought about the events of the last few days -- the determination to find Apion, the friendly but unnerving Apollonios, the horror of his sudden arrest and the wonder of his equally sudden freedom. There seemed a strange sense of foreboding in the air, as if the scene he was looking at was slowly decaying before his very eyes. Perhaps, he thought, Zeno had been right, and the Romans were taxing and exploiting Egypt into ruin. Would the desert someday encroach upon the fertile ground? How long would it be before all he could see would be covered with sand?

Several local farmers looked at Justin quizzically as he walked along the canal. Once he stopped and called to a more friendly-looking man,

"Is this the way to Theadelphia?"

"That it is," replied the farmer, "And where are you from?"

"Visiting from across the sea." Justin replied, not daring to reveal his city of origin. Nor did he speak again until he came to the town and asked at a shop.

"I am looking for a man named Ninnaros. 'The stump-fingered,' they call him."

"Ah, it's 'stump-fingered' you're after." Then, leaning over his counter, the shop-keeper said in a whisper, "Who are you, and what do you want with him?"

"Justin, friend of Apollonios of Tebtunis, with a delivery of a book that belongs to him." Justin sensed that Theadelphia was a town where no secret would be kept for very long.

"Book? May I see it?"

Justin was uneasy about showing the stranger the Homer, but it quickly became clear that the man could not read, and he had no interest in it. He simply needed to know everything about everyone in town.

"Follow me," said the strange Egyptian, and he led Justin down a narrow dusty lane. A knock on the door produced a man who could well answer to the name 'Stump-fingered.'

"A visitor with a book for you." said the shopkeeper. Before Justin could extend his hand or introduce himself the two men launched into a high-pitched argument in a language he could not understand. It went on for several minutes, and then the shop-keeper left in a huff.

"I am sorry to disturb you," said Justin.

"Come in," said the little man, "You bring a book?"

"Yes, from Apollonios of Tebtunis. Says it belongs to you, and he did some correcting. Homer's *Odyssey*, Book Six." Justin handed him the book.

The little man opened it with his small fingers, and exclaimed, "Indeed, he has corrected it. But he hasn't been very neat about it." Then looking up at Justin he asked, "How did he persuade you to bring it all this way? What did he pay you?"

"Nothing," said Justin. "I was actually his guest, and was headed this way on an errand, and he said you might be able to help. So I agreed to bring this to you."

"Me? Help with an errand? What sort of ...."

"I am looking for a place near here called "The House of Valentine," said Justin.

The little man suddenly looked frightened. He said in fearful voice, "I couldn't possibly take you there. No. You know what they say. You can get in, but you won't get out. What do you want with the House of Valentine?"

Ignoring the last question, Justin continued, "Yes, but Apollonios tells me that you know a man who can and will take me there...a giant man, he says...one they will fear."

"Yes," said the man thoughtfully. "Yes, I know who he means. The man lives near Crocodilopolis."

"Crocodilopolis!" exclaimed Justin, "But Apollonios told me to avoid that place!"

"Mind you, I don't like going there either; not since I had that terrible bout with too much bad wine and too many loose women. That's before I took up being a Christian."

Justin's was heartened to hear the familiar beloved name in such a strange and remote place, but before he could say a word Ninnaros went on,

"You're a Christian, I saw it in your face."

"I am," Justin replied, "And I rejoice to meet a brother."

Ninnaros placed the *Odyssey* on his little table, and picked up a small codex next to it, "Then it won't be Homer that you'll be wanting to read. No, and nor do I any more. Now that this one's corrected, however poorly, I can sell it to a woman who lives near here in Euhemeria. She collects all the old poets, especially Sappho." Then he added in a knowing whisper, "She's a bit strange, if you know what I mean." Then he added in a normal voice, " But she will pay me a good price for it. Instead, you'll be wanting to read this Gospel about Teacher Jesus. Here you are, sit down and read this and I'll fetch us something to eat. We'll need an early bed and an early start if we are to make it to Crocodilopolis."

Ninnaros disappeared, and Justin sat down and opened the little codex. He read:

"And behold a leper approached him and said, 'Teacher, Jesus, while journeying with lepers, and eating with them in the inn, I myself became a leper. If, therefore, you are willing, I am cleansed.' The Lord therefore said to him. 'I am willing. Be

301

cleansed. And immediately the leprosy departed from him, and the Lord said, "Go, show yourself to the priest and make an offering for your cleansing as Moses commanded, and sin no more..."

To Justin this sounded much like the gospel, but not a story that could be found in any one of the four gospels. He read in another place:

"A man came to tempt him saying, 'Teacher Jesus, we know that you have come from God, for the things which you do bear witness beyond all the prophets. Tell us then: Is it lawful to render to kings what pertains to their rule? Shall we render it to them or not?' But Jesus, knowing their mind, said to them in indignation, 'Why do you call me teacher with your mouth, when you do not do what I say? Well did Isaiah prophecy of you when he said: 'This people love me with its lips, but its heart is far from me; in vain do they worship me, teaching as doctrines merely human commandments."

Justin looked up from the strange codex. His mind was racing. Here were many phrases from the teaching of Jesus, but out of context, and patched together in an odd way. Then there was that text from St. Mark and Isaiah "This people loves me with their lips..." Here the codex read "loves." not "honors." It caused him to remember his conversation about this variation with his bishop, many months ago, and far away in Rome. He remembered how Eleutherus had chosen this reading over the other after much thought, but still to this day wondered which one was right. But the thought of his dear Bishop Eleutherus brought a sense of reality to a scene that seemed very strange: A strange land, a strange host, a strange Gospel, and the promise of stranger things still to come. He thanked God for Eleutherus and Irenaeus, and all those who stood for the truth in the four gospels.

Just then the door opened and Ninnaros brought the food and drink. During the meal that followed Justin asked, "Dear friend in Christ, where did you find this book?"

"Oh," replied Ninnaros. "I copied it myself, from the gospel we read in our local church here at Theadelphia. It is a great comfort to have my own copy of the words and deeds of Jesus."

"I find my own copy of the Gospel a great comfort too." said Justin, but he decided to keep to himself his impressions of the

302

strange book. He went to bed turning these things over in his mind, and wondering what more strange books were to be found in the Fayum.

CHAPTER 63

The sight of a small Egyptian and a tall Roman moving across the Fayum on a camel must have seemed very strange to the farm-hands or tradesmen on the path between Theadelphia and Crocodilopolis. Had they overheard the conversation, it would have seemed stranger than the sight.

"So, then, Ninneros, what is your trade?" asked Justin.

"I am a tax collector."

"A tax collector?" Justin continued, "I have heared the term used often here. Indeed, I have heard much about taxes since coming to Egypt." His mind was still fresh with the memory of his imprisonment in Tebtunis.

"Yes," said Ninnaros, "I do fairly well. So, my friend, we ride a camel, rather than go on donkey or on foot."

"And you, my friend, are like Zacchaeus, the tax-collector in the gospel who found Jesus." Justin said in an affable tone. But then he realized that the remark could have been taken as an insult, for Zacchaeus was very small, as was Ninnaros, the stump-fingered, and the latter might not have appreciated the reference to his stature.

"Zacchaeus?" asked Ninnaros, "Who is this Zacchaeus?"

"You know," the surprised Justin continued, "Zacchaeus, the tax-collector in the Gospel of Luke, who climbed up in a tree to see Jesus." Justin decided not to refer to his size.

"Gospel of Luke? I do not know the Gospel of Luke." Ninneros said, "Though I once heard a man from Oxyrhynchus speak of it. You know, there are many gospels, or so I'm told, but I'm content with the one I have. Now you take the big man we're off to see in Crocodilopolis. He reads another gospel. I think he calls it the Gospel of Peter, but I'm not sure. He showed me a copy, but it is very different from my gospel. And then there's the

305

gospel, or so they call it, that they read at the House of Valentine. Mind you, I haven't seen it. You can't see it unless you go there and find the maze, the labyrinth, and in the maze you find the book. I think they call it the "Gospel of Truth." But mind you, I haven't gone, and I won't go, and I don't think it's a very good idea for you to go there either. Oh, you never told me why you were going."

"I need to find a man who has gone there." replied Justin, still cautious about the exact nature of his errand.

"That wouldn't be the young man Apion, would it?" asked Ninnaros.

Justin started. "Yes, but how do you know Apion?" Justin was amazed at how much life was carried on by rumor and gossip in Egypt.

"Apollonios sent him a few months ago, with the same strange request, to transport him to the giant at Crocodilopolis, for conveyance to the House of Valentine. But mind you, I didn't linger in Crocodilopolis then, and I won't this time either...nor should you if you know what's good for you...And I wouldn't have anything to do with that House of Valentine...and that young Apion, so eager to get there! I think he wanted to join them. He's probably seen the Gospel of Truth!"

"What did he look like?" asked Justin, hoping to gain a better picture of the man he would need to find once he got in to the House of Valentine.

"A handsome, tall man with dark hair, and deep-set eyes," relpied Ninneros. Justin recognized the features, and realized that Apollonios had guessed the nature of his quest.

Crocodilopolis was reached without incident, but not without further warning from Ninneros, who fled back to Theadelphia as soon as the link had been made with Heron, an Egyptian man of massive proportions.

"Come in, my little Roman friend," said Heron in a loud and confident voice, "So it's the House of Valentine you want to enter, is it? No problem. Will you be staying, or do you want to get out?"

"Oh I will not want to stay," said Justin.

"Last man I led there was so eager to get in, but wasn't worried about his exit. You know what they say in the Fayum about the House of Valentine, that you can get in, but you can't get out.

Well, that's no problem for me. I've been in and out many times. They fear me, you see, my size, and my power. So I'll take you there, but why do you want to go?"

"I am searching for Apion, the man you mentioned." replied Justin.

"Yes, the son of the bishop," said Heron, "that is, of the dead bishop of Alexandria. I told them at the House of Valentine, you know, about the death, but I don't know if they will have told him. They have hidden him away for training, so he will be hard to find. But I'll find him. And I will also find their gospel. They won't let me see it, so I won't let them see mine. But it's time for me to see their gospel, whether they like it or not. So I am glad to take you, on a quest for this poor Apion, and to find the book at the end of the maze, and to learn their secrets. I can do it, for my gospel is a gospel of power, my little Roman friend."

Justin was annoyed by the persistent, condescending, "my little Roman friend," but figured that Heron probably was able to use the word "little" for just about anyone. His curiosity got the better of him, and he asked, "What is this gospel of power?"

"Oh," replied Heron, "Don't you know the Gospel of Peter? It is the Gospel of Power! For it says that when the Lord was crucified, he cried out on the cross, 'My power, my power, why have you forsaken me?" Justin recalled hearing this form of the saying from Aulynchus, who had learned it from Peregrinus.

"There is power in the cross," Justin replied, "And St. Paul called it the power of God, but he also spoke of the cross as the foolishness of God and the weakness of God. Did he not elsewhere write to the Corinthians that God's power was made perfect in weakness?"

"Well, my little Roman friend, you have your weakness, I'll take my power. Weakness will not help you in the House of Valentine. What you need is a show of power. You remember how when Jesus was raised, the soldiers who were keeping guard heard a loud voice in heaven, and they saw the heaven open and two men come down from there in a great brightness and draw near to the sepulchre, And the stone which had been laid against the entrance to the sepulchre started of itself to move sideways, and the sepulchre was opened, and both men entered. This is all in my

Gospel of Peter, the Apostle, my little Roman friend. So then, when the soldiers saw this, they awakened the Centurion and the elders, for they also were there to mount guard. And while they were narrating what they had seen, they saw three men come out from the Sepulchre, two of them supporting the other and the cross following them, and the heads of the two reaching to the heaven, but that of him who was being led reached beyond the heavens. And they heard a voice out of the heavens crying, 'Have you preached to those who sleep?' And from the cross there was heard the answer, 'Yes.' " Heron's voice thundered as he said "Yes!" And then he added in booming voice, "Power, I tell you, my little Roman friend."

"And how long have you been reading this Gospel of Peter?" asked Justin.

"About eight years," replied the giant. "Here's how it happened. My father was a pig-farmer, Pasion was his name, son of Heraclides from the Hellenion quarter of the metropolis. I helped him in the business, and have since taken over. Well, my little Roman friend, my father and his friend, Onesimus, from the Gymnasium quarter, also a pig-merchant, were returning from the village of Theadelphia. About dawn they were attacked half-way between Polydeucia and Theadelphia by thieves, who bound them and the guard of the watchtower, and assaulted them with many blows, and wounded my father very badly, robbed him of his pig and carried off his tunic. We all suffered terribly from it, and eventually my father died. Finally they found the culprit and brought him to justice. But I vowed that I was not going to be overpowered like that. Not me, my little Roman friend. So I set out looking for the real source of power. And then I came upon this group in the metropolis who said that the Power belonged to the Lord. They showed me this gospel, the Gospel of Peter. I found the power I was looking for. Yes, the power forsook him on the cross. But the power preached to the dead, and came forth triumphant. This is the power that none can resist. With this power I will push through the house and the maze, and find the book, this Gospel of Truth."

"I have seen the Gospel of Truth," said Justin.

"You have?" asked the astonished giant.

"Yes, in Rome. Valentinus, who wrote it showed it to me himself."

"Valentinus? *the* Valentinus?"

"Yes, you see, Valentinus lived in Rome, and taught there for many years, and the church leaders had a long consultation with the Gnostic leaders, of whom Valentinus was the most powerful. This must have been twenty years ago, in the last days of Anicetus. My father, who died defending the faith of Christ, was in on the consultation, and took me along with him, though I was only fourteen. I think Valentinus felt that since I was young, I might be easier to persuade. So I read his Gospel of Truth, but found the picture of Jesus unreal, and not at all like the Jesus in the four gospels which are read everywhere in the churches."

Justin was pleased that this little piece of information had disarmed Heron for a moment. But he valued the giant's help, and so he added, "But by all means see it if you wish, and I will be grateful to have your assistance in finding Apion."

"I doubt you'll persuade him to come out, if that is what you are aiming at." said Heron.

Justin looked at the ground, thinking of the strange gospels he had seen in the Fayum. Then he looked straight at Heron and replied, "It's worth a try, my big Egyptian friend."

CHAPTER 64

In the early morning light of the Fayum Justin sat copying the text of St. Mark. He was seeking to make good his promise to the magistrate at Tebtunis to supply him with a copy of the gospel. It felt wonderful to be copying the scriptures again, for he had not done so since leaving Rome. As he penned the opening line "The beginning of the Gospel of Jesus Christ, the Son of God..." he was reminded of how he first met Juliana, and how he noticed that her beautiful codex lacked the phrase "The Son of God." He reflected on how this had started him on his quest for the true text of the gospel, and his quest for Juliana. These two quests, which seemed to blend into one, had brought him to where he sat in the light of a February morning, on the day he was to enter the House of Valentine.

Then he remembered the letter from his teacher Irenaeus, which he had received in Alexandria. He thanked God for the magistrate in Tebtunis, both fair and cultured, who had left intact the contents of his satchel, and through reading the Gospel had found him innocent. He took out the letter and read again the section where Irenaeus mentioned the Valentinians and their "Gospel of Truth."

"Indeed they have arrived at such a pitch of audacity as to entitle their comparatively recent writing 'The Gospel of Truth,' though it agrees in nothing with the Gospels of the Apostles, so that they have really no Gospel which is not full of blasphamy. For if what they have published is the Gospel of truth, and yet is totally unlike those which have been handed down to us from the apostles, any who please may learn, as is shown from the Scriptures themselves, that that which has been handed down from the apostles can no longer be reckoned the Gospel of truth..."

"We'd better be off before it gets too hot!" boomed the voice of Heron, and the two men set out into the desert. After about an hour they saw it. The House of Valentine at first appeared as a series of specks on the horizon, almost a mirage. Then it came clearly into view, a stone fortress, standing sentinel in the desert, and glistening in the morning sun. It seemed at once silent, secret, forbidding, impenetrable. A momentary fear gripped Justin, but there was no turning back. He must face the Gnostics and find Apion. In no time they seemed to be at the door, and Heron gave a firm knock. There was no answer at first. Another knock and then another produced a man, dressed in white and speaking in a whisper.

"Greetings, Heron. And what is your business today? Have you brought us another seeker?"

"He is a seeker, to be sure," replied Heron, "And he is seeking the man I brought some time ago, Apion by name."

"He is not to be seen," replied the man. "No one being initiated may be distracted from his quest for gnosis."

"I bring a man with news for him," continued Heron.

"We will take the news to him," the man replied, "at a point when he is able to receive it."

"I am afraid it is something we must tell him ourselves," said the giant of Crocodilopolis, in as giant-like a tone as possible. Justin could tell that the doorman was somewhat intimidated. He replied sheepishly,

"Could I please ask you to wait outside, while I ask the Teacher whether this would be permitted." Heron complied, and Justin felt as though he were invisible. Perhaps, thought Justin, invisibility in this instance is an enviable state.

Once the door had shut firmly before them Heron said to Justin in a whisper. "They will never let us see him. But I know another way in. There are many secrets in the House of Valentine!"

"But are we not putting ourselves in some danger?" asked Justin.

"No problem, my little Roman friend," replied Heron. "I know another way into the house, and I have studied all the secret passages. I know the labyrinth, and I know where the chamber is where they keep the initiates. I know where they keep the Gospel of Truth."

"How do you know all this?" asked Justin.

"I have talked with the man who built this house. I've spent hours with him. He showed me all the plans, and told me where the wall is weakest. If they will not let us in, we'll push our way in, with a show of power, and then, my little Roman friend, you will find Apion and I will find the Gospel of Truth."

"I think you may be disappointed," said Justin.

"You may be too!" said Heron, "Now follow right behind me." Justin had no choice but to follow Heron around to the left side of the structure.

"Now just here is a secret door. It is often kept unlocked, but is always guarded. Since it is the middle of the day, the guard is weary and will be napping, so we will push like this..." Heron leaned his great weight against a section of the wall, and it yielded before him. He stepped into a dark hallway, and Justin followed. As predicted, the guard lay sleeping, and the two men crept by him. A turn to the left brought them into an empty hall, with several doors on either side. Silently Heron slipped down to the third door on the left, and whispered to Justin. "Your man is in there."

Just then noises were heard, and two men appeared in the hall.

"What are *you* doing here?" one of them shouted, as he moved swiftly toward the two intruders.

"We must see Apion, and we must see the Gospel of Truth." Heron replied, now in full voice.

"That would be impossible!" insisted the man.

Apion lifted him in the air by the collar, and said, "We will see them. First the man. He is in there, I believe." both men were paralized with fear. "Open it!" boomed Heron.

The man still on his feet went to the door to open it, while the other, still aloft, cried. "No, you can't, I mean, well, alright. But only for a short time, and he must begin his training all over again. At once when he sees you he becomes fleshly."

Justin thought to himself, "You mean he becomes real again," but he said nothing.

The door opened, revealing a tall young Egyptian, with facial features strikingly like Juliana. Apion was startled by the interruption, and fearful at the sight of the giant, though he recognized him.

313

"A man to see you," said one of the trembling attendants, as he slipped into the room with Justin. Heron caught the man's arm and pulled him back, exclaiming, "He must see him alone." The door slammed shut, and Justin found himself alone with Apion. The suddenness of it all, the violence, the secrecy, the darkness, all made it seem unreal, but here was his moment.

"I am a friend of your cousin Juliana, I come on her behalf."

Over the noise of shouts and scuffles in the hallway Justin went on, confident that Heron would take care of himself.

"First of all, I am sorry about your father."

"What about my father?" said the man in a tender, appealing voice.

"Did you not know that he died?"

Apion gasped, and stood in silence and shock, "Father, dead?" he whispered.

"Yes, I'm sorry, he died about two months ago."

"It was I that killed him. It was grief over me, and my joining the House of Valentine. I knew it would hurt him but I didn't know..."

"And they didn't tell you?" asked Justin

"No," said the tearful Apion, still looking around in a daze. "No, they have not told me anything, except to read these books, and to attain true gnosis, and that then I would see the Gospel of Truth."

"I have seen the Gospel of Truth," said Justin, remembering the value of revealing this piece of information in his conversation with Heron, and still able to hear noises of battle in the hallway. But losing no time he added, "Valentinus showed it to me himself in Rome twenty years ago. I was disapointed and unconvinced then, and I trust you will be now."

Apion looked up, his tearful face now stunned by Justin's boldness. The Roman continued:

"How can they talk to you of truth, when they are determined to hide the truth from you?" Not waiting for a reply, he continued, "And Juliana is quite upset and longs for your return and restoration. She loves you very deeply, Apion."

Apion sat on the little bench in his cell, and put his head in his hands. Justin put his arm around him and said nothing. Several

314

precious minutes were lost in the wait, but Justin sensed that silence was essential. He had made all his points. He had to wait for Apion.

"The door burst open, and in the hallway Justin and Apion saw the whole assembled Valentinian community, held at bay and terrorized by the giant of Crocodilopolis.

Their trembling leader spoke. "You may see the man but you may not see the book."

"He is at liberty to leave, then?" asked Heron.

"No, he is not." replied the leader.

"But I want to leave!" cried Apion. "Why did you not tell me about my father's death? Why have you kept me in this cell to read this "Gospel of Philip," as you call it, and this "Secret Book According to John?" Why have you not really treated me as one of yourselves? Why have you promised me freedom and given me slavery?"

"But this is how you become one of us," the leader replied.

"Well, I am not sure. I want to go, and I have wanted to for some days. I want to see my cousin, whom I love so much, and I want to go and mourn the death of my father. I want to see Alexandria and Oxyrhynchus. I want to see the sky and feel the sun and swim in the Nile. I want to see the trees, and hear the birds, and enjoy the world that God had made so good and beautiful."

"But we must flee the world." answered the leader.

"You flee it, I am returning to it!" said Apion.

"You can't hold him against his will," pleaded Justin.

"And you *won't*," boomed Heron.

"And you won't see the Gospel of Truth!" shot back the leader.

Heron and Justin escorted Apion down the hall, and out the door they had entered. The giant was the last to leave, and as he left he called back in a voice designed to strike like a thunder-clap. "I'll be back for the book!"

The three men set off for Crocodilopolis in the blinding, brilliant noonday sun.

315

CHAPTER 65

Both Apion and Justin were eager to leave Crocodilopolis, and the Bahr Josef provided swift passage out of the Fayum. But a brief stop at Hawara for food and rest meant one more encounter with the mysteries of the region.

The keeper of the canal-side inn had a laugh that aroused fear, and a leer that aroused suspiscion.

"Over there's the maze, " he said, "The labyrinth," bringing back vivid memories of the House of Valentine. "And here the Crocodile god Sobek is held in high honor. In that temple and labyrinth and tomb there is much to inspire, much to fear. The entrance columns of pure white limestone will dazzle the eyes. The great blocks of granite, of which the bulk is made, are indestructable. Though one may detest and fear the thing, and many of us do, with its many halls and chambers, one really must see it."

"I think we've seen enough mazes to last us for a while," answered Apion.

"But you really must see how the priests care for the sacred crocodile," said the inn-keeper with his sinister grin.

"We have no time to lose," said Justin.

"It's your loss," said the host as he poured fresh glasses of undrinkable beer.

So the two men set off and found the Nile. All the way down the river Justin listened to Apion as he told his tale, often in tears: "I've really wasted my life. I have been a wayward and rebellious son; no doubt I sent my father to his grave, and grieved my cousin, my best friend Juliana."

"If I know Juliana, I'm sure she will welcome you as if you had never been away."

317

Apion seemed comforted by the words. "How do you know Juliana?" he asked.

"She came to Rome with her father, Demetrius, who had some business there." Justin's voice was strong with feeling as he recounted the tale. "I am a scribe for the church in Rome, and she and I discovered a common love for the copying of the sacred scriptures."

"So *you* are the scribe from Rome." Apion was now less tearful, and more animated in his speech. "I tell you, when she returned from Rome late last summer, she was full of talk about her meetings and conversations with you, and about the differences in your manuscripts. We were all a bit amazed. You see, Juliana has gone everywhere with her father, and has met so many people in the different churches. But this was the first time that she spoke at length and with real feeling about any of the men she had met. She wanted to talk a lot with me, for I was her closest friend, and she turned to me after that unsuitable Hermas spurned her. But I was too distracted with the Gnostics, so I didn't listen too well. Nonetheless, there was no mistaking it. She told how she loved those conversations with you. She loved the way you both honored her and challenged her. She loved your devotion to the gospels and your commitment to fidelity in transmitting them. She so hoped you might visit her some day, and her hopes, I see, were not in vain."

Justin sat speechless, deeply moved by these revelations.

"Yes," Apion went on, "She has had many visits from men, from churches all over the empire. That's not surprising. And you know why they come. Of course they want to see Pantaenus and the catechetical school. Of course they want to be a part of the growing work here in faith and learning. But they really have come to see her. There have been readers and deacons aplenty. Even one bishop came! Of course, it was to consult with my father...."

Apion's eyes began to water, and his voice to break at the mention of his father, but he carried on. "Even one Bishop hoped to win her heart. But Juliana would not be drawn. And as for that wonderful group of cultured friends with whom she is seeking to share the Christian hope, not a one of them stands a chance. You should have seen how much Apollonios sought to win her affection! Of course she loves them all dearly, and they know that, but as friends. None has really won her heart."

"Do you think she would be pleased if she knew that you were sharing all this with me?"

"I don't know, Justin. But I do know this. That you have taken a real risk to come and find me in the House of Valentine. I do not know whether she asked you or paid you or what happened, but you came and rescued me, and I know that she will be very grateful to you, and that will only add to her already very strong affection for you."

"She told me how you had gone," recounted the scribe, "and I heard the cry of her heart, and I determined to come and find you. I *had* to do this. I did not even talk to my friend Marcus, who has traveled to Egypt with me. I just left him a note and went. I knew that God would be with me, whatever the outcome. I thank him now for the way this has worked out. O give thanks unto the Lord for he is gracious, for his mercy endureth forever."

"So you are a lover of the psalms, too." Apion went on with tearful eyes. "You know, Justin, Juliana loves the Psalms. She would often sing them to me. And in the last few months, while I have been in such confusion and turmoil, I would recall the words of a psalm, and remember hearing them in her glorious voice, and that was an anchor for me throughout all my times of uncertainty and pain. It was remembering her singing of the Psalms that made me begin to question the wisdom of my joining the Gnostics. O, mind you, I find much of what they say appealing still. But on remembering the reality and the beauty of the psalms, and how much they were at the heart of the church's worship, and not so much so among the Valentinians, at least these ones, I began to re-think. And then I saw you, and you mentioned her name. At that moment I knew I must leave, and this was my opportunity to do so."

The genuineness of Apion was very striking, and Justin was grateful to him for making plain how things stood, even if he felt he knew more than he ought to. Apion continued,

"So will you tell her that you love her?"

319

Justin could hardly believe that the question had been put so bluntly. But it was overdue. From the moment Justin had left for the Fayum, it was inevitable that he would. No, he thought, it was from the moment he had arrived in Alexandria. But even this seemed wrong. He now knew that even from the moment he had met her in the house of his beloved Bishop Eleutherus, something had begun that was about to come to fruition.

"Eleutherus," Justin said aloud.

"What was that?" asked Apion.

"Oh, nothing," replied Justin. "Yes, I will tell her how I feel. And when I have, I shall return to Rome and lay my plan and proposal before my beloved Bishop Eleutherus."

CHAPTER 66

Clement heard a loud knock on his door. As he opened it part way he saw a tired and weary traveler.

"Justin!" he exclaimed, and he called out, "Marcus, Justin has returned."

As the door opened fully, Clement saw the other figure.

"Apion!" He said yet more loudly, and then stood in stunned silence. Justin enjoyed the moment, knowing he had performed a minor miracle in rendering Clement speechless. Then Marcus arrived, and Justin said,

"Marcus, may I introduce Apion."

"Come in," both men said at the same time. Marcus carried on, "My brother, you are safe! and I am very pleased to see you have brought Apion with you. Juliana will be beside herself with joy."

Clement chimed in, "Come in and wash, refresh yourself, and then tell us of your travels. Oh, Apion, it is so good to see you again. I understand that you have been in the House of Valentine?"

"I have," replied Apion, "But with the help of my Roman brother Justin, I have returned, and I am pleased to be back."

Much time was spent recounting the tale, during which it became clear that the appeal of Gnosticism, though not of the brand of the House of Valentine, was still very strong for Apion:

"You see, I first began to think about *gnosis* when I met the most appealing teacher in this city. Heracleon was his name."

Marcus sat still, trying to hide his reaction.

"Heracleon taught me about the Pleroma and my need to become truly spiritual. It was through him that I met some people from the House of Valentine. As they described their life of an undistracted quest for gnosis in the desert, it began to appeal to me more and more. Heracleon had been explaining the story of Jesus and the woman of Samaria at the well. And when he came to the end of the story where it says, 'And they went out of the city,' he said, 'This means that they went out of their first way of life, which was worldly, and they came through faith to the savior.' I knew at once that I should leave the city, that I should abandon my old way of life, and should seek to be united with my pleroma. They offered me a welcome in the house of Valentine, and so I went. The only thing that gave me pause was the knowledge that it would hurt Juliana. Of course, I didn't think of my father."

His voice began to break, and his eyes water.

"But now that I have returned I shall have to take some time to think all this out. Now, however, I must go and see Juliana."

"She is away right now," said Marcus.

"Away?" asked both Apion and Justin impatiently.

"Yes, she has gone to Naucratis, to the birthplace of Pollux, where they are having a celebration for him before he departs for Athens." Marcus was glad to be able to recommend that Justin get Apion out of Alexandria.

"Athens?" inquired Apion. And then he added, "Pollux is an old mule!"

Clement chimed in, "Didn't Justin tell you that that old mule Pollux has been appointed Professor of Rhetoric at Athens? What *did* you talk about all the way down the Nile?"

"Mostly about me, and my wasted life," said Apion, "But also about God and life and love...and about Juliana."

Marcus caught Justin's eye, and without a word much was said.

And much more was said when they were at last alone together.

"Justin, you gave us all quite a scare. And when I got your note I went right away to tell Juliana. She was fearful indeed, knowing as we do how dangerous things are in the Fayum, and how uncertain life is for those who enter the House of Valentine. But she was deeply moved by your gesture, and spoke frankly about her feeling. I must let her tell her own story, but I suspect it will not disappoint you."

"Yes, and this is what Apion indicated to me," said Justin, "and you can imagine how encouraged I am." Then Justin's tone became more pensive, even solemn. "There were moments when I was in danger."

"Yes I know," said Marcus. "As soon as we heard the news of Zeno's death and of your arrest on suspicion of murder we left Oxyrhynchus for Tebtunis. But when we reached the vineyard of Apollonios, you had been freed and had just left that morning. We deemed that there was no catching you, so Juliana and I secretly entrusted you to the Lord, confident that, as you had indicated, he would be with you and keep you."

"Marcus, do you think I should go and find Juliana?" asked Justin a bit anxiously.

"Yes," said Marcus, "You must go to Naucratis, to the home of a certain scholar named Athenaeus, where the party is being held. You must take Apion with you, and you must not delay. The sight of the two of you together will be joy unspeakable to her."

Justin stood in silent thoughtfulness. Then he said to Marcus. "Thank you, my brother in Christ, for all your patience, and prayers. Thank you for putting up with me and the affair of my heart. Thank you for speaking on my behalf and for standing with me in prayer on my quest. I delight in the friendship we have in Christ."

"You know, Justin," said Marcus, "You know I prize friendship most highly, perhaps above all the gifts that God has given, and I count you my very dearest friend. So you can imagine that I was taken aback, even hurt slightly, when you left Oxyrhynchus without telling me, and left only a note. But then I chided myself for feeling this way. For I too have acted at times without telling you. Indeed I must share something with you now, something I have never told anyone. For several years in Rome I developed a close friendship with a leader among the Gnostics, who shared my love for the Gospel of St. John. We met once a week and had long conversations, and we both enjoyed the association. I was saddened when he left Rome, but I knew it was better, especially given the growing rift between the Gnostics and the church. But here in Alexandria, Justin, here in Alexandria I have run into him once more, and while we still have the same mutual respect, there is not the unity in the truth, which is the basis

323

of real friendship. However, I still admire him deeply. Justin, this man is the very leader of whom Apion spoke, Heracleon."

"Heracleon?" exclaimed Justin.

"It is true, Justin, and I ask your forgiveness for not telling you. It was my weakness not to have said anything about my friendship with Heracleon for these five years. But now I speak freely. For I know how vital it is to secure Apion's return to the church, and I know that I will no longer have close association with Heracleon, and I also count your friendship, and our openness with each other my chief delight."

"It is a delight to me as well," said Justin, "And so the Lord means for us to delight in friendship. For did not Jesus call his disciples friends, and confer on them thereby a special honor?"

"He did," replied Marcus," and in the Psalms we sing, "O how good and pleasant it is, when bretheren to dwell together in unity!"

"But there is even a more essential delight, and it is the key to all else in life." Justin's' voice was full of emotion, almost to the point of tears. "In the thirty-seventh Psalm David writes, "Delight in the Lord, and he will give you your heart's desire."

CHAPTER 67

"You have come to the ancient city of Naucratis, the great Egyptian center of Greek culture, which flourished before Alexander founded the new town in his honor!" The words spoken with strong local civic feeling were those of a young man who took pride in his name. Extending his hand to Justin and Apion, he went on. "I am Athenaeus..." But he was interrupted by another aged man who had left the party to greet the newcomers.

"New town indeed! Alexandria is the cultural capital of the world. My young friend Athenaeus has no sense of proportion. And he ought to know better, for he has spent much time in our library, the library made famous the world over through the munificence of Ptolemy Philadelphus and the scholarship of Zenodotus of Ephesus, Aristophanes of Byzantium and Aristarchus of Samothrace!" The old man then introduced himself. "I am Apollonius."

"Apollonius the Grumpy." added the young scholar.

"And we are Justin from Rome and Apion from Alexandria, in search of one Juliana, daughter of Demetrius of Alexandria and Oxyrhynchus. This is the party in honor of Pollux, is it not?"

"Yes, it is," replied Athenaeus, and then he continued, taking Justin by the arm, "So you are from Rome. Well, as soon as this feast is over I am going to move to Rome. If Pollux can go to Athens I can go to Rome. Tell me about Rome, the food and the wine, the districts and the libraries, the festivals and the philosophers."

"I would be glad to tell you what I know, sir," Justin replied, "but just now I am eager to see my friend Juliana."

Athenaeus continued undaunted, "I understand that goose-liver is much esteemed in Rome..."

"Ah yes, but I must..."

"And the fish, tell me about the fish. I understand that fish may be had in marvelous abundance, and is set forth in your banquets with great wealth of display."

"Please, now, if you don't mind..." said Justin.

"And the mussels," Athenaeus went on, "The mussels, are they really similar to the so-called Tellinae, as Aristophanes the grammarian says?"

Justin was growing impatient. He shifted from one foot to another, seeking to move past his host and into the room where he would find Juliana. But Athenaeus seized the corner of his garment:

"And tell me of the figs grown near Rome, which are held in esteem, the Chian and Livian figs..."

Justin muttered to himself, "The fruit of the Spirit is patience and self-control." He attempted to extract himself from the grip of his obsequious host. Apion actually slipped past the three and into the banqueting room. But for Justin there was no escape.

"And peacocks..." continued Athenaeus, now eagerly grasping Justin's elbow, and salivating as if he was contemplating some delicious meal. "Tell me of the peacocks. Are they really so numerous in Rome that even the poet Aristophanes has taken note of it in *The Soldier*, and does not Menodotus of Samos in his work on objects at the temple of the Samian Hera say that the peacocks are sacred to Hera? Why, it is a golden species, the beautiful, spectacular peacock. Indeed, it stands on the coins of Samos. Tell me, are peacocks really everywhere to be seen in the great city?"

"Yes indeed!" said Justin, unable to hide his frustration any longer. "And now, I *must* be after my friend. We have come in search of his cousin, Juliana, and I can be detained no longer."

Atheneus released Justin's arm, still chattering. As the scribe moved into the main hall, a further word chased after him, now with a shout: "You must tell me of the Saturnalia and the Bacchanalia!"

The bustle of the many guests and the smell of foods dazzled Justin for a moment. Then, across the room, he caught sight of Juliana and Apion slipping out the far door and into the garden, and deep in conversation. He waited, his heart racing, but his mind telling him he must not interrupt. The minutes seemed like hours.

At last he could wait no longer. He began to move through the crowd toward the garden.

"Did you find your friend?" came an affable shout from behind. It was Athenaeus. "Well, come meet the guest of honor, Julius Pollion of Naucratis."

"I have already met him," Justin shot back. But again his arm was seized, and it was off to meet Pollux.

"You know this man, I believe," shouted Athenaeus to Pollux.

"Justin," exclaimed the new Professor. "Justin, we hear that you have been off in the Fayum!" But before Pollux could say any more Athenaeus was chattering again:

"This man Justin is from Rome, and will tell me everything about the city that is soon to be my home."

"Yes indeed," said Pollux, "But you must not tax him."

"Just one more question about entertainment," said the host, who was not to be put off. "Tell me, if you would, is the Fanian law still enforced -- the law that ordained that not more than three persons outside the family should be entertained, except on market-days, when there may be not more than five. Now I understand that these last occur three times a month..."

Justin was not paying attention. But he deemed the delay to be God's provision, so that Apion and Juliana would have the full time needed to talk in private. Then it would be his turn. He stood in quiet confidence that the God who had been with him from the beginning was with him at this hour.

"Justin!" The voice of the approaching Apion told Justin that his moment had arrived. "Justin, Juliana would very much like to see you in the garden."

Athenaeus released his grip, Justin was through the doors and found the waiting Juliana. They stood in silence for a moment. Then Juliana spoke

"Justin, I am deeply grateful to you. But I never would have forgiven myself if you had not returned."

"And I never would have forgiven myself if I had not gone," said Justin, "Nor could I now leave Egypt without stating clearly what is on my heart. I love you very deeply, and long that you should be my wife, according to the ordinance of God. From the

327

day I met you until today, when I am standing before you, I have sensed a growing affection, and a deepening bond between us."

"And I have also," said the ever-confident, but tearful Juliana. "I have met many fine Christian men around the empire, and a number have come here to visit me. But none has touched my heart and challenged my mind like the Roman scribe who first stood firm for his church's way of reading St. Mark, and then listened to our way of translating, with sympathy and respect, and then risked his life in answer to the cry of my heart. We may always disagree about whose manuscripts are true to the Apostles. But we will never disagree about our love for each other. I will to be your wife, Justin, although, of course, I must first consult my father. He has always said that I should have it as I desire. But I will go to him straightaway and seek his blessing."

"And I must seek the blessing of my bishop. But if I know Eleutherus, he will be overjoyed. And just as he has adopted me as a son, he will welcome you as a daughter. But Juliana," continued Justin with a twinkle in his eye, "You may have to put up with a longer, less elegant Gospel of Mark.."

"And you with a shorter one, in more polished style." She replied.

As Rhoda observed at a distance the two friends offer each other a warm embrace, she thanked the God who answers prayer. And Justin and Juliana slipped discreetly back into the feast to rejoin Apion, and to toast to the honor of Pollux.

Now Justin actually welcomed the question from a familiar, gushing voice: "Tell me, how are leeks cooked in Rome?"

328

CHAPTER 68

It had not been an easy day for Demetrius, but he had tried to remain cheerful about it. The books in the shipping office would not balance, and nobody seemed to be able to find the error. The notice had come of yet another tax increase. Grain was late in arriving from his estate in the Fayum, and the ships would not be ready to sail when the sea -lanes opened. Several hands had fallen sick, and the winter months had meant the loss of three of the crew to other pursuits. One of the ships had begun to leak and another was overdue for major repairs. The money in Demetrius' coffers was still plentiful, but a few more years like this past one would change all that. There was a general nervous anxiety beginning to settle in for the whole business community of Alexandria.

About mid-day matters had been made much worse when a messenger burst into the shipping office and announced, "A ship in the harbor has just caught fire, dangerously close to one of our vessles loaded with grain."

Several panic-stricken workers ran to the dock, now crowded with spectators. In the middle of the harbor was a small craft engulfed in flames. The intense heat could be felt all the way to the shore. On the nearby grain-ship the crew battled nobly to put some distance between themselves and the inferno. Demetrius arrived at the quayside in time to see the exploding craft scatter burning debris perilously close to the boat that was his only hope for profit in the coming months. Then the fire died down and the crowd dispersed, with the exception of a small group of people standing around a large man who was making some declamation.

"Demetrius," called a voice, and the merchant turned to see James, Juliana's trusted servant. "Demetrius, I wish your health.

Juliana has returned from Naucratis and wishes to see you privately about a matter of great importance."

"Can it wait, James?" called back Demetrius in a voice full of frustration. But then he added. "No, I will come. The troubles here can wait. I cannot solve the problems by staying here, and if it is a matter of great importance to Juliana, then it calls for my attention now."

In the walled garden of their Alexandrian house Demetrius found his daughter sitting with an air of even greater confidence than usual. She rose to greet him:

"Father, I am so sorry to interrupt. I have just learned of all your troubles in the business, and of the dreadful fire, and I can wait."

"Have I not always told you, my beloved, that you are never in the way. You are life. Everything else is interruption!"

"Then I must tell you without delay, Father, that I have found the man I wish to marry."

"And why did you wait so long to tell me, my beloved. I have known that this was coming for some time. Is he not that fine Roman scribe? His heroic rescue of Apion is all the talk in the church. But that story is only the beginning of his virtues. He is a noble Christian man, and you have my blessing in your choice."

"But Father," she went on as she embraced him, "Father, it will mean that I must move to Rome, and leave you here alone." And then she repeated in tears, "Alone..."

"Now Juliana," Demetrius continued, "I am not alone, I am well looked after here, and I have enough problems to keep me busy. And, of course, I now have an excuse to visit Rome more often. More frequent visits from me may in fact aid the work here. Juliana I am truly joyful, and wish you and Justin joy. Is he here in the city? When may I greet him, and welcome him as a son of my own?"

"He is staying with Clement, but he is coming here to dinner with Marcus, his companion, and with Apion. Can you join us, Father? Please say that you can!"

"I may have to come late, but I will come. I would not miss it."

"Of course, Justin will have to ask his Bishop's permission, when he returns to Rome," said Juliana.

"If I judge Eleutherus aright," said Demetrius, "And in my business everything depends on one being a good judge of character. If I judge correctly, Eleutherus will give his enthusiastic support. Was it not he who first introduced you to Justin? He might as well have arranged the marriage himself! He struck me as a man of great sympathy and wisdom. You need not fear. But now, I must be back to the shipping house, or I will not be able to be at the great feast this evening."

Juliana sat in the garden, soaking in the afternoon sun. She thanked God for all his blessings. She thought of her mother, Anna, and wished that she could have been there with her to share these days. But she remembered that those who are asleep in Jesus are still one with the living, in a great fellowship of saints. Somehow she knew that her mother was rejoicing too. She opened her beautiful copy of St. Mark's Gospel, and began to read, in the place where Jesus quoted Genesis:

"But from the beginning of creation God made them male and female. For this reason a man shall leave his father and mother, and the two shall become one flesh. So they are no longer two but one flesh. What therefore God has joined together, let no man put asunder."

Juliana thought on these verses, and savored the memory of a delightful hour she had spent with Justin in the garden in Oxyrhynchus comparing their texts and debating who was right, for his copy of St. Mark had followed the fuller wording of Genesis, and read: "Therefore a man shall leave his father and mother and be joined to his wife, and the two shall become one flesh." She remembered playfully chiding him that some Roman copyist, probably by accident, had written in the extra line to conform to the way it read in Genesis, while in her heart secretly longing that it should in fact be what St. Mark wrote. After all, she not only loved the sentiment, she also loved the man who was reading it. She also loved the debate. And now she knew that as long as they both should live the debate, the banter, the game, the dance of love and thought and prayer and faith would go on. They would seek the true reading together.

331

That evening at the dinner Demetrius arrived sooner than expected. After greetings and toasts and prayers, the talk over a second glass of wine turned inevitably to the events of the day.

"I heard that you had quite a fright today, Demetrius," said Justin.

"Indeed I did, and the day would have been ruined had not my daughter sprung on me her glorious news. On top of accounting, tax and crew frustrations, we had a most horrific fire in the harbor. It nearly destroyed our one grain-laden vessel! When I returned to the shipping office, I learned that the burning craft had been set on fire by its captain! Fancy that. He claimed to be a Cynic philosopher, and was determined to burn his last possession in dramatic declamation of his belief. They say he burned it by using the old method of Archimedes. With the help of students, holding a series of mirrors, he concentrated the sunshine on his craft until it went up in flames! Now I try always to respect a man's religion and philosophy. But is this not a little absurd?"

Justin looked at Marcus, and they both, without a word, decided that this was not the time to tell the full story of Aulynchus.

CHAPTER 69

Justin and Marcus were sad to leave the house of Clement. The learned and affable young scholar who had become a dear friend gave promise of being the most knowledgable man in all the church. As a parting gift he gave to the Romans a copy of the Gospel according to St. Luke, which had recently been copied in the Alexandrian Scriptorium.

Others had arrived at the dock to wish the scribes farewell. Leonidas had come with his little son, already showing signs of being precocious. Apion was there to extract a promise that Justin and Marcus would return, and to hear the offer of a warm welcome whenever he could come to Rome. The scribes then boarded the grain ship of Demetrius, together with its owner and his daughter, who would also make the journey to Rome. The bustle at the dockside was interrupted by a loud shout. It was Nicholas of Sparta, who had just run down the Nile from Ethiopia, with letters for the Church at Rome. He was welcomed on board, and preparations were made to head out to sea.

Justin and Juliana stood together on the deck talking of many things. Then they sat and Justin opened the codex of St. Luke. He was quite prepared to find a text different from his own, but he was eagerly looking forward to thinking out the puzzle with his beloved Juliana. To him it was clear that each variation had its own story to tell. He leafed through to the very end of the Gospel of St. Luke. What he saw raised fresh questions, and promised many more conversations. At the very end, the book read:

"And he led them out as far as Bethany, and lifted up his hands and blessed them. While he blessed them, he departed from them, and was carried up into heaven. And they worshipped him. And they returned to Jerusalem with great joy, and were continually in the temple blessing God."

333

The words jumped off the page at him. For he knew that his copies lacked the expression "And he was carried into heaven," and the phrase "And they worshipped him." Some time he knew that he and Juliana would think through this difference together. But this was not the time. He stared at the text of St. Luke. In his heart he hoped that these words were what St. Luke wrote. He knew that his church, and especially his father, had been scrupulous and faithful in the transmission of the text of the gospels. But this text at this place in this Alexandrian manuscript might be right!

"We do not read these wonderful phrases," said Justin, and then he silently chided himself for having said it. But there was no need to chide. Juliana loved the debate, and welcomed it.

"You don't read them?" she said with a playful gleam in her eye. "But they are in all our copies, and all the best copies I have seen around the empire."

"When we get to Rome," said Justin, "we shall have to think this out. Perhaps there will be some other places in St. Luke where our manuscripts differ, and which may help us sort out this mystery."

A loud whistle interrupted the talk. Then a shout was heard from the dockside. It was a herald with some awful tidings: "We have just heard the news. The Emperor Marcus Aurelius has died, and his son Commodus reigns in his stead!"

What followed was general panic on the dockside, and among the crew. Marcus Aurelius was learned, philosophical, a true Stoic. Commodus could not be counted on for the same degree of cultured and refined humanity. Oh, it was true, he had had the best teachers, Pollux being among them, but he was not so much a man of ideals. He was a man of baser feeling, and capable of cruder actions. Marcus Aurelius had allowed some persecution of the church, but generally was restrained. There was no telling what Commodus might do.

"The Emperor dead? Commodus reigning in his stead? Disaster!" Nicholas of Sparta spoke the feeling of all on the ship. He went on: "Why, Commodus is a mere boy. He cannot be more than eighteen. Oh, in physique he struts around like a god, and certainly looks more god-like than his father. He affects the style of some sun-god or some sun-king from the east. He walks

334

through the camp with gold-dust in his hair; he competes successfully with gladiators in the arena. He transfixes ostriches, running at full speed, with specially designed arrows. He is not much of an administrator or a military officer, and will leave all that to others. He already has over three hundred selected women in his harem, and he loves games and parties. They say one of his ladies may be a Christian, but who knows how it will fare for us? Maybe less persecution because he is lazy and cares little for his father's sense of civic duty; maybe more because he is capricious and unprincipled."

Justin interjected. "Nicholas, we can only trust God, and remind ourselves of the Psalm which says, "Be strong in the Lord, and he shall comfort your heart; and put your trust in the Lord."

As preparations were made to weigh anchor, those on deck went below to stow their belongings and prepare for dinner. Finally only Marcus and Juliana were left on deck, looking out over the city in the early evening light.

"Marcus, you have been a splendid friend, not only to Justin, but also to me." The voice of Juliana was full of sincerity. "And I do trust that in time, perhaps soon, God will reward you with the same joy that Justin and I know."

"Ah yes," said Marcus with a sigh, "Perhaps...Perhaps." He was silent for a moment. Then he added. "But Juliana, did not St. Paul write to the Corinthians that it was best to remain single, especially if one is to be fully engaged in the Lord's work, and that "In view of the present crisis, it is well for you to remain as you are?"

"But Marcus," answered Juliana. Then she almost said, "You mean, of course, this *impending* crisis." This was the way, based on classical usage, that she was accustomed to translating the phrase in St. Paul. But this was not the moment for talk of readings and translations and interpretations. There would be plenty of time for all that. So she said instead, "But Marcus, do you not recall the word of the God at creation? Did he not say, 'It is not right for man to be alone.'? And is not this his normal intent for all his people? Oh Marcus, do not close yourself off to this splendid gift, if it is God's gift to you. And Marcus, did St. Paul not also write to the Ephesians as well as the Corinthians? Did he not tell them that God is able to accomplish abundantly far more than all we can ask or think?"

Marcus stood silent for a moment, gazing at the city, where a few lamps had begun to give their light. "Yes," he replied, "And, Juliana, with you as my near neighbor, I shall probably be regularly challenged to think."

"Indeed," said Juliana, "You might even be provoked to ask!"

CHAPTER 70

Almost all the lights were lit in the city of Alexandria as the large grain ship weighed anchor and headed out of the harbor. Justin was alone on the deck, staring first at the city, and then out into the sea. He looked up into the sky, studded with the lights that the Lord had put on for the night. He looked down into the water, over whose rippled waves danced the reflection of the city lights and the beacon lights of the great lighthouse.

Justin had remembered this remarkable lighthouse when he had entered the harbor, all storm-drenched and weary from his journey four months ago. He stared at the edifice, one of the wonders of the world, a thing at once of beauty and utility. He thought of all that he had seen and done and felt since he had last seen that light. There was the scriptorium at Alexandria, with its strange yet wonderful vision of sharing the good news with the cultured. There was the circle of scholars at Oxyrhynchus, where Juliana was standing for the truth of Christ among her pagan friends. There was the rowdy, mysterious, dangerous alluring life of the Nile and the Fayum. There was Zeno (poor Zeno) there was Ninnaros, there was Heron. Then he thought of the storming of the House of Valentine, and of the rescue and return of Apion. Above all there was the steady advance of a deep love and friendship with Juliana, which would now be theirs as long as they lived.

But what would become of them all in years to come? Would they see Clement again? Would Apion stay with the church? Justin was glad that Juliana's cousin had found lodging with Clement. Would Aulynchus still be declaiming his Cynic views when they were next in Alexandria? Would the churches stay in close communication, still compare texts and ideas, and still stand for the truth, or would some begin to lean more toward the Gnostics or the Montanists or the Encritites? Would he and Marcus and Juliana and Rufus and their friends continue to copy their sacred scriptures unhindered? Or would a fresh wave of persecution under Commodus force them underground, or even threaten the very life of the church? To all these questions Justin could give no certain answer, but he knew that whatever came, God would be with them. He remembered the words of Jesus at the end of St. Matthew's Gospel, "Lo, I am with you always, till the end of the age."

The lighthouse was now behind them, and its brilliant beam began to be more faint. The night had fallen, and the stars were a sure guide to the mariners on the great grain ship. As Justin strained to see the last flecks of Alexandrian light, Juliana slipped up behind him and took his hand. Neither said anything for a moment. Then Justin sang the words of a Psalm to a haunting tune:

"For with thee is the well of life;
And in thy light shall we see light."

NOTES:

These notes are intended to offer the reader the opportunity to follow up the historical details in both scholarly and popular studies of the late Second Century church and empire. This book is written with the conviction that God both inspired the New Testament writings and guided the process of their transmission. My own technical research on the New Testament text has led to an ever-increasing confidence in its trustworthiness and reliability. What the apostles wrote is basically what we read in our modern critical editions of the Greek New Testament

Abbreviations:

ANF: Ante-Nicene Fathers
ANT: J.K.Elliott, *The Apocryphal New Testament,* (Oxford, 1993)
BMM: Bruce M. Metzger, *The Text of the New Testament*, 3rd ed. (Oxford, 1992).
BMMT: B.M.Metzger, *A Textual Commentary on the Greek New Testament* (New York, 1994)
C: Philip Carrington, *The Early Christian Church,* (Cambridge, 1957) Volume 2. "The Second Century": A learned and enjoyable account of the Second Century Church.
DCB: *Dictionary of Christian Biography,* Smith and Wace, eds, (1877-1887) Older, but full of useful details and sound judgments.
E: Eusebius, *The History of the Church,* G.A. Williamson, (Penguin, 1965) an indispensable resource.
EEC: *Encyclopedia of Early Christianity*, ed. Everett Ferguson, 2nd. ed. 1997.
LCL: *The Loeb Classical Library.*
OCD: *Oxford Classical Dictionary*, 3rd edition (Oxford, 1997)
ODCC: *Oxford Dictionary of the Christian Church* F.L.Cross and

E.A.Livingstone. The standard reference tool in church history (3rd. ed., Oxford, 1997)

P.Oxy: *Oxyrhynchus Papyri*, B.P.Grenfell and A.S.Hunt,eds. 66 Vols.

(Egypt Exploration Fund, 1898-present).

P. Yale: *Yale Papyri in the Beineke Rare Book and Manuscript Library*, Volume I, eds. J.F.Oates, A.E. Samuel, and C.B.Wells, ((New Haven, 1967). Vol II ed. S.A.Stephens (Chicho, 1985).

Chapter 1: Irenaeus was the Bishop of Lyons in Gaul from 178 until about 200 A.D. He wrote an important book called *Against Heresies* (Hereafter A.H.) On the persecution in Gaul see E.p.199ff. The Psalm is 44:22. Valentinian Gnostics: followers of Valentinus. (EEC p.1155) "Codex" is a term for a book, as opposed to a scroll.(EEC p.267).

Chapter 2 : Oxyrhynchus was a city 250 miles south of Alexandria in the Nile valley. Here the rubbish mounds, built on dry sands, have preserved thousands of ancient manuscripts (Biblical, classical, documentary) many from the late second century.(EEC p.842). On women in Egypt in general see J. Rowlandson, *Women and Society in Greek and Roman Egypt, a sourcebook* (Cambridge, 1998). For the existence of women scribes in the Second Century church I am indebted to a paper by Kim Haines-Eitzen, given at the Society of Biblical Literature in 1996, a copy of which she kindly sent to me. Juliana quotes Mark 4:31. For women in the early church see the recent fascinating study by Rodney Stark, *The Rise of Christianity*, (Princeton, 1996) pp. 95-128. On Abortion see M. Gorman, *Abortion in the Early Church* (Downers Grove, 1992). On exposure of infants, especially women, see Stark, op.cit. p.97, who cites Papyrus P. Oxy IV 744(1st Century B.C.). "If you are delivered of a child…if it is a boy, keep it…if a girl discard it." The picture is not improved if the offspring is from a slave mother (see Stephanie West in ZPE, 121(1998) pp.167-172)). On the revolt in Egypt see *Cambridge Ancient History* (Cambridge, 1936) p.649ff.

Chapter 3: On Eleutherus see C. pp.254, 264. Carrington gives a beautiful portrait of this man who was Bishop of Rome from 174-189. See also DCB 2. pp.79-81. On Marcion see E. IV.11, p.163ff. (EEC p.715) The gospel codex opens to Mark 10:45.

Chapter 4.: For the various different heretical movements see B.D. Ehrman, *The Orthodox Corruption of Biblical Texts* (Oxford, 1993). On copy tables: Scribes in the early church normally used lap boards, See H.Y.Gamble, *Books and Readers in the Early Church*, (New Haven, 1995) p.90. In our story Romans use desks, Alexandrians lap boards.

Chapter 5: A good introduction to New Testament textual research is Bruce M. Metzger, *The Text of the New Testament, its Transmission, Corruption and Restoration*, Third Enlarged Edition (Oxford, 1992). This is the best introduction to this field of study. Fuller and more technical discussion of particular variations may be found in B.M.Metzger, *A Textual Commentary on the Greek New Testament* (BMMT) (New York, 1994). This is a companion to the fourth edition of the United Bible Societies Greek New Testament, which I use together with the 27th edition of the Nestle/Aland Greek New Testament. For Mark 1:1 see BMMT pp. 62. On Mark 16:9-20 see BMM p.226ff. On the eagle and the lion see Irenaeus, *Against Heresies*, II.11.8(ANF Vol.1,p.428).

Chapter 6: The texts are Psalm 7:1; Romans 8:34. For the variations of text, and possible motives see B.D.Ehrman, *op.cit.*, pp.151-152 and my own criticism of Ehrman's approach "Did The Orthodox Scribes Corrupt Holy Scripture?" forthcoming. I argue that we find evidence in the text of Irenaeus of a scrupulous fidelity to the text as he received it.
"My God, My God... Psalm 22:1 is quoted in Mark 15:34

Chapter 7: The Bibleothecae Ulpiae is described in J. Carcopino, *Daily Life in Ancient Rome* (New Haven, 1940) p.4.
Chapter 8: On Montanism see ODCC. E. 5.16ff. EEC pp.778-80. On Mark 7:6 see BMMT. p.94 (The first edition of

341

this volume, 1973). In Codex Bezae Cantabrigiensis, the great fifth century Greek/Latin manuscript of the Gospels and Acts, the Greek reads "love," the Latin column reads "honor." Keep your eye on this variation. We will meet it again in this story.

Chapter 9: On the variation at Luke 3:22 see BMMT p.112. "This day have I begotten thee" is the reading of Diognetus, Justin Martyr (Dialogue with Trypho 88) and a number of early Christian writers. Rufus quotes St. Paul at 1 Tim.2:12, Juliana cites Ephesians 4:15.

Chapter 10: For the worship of the Roman congregation in the mid-Second Century see Justin Martyr, *Apology*, 1. 67. The old Western order of the gospeles was Matthew, John, Luke, Mark. Juliana quotes Psalm 39:1

Chapter 11: On the Mithra cult, popular among soldiers, see EEC pp. 762, 790. On Christians in the army, and particularly the "Thundering legion" see C Vol 2 pp.224-6.

Chapter 12: Mark 12:36 = Psa. 110:1 See BMMT (First Edition, 1975)p.111 . On nectar, the drink of the gods, see the early Third Century writer Athenaeus *The Deipnosophistai*, II . 39. LCL (Vol 1) pp.168-169. On Idols Juliana cites 1 Cor.8:4.

Chapter 13: On *areskeia*, Col. 1:10, see H.C.G. Moule, *Colossian Studies* (London,1898)p.60, Moule speaks of a service that "has almost hidden authority away in friendship." On Christians and Jews in Egypt see EEC pp.363-366, and especially the works in the bibleography by B.Pearson. "Now the birth of Jesus Christ..." is Matthew 1:18.

Chapter 14: On the improvement of the style in in the Greek New Testament text see the studies of C.H.Turner and G.D.Kilpatrick edited by Keith Elliott in *Language and Style in the Gospel of Mark* (Leiden, 1993). The main thrust of these essays is accepted in the course of our narrative and is especially illustrated in the last part on Egypt. For Psalm 22:1 at Mark 15:34 see

BMMT p.99-100. Justin quotes Psalm 119:31. The variations discussed by the scribes are at Mark 2:1-2. On these stylistic features see C.H.Turner, *St. Mark* (London, 1930) p.52. St. Mark uses "immediately" in the same way many today pepper sentances with "like" and "you know."

Chapter 15: Marcus quotes Isaiah 53:6, Justin quotes Psa. 84:11-12.

Chapter 16: For Florinus see ANF I, p.568. For the Gnostic Myth in its variety see B. Layton, *The Gnostic Scriptures* (Garden City, 1987). The passages quoted are on pp. 105 and 118.

Chapter 17: Psalm 119:49-50; Matthew 7:15-16. The "prophecy" of Sophia is found in E. Pagels *The Gnostic Gospels* (New York, 1981) p. 66, A valuable introduction to Gnosticism in general, despite the polemical slant. Vesuvius was the volcano that erupted in 79 A.D, inundating Pompeii and Herculaneum in S. Italy. For Irenaeus' Letter to Florinus see ANF I p.568. The debate between Rufus and Florinus was on John 1:13 See BMMT p.168. See also Bart D. Ehrman, op.cit. pp. 26-27, 59. Despite Ehrman's weighty presentation, there is no evidence of official church sanction of the alteration of scripture texts among the Orthodox. Some zealous copyists may have made changes for doctrinal "improvement" in their private copies. See my comment in *Novum Testamentum*, XXXIX (1997) p.90.

Chapter 18: The raising of Jairus' daughter is at Mark 5:21-43 and Luke 8: 41-56, cf. Matt. 9:18-26. Codex Bezae and a number of Old Latin manuscripts omit the name Jairus in Mark (D a e ff i r1).

Chapter 19: For times and methods of travel see Lionel Casson, *Travel in the Ancient World* (London, 1974). For book production see H.Y.Gamble, *Books and Readers in the Early Church* (New Haven, 1995). On communication in the Empire of the New Testament era see M.Thompson, "The Holy Internet" in

R. Bauckham, *The Gospel for All Christians* (Grand Rapids, 1998) pp.49-70. Albinus quotes from Virgil, *Georgics,* 2: 184-190.

Chapter 20: Albinus quotes Virgil, *Georgics,* II, 152-155, tr. by John Dryden. Psalm 62:1-2.

Chapter 21: For Puteoli see OCD p.1280. St. Paul came to Italy through this port (Acts 28:13) on an Alexandrian freighter.

Chapter 22: The passages are Virgil, *Georgics,* 1: 438, Psa. 107: 23-31, Virgil, *Aeneid* 1. 142, Mark6:50. Cyrus: Isa. 45

Chapter 23: For ships of the Mediterranean see W.W.Mooney, *Travel among the Ancient Romans (Boston, 1920)* pp.143-148. Albinus quotes Virgil *Georgics* 4.195. For the port of Lechaeum see OCD on Corinth.

Chapter 24: For Corinth see G.D.Fee, *The First Epistle to the Corinthians* (Grand Rapids, 1987)pp.1-15. E. 4.23(EEC p.290). Albinus quotes Virgil, *Aeneid,* III. 56. Mark 1: 41

Chapter 25: For Dionysius of Corinth see C. pp.197-200. E. 4.23. DCB 1. 849-850.

Chapter 26: Tatian was a founder of the Encritites (EEC p.370) and author of the Diatessaron (One narrative woven out of four gospels) C. p.207-212.

Chapter 27: Irenaeus on the four gospels see ANF I, p.428.

Chapter 28: On Athenagoras see C. 239-241. EEC p.140. For his writings see ANF 2, pp.123-162, see Chapter VI of "A Plea for the Christians" pp.131-132. Isaiah 44:6, Isaiah 46:1, Psa.115:3-4. on "Absurdities of the heathen gods," Athengoras, "Plea" Ch XX ANF 2, pp.138-139.

Chapter 29: On readings characteristic of Tatian and the Encritites see B.M.Metzger, *The Early Versions of the New Testament* (Oxford, 1977) pp.34-35. My view of the beginning of

Gospel harmonies follows that of F.C.Burkitt *Cambridge Ancient History*, XII (1939) pp.493-495. Marcus quotes Psa.69:22.

Chapter 30: On God as musician see Athenagoras, *Plea,* XVI, ANF 2, p.136. On Theophilus of Antioch see C. 212-214. E. 4. 20,24 On Quadratus see E.4.23 , On Pinytus of Cnossus in Crete see E. 4, 23.

Chapter 31: For trade and piracy see F.Meijer, *A History of Seafaring in the Classical World* (New York, 1986) pp.187-195.
"My power, My power...etc." is the wording of the cry of Jesus on the cross in the apocryphal "Gospel of Peter" see ANT, p.155 (see notes on Chapter 63) Justin quotes Psalm 27:1. Caesar's capture is found in Plutarch, LCL VII, pp.444-447. Marcus quotes Gen. 50:20 and Rom.8:28. Justin quotes Mark 9:24.

Chapter 32: On the Cynics and Diogenes Laertes see OCD and the helpful article by Abraham Malherbe in the *Interpreters Dictionary of the Bible*, 1st ed. For Peregrinus see Lucian LCL Vol.5, pp.1-51, and OCD. Aulynchus quotes a version of Matt. 10:28, that has lost a line. Some scribe's eye will have moved accidently from the first "fear" to the second, omitting the intervening words. This is called homoeoteleuton. It happened a lot in ancient copying. See A.C.Clark, *The Descent of Manuscripts* (Oxford, 1912) for fascinating examples in the best manuscripts. Examples of this omission by similar line ending in the principal uncial manuscripts of the New Testament are found in that same author's *The Primitive Text of the Gospels and Acts* (Oxford, 1914). The "old saying" is Deut. 21:23 (= Gal.3:13).

Chapter 33: On the church in Crete, and Bishop Pinytus of Cnossus, see E. 4, 21, 233 (pp.181, 184) EEC p.302.

Chapter 34: The passage quoted by Justin is John 7:53-8:11, a famous textual crux. Some early manuscripts of John omit it, and others put it in another place, while still others place it in Luke. For discussion see BMMT pp.187-189. It is found in some early "Western" witnesses. I take it to be not by John, but rather a floating piece of genuine Apostolic tradition, which was attached from earliest times to the fourth gospel. Justin quotes Titus 1:12.

Chapter 35: See OCD for Selene. In myth she is the Greek moon-goddess who drives the moon chariot. An appropriate name for our ficticious character.

Chapter 36: Paul's speech to the Ephesian elders is found in Acts 20:17-38. Hegesippus was a collector of early church traditions, whose five notebooks were much used by Eusebius. See E 4.7, (p.160) On Polycrates see E 5.24.1 (pp.230-232). Victor was a North African leader who became Bishop of Rome in 189, upon the death of Eleutherus. "Father, Forgive them..." is Luke 23:34, which was known to Hegesippus and Justin Martyr, but is missing from some early manuscripts (P.75, B, D), see BMMT p.154. "God has not forsaken..." is Romans 11:2. On James the Just, a tradition that Eusebius found in Hegesippus, see E. 2.23.17 (p.101).

Chapter 37: The Psalms they sing are 114-118, Among those sung by pilgrims to the Passover. Julia's phrases from St. John's Gospel end with John 17:21. On the relationship of oral to written tradition see A.F.Walls. "Papias and the Oral Tradition" *Vigiliai Christiani* 21 (1967) pp.137-140.

Chapter 38: On the "New Prophecy, as Montanism was called, see ODCC, EEC p.778. and C.pp.139-144, 180-186. Justin dresses singing Psalm 31:1. Papuza in Phrygia was the city where Montanus set up the center of the New Prophecy. Tertullian, the great North African theologian of the late Second and early Third centuries, joined the Montanist movement around 208 A.D. For Tertullian as a young man see volume 2 of this series. *The Pelican and the Phoenix* or "Scribes in Africa."

Chapter 39: On the Synod in Hierapolis see DCB, vol. 1, p. 132. This was probably the first church synod of so large a scale. On the changes in Acts championed but not created by the Montanists see J. Rendell Harris, *Codex Bezae* (Cambridge, 1891) pp.148-153. For Priscilla and Aquila, and the textual variant at Acts 18:26 see BMMT p.413. Melito's prophecy is from his "Homily on the Passion" published in 1940. This section is quoted from M. Green, *Evangelism in the Early Church* (London,1970) pp. 201-202. On the Thecla cult see ODCC. and S. Davis *The Cult of St. Thecla, Apostle and Protomartyr, A Tradition of Women's Piety in Late Antiquity,* Yale PhD Thesis, 1998, Forthcoming.

Chapter 40: On Pergamum see OCD. On the letter to Pergamum, Rev. 2:12-17. Albinus quotes Virgil *Aeneid* II, 290-295. Justin replies with Hebrews 13:14. On Galen's view of Christianity see R. Wilken, *The Christians as the Romans Saw Them* (New Haven, 1984) pp.68-93.

Chapter 41: The *Attic Nights* of Aulus Gellius is LCL Book II, p.228-229. The name "Cynic" comes from the Greek word for dog. For the "Gospel of Thomas," the best known apocryphal Gospel, written in the Second Century, see ANT pp.123-147. The sayings quoted are 71 and 114. For Jesus as a Cynic see J.D.Crossan, *Jesus, A Revolutionary Biography* (San Francisco, 1989) pp.114-121. For the fine reply that shaped this chapter see N.T.Wright, *Jesus and the Victory of God* (Minneapolis, 1995) p 73. Wright mused, "If we can imagine for a moment a genuine Cynic being presented with a copy of *Thomas*, it does not take much thought to envision him responding with a fairly caustic put-down," pp.73-74.

Chapter 42: On Antioch see G.Downey, *A History of Antioch in Syria from Seleucus to the Arab Conquest* (Princeton,1961). Theophilus of Antioch see C. 212-214. EEC p.1122. The Bishop's banquet is patterned on a middle Eastern feast as described to the author by several who have attended them. For Theophilus see R.M. Grant, *Ad Autolycum* (Oxford, 1970). An excellent introduction to the riches of early Eastern Christianity and its biblical text and interpretation (Syriac, Arabic) is Kenneth E. Bailey, *Finding the Lost* (St. Louis, 1992) This book gives penetrating insight into the parables of Luke 15 (Prodigal son, etc.) A must-read , and not just for scholars!

Chapter 43: For Bardaisan see the article in DCB by F.J.A.Hort (A dated but splendid piece of scholarship!) The hymn is my own composition, built up from phrases attributed to Bardaisan. On the Good Shepherd see Luke 15:1-7 and 1 Peter 2:25. Serapion became Bishop of Antioch in A.D. 199. see E. 6.12, pp. 251-252. Berytus is modern Beirut in Lebanon. On the Hebrew Matthew see E. 5.8 (p.210). The Rabbinic saying is in the Talmud: see Soncino *Talmud, Nezikin* III, p. 238. Theophilus' questions are from *Ad Autolycum* 3,2, ANF Vol. 2 pp.111, 98.

Chapter 44: Justin quotes Isa. 42:5. On the punctuation of John 1:3-4 see BMMT pp.167-168.

Chapter 45: On Caesarea see OCD and ODCC (EEC p.199). In Matthew 13:35 the attribution of the Psalm to Asaph and the addition "of the world" are fascinating. For both see BMMT pp.27-28. Marcus sang Psa. 27:1. Bardaisan's phrase is from his *Book of the Laws of Countries*, quoted by Hort in DCB Vol 1. p. 257.

Chapter 46: On Alexandria see OCD and EEC pp.30-34.. On the reading "to be the Christ" at Mark 1:34 (parallel Luke 4:41) see B.D.Ehrman, op.cit. (Oxford, 1993) pp.159, 179 n.183. Marcus quotes James 3:8.

Chapter 47: On the Alexandrian Catechetical School see ODCC. Nicholas quotes Hab.2:2-4. On the reading "my faith" in Heb.10:38 (= Hab.2:4) BMMT p.601. Dionysius' letter to the Spartans is cited by E. 4.23 (p.183). This may be the first use of the word "Orthodox." On women scribes see paper by Kim Haines-Eitzen, (Notes on Chapter 2).

Chapter 48: For the early Alexandrian type of manuscript see P.W.Comfort, *The Quest for the Original Text* (Grand Rapids, 1992). On Clement of Alexandria, one of the greatest figures of the late Second and Early Third Century Church, see ODCC and C. p.273 (EEC pp.262-264). A Greek fragment of Irenaeus *Against Heresies*, dating from the late Second Century, has been found in Oxyrhynchus (P. Oxy 405). On Marcus the Magician see ANF I p.334. For Irenaeus' description of the Gnostic Myth see Irenaeus A.H. 1.29.1, ANF I p.353. B. Layton, *The Gnostic Scriptures* (Garden City, 1987) gives a sympathetic and fair introduction to Gnosticism. For a recent "evangelical" assessment see E.M. Yamauchi's article in *New Dictionary of Theology* (Downers Grove, 1988) pp.272-274.

Chapter 49: The unnamed student quotes Matt. 7:29. Pantaenus' exposition of Psa 19:5 is found in DCB p.Vol.4, p.183. On Pantaenus' use of the Hebrew Matthew in India see E.5.10.3 (p.213). Justin's *Dialogue with Trypho,* is found in ANF I pp.194-270. Sect. 126 is on p. 262.

Chapter 50: Leonidas was absent due to the birth of his son Origen, the future theologian and biblical scholar (see ODCC). The story of the wooden horse is found in Homer's *Odyssey,* 4,271-289; 8,492-520. The copying begins at John 1:34. For my view that all the variant readings are original, and that each dropped out for different reasons in different copies see Kathryn Greene-McCreight and Christopher Seitz, *Theological Exegesis, Essays Honoring Brevard Childs* (Grand Rapids, 1998) pp.300-308. On the influence of Atticism on the text of the Greek New Testament see G.D. Kilpatrick, *The Principles and Practice of New Testament Textual Criticism* (Leuven, 1990) pp.15-73. G.D. Kilpatrick was my supervisor at Oxford from 1974-1978. See also S. Swain, *Hellenism and Empire* (Oxford, 1996).

Chapter 51: Justin's codex was an early Alexandrian type like our papyri, P66 and P75. The variant reading "the prophet" is found in some manuscripts of John 7: 52. On the long passage, John 7:53-8:11 see the notes on Chapter 34. On the punctuation and text of John 1:3-4 see BMMT p.167. On Heracleon see ODCC. The "House of Valentine," though a literary invention, is probably the sort of community that was developing among

Gnostics in rural Egypt. The hunger for community eventually found its expression. Nag Hammadi among the Gnostics and the Pacomian monastic communities among the Orthodox are clear examples of a later date.

Chapter 52: For Heracleon, who is quoted extensively by Origen, see Werner Foerster, *Gnosis* (Vol.1) tr. R. McL Wilson, (Oxford, 1972) pp.162-183. Selections for this chapter are taken from pp.168-171.

Chapter 53: Details of the boat are found in P. Merton 19, a record of its sale to Diodorus on 31 March, A.D. 173. H.I Bell and C.H.Roberts, *A Descriptive Catalogue of the Greek Papyri in the Collection of Wilfred Merton, F.S.A.* (Vol I, London, 1948) pp.78-79. The passage from Pliny's *Natural History* is found in the LCL Book XIII. 22ff. On papyrus see Naphtali Lewis, *Papyrus in Classical Antiquity* (Oxford, 1974).

Chapter 54: For wine see Pliny's *Natural History*, Book XIV, LCL, pp.235-245. The "Scribes and Scholars of Oxyrhynchus" are mentioned in Oxyrhynchus Papyrus 2192. A summary and bibliography are found in E.G.Turner, *Greek Papyri* (Oxford, 1980) pp. 86-87.

Chapter 55: See E. G. Turner, "Roman Oxyrhynchus," in *Journal of Egyptian Archeology*,38(1952) pp78-93. For the *Chariton* mime see D.L.Page, *Greek Literary Papyri*, LCL, Vol 1, p.336. The three New Testament Manuscripts are P67, P52, and P90. On P67 see G. Stanton, *Gospel Truth* (Valley Forge, 1995) for the controversy. P52, the Rylands fragment (P. Ryl.457), a fragment of John 18 (c. A.D. 125) housed in the John Rylands Library in Manchester, England, is our earliest New Testament fragment. P90 (P. Oxy. 3523) from the late Second Century is in the Ashmolean Museum in Oxford.

Chapter 56: For the Ten Attic Orators see OCD. The views of Celsus are cited in R. Wilken, *The Christians as the Romans Saw Them* (New Haven, 1984) pp.96-97. Juliana quoted Philippians

4:8-9; Isaiah 46:1-4; 9-10. Clement of Alexandria, *Exhortation* 7, ANF Vol. 2, p. 192.

Chapter 57: Pollux, *Onomasticon*, IX, 32. ed. A. Bethe (Teubner, 1831) my own translation. The letter about books, c. A.D. 170 is P. Oxy 2192. The books, of which Second Century fragments remain, are:
1) Homer, *Iliad* 5, 578-586, P. Yale I 6 (P. Oxy 757).
2) Demosthenes, *On the False Embassy 58-65*, P. Yale I 22.
3) Pindar, P. Yale I 18, (P. Oxy 408).
4) Plato, *Republic* X, 607E-608A, P.Yale I 21 (P. Oxy 24).
5) Aristotle, *Protreptics* ,(P. Oxy 666).
6) Thucydides IV 38.5-40.2. P. Yale II 99.
7) Xenophon, *Cyropaedia,* I.6.3-11 (Codex, Dublin, P.Oxy 697.
8) Euripides, *Hypotheses* (P. Oxy 2457).
9) The Joke is P. Yale I 25.
10) Homer, *Iliad*, 24, 318-384, P.Yale II 96..
I have held and studied most these fragments. These very copies may have been owned, held and studied by Pollux, Harpocration and the others!

Chapter 58: Juliana quotes Romans 5:8. Sophocles' "Satyr play," *The Searchers*, P. Oxy 1174, was unknown until the discovery of this late Second Century Papyrus at Oxyrhynchus, published in 1912.
Justin quotes to himself Psalm 8:3-4.

Chapter 59: For the Fayum see the article in OCD and B.P.Grenfell, A.S.Hunt and D.G. Hogarth, *The Fayum Towns and their Papyri* (London, 1900).(=P.Fay.).

Chapter 60: The song of the boatman is found in D.L.Page, *Greek Literary Papyri*, Vol.1,LCL. pp.508-512. The books Apollonios shows are two first century copies of the Odyssey 7: 176-185 (P.Yale II 98) and 6: 286-300 (P.Fay. VII) For the name Ninneros see P.Fay. 224, p.303,

Chapter 61: For examples of Second Century arrest warrants in Egypt see P.Oxy. 2572-2576. Justin quotes Psa.27:1, Psa. 69:1, 1 Peter 4:15-16. On Mark 15:28, which I believe Mark wrote, see*Evangelical Quarterly*, LXI (1989) pp.81-84. On Mark 10:19 and the variations of text, the most penetrating discussion is C.H.Turner, *St. Mark*, in *A New Commentary on the Holy Scripture*, ed. C.Gore, etc. (London, 1930)pp.87-88.

Chapter 62: For the Homer,*Odyssey*, Book 6, found at Euhemeria, near Theadelphia see B.P.Crenfell, et.al. *The Fayum Towns and their Papyri*, pp.93-5 and Plate IV. The "gospel" Ninneros was reading is the "Egerton Papyrus 2" (c 150 A.D.) See ANT pp.37-40. On this and other "Apocryphal" gospels see the helpful article by R.J. Bauckham in *Dictionary of Jesus and the Gospels* (IVP, 1992)pp.286-291. The reading corresponding to Mark 7:6 (Isa.29:13) is uncertain in this papyrus. Editors give "honor" as the reading. But "love" would fit the space equally well, and I have conjectured it for the sake of the story. What do you think?

Chapter 63: Zacchaeus is found in Luke 19:1-10. Heron's gospel is "The Gospel of Peter," a second-century apocryphal work. see ANT pp. 150-158. For the assault of the pig-merchants see P.Fay. 108 (B.P.Crenfell, et. al. op.cit. p.259).

Chapter 64: The House of Valentine is my own invention, but for the existence of such mazes in Egypt see notes to Chapter 65. Justin reads Irenaeus A.H. 3.11.19. see B. Layton, *The Gnostic Scriptures* (Garden City, 1987) pp.325-353 for "the Gospel of Philip."pp. 23-51 for "The Secret Book According to John."

Chapter 65: For the Labyrinth see A.B. Lloyd, *Herodotus Book II,* Commentary in 3 vols. (Leiden, 1988) Vol 3 pp. 120-123. Justin quotes Psalm 136:1 for the scarsity of Psalms references in the Gnostic writings see B. Layton, op.cit. p.322..

Chapter 66: For Heracleon on John 4 see W. Foester *Gnosis* (Oxford, 1972) pp. 162-183. On Naucratis, an old Greek colony and cultural center predating Alexandria, see OCD. On Athenaeus see OCD and the seven volumes of his *Sophists at Dinner* in LCL, edited by C.B. Gulick. Marcus quotes Psa 133:1, Justin cites Psa. 37:4.

Chapter 67:.Athenaeus wrote a long dialogue entitled *Deipnosophistai*, or *Sophists at Dinner*, a sort of early third-century "Galloping Gourmet." It is still extant, and the seven volumes in the Loeb Classical Library cover all sorts of subjects, quote hundreds of ancient authors, and give a picture of life in Rome in the late-second, early-third century. In our tale Athenaeus is just beginning to collect his material. The references in this chapter are to 1)Goose Liver Vol. 4 p.237 2) Fish, Vol.3 p.11. 3) Mussels, Vol 1. p.369. 4)Figs Vol.1. p. 327 5) Peacocks Vol 7. pp.11-13 6) Saturnalia and Bacchanalia, Vol.6, p.449. 7) The Fannian Law, Vol 3, p.233. Apollonius the Grumpy (Dyscolus) a Gramarian from Alexandria, who flourished in mid-second century, would by this time be a very old man. The date of his death is uncertain, so we have kept him alive for this party. He wrote obstruse gramatical treatises, bits of which survive in later anthologies.

Chapter 68: On the variation at Mark 10:7 see BMMT p.88. On Archimedes' method of burning the ship with mirrors see *New York Times*, Oct. 27, 1998, p.F 5.

Chapter 69: Leonidas' precocious son is Origen. The textual variations at Luke 24:51-52 are among the famous "Western non-interpolations," where, surprisingly, the normally longer Western manuscripts are shorter and the 'Alexandrians are longer. To find out more about them, read Vol.2 in this series, *The Pelican and the Phoenix*. The description of Commodus, who succeeded his father, Marcus Aurelius, as emperor, when he died at Sirmium on March 17,180 A.D. is found in C. Vol 2, p.271. The scriptures quoted are Psa. 27:16, I Cor 7:26 (See commentaries on translation question) Gen.2:18, Ephesians 3:20.

Chapter 70: Justin quotes Matthew 28:20, Psalm 36:9

CAST OF CHARACTERS

*: Historical character found in ODCC or DCB
**: Historical character found in OCD
***: Historical character not found in dictionaries
No star: Fictional character

* Abgar
* Agrippinus
Albinus
Anaximines of Alexandria
Anna
Apion
Apollonarius of Corinth
***Apollonides
Apollonios of Tebtunis
** Apollonius the Grumpy
*** Apollonius son of Serapion
Ariston
* Athenagoras.
** Athenaeus
Aulynchus
* Autolychus
* Claudius Apollinarius of Heirapolis
* Bardaisan
* Basilides
Ben Jacob of Berytus
* Bishop of Ephesus
Blastus
Castor
*Celsus
Chloe

355

Christophilos
* Claudius Apollonarius of Heirapolis
* Clement of Alexandria
** The Emperor Commodus
Deacon of Ephesus
Demetrius
*** Demetrius the Bookseller
*** Didymus
*** Diodorus
***Dionysios
* Dionysius of Corinth
* Eleutherus
Eucharion
Fayum farmer
* Florinus
Fortunata
Gaius
** Galen
M. Suplicius Garbo
** Harpocration
* Hegesippus
Heliodorus
* Heracleon
Hermas
* Hermogenes
Heron the giant
* Irenaeus
James
Jason
Julia
* Julian
Juliana
Justin
* Justin Martyr
*Leonidas
Lucius
Macrinius
Magistrate at Tebtunis

Malichos
* Marcion
Marcus
* Marcus the Magician
** Emperor Marcus Aurelius
* Maximilla
* Maximin
* Melito of Sardis
Merchant at Theadelphia
** Moeris
* Montanus
Nerus
Nicholas of Sparta
Ninneros the Stump-Fingered
* Pantaenus
* Papias
*** Pasion
*** Onesimus
Paulus
** Peregrinus
** Phrynichus
* Pinytus of Cnossus
** Pollux
* Polycrates
* Prisca
Rhoda
Rufus
Sabina
Selene
*** Seleucus
* Serapion
* Soter
Taesion
* Tatian
** Telephus
* Thecla
* Theophilus of Antioch
Timothy

Titus
* Valentinus
* Victor
Zeno

The end

Route of the scribes, A.D. 179-180

(Not to scale)

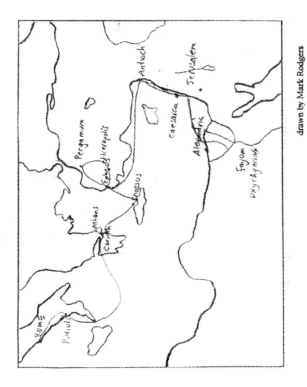

drawn by Mark Rodgers

ABOUT THE AUTHOR

Peter Rodgers is the Rector of St. John's Episcopal Church, New Haven, Connecticut and an Associate Fellow of Timothy Dwight College at Yale University. He holds degrees from Hobart College, General Theological Seminary and Oxford University. Before coming to St. John's in 1979 he was curate for student ministry at the Round Church in Cambridge, England. He has published several journal articles on the text of the New Testament and is the author of *Knowing Jesus* (InterVarsity 1982, Forward Movement 1989).

Printed in the United States
65468LVS00003B/55